Confessions
from the
Quilting
Circle

MAISEY YATES

Confessions
from the
Quilting
Circle

ISBN-13: 978-1-335-44899-6

Confessions from the Quilting Circle

HQN
22 Adelaide St. West, 40th Floor
Toronto, Ontario M5H 4E3, Canada
www.Harlequin.com

Printed in U.S.A.

To my nonnie, Lila Pauline.
I wish we could have shared more stories with each other.

Confessions

from the

Quilting

Circle

1

March 4th, 1944

The dress is perfect. Candlelight satin and antique lace. I can't wait for you to see it. I can't wait to walk down the aisle toward you. If only we could set a date. If only we had some idea of when the war will be over.

Love, Dot

Present day—
Lark

Unfinished.
The word whispered through the room like a ghost. Over the faded, floral wallpaper, down to the scarred wooden floor. And to the precariously stacked boxes and bins of fabrics, yarn skeins, canvases and other artistic miscellany.

Lark Ashwood had to wonder if her grandmother had left

them this way on purpose. Unfinished business here on earth, in the form of quilts, sweaters and paintings, to keep her spirit hanging around after she was gone.

It would be like her. Adeline Dowell did everything with just a little extra.

From her glossy red hair—which stayed that color till the day she died—to her matching cherry glasses and lipstick. She always had an armful of bangles, a beer in her hand and an ashtray full of cigarettes. She never smelled like smoke. She smelled like spearmint gum, Aqua Net and Avon perfume.

She had taught Lark that it was okay to be a little bit of extra.

A smile curved Lark's lips as she looked around the attic space again. "Oh, Gram…this is really a mess."

She had the sense that was intentional too. In death, as in life, her grandmother wouldn't simply fade away.

Neat attics, well-ordered affairs and pre-death estate sales designed to decrease the clutter a family would have to go through later were for other women. Quieter women who didn't want to be a bother.

Adeline Dowell lived to be a bother. To expand to fill a space, not shrinking down to accommodate anyone.

Lark might not consistently achieve the level of excess Gram had, but she considered it a goal.

"Lark? Are you up there?"

She heard her mom's voice carrying up the staircase. "Yes!" She shouted back down. "I'm…trying to make sense of this."

She heard footsteps behind her and saw her mom standing there, gray hair neat, arms folded in. "You don't have to. We can get someone to come in and sort it out."

"And what? Take it all to a thrift store?" Lark asked.

Her mom's expression shifted slightly, just enough to convey about six emotions with no wasted effort. Emotional economy was Mary Ashwood's forte. As contained and practical as

Addie had been excessive. "Honey, I think most of this would be bound for the dump."

"Mom, this is great stuff."

"I don't have room in my house for sentiment."

"It's not about sentiment. It's usable stuff."

"I'm not artsy, you know that. I don't really...get all this." The unspoken words in the air settled over Lark like a cloud.

Mary wasn't artsy because her mother hadn't been around to teach her to sew. To knit. To paint. To quilt.

Addie had taught her granddaughters. Not her own daughter.

She'd breezed on back into town in a candy apple Corvette when Lark's oldest sister, Avery, was born, after spending Mary's entire childhood off on some adventure or another, while Lark's grandfather had done the raising of the kids.

Grandkids had settled her. And Mary had never withheld her children from Adeline. Whatever Mary thought about her mom was difficult to say. But then, Lark could never really read her mom's emotions. When she'd been a kid, she hadn't noticed that. Lark had gone around feeling whatever she did and assuming everyone was tracking right along with her because she'd been an innately self focused kid. Or maybe that was just kids.

Either way, back then badgering her mom into tea parties and talking her ear off without noticing Mary didn't do much of her own talking had been easy.

It was only when she'd had big things to share with her mom that she'd realized...she couldn't.

"It's easy, Mom," Lark said. "I'll teach you. No one is asking you to make a living with art, art can be about enjoying the process."

"I don't *enjoy* doing things I'm bad at."

"Well I don't want Gram's stuff going to a thrift store, okay?"

Another shift in Mary's expression. A single crease on one side of her mouth conveying irritation, reluctance and exhaustion. But when she spoke she was measured. "If that's what you want. This is as much yours as mine."

It was a four-way split. The Dowell House and all its contents, and The Miner's House, formerly her grandmother's candy shop, to Mary Ashwood, and her three daughters. They'd discovered that at the will reading two months earlier.

It hadn't caused any issues in the family. They just weren't like that.

Lark's uncle Bill had just shaken his head. "She feels guilty."

And that had been the end of any discussion, before any had really started. They were all like their father that way. Quiet. Reserved. Opinionated and expert at conveying it without saying much.

Big loud shouting matches didn't have a place in the Dowell family.

But Addie *had* been there for her boys. They were quite a bit older than Lark's mother. She'd left when the oldest had been eighteen. The youngest boy sixteen.

Mary had been four.

Lark knew her mom felt more at home in the middle of a group of men than she did with women. She'd been raised in a house of men. With burned dinners and repressed emotions.

Lark had always felt like her mother had never really known what to make of the overwhelmingly female household she'd ended up with.

"It's what I want. When is Hannah getting in tonight?" Hannah, the middle child, had moved to Boston right after college, getting a position in the Boston Symphony Orchestra. She had the summer off of concerts and had decided to come to Bear Creek to finalize the plans for their inherited properties before going back home.

Once Hannah had found out when she could get time away from the symphony, Lark had set her own plans for moving into motion. She wanted to be here the whole time Hannah was here, since for Hannah, this wouldn't be permanent.

But Lark wasn't going back home. If her family agreed to her plan, she was staying here.

Which was not something she'd ever imagined she'd do.

Lark had gone to college across the country, in New York, at eighteen and had spent years living everywhere but here. Finding new versions of herself in new towns, new cities, whenever the urge took her.

Unfinished.

"Sometime around five-ish? She said she'd get a car out here from the airport. I reminded her that isn't the easiest thing to do in this part of the world. She said something about it being in apps now. I didn't laugh at her."

Lark laughed, though. "She can rent a car."

Lark hadn't lived in Bear Creek since she was eighteen, but she hadn't been under the impression there was a surplus of ride services around the small, rural community. If you were flying to get to Bear Creek, you had to fly into Medford, which was about eighteen miles from the smaller town. Even if you could find a car, she doubted the driver would want to haul anyone out of town.

But her sister wouldn't be told anything. Hannah made her own way, something Lark could relate to. But while she imagined herself drifting along like a tumbleweed, she imagined Hannah slicing through the water like a shark. With intent, purpose, and no small amount of sharpness.

"Maybe I should arrange something."

"Mom. She's a professional symphony musician who's been living on her own for fourteen years. I'm pretty sure she can cope."

"Isn't the point of coming home not having to cope for a while? Shouldn't your mom handle things?" Mary was a doer. She had never been the one to sit and chat. She'd loved for Lark to come out to the garden with her and work alongside her in the flower beds, or bake together. "You're not in New Mexico anymore. I can make you cookies without worrying they'll get eaten by rats in the mail."

Lark snorted. "I don't think there are rats in the mail."

"It doesn't have to be real for me to worry about it."

And there was something Lark had inherited directly from her mother. "That's true."

That and her love of chocolate chip cookies, which her mom made the very best. She could remember long afternoons at home with her mom when she'd been little, and her sisters had been in school. They'd made cookies and had iced tea, just the two of them.

Cooking had been a self-taught skill her mother had always been proud of. Her recipes were hers. And after growing up eating "chicken with blood" and beanie weenies cooked by her dad, she'd been pretty determined her kids would eat better than that.

Something Lark had been grateful for.

And Mom hadn't minded if she'd turned the music up loud and danced in some "dress up clothes"—an oversized prom dress from the '80s and a pair of high heels that were far too big, purchased from a thrift store. Which Hannah and Avery both declared "annoying" when they were home.

Her mom hadn't understood her, Lark knew that. But Lark had felt close to her back then in spite of it.

The sound of the door opening and closing came from downstairs. "Homework is done, dinner is in the Crock-Pot. I think even David can manage that."

The sound of her oldest sister Avery's voice was clear, even from a distance. Lark owed that to Avery's years of motherhood, coupled with the fact that she—by choice—fulfilled the role of parent liaison at her kids' exclusive private school, and often wrangled children in large groups. Again, by choice.

Lark looked around the room one last time and walked over to the stack of crafts. There was an old journal on top of several boxes that look like they might be overflowing with fabric, along with some old Christmas tree ornaments, and a sewing kit. She grabbed hold of them all before walking to the stairs, turning the ornaments over and letting the silver stars catch the light that filtered in through the stained glass window.

Her mother was already ahead of her, halfway down the stairs by the time Lark got to the top of them. She hadn't seen Avery yet since she'd arrived. She loved her older sister. She loved her niece and nephew. She liked her brother-in-law, who did his best not to be dismissive of the fact that she made a living drawing pictures. Okay, he kind of annoyed her. But still, he was fine. Just... A doctor. A surgeon, in fact, and bearing all of the arrogance that stereotypically implied.

One of the saddest things about living away for as long as she had was that she'd missed her niece's and nephew's childhoods. She saw them at least once a year, but it never felt like enough. And now they were teenagers, and a lot less cute.

And then there was Avery, who had always been somewhat untouchable. Four years older than Lark, Avery was a classic oldest child. A people pleasing perfectionist. She was organized and she was always neat and orderly.

And even though the gap between thirty-four and thirty-eight was a lot narrower than twelve and sixteen, sometimes Lark still felt like the gawky adolescent to Avery's sweet sixteen.

But maybe if they shared in a little bit of each other's day-to-day it would close some of that gap she felt between them.

Lark reached the bottom of the attic steps, and walked across the landing, pausing in front of the white door that led out to the widow's walk. She had always liked that when she was a kid. Widow's walk. It had sounded moody and tragic, and it had appealed to Lark's sense of drama. It still did.

She walked across the landing, to the curved staircase that

carried her down to the first floor. The sun shone in the windows that surrounded the front door. Bright green and purple, reflecting colored rectangles onto the wall across from it. The Dowell house, so named for her mother's family, had been built in 1866, and had stood as a proud historic home in the town of Bear Creek ever since.

The grand landscape, yellow brick that had mottled and taken on tones of red and rust over the years, was iconic, and had appeared on many a postcard and calendar. It had been part of her gram's family, but to Lark it had always been Grandpa's house. When he'd died ten years earlier, it had surprised everyone that the ownership of the place passed to Gram, considering the two of them had been divorced for over forty years at the time. But it had been clear that however deep Lark's grandfather's bitterness had been, it hadn't extended to making sure his former wife didn't get the home that had been passed through her family for generations.

But even after Lark's grandfather had passed, Addie had never lived in it. A couple of times Lark's uncles had stayed there when they'd come to town for visits, but for the past two years it had been largely closed up. And the attic had clearly been used as her grandmother's preferred storage unit.

It was The Miner's House that her grandmother had called home. She had made a little candy shop in the front, and had kept a bedroom in the back. The yard had a small dining set and the porch had rocking chairs. That, she'd said, was all she needed.

But as a result, The Dowell House was in a bit of disrepair, and in bad need of a good dusting.

Lark walked through the sitting room, and into the kitchen. The two rooms were divided by a red brick wall with another stained glass window set into it, and a large arched doorway. At one time, it had been an external wall and door, the change just part of one of the many expansions and remodels that had taken place over the years.

Another thing Lark had never given a whole lot of thought to. Because it was simply how Grandpa's house had looked. Now, she saw it for the slight architectural oddity that it was.

She could see her sister through the window, the pane cutting across her face, the top of her head green, and the bottom half purple. Lark walked into the kitchen, where her mother was already seated at the table, and her sister was in the process of wiping it off. She had brought... They looked like insulated bags, which Lark could only assume had food in them.

"I figured you guys would be pretty hungry by now."

"I'm always hungry," Lark said. "And hi." She closed the space between herself and her sister and drew her in for a hug.

"Good to see you." Avery dropped a kiss on to her head.

Lark took a step back. Avery looked tired, her blond hair piled on top of her head, an oversize sweater covering her always thin frame. She had on a pair of black leggings and a pair of black athletic shoes. She looked every inch the classic image of the supermom that she was.

Avery had all the self possession and poise of their mother and the effortless femininity of their grandmother. She'd been popular and stylish with ease and Lark had envied her. When Lark had reacted to things it had always been big, and often messy. Until she'd learned to get a grip on herself. Until she'd finally learned her lesson about what could happen when you acted, and didn't think it through.

"But what food did you bring?" Lark asked.

"I had a potpie in the freezer. I also brought salad and rolls. I figured Hannah would probably be hungry too, after flying cross-country."

Her sister had also brought wine, and sparkling water. Lark helped herself to the water. Without asking for assistance, Avery finished cleaning off the table, then produced paper plates. "I didn't know what kind of a state the dishes would be in. And I

didn't know which appliances in the house were functional. I
don't hand wash."

"No. Why would anyone? It's why God gave us dishwashers."

"Agree. Mom?" Avery asked. "How much potpie do you
want?"

"I can serve myself."

"No," Avery said. "You don't have to. Just sit. I'll get you
some wine." Avery was a flurry of movement, and even when
Lark and Mary had their food, Avery didn't sit. She opened up
the cupboards and looked in each of them, frowning. Lark could
almost see an inventory building in her sister's head.

"What exactly are you doing?"

"I've been thinking," Avery said. "Didn't you talk to Hannah at all about what her idea was for this place?"

"No." Lark felt vaguely wounded by that. There was a plan,
and Hannah hadn't said anything to her?

That made her feel more like the baby sister than anything
had for a while.

"Finally!" Laden with suitcases, Hannah pushed the door open
with her shoulder, her bright red hair, a shade or two down the
aisle from the color their grandmother had used, covering her
face. "I couldn't seem to get a car. I had to rent one."

Her suitcases were flung out in front of her, her violin in a
black case slung over her shoulder. Lark didn't see a purse. She
was sure her sister had one, but the violin was obviously her
most important possession.

"Yeah, I don't think ridesharing has really caught on around
here," Lark said.

"Do you mean those apps? Aren't all the drivers serial killers
or something?" Avery asked. Everyone looked at her. "One of
my friends shared a post about it online."

Hannah and Lark exchanged a glance.

"Well, I've managed to use it for about five years now and
not get serial killed. But I'm keeping my fingers crossed," Han-

nah said. "It will be good to have a car, but I don't really want to pay for a rental for the next three months."

"Dad said you could borrow the car," Mary said.

"Thanks," Hannah responded.

"I drove," Lark said, only then registering that her sister had not in fact asked if she needed the car. "So I have my car," she finished lamely.

Dad and Hannah had always had their own special thing. Not that Lark thought he loved Hannah more. She just wasn't shocked that he'd set the car aside for *her*.

"That smells good," Hannah said. She grabbed a paper plate and served herself a large portion of salad, and a small wedge of pie, passing on the wine and taking a sparkling water the same as Lark.

Soon they were all sitting around the table, except Avery, who was standing, leaning against the kitchen counter, holding a glass of wine.

"Do you want to sit?"

Avery blinked. "Oh," she said. "I just get so used to not having a chance to sit."

But she didn't move from her position.

"Avery says you have an idea?" Lark pointed that statement at Hannah.

"Oh," Hannah said. "Yes. I do. Well, we're doing a scaled back concert series this summer, and I wasn't needed for the next three months." Lark couldn't read her sister's emotions. She was laying it out matter-of-factly, but Lark had the sense she wasn't all that happy to have three months off. "I'm clear until end of August."

"You can just...leave for a few months?" Avery asked.

"I don't even have a houseplant," Hannah said. "Easily mobile by design, thanks." Lark knew that sometimes the orchestra sent people to other orchestras on loan. Her sister had spent seasons in New York, London and Moscow.

On paper, she and Hannah were pretty similar. Creative professions, the chance to move around. But there was a tenacity and intensity to Hannah that had skipped Lark. Avery had it too. She just channeled it into school events.

But Hannah was an island. An island of isolated, locked down emotion. Whatever her sister really felt about things was tough to get a handle on. She might be outspoken, but that wasn't the same as sharing feelings.

Hannah was allergic to feelings.

"I have the summer, free and clear. And I thought I could spend that time helping revamp everything here and… When it's over we can turn this into a vacation rental."

"It's a great idea," Avery said, using her school meeting voice. "Because none of us want to live here, right?"

"No," Mary said. "I'm not antsy to move back into my childhood home."

"David hates this house," Avery said. "The last thing he wants to do is fuss with potentially faulty plumbing on a day-to-day basis. Old houses are charming and wonderful, but they can also be a pain in the butt. Hannah isn't staying. Lark, I assume you're going back to New Mexico."

"I think it's a good idea," Lark said, bypassing the question she'd been asked. She was happy to linger over their plans for a moment, which would give her more space to address her own next. "A vacation rental. The house is famous. I think people will really enjoy staying here." She took a deep breath. "I want to stay here. In town. Permanently."

Avery and Hannah looked shocked. Her mother's expression was smooth, except one divot on the right side of her mouth, which suggested pleasure.

"Have you ever been to a Craft Café?"

That earned her a couple more blank stares.

"They're these cafés where you can come in and work on crafts. I think that's pretty self-explanatory."

"Does anyone *do* that?" Avery asked.

"Yes. They're getting more popular in places, and I think it could work here. We get all the tourism in the summer, and the kinds of people who move here are... Well, they have a lot of leisure time on their hands. They're either retired, or they have family money of some kind."

"What about your illustrations?"

Her heart squeezed uncomfortably. "I... I'm taking a break from it. But I have the money to put into the place. I don't need to use Gram's. But we all own The Miner's House and I am proposing that I use it for business. So, I need all of you to be on board with it."

"I don't have plans for it but..."

"Do you have a business plan?"

Her mom and Hannah spoke at the same time.

"I do have a business plan," Lark said.

And she was thankful for her friend Rusty who had told her in no uncertain terms that "starting a crowdfunding campaign is not a business plan."

Then had helped her make an actual business plan.

"And I know it's going to take some time and money to rehab the place, but, if we're working on the house here, I can easily get the same crew to go down the street and do some work there too. Two houses, one stone. Or one phone call."

She took a breath. "I sold everything. I mean, all my furniture. And my lease was up. I... I want a fresh start here."

The deep irony of looking for a fresh start here. This place that had made her, then unmade her. Tearing out each and every stitch that had held her together so she'd been forced to go off in pieces and find a way to repair what was.

It wasn't holding. That was the problem.

All these years later. Nothing was healed, just hidden.

She felt like she'd left pieces splintered of herself all over the country. On rivers and lakes in the Midwest, in the Atlantic

Ocean. In different towns and different cities, different jobs and groups of friends.

She'd been searching for things there, but it had only left her more fragmented. And none of it had brought her healing.

She'd been everywhere else looking for it. But she hadn't been back home, not really. Visits with her parents, the will reading, the funeral, that wasn't the same as really being here. When she came back she didn't spend time on Main Street in town, didn't visit old friends. She usually holed up in her parents' house and went between there and The Miner's House to spend time with Gram.

"If you can open this shop, you'll stay?" Her mother's expression was neutral, and Lark couldn't really tell what her feelings were on the subject.

"Yes," she said.

"Then try it," Mary said. "Why not?"

"A ringing endorsement," Lark said. "What about you two?"

"I figured I'd just line up the renovations for The Dowell House," Hannah said, in her typical, straightforward fashion. "Avery and I have already gone back and forth on furniture, and I ordered some."

"You didn't ask me?" Lark asked.

Avery and Hannah both had the decency to look slightly guilty. "I didn't think you'd care," Avery said.

But they hadn't asked.

Their skepticism about her ability to run a business combined with this felt...

Like something you've earned?

She ignored that. Even if it was true.

She felt nearly divided sometimes, into before and after. Before she'd left home, and after. When she'd been young she'd been...well, young. And probably a little bit spoiled because she was the youngest. She'd always wanted to have fun, to have good feelings because bad ones had been unbearable and she didn't know how to keep them in, and when they came out it was always a whole meltdown.

And then after...

She'd just stopped letting herself show those feelings. She'd stopped...letting herself want so much. And if her family thought she was sort of a shiftless drifter then fine. It suited her. It kept her a little mysterious, which also suited her.

Except now you're mad about it. And hey, you've moved home. So much for your distance.

"Do whatever you want with The Miner's House," Hannah said. "I can't run a shop and I don't need a little house."

"Same," Avery said.

It was, maybe, the most tepid unanimous yes of all time, but Lark would take it.

She put her hand on top of the swatch book, and held the silver Christmas ornaments to it, looking at the silver glinting against the worn leather. Her grandmother would approve of the idea, she knew she would.

Gram had loved art. And she had fostered the love of it in Lark. In all of them, really. The Miner's House had been the only place the three of them had ever gotten along.

"I'll keep a bowl of candy on the counter," she said.

Because her gram would want the kids to be able to come in for candy still.

She just knew it.

"What's that?" Mary pointed to the book that was on the table next to Lark.

"It's not your business plan, is it?" Hannah asked.

Lark rolled her eyes. "No. Even I'm not a big enough hipster to put my business plan in a leather bound book."

"I don't know about that," Avery said.

"I don't know what it is. I grabbed it off the top of the craft boxes before I came down. I wanted to see what was in it."

It was worn, the edges looking chewed and tattered. The

leather cover was pale in the places where someone's hands might have rested while holding it. She opened it up, and saw small, neat handwriting on the first page.

Memory quilt.

On the next page was a graph. A design for a quilt, with each piece laid out on the grid.

"Grandma was making a quilt," she said. "This is…"

She turned the page. There was a scrap of lace affixed to it, and underneath it in that same handwriting it said: *wedding dress.*

"It's like a swatch book. With fabric for the quilt."

"That's interesting," Hannah said. She got up from her seat and moved down to the end of the table, peering over Lark's shoulder. "What else?"

She flipped the page where there was a very colorful fabric in silk and velvet. "'Parlor curtains.'" She went to the next page, which had a fine, beaded silk. "'Party dress.'"

"There's all kinds of stuff like this up in the attic," she said. "Remember when Gram used to let us go through her collection and choose things to craft with? Broken earrings and old yarn and fabric. And always tons of unfinished projects lying around. Obviously she intended to make this quilt. Maybe she even started it. And it's somewhere up there with all of the… the unfinished things."

Unfinished.

That was the word that kept echoing inside of her.

Because it was why she was here. She was one of the unfinished things.

Being here, opening the café, it would give her a chance to finish some of what her grandmother had started.

Maybe along the way she'd manage to join up some of the unfinished pieces inside her own soul.

2

April 15th, 1864

How far is the trip to Oregon? I have heard it's long, and perilous.
It is kind of you to offer to pay for my passage, but I will sell most
of what I own before departing. There is nothing left for me here,
and no reason to come back. If you have a parlor or sitting room,
I might bring my curtains.

Signed, Anabeth Snow

Avery

Avery stopped at the store on her way home to pick up two
things, which turned into roughly fifteen things. That was always how it worked. Go in for milk and realize you need bread,
cheese, salad and hey those tomatoes look good too. And so had
the four boxes of cookies she'd thrown into her cart too.

The automatic light on the porch illuminated when she

walked up the paved path that led to the neat little front door. Like every house in the square, it was immaculate. Painted in Victorian colors that would have been used during the era, in accordance with the historic colors ordinance. Which was an actual ordinance that the City Council enforced with a great deal of vigor.

She didn't mind.

It made everything look like a postcard.

This was her dream. This clean, beautiful street with neatly kept hedges and trees planted every three feet. Small but lush green lawns that didn't dare have so much as a stray leaf on them.

She'd grown up in a slightly older part of town, 1970s tract houses that felt flat and rectangular, rather than grand like the homes that populated her neighborhood. And of course, she had always asked her mother why her parents had chosen to live in houses with green check carpet. At the time, she hadn't understood about money. She did now.

But thanks to David's job, they could well afford this. These houses weren't historic, of course, not really. They only looked like it. And inside they were outfitted with every modern convenience imaginable. And reliable plumbing.

For which she was grateful. It was better than historic.

Avery's parents had worked hard to give them a good life but she'd had a sense of dissatisfaction with it ever since she'd seen the way other people lived. Maybe it hadn't been fair, but Avery had known she'd wanted more from an early age.

Her mom had always been so practical. She'd never wanted to spend money on trendy clothes. She'd cut their hair herself. Mary Ashwood had let her own hair go gray the minute nature ordained it, while so many of her friends' moms had stayed frozen in a time capsule brought to them by the beauty salon.

Avery had wanted that life. Bright and shiny and perfect.

She had it now.

Her hands full of paper bags, she leaned her shoulder against the cranberry color door and maneuvered so that she could wrap her hand around the knob, turning it and shoving it open.

"I'm home," she called.

Not surprising at all, Hayden and Peyton said nothing. Also unsurprising, David assumed she was announcing it for the benefit of the children, and he said nothing either. Though, she heard his footsteps in the kitchen.

She walked through the entry, toward that room, and paused in the doorway. She put her hand on the door frame, brushing her fingertips over the wood.

The paint was chipped.

She frowned, then stepped forward. "I stopped to pick up a few things."

"The kids are eating us out of house and home," David said.

"They're teenagers." She shrugged as she set the bags onto the island. "It's what they do."

"Sure," he said, his focus on his phone.

She busied herself putting the groceries in the fridge and the pantry, her mind blank for the first time all day. It had been filled with everything she'd had to do and this was the first time she'd slowed down long enough to have her own thoughts. If she wanted to.

But she was too tired for thinking today.

When she exited the walk-in pantry, her husband had put his phone away.

He looked at her and smiled. Something inside of her lit up.

He was just as handsome as the day she'd met him. They'd been young. Just finishing up college. He wasn't from Oregon, but he had always wanted to go there. It so happened Medford had a good couple of hospitals, and there was ample opportunity for a new surgeon who was young and full of enthusiasm.

So she had moved back home. And he had moved with her.

"How is your mom?" he asked.

"She's good. I mean, fine. You know how my mom is. She's

a big believer in sucking it up and soldiering on. She doesn't talk about her feelings. But I think Gram's death affected her a little bit more deeply than she expected it to. Considering they weren't exactly that close."

"Your gram always came to Sunday dinner, it's not like they were strangers."

"No, no I know." But Avery also knew they were distant from each other. Gram was so easy with her, and with the kids. But a tightness came over her face when Mary entered the room.

And with her mom, who could even tell?

Avery sighed, sadness settling over her. This Sunday would be a dinner-at-Mom's Sunday. They'd had one other since Gram's death and Avery missed her sweet presence so much. Missed her giving the kids craft projects to do. Missed her rocking in that ratty old recliner her parents had had in the living room for at least thirty years while she ate her dessert.

Pie had been her favorite. Pumpkin.

Avery had learned her recipe years ago, and she'd made it for her extra in the months leading up to her death because she'd felt her slipping away and...

And there had been nothing she could do about it. Of course not. Gram was in her nineties and it was how life was. But Avery resented it.

Gram had been her link back to such a beautiful time in her life. To moments when she'd felt close with her sisters. When her biggest worry had been getting through snapping enough peas for dinner so she could go sit in the sunshine with a book or with her cross-stitch.

When she'd dreamed of going to college and maybe going somewhere new after. When she'd dreamed of being an actress or a writer. Something fabulous and exciting that had just felt so possible in the warmth of a sunbeam in a grandmother's tiny backyard.

"What all did you do today?" David asked, his voice filled with concern.

"Had a meeting at school. I went to coffee with Alyssa to talk about organizing speakers for the Writer's Festival for next school year. I scrounged up some dinner for you guys, and got some food together to take to mom and Avery and Lark. Visited with them for a while. Grocery store. Then home." She paused for a moment. "What about you?"

"Surgery all day."

"Did it go well?"

He shrugged. "I'm a doctor. I'm not really seeing people at their best. I figure it goes well every time. Without help, there'd be no hope, right?"

She wondered if that meant someone had died, and he didn't want to talk about it. It was hard to tell with him. It was why she always hesitated to ask about his day.

"I brought you flowers," he said. "I know it's been a rough few weeks."

She blinked. "You did?"

"Yeah," he said.

He moved to the side, and on the granite countertop, she saw a crystal vase, filled with red roses. "They're beautiful."

"You know I love you," he said, wrapping his arms around her then, and bringing her in for a kiss. A deep sort of validation filled her. He was such a handsome, accomplished man. And he'd given her all this.

And flowers.

"I know," she said. "I love you too."

"You do so much. For me, for the kids."

"Thank you," she said, a smile curving her lips.

"Did you guys decide what you're going to do with the houses?"

"Well, we're going with the vacation rental for The Dowell House. I think it's the best idea."

"Sure," he said. "A good way to bring in some revenue from something that would otherwise just sit there."

"Yeah. Lark had an idea for The Miner's House. I… I don't know anything about the kind of business she's proposing, but I figured there was no harm in her trying something."

"Does she have a business plan?"

"I asked that too. Apparently she does."

"No offense to your sister… But she's not the most responsible."

Avery wanted to defend Lark. It was only natural. They were sisters, after all. But David really didn't understand her sisters. Hannah, at least, had a real, tangible job. But no matter how many times she showed David the illustrations in books that were done by Lark, he still seemed to think she drew pictures for a living, and that it was so sporadic there was absolutely nothing dependable about it.

But Lark was Lark. The baby. She was a giant emotional response, all heart and no planning. And she never got in trouble for it. Life never seemed to throw her a consequence of any kind. No, she wasn't the overachiever Hannah was, but managed to coast and always end up in a fine enough place.

It had been so annoying when they were kids.

When Avery was younger if she would have flipped a fit the way Lark did, she'd have gotten grounded for life.

"So she's not drawing anymore?"

"She said she was on a break."

"Really."

"She didn't offer any more information than that. Anyway, she wants to open something called a Craft Café? She said she's going to invest all of her own money."

She could practically hear him rolling his eyes. "Well, see that that's it. Because you know, with ventures like that, someone might think they have all their own money, but if she gets in too deep, you know she's going to ask us."

"I know," she said. But she wasn't sure she actually agreed. Still, David believed it, and it was easier than having an argument.

"We'd be better off selling it. Her turning it into another rental."

"Just give her six months. She wants to stay. She wants to stay, and I can tell my mom is desperate for her to."

"And then she'll leave. Just like your grandma did. And that will break your mother's heart."

Avery sighed heavily. David was probably right. Lark didn't have a great track record when it came to staying in one place. "She'll have me. She always does."

"Yes. It always falls to you to be there for your mom when your sisters don't bother to come home for things. You're the one that takes care of your parents and goes to every holiday, and now if Lark ends up saying she's staying and then doesn't, you know you'll have to fix it. She doesn't say it bothers her, but you know it does."

Because however her mom acted, things did hurt her. And Avery could tell when they did. "It's my family…"

"*We're* your family," he said. "You have a family. Your sisters don't have husbands and children."

"Hannah plays in a symphony orchestra. One of the best in the country."

"That's not the same as the kind of obligations you have."

She looked at her husband of seventeen years. "No," she agreed. "It's not."

"She's married to her job."

She nodded silently. "And I can't really imagine that Lark will ever settle down."

"Too much of a project," David said.

"Hey. She is my *sister*."

"Yeah, I know. My sister is a project too."

She looked at the flowers and sighed. "Everything will be

fine. She'll try her business, and whatever happens will happen. I promise it's not going to distract me too much." He kissed her again, and she pushed everything out of her mind except that. Because she did love to kiss him. Still.

She might not be able to go back in time and sit in that simple sunbeam with Gram, but her life was pretty good.

Hannah

It didn't matter how many years it had been since she'd moved away, and how many times she'd come back during that time, it always felt weird to walk into her childhood home feeling more like a guest than an inhabitant. Stranger still dragging her suitcases into the childhood room she had shared with Lark.

That shared space had caused so many fights.

I'm drawing, Hannah! Stop playing!

She could practically hear Lark's complaints echo off the walls all these years later. Lark had never understood Hannah's obsession with the violin, and had often made it worse by trying to connect their two passions.

We're both creative!

Of course, Lark didn't have to spend hours doing scales to make sure she was precise. Perfect. Lark didn't understand that music wasn't a free-form scribble. You had to build a foundation on perfection.

And her mother had always sided with Lark.

She's tired, Hannah, you have to stop now. It's late.

Of course, Lark was the baby. And the baby always got what she wanted.

So Hannah had gone out wrapped in a winter coat and rage and played angrily on the back porch until their neighbor had yelled at her out of his living room window.

At least they didn't have to share now. Lark was staying in The Dowell House already, but Hannah had told her mother she'd stay at the house before she'd known that The Dowell House was in habitable condition—something she'd been concerned about since no one had lived there since her grandfather's death about a decade ago.

She'd done a quick walk-through after the funeral, and she'd ordered beds and other furniture, purchased with money left by Gram, and it would all be here later in the week, and would round out the extra bedrooms in the house that were currently empty.

Hannah had promised her dad she'd stay the first night, but then she'd be moving into The Dowell House along with her sister.

Her and Lark's old room still had two twin beds, shoved against opposite sides of the room. Though, Lark's white comforter with rainbow brushstrokes and Hannah's blue plaid with yellow sunflowers had been replaced by quilts. Hannah sat down on the edge of what had been her bed and touched the quilt.

She could feel Gram's warmth in the stitches. Could remember when she'd first put a fabric square and a needle in Hannah's hands.

Hannah hadn't been very nice about it, or very appreciative.

I have to practice violin, Gram. I don't have time to learn to quilt.

Well, I have a quilt that needs finishing, and I have five pounds of potatoes that need peeling. So, pick your poison.

Hannah had chosen the quilt.

She had learned to knit that same summer. In the intervening years she hadn't picked up a craft once. It was all so domestic. And she was committed to her music. She didn't need fractured focus. When she wasn't practicing her music, she was networking, going out and making the most of living in Boston.

If she felt like bringing a man home, it was easy enough to meet one that she never even had to see again.

The joys of the city.

But she didn't sit home making anything but music.

Even when she came to visit for the holidays, Gram had tried to get her to pick up a needle and thread. She remembered last year at Christmas they'd wound up crammed into the living room at her parents' house, Gram sitting in a rocker with a TV tray in front of her. A slice of pie on a plate, and a needlepoint sampler next to that.

Avery and her kids had sat dutifully on the floor doing versions of the same thing, while Lark had sat next to them, knitting.

Hannah had gone into the kitchen with her mom, dad and David.

She wished she hadn't now.

It was the last time she'd seen Gram.

I don't know why you seem to think you only need to be good at one thing. If you have the capacity to learn how to create many things, music, hats, and quilts, why wouldn't you?

That was what Gram had asked her when she complained about learning to knit.

She understood what her grandmother had wanted. But she had to be single-minded. She wasn't just a casual musician. She breathed it. It wasn't always a creative outlet, or a joy. It was painful sometimes. Monotonous, because anything you did day in, day out could be.

Greatness required sacrifice, and she'd been willing to make those sacrifices.

Well-rounded was for other people.

"Knock knock." Her dad said it, rather than actually doing it, because the door to the bedroom was still open. "Good to see you, Hannah Banana."

"Hi, Dad." She got up off the bed and went to hug him.

"Do you want to come have a cup of tea? Just finished in the shop."

"You're having tea?"

"I'm having a beer."

"Pfft. I want beer. What are you building?"

"Signposts. I was enlisted to help Patty in this sign making business she started. She does the artwork. You know how she gets. She comes up with an idea and then she goes into it full-bore. She's been keeping me going hard for weeks."

"Good thing," Hannah said. "What else have you been up to?"

"Photography, which is a lot of hiking. Cooking classes."

"Cooking?"

"If I don't learn now I won't learn. Might as well."

"I guess. Is Mom doing any of it with you?"

"You know how she is. She likes her routine. And if she went to a cooking class and couldn't figure it out she'd break all the eggs in a temper and storm out." He laughed when he said it.

Hannah walked out of the bedroom, flipping the light off, the darkness taking her memories along with it. The shag carpet beneath her feet was plush, completely different to the wood floors in her apartment. The linoleum in the kitchen was the same ochre that had been there since she was a child. It was a bit scarred and worn now, but it spoke of home, and she liked it.

The kettle on the stove was already whistling, and her mom was standing there waiting. Then she poured her a generous amount of hot water and plunked a Lipton tea bag into the cup.

Hannah's British friends in the symphony would recoil in horror. Even more so if she confessed to them that half the time her mother made the water for the tea in the microwave.

The kitchen felt so small now. Every time she came home it surprised her. The cast of the light was yellow, the wood too warm. It was nothing like her big, open apartment with black and chrome and high ceilings that carried her music up and filtered it down all around her so she was consumed with it.

A space all her own.

A space dedicated to what mattered to her.

One where no one ever told her to stop playing.

"I'll have a beer," Hannah said, when her mom went to pour a second cup.

Her expression was vaguely disapproving. "You smell like cigarettes."

"Am I fifteen?"

Her dad turned to her, holding the beer and handing it to her. "Does being over eighteen make you immune to the negative effects of cigarettes?"

"How's your cholesterol, Dad?" she asked sweetly. "And did you have steak for dinner?"

"It's not your job to monitor my health, Hannah Banana."

"Well, seems fair since you're doing it to me."

"And are you seeing anyone?" he asked.

"Saw a man a for a whole night a couple of weeks ago."

That earned her a gruff grunt.

But a smile tugged at the corner of his mouth. Because as much as she knew he disapproved, even when she was irritating him she knew he enjoyed it. He had raised his daughters to be strong women with their own minds.

Even when those minds weren't quite the same as his.

And in her mind, marriage was silly. It was for people who wanted houses in neighborhoods like this one. Who wanted kids and who wanted to be normal.

She wanted to be something more than normal.

Her dad took a sip of his beer. "I just hate the idea of you being all alone over there."

"I have a lot of friends. Playing in a symphony is a whole group thing."

"It's not the same as being in love," he said.

Her dad was a romantic, beneath all his alpha bluster. Hannah had always found that funny because her mom really wasn't. Joe Ashwood liked to bring his wife flowers just because and Mary appreciated them…but Hannah had a feeling she'd never have asked for something so frivolous.

Hannah appreciated her dad, but she wasn't like him.

She could remember when she thought love was supposed to be bright and blinding like a summer day. That it was supposed to consume you and keep you up at night. That it was okay if it hurt, or didn't fit quite right.

That it burned with the ferocity of the rest of her dreams. But she knew better now. That was... It wasn't anything you could live with.

Not when you wanted something else. Not when you had a big and bright dream to follow.

But even though she'd let that go, being in Bear Creek always reminded her of that kind of summer. That kind of feeling.

It was uncomfortable, but an uncomfortable she accepted as part of coming back. It was why she only did it once a year.

Knowing she was settling in for a couple months was unsettling.

"How's the fiddling going?" Her dad leaned against the counter and crossed his arms, fixing her with his thousand-yard blue stare that had never failed to strike fear into her heart when she'd been a teenager, contemplating any level of rebellion.

Fortunately, her *fiddling*, as her dad persisted in calling it—for the sole purpose of irritating her—had kept her too busy to get into classic rebellions.

"Good. I am..." She took a breath. She'd been avoiding saying this out loud. Now she wondered if she should. If she was making it a big, superstitious thing when it really didn't have to be. "There's a principal spot open. I've been first chair now for a couple of years, and... I think this is it. I think this is... I think I'm going to get it."

She'd said it now. It was there. Out in the universe.

"That's... That's great news," he said. "Why didn't you tell us earlier?"

"Because I'm nervous about it. I might not get it." But even as she said that, her stomach twisted, and the echo inside of her was fierce and strong.

That was unacceptable. She had to get it. She had to. There wasn't another choice. She hadn't started this journey and kept on it so doggedly to not get this spot. She'd been with the Boston Symphony for over ten years, and she had more than proven her worth.

This was her dream. Her *practical* dream. To be the lead position in the orchestra.

She knew it wasn't common for a violinist to ascend to the heights of world fame as a soloist, and sure, she'd held some of that hope in her heart. Everyone had those kinds of dreams. But this was possible. More than possible, it was likely.

It was what she'd been working toward since she'd left Bear Creek.

And the timing for her to get away for a while as the board reviewed everything was actually great.

"You'll get it," her dad said. "You know you will."

Unfailing confidence in her. He'd always had that. Pressure accompanied the warmth in her chest and she found it hard to breathe around it.

"You've worked for it," her mom said.

"You've always been special," Dad said.

Special.

Her mom had always worried her dreams weren't practical. But her dad had always said that. *Special.*

But she'd believed it. She'd known it, down in her bones. That she wasn't meant for this place. That she was bigger than this house, this town.

This had been her obsession, her focus, for nearly thirty years. And anything other than the top was a failure.

And Hannah could not fail.

3

April 12th, 1944

I know you cannot control when you return. And I know you will come back to me. But it will be impossible to hide this secret forever, and I fear what it will mean for us, and for our baby, if the world knows he came into being outside of marriage. Your parents hate me already. What will they do if they find out about this?

Love, Dot

Lark

"Where is Avery?"

"She has school run." Lark looked around the attic, mentally formulating a plan of attack.

"Isn't Peyton old enough to drive?" Hannah asked.

"Almost at least. But I think Avery likes doing it."

Hannah frowned. "I think that's something I would *not* enjoy."

Lark shifted. "No. Probably not."

She kept her eyes on Hannah as Hannah scanned the room and she could almost see the mental to-do list her much more organized sister was building as she took a quick inventory of everything stacked in front of them. "This is a lot of stuff."

They'd gotten a massive furniture delivery today, and Lark couldn't even be annoyed because the rich velvet chaise, the beautiful four poster beds and plush sectional were exactly what Lark would have chosen if she'd been consulted.

It was always weird to her, when the three of them had taste that crossed over.

"I was thinking about it last night," she said, quickly. "If we start taking things over to The Miner's House I can sort through it during slow times. I know Gram's bedroom is still completely filled with her things. I peeked in there last night but I couldn't quite bear going in."

Hannah looked down. "Yeah, I...don't think I'm quite ready for that." She frowned. "Do you feel guilty? About how little we visited?"

"I always at least came for Christmas and the Fourth."

"Better than me. I was down to Christmas, and only after the holiday concert series ended in Boston."

"We both saw her last in the same visit," Lark said. "Remember, she said your hair was looking too ordinary."

Hannah grabbed hold of the end of her ruby hair. "Yep. Too dull for Gram." Sadness lowered her features. "She wanted me to sit and needlepoint with her and I didn't want to."

"Well, you're here now. You're moving over here tonight, right?"

"Yes."

"We can have a slumber party."

"Are you staying here for the whole renovation?" Hannah asked, her brow pleating.

"I was planning on it."

"I'm not sure if it's going to be hugely livable."

"I'm very comfortable with camping, Hannah."

Hannah's lips pulled down into a frown. "You think you're going to walk to the creek and bathe?"

"Sure. Why not? We used to skinny dip in the creek all the time." At least they had until Hannah had gotten too busy to hang out with Lark anymore.

Until she'd gotten consumed by her music, and then there had been Josh—until Hannah had cut even him out. And between him and music there hadn't been time for her to devote a breath to anyone else. Let alone an afternoon with her sister.

Hannah laughed. "True. I remember being scared boys were spying on us. Then a couple years later I was a lot more worried they *weren't* spying on us."

"Yeah I think the boys were mostly ignoring us, to be honest."

One boy in particular. But thinking about him was like a series of chain reactions, and Lark didn't want to step down that path. So she didn't even put one foot on it.

"In a month or so I'll work on finding a house to rent here," she said. "And until then I guess we're roommates."

"Oh wow," Hannah said, looking a bit stricken. "It's like being kids again."

"Except we have our own rooms. This place is plenty big."

"You think that your craft business is going to make enough money for you to rent somewhere else?" Hannah asked.

"I have money," Lark said. "Don't worry about me."

Her sister paused. "You have that kind of money?"

"I had some successful projects," she said, feeling a little defensive and hating to be put in that position.

She'd decided a long time ago that it was powerful to be *fine, thank you very much*, and have no one else be able to quite pin her down.

But now that she was looking at proximity with her sister for some time, it was annoying.

"You never say," Hannah said. "I keep everyone posted on what's happening with the orchestra. But why are you coming back *here*?" Hannah's tone dripped with disdain. "Why are you... Changing everything?"

Lark couldn't seem to shift the deep sadness that welled up inside of her. Six months ago she'd been hit with an overwhelming realization that what she was doing wasn't what she loved. Not anymore.

That in some ways it was keeping her broken, not healing her.

And once she had realized those things, it had felt like a slog to finish the project she was contracted for. And she...she was not a precious artist. She was a commercial artist.

She enjoyed making art that she could be paid for, art that met her admittedly meager needs. She could enjoy art in any variety, and enjoyed the challenge of adapting to different styles, and different directives for different projects. But once it was gone, it was gone, and once the sadness had taken hold it was too much like old memories.

And every time she picked up a pen she felt like she was sitting in them. The entire point of staying away from Bear Creek had been outrunning bad memories. But it wasn't working anymore. They'd been ankle deep for years, and now she felt them creeping up, higher and higher and she worried soon she'd drown in them.

So when Addie died, and had left her this place, she had figured...might as well wade right in.

"You know me. I like to...follow my feet and see where they lead me. I was itching for something new."

"Just like that?"

"It's not really like being first chair in a major symphony orchestra," Lark said, touching her sister's hand. "I get contracts from a lot of different companies and publishers. I can easily step back in."

"I don't know how you do that. Just... Move. Change things. Assuming that you won't lose any ground."

"I don't know that I was ever trying to gain ground," Lark said.

Hannah frowned. "That's what I'm always trying to do."

"I guess that's the difference. You're climbing a ladder, and I'm just...driving on the highway. Nowhere so far has been better, just different."

It tasted a little disingenuous on her tongue. And she had to wonder if it was more accurate to say she was *running* down the highway. Leaving her past behind.

She just...as annoying as it was for them to underestimate her the alternative was emotional honesty and Lark had some things to work out in herself before she got there.

"Okay, do you want to help me box this stuff up?"

"Sure."

The stuff was already boxed, technically, but it wasn't exactly transport ready. They both knelt down on the rough, hardwood floor and opened up boxes, sifting through the contents. Silks, yarns, roving and gingham. Thread, wire and twine. Beads, pliers of all varieties, strips of leather and metal stamping kits.

It was so similar to the craft kits she'd started assembling right after Gram's funeral. When the dream of the Craft Café was the only thing that kept her from sinking into full-on grief. Seeing it now gave her a renewed sense of purpose.

They shifted to another section and began unearthing scarves, half-finished sweaters that were on cables. There was even one that was entirely finished, just not cast off, still on the needles.

Lark touched the nearly finished sweater and chuckled. "I've never related to Gram more."

"I feel lied to," Hannah said. "She was always such a stickler to me."

"She probably knew it was what you needed to hear. If you

would have known that knitting would be a haphazard disaster of unfinished projects you would never have wanted to do it."

Hannah looked surprised. "That is true. I really don't like things being left undone."

"Neither do I," Lark said softly, touching a particularly beautiful, half-made pink cashmere sweater. "I seem to do it often enough, though."

She hadn't always. These things, arts and crafts, quilting and knitting...they'd done them all together once upon a time. Because no matter how different they all were, no matter how busy, they'd had time for Gram.

And she'd set them all down with a project and watch as their strife turned into teamwork. Turned into a kind of shared joy and purpose that they never found together outside of sewing or knitting.

Lark moved over to the next stack of boxes. "Oh," she said. "It's fabric."

Fabric that was neatly folded into bins, with handwritten labels affixed neatly to the top of them. "'Parlor curtains,'" she read. "'Party dress.' This is the fabric that she was going to used to make the memory quilt."

"I haven't... I haven't gone near anything like this in years. Not since I left home."

"Really? Why no—"

"He gets done at 5:30." Avery's voice filtered up the stairs. "He can wait around for like ten minutes. No I...you know, I'll call Karen." She pushed her way into the attic, her phone still pressed up against her ear. "No. Nonono. it's fine. It's *fine*. It's just that I told my sisters I would help sort through things tonight. I didn't want to have to..." The sentence stopped sharp on a harsh breath. "Dinner will be ready. It's in the Crock-Pot." She closed her eyes. "It won't be Crock-Pot dinner tomorrow night. I promise. Don't worry about it." She paused. "I love you too." She hung up, and blinked three times as if to try and forcibly brighten her expression. "Scheduling drama."

Lark wondered if that dismissal, airy and light like she was brushing a cobweb away from in front of her, worked on her friends. She might not have spent a ton of time with Avery in the last ten years, but she'd grown up with her sister.

And she could tell the conversation was bothering her deeper than she was admitting. She wasn't used to seeing tension between Avery and David, but she usually saw them at holidays, when David was sitting with her dad or the kids with a beer in his hand. Relaxed. She wasn't part of their real lives, with schedules and work and things.

"Your husband doesn't want to pick up his son?" Hannah asked, arch and judgmental in a way Lark could never pull off.

That had always been Hannah's way. She wasn't mean, but she didn't go out of her way to be...gentle either. Hannah's opinions often fell like an ax and God help you if your neck happened to be under them.

Lark had spent most of their childhood mortally wounded by Hannah's sharp tongue.

She could remember one fight they'd had about Hannah's incessant, obsessive practicing.

I'm not scribbling on a piece of paper and calling it art, Lark. This is a discipline, not a kindergarten project.

And all her defenses had gotten jumbled up inside of her. About how art was a discipline, and you did have to learn it. About how there was real school for it. Real work. Because her tears had clogged up her throat and she hadn't been able to say a thing.

That was when she'd do something like hide Hannah's rosin or put a caterpillar in her underwear drawer.

Actions spoke louder than words, after all.

And because actions spoke louder, she'd just worked harder on her art—in between bouts of petty vengeance. She'd ended up getting a scholarship, same as Hannah. But she'd never felt like her sister had really…understood.

And all of her big attempts at being heard, being seen…being something. They hadn't worked out well.

"He's a doctor," Avery said. "He's busy. It's not like he's been out golfing all day. He's been in surgery. He has some things to finish up. Paperwork."

"Oh, right," Hannah said. "You know, your time is important too."

"I'm not…" Avery waved away more imaginary cobwebs. "In people's spines."

"If he's *in* someone's spine, I think there's a problem," Hannah said.

"He should be more considerate of your time," Lark said.

Avery's expression honed itself into a finely sharpened point, and she turned it straight onto Lark. Hannah had likely gotten away with being snarky, because Hannah was always snarky.

It reminded her so much of their mother that it shocked Lark into silence for a moment. "He's a doctor," she said again. "The kind of pressure he's under is a lot more intense than…"

"Raising his children?" Hannah asked.

"I thought you liked David," Avery said, frowning at Hannah.

"I do," Hannah said. "But I don't like this. I don't like you just dismissing your whole life because David is an important doctor."

"I'm not dismissing my whole life. I need some extra help picking my son up. That's all. And if I didn't want to be here so badly, I wouldn't need help."

"You gonna text Karen?" Lark asked.

"Yes," Avery said, stabbing at her phone, then staring at it for about thirty seconds before stabbing at it again. "There. Handled. Okay, where are we at up here?"

"I just found the fabric that Gram was going to use to make the quilt," Lark said.

"That sounds like more fun than discussing my schedule."

"I'm thirsty," Hannah said.

"I brought wine."

"Nothing stronger?" Hannah asked.

"Sorry," Avery said. "I left my flask in the other minivan."

"You joke, but probably half of the moms in that hellscape you call a pickup line have gin in their water bottles."

"Oh, more than half," Avery said.

Hannah lifted a shoulder. "I find it interesting that so many women fade into a life that requires they dull their senses for half of it."

"Fade into a life?" Avery asked. "Is that what you think I did?"

"No," Hannah said, sounding defensive but not totally convincing.

Avery's expression was flat, unamused.

"I made the choice to come back," Avery said. "There was no *fading* anywhere."

The growing tension between her sisters built up a knot in Lark's chest. Hannah and Avery were both blunt, and would go right in for a fight without even pausing to think about it. They also got over it when it was done. They always had.

And of course neither of them realized that Lark had wanted, more than anything, to *fade* into the kind of life Avery had. If it were that simple, she'd have done it.

"I'll have wine," Lark said.

She grabbed a glass out of the bag and held it up to her sister. Hannah, meanwhile, dug in the corner for a blanket, and then looked up impishly.

"Remember how we used to use this clothesline?" She flipped her finger over the top of a cord that hung stretched across one section of the room.

"Yes," Lark said.

She slung the sheet over the top of the line, then took a stack of boxes and used it to anchor four corners of the sheet.

"The tent."

"A wine drinking tent," Avery said. "Excellent."

They exchanged glances, and Lark was the first person to get underneath.

"Remember when we'd have sleepovers with Grandpa and we'd come up here and tell scary stories until Lark cried?" Avery asked.

"I didn't cry!" Lark frowned. "And if I did it's because I was *a child* and you were all being mean."

"We had a fort like this at Gram's too," Hannah said. "Just in the backyard."

The silence that stretched between them was heavier then. Filled with memories.

"I remember that. She'd sit in it with us," Avery said. "And tell us about the great Dowell family."

"So many legends about the men and how great they were at…hunting skunks." Lark shook her head. "I always thought it was weird there were no stories about the women."

"What was always weird was having Gram and Grandpa just down the street from each other. But never speaking."

"You can't really blame him," Lark said. "She left him. As much as Grandpa was an old-school gentleman he held a grudge."

"I've always had a hard time with that," Avery said softly. "I love Gram. I always have. When we were teenagers it was easier to be close to her than it was Mom but… But you see things differently when you have your own kids."

Lark bit down on the inside of her cheek as Hannah shot Avery a quick, irritated glance.

"I'm perfectly capable of understanding why it's upsetting that somebody left their daughter without having children of my own, thank you," Hannah said, her tone tart.

"That's not what I meant," Avery said. "It's not. It's just… I think about it a lot. I put myself in that position. And I don't understand."

"Do you really not?" Lark asked. "You never wanted to just run away from everything?"

Avery frowned. "No."

"I do," Lark said. "I want to run away from things all the time." *Currently this conversation.* "Neither of you ever just want to...detonate a bomb in the middle of everything and start over?"

She was genuinely curious. For her, settling in the town was a big shake-up. As big as the first one, really. When she'd left home at eighteen for school. When she'd decided she wouldn't live in Bear Creek, not again. When she'd figured out how to care less. How to go with the flow more rather than...rather than hoping so badly for something she might not get to have.

"No," Hannah said. "I worked way too hard to change what I'm doing now. I get chances to change scenery for a season or two, but BSO is my home. It's my life."

"Never," Avery said, shaking her head.

"Never? You never want to act out of character? I don't know, the idea I could unmake and remake everything tomorrow if I needed to is what makes me feel less claustrophobic on a bad day."

"But picking up and leaving isn't acting out of character for you," Hannah said.

"Not true," Lark said. "I think for me uncharacteristic is what I'm doing now. Coming home after all this time."

And it scared her. But if she thought back to where she'd been before she made the decisions, she felt calmer again. She'd reached the end of the road she was on. She was exploring a new road here.

No one was forcing her to do anything. It was her choice, and she could make a new choice if she needed to.

"So this is what your bomb detonation looks like?" Hannah asked. "Camping out in your grandpa's attic and drinking wine? Super cool."

Lark made a scoffing noise.

"No, I don't ever want to do anything like that," Avery said. "Gram hurt Mom, even if she never admits it. And I…it was wrong what she did. Taking off and leaving my responsibilities could never be a fantasy. Mom might not have been the easiest person to talk to, but she taught us all how to be responsible, that's for sure."

Mary Ashwood had definite ideas of what she wanted for her daughters. Lark remembered the time her mother had told her she had to remember to think of others, to act with her head and not her heart.

Too emotional and untamed and she'd end up like Gram. Lark hadn't understood why that was bad. And that was the first time Mary had told her. That Gram had abandoned her as a child.

She'd said it all no-nonsense and brusque. Just relaying the facts.

But it had wounded Lark, deeply. To have her Gram knocked off her pedestal like that.

But it had certainly made an impression on her. To know that the woman she admired so much was capable of hurting her mother so much. Her grandpa. Her uncles.

If Gram could, Lark could too.

So she had to listen to her mother. She had to make sure she never did anything quite so reckless.

"Well. She knew that I would stay here. So I think it was pretty easy for her to support you."

"What does that mean?" Hannah asked.

"I'm just saying, I don't think it would've been quite so easy for her to let you go if I wasn't here."

"Did you want to be anywhere else?"

Avery shook her head. "No. I didn't. Anyway. I'm not sure how we got started on this. It's not important."

"I don't know. I think the fact that you brought it up proves that it's at least a little bit important," Lark said.

"I'm happy with my life," Avery said. "I didn't mean to imply otherwise."

"I know you're happy. That doesn't mean you never wanted anything else, though," Hannah said. "You have a great house. And husband. And kids."

"I know you're allergic to kids," Avery said.

"I'm not allergic to kids," Hannah said. "They just don't fit anywhere in my life."

Lark would have fit them in. But no one asked her.

It was weird, how they could feel so linked by their past, by the fact they were sisters, and yet have no real idea of who each other was now.

There had been a time when they'd known exactly what each other thought about everything. And then Avery going through puberty had widened the gap hugely, then Hannah going after her and leaving Lark behind.

It hadn't left a lot of time for sisters.

Lark had her own group of friends. Friends who were incredibly important to her. Friends who had introduced her to the benefits of hard cider and Doritos as a flavor combination.

Of course, that group had dissolved too.

"Kids don't fit into your life," Avery said. "You rearrange your life to fit kids into it."

"A fantastic reason to go on without then," Hannah said. "I'm just teasing. But my only goals right now revolve around the symphony."

Hannah had always known exactly what she wanted. She'd always had her music. And she had always known which direction she was headed. Lark felt like her life had been one big redirect after another. Thinking she was on one path, ending up on another. Flying off of the new one spectacularly and landing somewhere entirely different.

Avery had gone to school for English, but she'd also always

been very clear that she wanted to get married and have children. She'd come back to Bear Creek with a degree and a fiancé.

It made Lark feel like the cuckoo in the nest. If it weren't for Gram she would have felt like she was an entirely different species to her family.

"I like kids," Lark said. "And the idea of being in a shop the way that Grandma was… It makes me happy. I want it to be filled with people. Laughing and talking and creating. I want it to be…" She looked at the piles of things they had gone through already. "Her. Everywhere Grandma went she created something. It was like her hands were magic. That was what I learned from her. That hands could make magic, right here in the real world. And I want to give that to other people."

"I can mend socks and make costumes and do all kinds of things thanks to Gram," Avery said. "I'm not sure I find the kind of magic in it that you do, Lark, but it does make me feel closer to her."

"All this stuff," Lark said. "It's such a treasure chest."

"Loose ends," Hannah said, wrinkling her nose. Lark noticed her sister didn't have a comment on what it had meant to her. But she was right about one thing.

A lot of loose ends. So many of them. Down in Lark's own soul. And even in the story of their grandmother. And Lark found herself wondering if there was a secret in the things her grandmother had chosen to make. In the things she hadn't finished.

The family she didn't talk about. The wounds that she carried. How a woman who clearly loved so much, the kids in town and her grandchildren, had left her husband and her children for as many years as she had.

As Lark had gotten older, and understood more deeply why there was friction between her mother and grandmother, as she'd realized she loved both women and that Gram's actions were hard to reconcile, she'd wondered about her life. She'd wondered about why.

"We need to finish the quilt together," she said.

"I don't really quilt," Avery said.

"You know how. And, I'm making a whole space just for this kind of thing. Wouldn't it be great if we got together every week and worked on this? It's Grandma's memory quilt, and what better way to finish it than as a family?"

"I… Yeah," Avery said. "That does sound fun. We can spend time together."

"We're going to be spending time together while we renovate The Dowell House," Hannah pointed out. "And it's going to be a lot of work."

Avery held up her hands, which were freshly manicured. "Do I look like I'm getting involved in actual manual labor? We are going to end up paying someone else to do most of it."

"I know," Hannah said. "But it's still going to be time-consuming to oversee it."

"We have time to sit together and make a quilt," Lark said. "If we don't make the time…" She closed her eyes. "I feel like I've barely seen either of you since I left home."

"Because you haven't," Hannah said.

"I didn't see Gram enough. And now it's too late." Lark appealed to her sisters. "Remember sitting on the front porch of The Miner's House? And we would each get a little quilt square? And we'd actually sit together and we didn't fight or anything. It was good."

"I don't do this stuff anymore," Hannah said. "I might not be performing while I'm here but I can't stop practicing. I have to get everything with the house organized, I don't know that I want to undertake…quilting."

"Come drink wine then," Avery said. "You have to put your violin down sometimes. Do it at this appointed time."

"Why don't you want to do it?" Lark asked. "You liked it when we were kids."

"Until I found the thing I loved doing. Anyway, you know what I'm allergic to? Domesticity."

Avery rolled her eyes. "Well don't get too close to me. I might get some on you."

"You take everything awfully personally," Hannah said.

"And you're taking a little bit of quilting awfully seriously."

"Mom's not going to be super into it either," Avery pointed out, ignoring Hannah now.

"She barely knows how to thread a needle. And you know she's going to get mad about it because she hates it when she doesn't know how to do something."

Something shifted inside Lark's chest. "We'll teach her. Because Gram didn't. But she did teach us. And it's not lost. It's not too late."

Conviction burned in her chest, along with something else. A deep need to share this. To pass it on. Like the stitches on the quilt would stitch up something inside of her. Close something off that had been there, frayed and gaping for years.

"Okay," Avery said. "I'll do it. I'll convince her."

Lark raised her glass. "Excellent. The Ashwood family quilting circle will commence this week."

4

He says he wants to marry me. That will mean...staying here. I can't bear the thought of it. I love him, but I cannot imagine that life. In a kitchen, looking at the same view I've seen all my life with children tugging at my hem. Even he could not make it bearable.

Ava Moore's diary, 1923

Hannah

It seemed somehow quintessentially Bear Creek that there would be a generalized handyman. Who not only did basic plumbing, but other odd jobs. Drywall repair, electrical. It was the kind of thing some people found charming about small towns. And if Hannah squinted and tilted her head slightly, she could almost see it.

But mostly she found the lack of options here just...a lot of work. It wasn't like in Boston where she could order groceries, dinner, a car or a date all with her phone.

Though she supposed a handyman who was basically a human Swiss Army knife was a convenience of a sort.

And it was of course exactly what they needed to get The Dowell House functional again.

The wiring was finicky, owing to the fact that their grandfather had done a fair amount of work on the place on his own. And absolutely shouldn't have. The man wasn't qualified. Sometimes a light switch in one corner of the kitchen turned a light out in the parlor, and it was things like that that were going to make it difficult for guests to enjoy a stay.

What had surprised her was that there had been a website with a contact form, and she'd been able to contact the business through the internet and make an appointment that way.

In her opinion everyone should do it like that. If she could avoid a phone call, she would.

She wanted efficiency. Not small talk.

She was puttering around the kitchen when she heard the sound of a truck, a big truck, with a rumbling, clanking engine pull up to the property.

"You would think a handyman might make his truck sound like it wasn't on its last gasp," she muttered as she went over to the window and looked outside. It was indeed a big dually, all white and chipped with red lettering on the side that said All Around Handyman.

"Not a mechanic, though," she said against the window.

The figure inside shifted, and got out of the truck, rounding to the passenger side so that Hannah could get a better look at him. He was not, as she had imagined, a middle-aged gray-haired man with a beer belly. Rather the guy was young, with dark brown hair and broad shoulders. And when he turned to the side, she felt like she had taken a punch straight to her solar plexus.

That profile was as familiar as her own.

More.

She blinked rapidly, shocked that tears were filling her eyes. *Tears.* Over the ex-boyfriend that she had broken up with nineteen years ago.

It was just shock. She wasn't remotely heartbroken over Joshua Anderson. Not back then, not nineteen years later.

Then he turned fully, facing the kitchen window, and looked up. She felt like she was sixteen years old all over again.

And she knew that the face she saw, superimposed over whatever his actual thirty-six-year-old face looked like, was just the boy that she had fallen for, hard and fast, clawing tooth and nail to try not to. Because she had always known she was going to leave, and she had never, ever wanted to have a relationship with a local boy.

But she could remember then. That he was the most beautiful thing she had ever seen. That he had scrambled everything up in her brain, in her chest, and turned her well-ordered existence into a series of compromises and what ifs.

She'd been crouched in a corner at lunch, her sheet music in front of her as she ran through it all mentally. Over and over again.

"Why do you always eat alone?"

She looked up and her heart dropped. He was…devastating. She'd never understood that term to describe a boy before. Lark used it with ease. Every boy with eyes a certain shade of blue devastated her.

But Hannah herself had never been devastated until that moment.

"I'm busy."

He didn't take the hint. He sat with her. He didn't talk while she was looking over her sheet music, he just sat. Then he walked with her to class.

"I'm Josh."

And I'm too busy.

"Hannah."

She'd thought that was the end, but it was the beginning. Slowly those lunch dates had become daily, and she'd started talking to him instead of looking at her sheet music. She'd started spending some nights out with him.

Kissing him had made her breathless in a way only music ever had before.

Until she'd realized what was happening.

That he was a distraction and she'd fallen right into him in the most basic of ways.

She needed a cigarette. Badly.

She was suddenly doing mental calculations to figure out how she could sneak one outside while he was still here.

He walked along the side of the house, toward the front, and she followed, concealed now by the wall until she stopped in the living room, peering through the window from a great distance, watching as he rounded the corner and stepped onto the flagstone path that led up to the door.

Each footstep he took seemed to echo inside of her chest. And by the time he knocked on the door, she was so wound up that even though she had been expecting it she jumped.

She was being ridiculous.

Nineteen years since they'd broken up.

It had been nearly nineteen years since she'd so much as seen him. And, by extension, since he had seen her naked. Which meant it was probably not in the forefront of his mind. Though, now all she could do was imagine *him* naked.

She cut off that thought and went straight for the door, walking to the entryway and taking a brief moment to look at him through the one-way glass, which allowed her to see a purple and green tinted version of him, while she knew that he couldn't see her at all.

Then she opened the door. "Hi," she said, smiling as widely as she could.

She didn't know if that was weird or not.

"Hannah Ashwood." His lips tipped up into a smile, all arrogance and knowledge which had not been there when he was sixteen. "It has been a while."

"It has been," she said. She squinted, a sudden realization washing over her. "You knew that I hired you."

"Yes."

"I did *not* know that I hired you."

"Well, I like to make an entrance." And he did just that, walking right into the house, his broad frame filling the entryway.

It wasn't the lines on his face that made him seem different. It was the way he carried himself.

"I don't recall you being someone who felt the need to be theatrical," she said.

He'd been sweet and earnest, and they'd fought with intensity. And made up with even more of it. He'd always cocked his head to the side slightly, managing to be taller than her and somehow give the impression he was looking up at her.

Because he was trying to impress you. And he doesn't care anymore.

"This is the place you want me to work on?"

He didn't bother to comment on what she'd said about theatrics.

"I... Yes." Her head was still spinning. But of course he wasn't surprised. She had put her name on the contact form. His name wasn't listed on the business. Even if she hadn't put her name on there, he was well aware that her family owned this house. And given the way the gossip vine wound itself around the town, he was probably well aware that they were all here dealing with the inheritance that Addie had left behind.

So, while she felt the need to gather herself and redirect, Josh obviously didn't. And she was just going to have to pretend that she was fine. Truly, her response to this whole thing was disproportionate to the situation.

There was something about Josh that would always feel sad. Sad and unfinished, but no matter how their relationship had ended, it would have ended.

She had been just almost eighteen when they'd broken up. And she'd done what she had to do. She didn't regret it.

Because he was a handyman in Bear Creek, Oregon, and she played for the symphony in Boston. And there was nothing that could have ever brought those two worlds together. Her aspirations with his...his lack of them.

He'd just been *happy* here. And she had never been able to understand that.

"There's electrical, plumbing, drywall," she said, careful to keep the list neutral. "The roof might leak a little bit."

"It might?"

"I haven't been here in the rain, Josh, but if you would be so good as to check out the roof as part of your services, I would appreciate it."

"Hmm." He made kind of a dismissive grunt and looked around the entry. "It'll cost you."

"I know." Somehow, even as she said that, she felt a strong sense that he might have meant something deeper than money. *Stupid.*

"I look around, and then I'll send you an estimate. Does that sound good?"

"Yes. But… Be honest with me, is anyone else here going to be able to do all of this?"

"You can have people come in from Medford. I don't know that anybody else can do everything that you need doing on the place."

"So the bid is a formality."

"You can overpay to your heart's desire, Hannah, I really don't care."

Well. It was pretty obvious to her that he wasn't neutral. He might have shown up to take the job, but he didn't think of her as just another client. She wasn't entirely sure how she felt about that.

She cleared her throat. "Yeah. I'd rather not."

"Okay. I'm going to walk the place."

"Do you need me?"

He arched a brow. "If you think there are things that you should point out. Otherwise I'll try to see what I can find on my own."

She blinked, taking in the changes to his face. The lines that crinkled by his blue eyes, the deep grooves by his lips. He was the same height as he'd been in high school, but he was thicker now. Broader. He did physical labor, so she supposed that she shouldn't be surprised he was in excellent shape. But it was a little bit confronting.

He looked... Better. Better even than he had then.

What does it matter how he looks?

It didn't.

"I'll walk with you," she said.

She had managed to avoid the guy every time she had come back to town before now. And now she had hired him. And was apparently digging in to the hiring of him. Because not hiring him would be stupid, and would also reveal the fact that she...

She felt *something* when she looked at him.

That was silly. She'd been hit with a wave of nostalgia upon seeing him, because who... Who didn't feel that way about their first?

And there were just other things tangled up in him that she was never going to be able to sort out.

She cleared her throat. Awkwardly. "So. What's... What's been going on with you?"

He turned, one brow lifted. "Just... In the last nineteen years?"

"Yeah."

"Not much." He turned away from her.

"I'm in the Boston Symphony Orchestra," she said and wanted to pull the screwdriver out of the back of his pocket and stab herself.

He might not be trying to impress her, but apparently she wanted to impress him.

She did not do things like that, especially not with men.

Now he was just making her feel...not herself. Insecure and younger and not the accomplished, confident woman she was.

"I know you are. I think my mom has a picture of you on her fridge. That she took off of a brochure."

She laughed. "Really? I mean, I wouldn't have thought your mom would..."

"You thought she might hate you?"

"Yes."

"She did." He turned toward her again, and this time he smiled. "She got over it. Because it's been a long time. And mostly she's proud of you. Because you went and did what you said you would."

She noticed that he didn't say *he* was proud of her.

Do you need your ex-boyfriend to be proud of you?

"Right."

"Good for you," he said. "Not very many people do."

She didn't know what to say. Because she realized that she didn't actually know for sure what all he had wanted. He'd talked about staying close. He'd talked about loving this town.

I can't stay close.

But you'll be back.

Maybe I won't!

They'd fought about it. So much. He'd told her he'd wait, and she'd said he had to come with her.

To a college I can't afford? Where I can hang out and be your deadbeat, townie boyfriend?

Everything had seemed clear and easy before Josh and he'd made her feel like she was breathing around knives. She hadn't known what to do.

Until you blew it up.

"You...own your own business." Realizing full well that her

tone made it clear she'd just given him the verbal equivalent of a participation trophy.

"You don't have to pretend to be impressed, Hannah. I'm well aware that I don't impress you."

"I didn't say that."

"I knew it then. I know it now."

"Maybe I don't actually think about you that much."

That earned her another look. And something twisted low in her stomach. And she knew that she thought about him about as much as he thought about her. Which was perhaps more often than either of them would like.

She had hurt him.

She wished that hadn't been essential. But it had been. She'd had to make a clean break, a real break. Her violin wasn't the home wrecker. It wasn't the diversion. She'd given up her childhood for it already. Had given up normal long before Josh. Her sacrifices had already been endless. He had been unplanned and completely useless to her goals.

She'd made a choice to be tougher. To get refocused.

"I'm sorry that I was an asshole when I was seventeen. Who isn't?"

He huffed a laugh. "I swear I don't walk down the street with a Hannah shaped chip on my shoulder."

She believed that. It had been a long time. But he'd...known he was going to see her and he had to have had a feeling about that. Given his reaction to her.

She crossed her arms, as if she was trying to shield herself for the response of what she asked next. "Did you prepare a speech? For this. You knew we were going to see each other."

He turned to face her, crossed his arms over his broad chest. "Maybe."

"Let's hear it."

"No. Because this has already gotten weird."

"Joshua Anderson," she said. "If you have been saving up a speech for me for nineteen years then I deserve to hear it."

"Fine." He turned to her, shoulders square. "I'm happy. I did exactly what I wanted to do. I built a life here. I took care of my mom. My dad died, but I bet you didn't know that. But it made it so I couldn't leave, even if I had wanted to. I took care of my mom, and I took care of my sisters, and I'm proud of what I did. And you were right. We wouldn't have worked. Because I would have made you miserable, every day of your life. And you would have looked around at what I think is paradise and seen nothing but your broken dreams. So, thank you. For breaking my heart then. So that you didn't have to do it later."

Her lungs deflated. "I did not know your dad died. I'm sorry. My mom never told me." Her mom wasn't one to share news from town, that was for sure.

"She probably didn't talk to you about me. The same as my mom didn't talk to me about you for a really long time."

"For what it's worth," she said, "you were the worst part about leaving."

That was the truth whether she should have said it or not.

She'd done her best to be cruel when she'd separated from him and she certainly hadn't said that then.

But she'd wanted to blow it all into so many pieces they'd never be tempted to even try to put them back together. She had made too many decisions that she couldn't take back, and she had to move forward.

He cleared his throat. "Well, that got a little bit more personal than I meant it to. If you don't want to hire me, Hannah, that's fine."

"Do you not want to work for me?"

"Really, I promise you, I'm fine. It's been a long time."

"Yeah. But apparently I'm still the person that you argue with in the shower." Discomfort tightened inside of her, along with an arrow of sensation that seemed to strike right between her legs. "You know what I mean."

"Sure. But if it helps, there are a couple people I argue with in the shower. You're on the list, but not as high as you used to be."

She laughed. "Yeah. I almost never argue with you anymore."

"Why did you ever argue with me?"

She tried to force a smile. "I guess it's not really an argument. Sometimes I would just try to make you understand. That I was right. I guess you kind of know that."

He looked her over. "I do." He looked down, seemingly taking stock of his white T-shirt with dirt marks over it, his jeans with paint splatters. "Yeah, I do."

Then he turned away from her. "Tell me about this place, and your plans."

"We want to do a vacation rental."

"That's a good idea," he said. "Vacation rentals do pretty brisk business here. Especially during the summer months during the concert season." There was a mildly famous summer festival in Bear Creek where niche bands and bands who had once been popular played, and it brought a fairly decent crowd of people in.

"I bet. And with all the wineries in the area I'm sure it goes on even longer."

"You'd be correct. Tourism has really revived itself since you left."

"Yeah. I remember when half the buildings on Main were empty. Not anymore." He stopped in front of a crack in the drywall. "Yeah. That will need to be fixed," she said, feeling a little bit lame, because that was obvious.

But he didn't make her feel stupid. He went into some kind of professional mode, talking only about the repairs that were needed for the house and marking things down on a paper that he had on his clipboard.

"My sister is opening a Craft Café," she said. He didn't ask. But she was going to tell him. Because her skin felt too tight, and saying something seemed as good of a way as any to make it feel a little bit less so.

She didn't like this. This weird emotional reaction he was creating in her. She didn't do emotion unless she chose to, and she was not choosing it now.

"What?" he asked.

"I don't know. It's a café. Where people also make crafts?"

"I'm going to put that on the list of things I don't understand. Right next to avocado toast."

She laughed and tilted her head, tucking her hair behind her ear.

Are you flirting with him?

She was not flirting with him. She didn't do coy flirty stuff. If she wanted a guy she was honest about it. She had so many friends who saw dating as this big, high stakes thing. Because every guy was a potential life partner. But not for her. It made everything a lot more straightforward.

And made it so she didn't...play with her hair and get shy because it didn't matter if a guy wasn't into her. If not, she'd find someone else or they'd find her.

Yet, here she was.

Hotter to her now than he'd ever been and that was... unexpected. Not welcome.

"Right," Hannah said. "Well. She's very confident in it."

"If I remember Lark correctly, she was always...outspoken. Confident."

"Yeah."

"Different than you."

"I'm *confident.*" The plainspoken observation made her feel undressed. It was one thing to have to deal with a former lover and to cope with the fact they'd seen you naked—but he'd seen a pretty great version of her, so it wasn't embarrassing. It was the emotional intimacy they'd once shared that made her feel laid bare. "I've always performed in front of people. What would make you think I'm not confident?"

He lifted one broad shoulder and she tried to see what he did in that moment. Because she couldn't imagine very many other people looking at her—with her bright red hair and matching lipstick, black tank top and tight black jeans—and think she was...somehow lacking in confidence.

"Don't do that. Don't *shrug* at me. You think I'm not confident?" He was wrong. She'd been too confident if anything. So convinced she was special.

She still was. You couldn't get by in a career like hers without believing in hard work *and* magic. She knew too many people who worked hard and couldn't get to where she was.

"I think you weren't when you were seventeen. I don't have anything to say about who you are now. I don't know you."

His words felt sharp like a knife. Like they'd gone right between her ribs and twisted.

Because at seventeen she'd been no less *in your face* than she was now. She felt seen somehow and she didn't like it at all.

He hadn't said if he was single or married or with someone. If he had kids.

And she wouldn't ask.

They finished the walk through the house, and he handed her the paper from the top of his clipboard. "That's my very fast estimate."

"That was a fast estimate," she said, looking down at the figure. It was a lot, but not too much. And Gram had left money. "You're hired," she said, decisively.

"Just like that?"

"Yes. This part of the project is mostly me. So yes. You're hired." There was a budget, part of what Gram had left behind, and Hannah knew this was well within it, and also that her sisters would be fine with her making the decision.

"Great. I guess I'll be seeing you around, then."

"Yeah. I guess you will. I guess… We'll see each other."

His mouth cocked up to one side in a half smile. "Yeah. I guess so."

And by the time he left, she was breathless, and reverted in a way that made her want to slap herself. What was the matter with her? She'd gone and backslid into some high school state where half a glimpse of Joshua Anderson sent her into a tailspin.

But you're not in high school. You are a thirty-six-year-old woman.

A thirty-six-year-old woman who'd felt afraid to pick up a sewing needle last night when her sister had suggested they finish her grandmother's quilt. And she couldn't figure out why.

Because it's part of the Hannah you left behind.

So was Josh Anderson but he was apparently coming to refurbish this house.

And her phobias about the past actually did uncover some insecurity she wasn't comfortable with. She didn't want them to exist. Not at all.

She'd been soft then. Had been swayed by the romanticism he'd roused in her. Something she hadn't realized existed before then. She'd been…made normal by him in some ways. He'd made her want to hang out with friends on Friday nights and sneak off and have sex in cars.

He'd shown her that the soaring feeling in her chest she got from playing music, she could feel when he touched her body.

When he was inside her.

And she hadn't wanted to think about the reality of the situation, or that she couldn't be both a normal girl and an exceptional one.

But in the end, she'd had to choose. And that moment in her life when she'd been idealistic, when she'd hoped she didn't have to…

It had burned to the ground, and she'd emerged harder. Stronger.

She'd learned she couldn't let herself be pulled in too many directions. She'd learned you couldn't love too many things.

She'd put the past away, and she didn't get it out and turn it over, not ever. That was behind her. The past had nothing to do with her future, and her future was what mattered.

Which meant…making the past into something bigger than it was didn't have any place.

She took her phone out of her pocket and looked at the text box for the group chat called Sisters.

All right, she typed. What night are we quilting?

5

The wagon is reserved for children, and sometimes women, but I prefer to walk. I am not sure what I've agreed to or why. Grief makes fools of all of us. Or perhaps it is still love, reaching out from beyond the grave. At least out here it is easy to forget who I am. Abraham Snow's wife would not have made this journey. But his widow is.

Anabeth Snow's diary, 1864

Avery

"Grandpa is in his shop if you want to go see him, Hayden."

When her mom spoke, Avery's son brightened visibly. Getting her fourteen-year-old to brighten was no easy task these days. Hayden was all height with none of his breadth yet. Taller than she was, but narrow. He could be sweet, but sometimes… sometimes his bursts of testosterone stole the boyish roundness from his personality and replaced them with angry, impatient edges that his maturity level couldn't quite support yet.

It was such a weird thing, watching this boy you'd created grow into a man. She'd watched her daughter transform from a small rectangular shaped girl into a girl with the shape of a woman, who looked so much like Avery it sometimes caught her off guard.

Even stranger was realizing Peyton looked more like Avery did in her head, than she did in real life, because in her heart she still looked like that sixteen-year-old version of herself. Thirty-eight-year-old her wasn't fixed in her head yet. And by the time she was, she supposed she'd be forty-five-year-old her and then that would be another thing to get used to.

She could ignore time when it was her. Much harder when she looked at her kids. They were evidence of the passing years in a sometimes harsh way.

Most especially when they made it clear they didn't need her in the ways they once had.

"Okay," Hayden said, barely looking at her as he went back out the front door, and headed toward her dad's shop.

"He was desperate to get away from the women," her mom said.

"Yeah."

Hayden was mad, and not at her, at David. She wasn't supposed to be the one to pick him up from practice today. But David had been busy with paperwork at the hospital, stemming from a surgery that hadn't gone to plan. But Hayden didn't care about the reasons. Only that his dad hadn't been there for him.

Avery really didn't mind when her plans had to shift because of David's work. She didn't. She understood that his work was intense, and she'd chosen to marry him, knowing he'd be a doctor. But Hayden didn't understand.

She wasn't what he wanted. Wasn't the one who could fix it.

That hurt. Made her feel helpless and...

Tired.

"We're not going to stay long," Avery said. "I have to fix dinner. But I wanted to talk to you. Because… Lark has an idea."

"Lark has an idea and you're here to pitch it to me?" her mother said. "That doesn't seem like a very good sign."

"Lark wants to finish Gram's quilt. And she wants all of us to help."

She watched her mother's expression shift into something bland, which meant she was thinking mean things and didn't want to advertise it.

Avery knew, because she often did the same thing.

"I don't really want to mess with my mother's things," her mom said.

"Mom, I know." Avery looked at her mother, and she felt… Well, immensely guilty. Because she knew that this was a sore spot for her mom. It was also why she thought she should be the one to talk to her about it. "I understand that your relationship with Gram was complicated."

"It wasn't complicated," Mary said, her tone firm. "She had a relationship with the three of you and there was no cost to being civil. If your grandpa could be civil, always, in spite of his hurt, I could be too."

Her grandpa had been extremely upright. He'd had a classic view on manners and the treatment of others.

He'd passed it on to his daughter, who took his way of things as gospel.

Her mother was old-fashioned in her values, but without being overtly feminine. She'd learned to cook of a necessity, but she'd never been one to sit and have girl talk. She wasn't a big toucher, and she didn't show her emotions easily.

The admission that she'd had to work to be civil was a pretty big admission, actually.

"I know. You let Gram back in for us." She took a breath. "I know that you made as much of a relationship as you had because you wanted the three of us to know her. And I think that was incredibly kind."

"It is what it is," she said. "And now she's gone. It's going to take a while to figure out exactly how I feel about all of this."

That was as close to a heart-to-heart as her mom got.

"I know," Avery said. "And I'm sorry. But I do think that Lark is right. We can do this together. Finish the quilt together. We can teach you how. I can't fix what Gram did, that she wasn't in your life. But we can make something new together, out of all these old things. That feels a lot like fixing something." She blinked. "Or at least repairing it."

"I'll never forget it," Mary said. "When Mom came back, and wanted to see you. You were two years old. I could hardly believe she had the nerve to do that. But she…taught you things I couldn't. Things she didn't teach me, and I was never going to keep that from you."

"Mom, we love you so much. Nobody wants you to be hurt by this. But we would like you to do this with us."

"It's no fuss, Avery," she said, her manner getting brusque and making Avery think it was at least a little bit of fuss.

But she wouldn't say that, of course.

Avery looked at the time. She really had to go get moving on dinner.

Suddenly, Avery wanted to sit down. At her mom's kitchen table. And just stay. In this place where someone felt like it was easy to do things for her. Where somebody might fix her dinner. She had the strongest, strangest urge to go to her childhood bedroom and curl up in the bed in there.

"Thanks, Mom. I have to go." She took a step away from the kitchen, rather than moving toward it like she had just wanted to do. "I'm glad that you're going to do the quilt with us."

"Me too," Mary said. But her smile didn't quite reach her eyes. And Avery knew that like everything else, it was complicated.

But complicated was just the way life was.

You didn't get to go hide in your parents' house just because you were tired.

And you just said that you never felt tempted to run away.

All right, maybe sometimes she wanted a break. That wasn't the same thing. And she wasn't taking one. That was what really mattered. What you actually did.

And Avery always did what she was supposed to.

Mary

Mary walked up the front steps of The Miner's House with a bright ball of emotion burning inside her. She avoided this place. It had been her mom's candy store, and except for dropping off and picking up the girls, she didn't set foot in it. And, hadn't had occasion to in more than twenty years.

She could still remember her mom coming back. Mary had been pregnant and Avery had been a toddler.

Addie had rolled in, in that convertible of hers at nine at night.

Mary hadn't seen her mother since her wedding five years earlier. She'd been mad Addie had shown up for that when Mary had not sent her an invitation and she'd known it would be a problem for her dad.

But she'd come all the same, and just like now, on a breeze of spearmint, perfume and cigarettes.

She didn't invite her in. She stepped outside instead, wrapping her robe more tightly around her body. "Mom. What are you doing here?"

"I'm moving back. I'm... I'm moving home."

She hadn't noticed how old her mom looked five years earlier. How deep the lines by her mouth were. Her red hair was the same, and she was still trim and full of energy.

Her hair never changed. Mary had already vowed to gray gracefully instead of insisting on candy-apple red into eternity.

"I want to know my grandchildren."

The words stabbed through her chest. "Why? And why now? Why mine? Why not move to Newport to get to know Bill's kids?"

"You have a daughter. I... I made a mistake, Mary. I made a lot of mistakes. Would you really keep me from knowing your kids?"

She thought of everything she'd missed not having her mother in her life. Could she keep her kids from having a grandmother when she wanted to be there for them?

Joe's mother had passed when he was in high school and Addie was the only grandma. Their only chance at that.

"I'll think about it. Come back tomorrow."

It was her dad who'd told her grudges didn't heal wounds. And she was sure he was right. But...either way she didn't feel all that healed.

It was nostalgic and terrible, a feeling of sadness and wistfulness rolled into one as she walked up the white steps and through the front door. She hated this. Hated all this grief. She couldn't control it or compartmentalize it. It just sat there.

The changes in the space shocked her enough to take over the feelings. "Lark," she said. "Did you do this?"

There was a heavy wooden bar where a shiny counter had once been, with tall stools positioned at it. Antique lights hung over the top of it. The entire thing felt warmer. Older and newer all at once.

Mary was in awe of what her youngest daughter had accomplished. It wasn't just all the work it had taken, it was...

It was the bravery.

Taking this place and turning it into something new.

Mary had always had complicated feelings about the candy store. That her mother had settled here when it was far too late for Mary to benefit from it.

That it was the place her girls had gotten along best.

Mary hated to admit it, but she'd felt betrayed by that sometimes. That Addie had been able to find ways to bring the girls together. That she'd done it with arts and crafts, which had felt beyond Mary's reach.

With chats and sewing, feminine things. The sorts of things

Mary had spent a lifetime feeling incompetent at and certain people around her knew it.

But now the building had brought Lark home.

"I did," her daughter said, coming in from the back.

She was so glad Lark was home. She worried about Lark because while her daughter had done what Mary considered to be an incredible feat—become a self-supporting artist—she was so isolated. So hard to reach when at one time she'd been so...

She'd been different. And Mary had never been able to figure out what had changed. Lark would have never admitted anything had.

And Mary didn't know how to...talk to her girls. She'd never learned that. Talking about feelings. She was always more comfortable doing something. Putting a Band-Aid on a scrape. Fixing peanut butter and jelly to ease their hurts.

And as they'd gotten older Band-Aids and peanut butter hadn't been enough.

More and more she'd felt like an outsider to their lives. And as they'd grown older they'd gotten closer to Addie.

Addie knew how to talk to them, she supposed.

Mary hadn't known how.

Lark smiled, easily, the way that Lark always did. Lark was her sunny child. She'd always had so much energy, and her moods were aggressively cheerful, until they weren't. Lark's meltdowns were rare, but they had always been epic. She had never been halfway on anything.

When Lark had gotten an idea she'd been halfway finished with it before she'd ever thought to ask. One time she'd cut up half of their family photos making a scrapbook when she'd been ten. Mostly that had just meant all of Mary's nice photos that had been waiting for a home in a photo album had been cut into shapes deemed artistic by a child, and destroyed in Mary's opinion.

Lark had once started a dog washing business without asking. Mary had discovered it when she'd come home to find a terrier in the bathtub and Lark making bandannas out of an old swimsuit.

Lark never meant to be bad. She never meant to cause problems. And any opposition to her schemes had been met with meltdowns.

Mary found herself missing Lark's tantrums.

She couldn't figure out why Lark being less moody made her feel more concerned. Had never been able to pin that worry down.

"It looks... It looks wonderful," Mary said.

The door opened behind her, and Hannah came through, along with Avery.

Hannah was a statement, as always, her bottle red hair never faded. She suspected her daughter touched it up at least once a week. She was dressed head to toe in black, and somehow managed to command attention, even wearing dark colors. But that was Hannah. Quietly intense and dramatic, but rarely showing it.

She was outspoken and quick to voice an opinion but when it came to deeper emotion she kept everything bottled up, and sometimes Mary could see that she was silently drowning, but also knew that asking her about it would only push her into deeper water. Further away.

It frustrated her that in many ways she and Hannah were probably the most alike, and somehow that made her the hardest to know.

It was one reason she'd been so thankful for Hannah's boyfriend, Josh Anderson. She'd had to pretend she didn't know Hannah was sneaking out to be with him some nights. But she hadn't wanted to push Hannah further away, and she'd so hoped that Josh reached her in ways she couldn't.

For a while, it had seemed he had.

Until Hannah had dumped him. Broken his heart.

Mary had gotten an earful from Cathy Anderson after that.

It had been the last time she'd spoken to the other woman.

Mary had told her that while she liked Josh well enough she didn't meddle in the affairs of her kids. And that Hannah had to do what she thought was right.

It didn't matter if Mary couldn't understand what Hannah's heart wanted.

Avery was both intimidating and a triumph for Mary. Evidence that having Addie back in their lives had done some good, but also...a feminine, pretty supermom type that Mary herself had always been intimidated by when she'd been raising her kids.

She'd never meshed well with groups of women. But she'd been raised in a house of men.

Her father had been a quiet man. A good man. But a man who had expected that when life was hard you picked up and carried on.

It was Addie who hadn't been able to do that.

Mary's mother had been so...volatile toward the end. Crying, laughing or shouting and nothing in between. In response, Mary's father had gotten more and more even-keeled till he was like a river that barely moved.

She knew he'd been hurt when Addie had left, but he'd stayed steady.

Mary had wanted to do the same.

"I have all the fabric laid out in the sitting room," Lark said.

Lark was fluttering. And she led them all from the entryway into a little room that had chairs set up in a circle.

"And look what I made!" Lark produced a large box, and inside were blossoms and vines, twined into...

Lark pulled one out and put it on her head, pale white and pink blossoms like cheery punctuation marks on her head. It reminded Mary of Lark's near daily tea parties when she'd been a girl.

Peanut butter and jelly sandwiches had been cut into tiny triangles, and milk poured into teacups. Lark had always been about the experience. Had always wanted even mundane moments to be parties. She'd guided and directed it all, and Mary had indulged it because when Lark was full of sparkle it was impossible to deny her.

Lark had brought something out in her then that she'd never been able to find before. Or since.

"Crowns!" Lark said.

"No," Avery said, her lips firming into a line.

Hannah lifted a shoulder, then rooted around in the box until she found a crown with yellow flowers, which she perched on top of her bright red hair. "I'm here. I'm quilting. I might as well."

Mary looked at her daughter. "You can't possibly expect me to wear a crown while trying to do something I've never done before in my life."

It was too easy to imagine herself. Her face wet with tears while her mom yelled at her about the ruined sampler.

She'd only wanted to learn to needlepoint like Addie.

It's ruined now! Mary, why do you have to ruin everything of mine!
She clenched her hands into fists.

She could remember the yelling. Her tears.

I don't have the patience to teach you and God knows you can't learn.
And the next day she'd been gone.

Mary knew full well it wasn't why.

She knew it with her head.

It was a lot harder to know it in her heart.

"Mom," Lark said, heading over to the box and plucking out a delicate pink crown. Then she closed the distance between them, and set it on her head. "That is the best time to wear a flower crown. When you have absolutely no idea what you're doing. That's why I wear one every chance I get."

Her daughter's eyes glittered, but there was something else there too. A something that had been there for years, that Mary couldn't ever quite reach.

Lark had always been pure in her emotions. Mary had seen her daughter full of brilliant joy, and also screaming down the house in a rage. She no longer flew off the handle, but she was no longer pure in her joy either.

And Mary found herself keeping the crown on her head.

She had worried about Lark's impetuous nature leading her to heartbreak. Had worried Avery's desire for the finer things would leave her perpetually unsatisfied. Both characteristics had reminded her of Addie.

She'd worried less about Hannah, who had charted a course when she'd been a child and gotten right to work on meeting her goal. She had some concerns about Hannah's happiness at times, because you never could tell, but when it came to life, she knew Hannah would be okay. She didn't worry about Avery anymore. She'd been a silly girl in high school, but marriage and motherhood had taken that and honed her into the perfect suburban specimen. She was everything Mary had never known how to be.

Friends with other mothers, perfectly put together. A gourmet cook. Perpetually on the ball with her kids' busy schedules, and took time to get manicures with her daughter on top of it. Actually *liked* getting manicures.

Mary might have had trouble connecting with Avery at times, but she must have done something right with her.

"Avery," Lark said. Her tone was cajoling, but Avery was unmoved.

"No. I don't go to costume parties."

"This isn't a costume."

"Okay," she said, still unmoved, taking a seat in the circle.

Mary sat next to her oldest daughter, and watched as Hannah and Lark moved some boxes around.

"There's fabric in each of these," Lark said. "I thought tonight we might go through some of it and choose what we like, and also go over some basic techniques."

Mary felt that familiar sense of hollowness in her stomach. The one she often got when she was faced with an unfamiliar task. There were so many things that girls around her had simply known because they had grown up with mothers. She knew, logically, that there was no shame in not knowing how to do something.

But not having a natural confidante growing up had forced her to turn inward for strength.

When she'd collapsed on the ground weeping after her dad had told her Addie had left for good, he'd told her crying didn't fix a thing. He was right, it didn't.

So through growing up, through periods and hormones and liking boys for the first time she'd just stuffed it all down.

Joe had been the first person she'd ever shared her feelings with really. They'd met when she'd taken a job at a local ranch doing odd jobs when she was eighteen, and he'd been...well he'd looked like a cowboy to her.

And he'd been perfect. Sensitive in ways she never had been and strong in all the right ways.

Still, the feelings of inadequacy she had around all the "normal" girl things she'd never learned never really went away.

And it always seemed to combine with that last memory of her mother. The way she'd found her so unteachable.

She was sixty-five years old. She didn't put a lot of stock into thoughts like that, not anymore. But even though the thoughts, the worries and the concerns had disappeared from her brain, they remained in the pit of her stomach.

Ideas could be unlearned, but feelings were a part of the very way your body was put together.

Lark pulled out the journal that she had that first day at The Dowell House. "This has the list of fabrics that Gram was intending to use. And they're buried in these boxes. There are other fabrics too, but we'll need more. Backing and a base fabric and all of that. But this is her drawing." She held up a grid that made little sense to Mary. "And these are the fabrics." She turned the page, and began to show the swatches. "There's no information or anything on here, just titles."

"How is this going to work?" Avery asked.

"We'll each work on our squares. Sometimes here, but we can take everything home, because when we're finished with the squares we'll join them all together on the quilt. So, if we can each choose a few fabrics that we like best, we can work them into the pattern that Grandma made. And it looks like we'll each be making...three squares, and there's a guide for a big centerpiece, but I can do that."

"Okay," Avery said. "That makes sense."

She stood up from the chair and gave Lark a distinct dirty look as she moved past the crowns, a clear warning that if she were to engage in a guerrilla coronation she would not blithely accept it the way that Mary had. "The parlor curtains," Avery said, squinting at the page. "Those are pretty."

In spite of herself, Mary was curious, and she found herself getting up out of her chair and moving closer. The parlor curtains were a rich burgundy velvet brocade. It didn't surprise her that it appealed to Avery, who liked a traditional looking home, and probably liked the feeling that there was something connected to a family. But a fancy one.

"Those are in this bin," Lark said, indicating a box of fabric. "If you want to take it home and then go through it, and see what else is there..."

"Sure," Avery said.

"What's this one?" Hannah leaned over and tapped a piece of peacock blue fabric that was filled with silver beads. "The party dress."

Mary noticed that Hannah didn't seem quite as into this as Avery or Lark, but she could also see a secret fascination shining in her eyes when she looked at that particular fabric.

"I assume it's a party dress," Lark said.

"Thanks," Hannah said, rolling her eyes.

"Well, I don't have any more information than that."

"I'll do that one. It's pretty."

"You'll have to dig until you find it," Lark said. And Hannah set about busily rifling through the boxes.

Then Lark leveled her gaze at Mary.

"What are you going to pick, Mom?"

"You're not going to choose first?"

"I can't decide. There's so much, and I really like all of it."

Mary took the book from Lark's hand and began to turn the pages. She stopped on some cream colored lace that seemed delicate and pale compared to the other fabrics. It simply said *wedding dress.*

She'd just take that. She didn't much care and there was no point waffling about it.

"I like this."

"Was that Gram's wedding dress?" Lark asked.

Mary shook her head. "No. It couldn't be. She and Dad didn't have a real wedding. She wore blue silk for that. They had a picture when I was small. I remember it clearly." Her dad had kept it, always. It had never made sense to Mary, not when she knew how angry he was with her.

Mary's father was not a man to speak ill of others, but the icy look in his eye when Addie was mentioned said it all. He'd never remarried. As far as Mary knew, he'd never dated again after his wife had left him. His anger had been like a stone. Silent and heavy and present, whether it was remarked on or not. And after he'd died fourteen years ago, Mary had taken it upon herself to hold at least one corner of her heart in contempt of her mother. Making absolutely certain that full forgiveness was never on offer.

That unspoken tension and resentment lingered in the air between them at birthday parties and holidays. She did more than simply cutting her mother out of her life. She had allowed her in while making her aware that all was still not well. It had felt satisfying when her mother had been there to witness it. And now that she was gone there was something unsatisfying about it. Strangely unfinished.

And it was the oddest thing, because Mary had never meant to resolve things with the woman who had abandoned her when she was four years old.

Because just as she couldn't go back and remake herself so those insecurities and feelings of failure didn't exist inside of her, an apology couldn't undo what had been done. Coming back couldn't restore what had been destroyed in the first place.

"I'm not sure where any of this fabric came from," Mary said softly.

"Honestly, with Gram it could have come from anywhere. It could be from different rummage sales. Or people she knew in town…"

"She liked to collect things," Mary said. "She could make anything sentimental." It was one of those things that had bothered her about her mother. That she could be so attached to objects, and had left people so easily.

She touched the small square of lace as if it might teach her something. As if she might be able to understand her mother's connection to such things.

She didn't. She couldn't. But she understood that this mattered to her girls. Standing here, in the middle of all this, feeling out of her element completely, for the sake of her daughters.

"I'll do this one."

After that, Lark began to talk about quilt construction, and the way that they would work a square. She had one partly finished, and began to explain the steps with the efficiency of a practiced teacher.

"Have you been teaching classes?" Mary asked.

"Here and there," Lark said. "Otherwise I wouldn't leave my

house. I mean, drawing in your own home and communicating with everybody over email is pretty solitary."

"I didn't know that you were teaching." Mary looked down at the practice square in her lap.

"It didn't really seem important."

She had the sense then, when she looked at Lark, of sun slipping behind clouds. Bright and warm, but elusive. But she lived far away for so long, Mary supposed it was only natural for her to forget to include her mother in the details of her life.

It was normal, not a slight.

Mary chastised her nervous fingers as they shook, trying to get the thread through the needle and finding little success. She said nothing, and instead watched her daughters chatter and laugh, looking more and more like the girls they had been as each minute passed.

And that's why she was here. Not to quilt or confront untied threads from the past.

It was for them. For her girls.

They were happy. Hannah was on the verge of being principal violinist, like she had dreamed of since she was a little girl. Lark, for all that it was easy to seem like she was her pie-in-the-sky daughter, had come up with a business plan, and money in hand to begin this next phase of her life.

And then there was Avery. Married to such a wonderful man, with her two beautiful children, Mary's grandchildren that she loved with all of her heart.

The girls were happy.

And the sharp, unsettled edges in her own heart didn't seem quite so important in the face of that.

6

You have never gone so far that you can't come back home again.

From a letter, unsigned and unsent

Lark

"Can I be your first customer?" Lark's dad sat down at the counter and picked up one of her printed menus. "This is great, Lark."

She had been ready for her soft open of The Miner's House Craft Café. She didn't do any advertising, she just quietly opened the door one sunny day at noon, with her family there to see it become official.

Over the past couple of weeks her dad had helped install the new counter, which had been built by a local furniture maker. Lark had assembled many of the craft kits that she had begun working on shortly after Gram's funeral. Her sisters had helped clean the public areas of the space. The front room, where there was a bar and different things for sale, jewelry made by Lark, and other local artisans, local honey and fire cider, along with other folk medicines that were brewed in town. She was set up to serve coffee and had gotten her liquor license so that she could serve alcohol.

There was also a display with craft kits—small needlepointing sets with patterns, thread and hoops. Beading kits and kits to make graphic ink designs using linocut. All things she'd been working on for the last few months ahead of coming back to town.

Hannah sat down on the stool next to their dad. "I'll have what he's having."

"Beer," Dad said.

"Beer," Hannah confirmed.

Her mom and Avery came in a moment later, and sat at the two bar stools down at the end. When Lark put the beer bottles on the counter, her mom gave her father a scathing look. "It's barely noon," she said.

"I'm retired," he said, lifting the bottle. "Time is relative."

"I'm a musician," Hannah said, also lifting the bottle. "I do what I want."

Hannah and her dad clinked their bottles together. "Cheers, Hannah Banana," he said. "And cheers to you." He extended the bottle toward Lark, and Lark felt herself warm with happiness.

"Are you going to do a craft, Dad?"

"Not likely," he said. "I have a shop for that."

For the first time, Lark realized that she probably got some of her creativity from her dad. He made things, it was just she didn't think of them in the same way she thought of her own art.

"Are you all set up? Or do you need anything else?" her mom asked.

"I'm going to add more art to the walls. Keep gathering kits and talking to local artists." She moved from behind the counter. "Come here."

When they'd been little, Gram had often given them ice cream and set them down at the table nearest to the front of the store where she could keep an eye on them, and given them crafts to do.

Back then, the back rooms had been Gram's living quarters. Lark had left her bedroom untouched, and it was still filled with her belongings. She couldn't bring herself to disturb any of them.

The other rooms, though, she had turned into more space.

She led her family back to the room that was connected to the front. Past that was a hallway, another seating area, and then one in the back with a table for large groups. Behind that were the kitchen and bathroom. The kitchen was small, but she didn't need much room, considering she would be doing more reheating than actual prep.

"Dad, this is where we quilt," she said, gesturing to the room just behind the bar. It was the space where they had once done crafts in their grandmother's candy store. Gram's store had ice cream in the counter, along with walls of candy bins. Shelves filled with candy bars, both modern and old-fashioned. All the rooms had contained tables and chairs, similar to the layout that Lark had now, though she had traded in the round iron tables with matching chairs for eclectic chairs that she had purchased at various yard sales and thrift stores, with scarred, secondhand tables.

"It's cozy," Avery said.

"I think so," Lark said.

"This is great. I have a lunch meeting. I need to go." Avery pulled her in for a hug. "Best of luck on your opening day."

"I'm reading at the library," her mom said. "I'll come back by later to see how things are going."

"Hannah Banana and I can hang out for a bit," her dad said, putting his arm around her sister.

"Maybe I'm busy," Hannah said.

"You're not busy. Go finish your beer. Maybe we'll have one of Lark's cheese plates."

Hannah and her dad lingered for another hour before they left, and during that time, a few customers came and went. She had quite a few people come in and ask what was happening, and what the business was. And several of them stayed in the late afternoon and had beer. By the time she closed up, she was feeling more than a little bit tired. She was ready to go back to The Dowell House and lie down in a dark room. But when she got in her car and tried to start it, it only sputtered.

She sighed heavily. She could walk back to The Dowell House. It wasn't far. But she had more supplies to bring over in the morning, and she really did need a car for carting things around.

She sat there for a moment, and then remembered. There had been a mechanic in town back when she'd been in high school. And she hadn't really taken note of if the building it used to be in was in fact still the same business, but it was only two doors down.

At the very least she could go ask for a jump.

Of course, it was after five and most things in Bear Creek, except the bars and restaurants, closed by then.

She got out of the car and looked down the street, and saw a light filtering through the window of what had once been the garage.

Well. She might as well go check it out.

She started down the street, and breathed a sigh of relief when she saw that the sign above the door still said R&J's Auto Shop.

And the sign on the door said Open.

She pushed the door open and looked around the room. The small reception area was empty.

Except for a small, orange plastic chair and a fake plant that had seen better days. It was shabby and dusty, and Lark had to wonder what the point of fake shrubbery was if it actually made the place look uglier.

The floor was white tile with mottled gray spots, which worked, because the trim that separated the wall and the floor was also gray, and the white walls were spattered with what was probably oil, but could have been high-octane coffee, judging by the vaguely burned bean smell in the air.

She wondered if they'd just forgotten to lock up and turn the sign over. Which was infinitely possible in her hometown.

The second hand on the clock ticked around twice, and she was starting to wonder if it was a sign that this wasn't happening and she needed to just walk on home. If the universe was going to prevent her from her quest, then she wasn't going to argue with the universe.

The universe had seen things.

But just as she was about to turn and leave, the door that separated the reception area from the garage opened.

It was *him*.

Oh, lord. It was him.

Ben.

Recognition was swift and brutal.

But when she looked at him, she did not see her friend from all those years ago. He was older, that was how time worked, after all. But time hadn't hurt his looks at all. Not at all.

Right. Well the last thing she needed to do was start melting over how he looked.

But there was something else that felt changed too. It wasn't her, that was for sure.

Apparently you could avoid your hometown for years, except to see your family. Limit the amount of time you spent wandering around. Do anything, absolutely anything, to forget the biggest heartbreak of your life.

And he could walk into a room covered in grease and oil,

wearing nothing but worn jeans and a dirty white T-shirt, and you could find yourself right back where you never wanted to be.

Hopeless and desperate for a man who didn't love you.

Fantastic.

His blond hair was darker, pushed back off of his forehead. His cheekbones were sharper, his face covered with stubble. But the scar on his cheek was still visible. She remembered how he'd gotten it. Running underneath the bleachers and colliding with a support beam beneath it. He hit the side of his face and tore it open and it had taken a fairly legendary amount of stitches to close it back up again. The end result was a groove that ran just beneath the corner of his eye to the edge of his cheekbone.

She remembered him before and after that scar.

He had a beard now. But that didn't do anything to hide the lips that she had spent a whole lot of her teenage years staring at, composing poetry about them. Poetry that would only ever exist in the secret pages of a diary that had been burned long ago.

She could look at him and see a map to her past, but it felt distant. Far away.

She could see the exact moment recognition sparked through him. His blue eyes flickered over her, then stopped, and then clashed with hers.

He didn't smile, and somehow she wasn't surprised. Because there was something about his bearing now that didn't suggest he smiled all that often. There was a groove worn between his eyebrows, but he was missing lines by the corners of his eyes.

"I heard you were in town," he said.

Well she'd heard blessed little about him. Certainly not that he was running this auto shop which would have *been nice to know.*

Sure, but you pretend you're not avoiding and you've done it so well no one has noticed that your friendship didn't just fade away from years of neglect.

Right. That friendship that had been one of the most important, essential friendships in her life. Except she'd gone and fallen in love with him when she was fourteen.

While he'd gone and fallen in love with the *other* most important person in her life. Her friend Keira.

And they'd been a golden couple.

Still were, she was sure.

"I am. Obviously. I... I'm running Gram's shop. Though it's not...candy anymore."

"I wondered."

"Well. Wonder no more." Wow. That was so lame. She was so lame.

The corner of his mouth lifted slightly, but she would never call it a smile. "What brings you in?"

"Oh. My car won't start. Which you know is... I mean I could walk back to The Dowell House. I'm staying there." *Too much information, Lark.* "But the car thing will be a problem at some point and I saw you were open and...and."

Ben had been her very first experience with hiding emotion. Letting feelings out had been a catharsis for her all her life and she'd never thought of them as dangerous.

Until keeping how she felt about him shoved down deep for fear it would ruin her friendships, and therefore her life, had taught her that she sometimes needed to keep things to herself.

And then...oh then when she hadn't. When she'd exploded and done the very thing she shouldn't have...

"Where's your car, Lark?" he asked. "I was about to leave, but you know I'll help you out."

There was something about the way he'd said that. A familiarity to his words that melted the years away.

And now it was just right there, in her mind, a full Technicolor view of that night.

With wine and potato chips and a movie playing in the background that neither of them watched. He'd just been so... Broken. Because Keira had left him and broken off their engagement. And Lark was going away to school, so he was losing her too.

She could still remember seeing him like that. Like he was missing a piece of himself. And she'd thought...finally. *Finally he's missing something too.*

Because she had been missing him her whole life, at least it had felt like it.

She'd let her desire free. All the spontaneity and feeling and need she'd pushed down with him—only ever him—and she had touched him.

Not like a friend. She had touched his face, like a lover might do, and dragged her thumb over his bottom lip. And the next thing she had known he was kissing her.

It was so much like every fantasy she had since she'd been fourteen years old that she hadn't been able to say no. She hadn't wanted to. Even though she'd been certain at the end of that particular road would be heartbreak she... She hadn't wanted to say no. So she hadn't.

So she'd given Ben Thompson her virginity on the floor of his parents' daylight basement with the DVD menu of *Mean Girls* playing on repeat in the background. Which was maybe the most dated memory she possessed. And also one of the sharpest. One of the most devastating.

And they had never talked about it. Not ever. Because by the time she had quit hiding from him he had gotten back together with Keira. And it had been time for her to go to school. So she had.

Hadn't come back even for their wedding.

Hadn't spoken to him since.

"Do you have to... You don't have to be home?"

With your wife.

Your wife, who I also care about and miss. Your wife who I've totally accepted you have because it's been sixteen years and of course it's fine and I'm not hung up on you at all even if you are still hot.

"Nope."

She wanted to ask questions, but she didn't.

"Great. Lead the way."

She walked out the door, and he paused, turning the sign so that it said Closed, and when the cold air hit her, so did the reality of what was happening. It settled over her suddenly that she was walking down the street with Ben Thompson and rather than feeling like she was back in her sixteen-year-old skin, she felt like that girl was watching her, like she was both the Lark she was now and that girl from then. There had been a time in her life when he had been the dearest person in her world.

Her friend. In a deep, real way. But the problem had always been that she had felt for him in ways that a friend wasn't supposed to.

And Keira had been her other person. Her friend from childhood she'd shared everything with. Until she'd found herself loving the same person she did, which took the sharing thing a little too far.

For Ben it had always been Keira, never Lark.

And if there was one thing she had never wanted to feel again for the rest of her life, it was that sense of being with him and not really being with him.

She shoved all that introspection aside, and focused on the sound of her feet connecting with the sidewalk. The sole of her shoe on the cement, the vague crunch of dirt and sand that was nearly invisible on the uneven surface.

She let it consume her. Her thoughts, her chest.

That mundane action. It was so much better than memories.

"This is it," she said, stopping in front of her little red hatchback.

"Okay then." She'd never heard two words so heavy with judgment.

He muttered an expletive under his breath as he rounded

to the front of the car and popped the hood. "What exactly is going on?"

"It won't start. I mean, it took a couple of tries this morning, and I went to the store, and when I came back I tried again and nothing."

"Probably spark plugs or wiring. Connections. That kind of thing."

"Right. Well, I don't know what any of that means, so if you just want to give me a bill when you figure it out, that would be great."

"You don't want to know what you're paying for?"

"I'm just telling you it's not going to make sense to me even if you explain it."

"Fair enough. I'd probably feel the same if you started telling me about the crafts that you do in here." He gestured toward the cottage.

"Well, give me too much detail about the car engine, and I will."

She watched him work, bent over the car, the muscles in his arms shifting. He had tattoos. He had not had tattoos when they were younger. She was fascinated. He'd put art on his body, permanent art, and art was only ever personal. But when you inked it down beneath your skin it had to mean something truly deep.

She wanted to ask.

He looked up at her and their eyes caught, and so did her question. He just stared at her for a long moment. She had no idea why this man had the power to tilt her world on its axis like this. With one look.

She was saddest right then that they weren't friends anymore.

"You look the same, Lark," he said, a husky note in his voice telling her his own feelings were tangled up right now too.

But that wasn't possible.

Or fair.

He never had been. Neither had her feelings for him.

"You don't," she said. "I mean… I…you have tattoos."

He looked down at his arms. "Yeah. So I do."

Why? What do they mean?

"When did you buy the shop?" She asked that instead, because asking about work was easier.

"Twelve years ago or so. Marco retired. At that point I'd been doing most of the work anyway for a while. It was an easy transition. And hey, people react differently when you say you own a garage than when you say you're a mechanic."

"There's nothing wrong with being a mechanic."

He huffed a laugh, but there was no smile with it. "Agreed. I wasn't talking about what I think."

"I'm a professional artist. I've heard a variety of reactions. Just in my own family."

"Good for you," he said. "That you ended up doing art, I mean."

His blue eyes lingered on hers for longer than she was comfortable with. She looked down at the sidewalk, her touchstone.

"Thanks. I mean, good for you too. I've always thought… Getting to own a little piece of Main Street is pretty amazing considering the history here."

"It is that. I certainly don't mind it." He straightened, wiping his hands off on a rag that had been in his back pocket. "I'll bring the parts over and fix your car up. You need some connections tightened and a couple new spark plugs. And you need your oil changed. But I'm going to have to get it into the shop for that. So let's get it running."

"Thank you."

"Did Addie leave you this place?" he asked.

"Not me by myself, no. But we're all kind of taking different roles in the inheritance. Hannah is spearheading turning The Dowell House into a vacation rental."

"Sounds like hell."

"Yeah, it kind of does to me too. But she wants to handle it. And Avery and my mom can manage it."

"Hannah's not staying?"

"No."

"But you are."

"I am. Hey, thanks. I have to... I need to get the café open. Just bring me a bill, or something. And tell Keira hi for me."

"Sure."

"Thanks. It... It was good to see you again."

"You too."

She turned away from him and walked into the café, and when she closed the door behind her and the silence settled around her she found it was difficult to breathe. She didn't understand how... How that had just happened and it had been so... Nothing. So casual and... Easy. Except it didn't feel easy. She felt like her insides had been rearranged. And yet, it had been easy to talk to him.

Not the same. Not even close. But not impossible either.

She might have called it a miracle if it didn't feel so anticlimactic.

"He's going to fix your car. You saw him."

She had. And she had survived it. And if it felt like there was something sharp in her chest that was difficult to breathe around for the rest of the day, she was still going to call it a win. Because she hadn't collapsed.

"All these years, and you managed not to collapse. One encounter with him isn't going to do it."

You're not in love with him anymore.

Bolstered with that, she began to unload the sparkling water from its case. This had been the right decision, coming home.

She was even more certain of it now than ever.

7

The grass is like the sea. It goes on forever and makes waves in the wind. The vastness of it terrifies me, and I don't know why I've left the comfort of everything I've ever known to take a teaching position in such a new, wild place. But home was not home to me. Not anymore. This alien prairie isn't home. Oregon won't be home either. I'm destined to be homeless forever.

Anabeth Snow's diary, 1864

Avery

Avery checked on her chicken, and then went over to the box of fabrics that she had brought over from her sister's place two days ago. She hadn't had the chance to go through any of it, and she was dying to.

She opened up the top of the box, and removed a bolt of marigold fabric, finding the brocade curtains beneath. She traced the blossoms and leaves with her fingertips, and then pulled one of the panels out, a piece of paper fluttering out from underneath.

She unfolded it, and saw that it was a small, handwritten note.

The parlor curtains, which hung in the window in Boston, then made a journey on the Oregon Trail, to hang in the windows here.

She looked up, out her own windows, past the sensible cream-colored curtains that were nothing half so dramatic as this beautiful set was. She looked at the sedate view. The perfectly manicured lawns and lovely homes. And she wondered what sort of woman would trade beautiful Boston views and bring these curtains, and herself on a journey across the country. Swapping out city views for what must have been something much more rugged.

Same curtains. Different windows.

She pressed the note to her chest for a moment, rooted to the spot. To her view.

And then the front door burst open and her kids came in, bickering.

Hayden threw his soccer bag down by the blue decorative table in the entryway.

"Good to see you too," she said to her son as he stomped into the house.

Her daughter was focused solely on her phone. "What's for dinner?" she asked.

"Chicken."

"Ew."

Avery let out a slow breath. "Did you want something else, Peytona?" She used her daughter's childhood nickname, as she looked her directly in the eye, since they were the same height now.

"Something that isn't gross?"

Avery shook her head. "I don't know what that means since everything from chicken to the wrong lip gloss is gross to you."

"I might be a vegetarian."

"Great, green beans then." She'd had green beans on her mind because of Gram. "Because I'm making chicken. I need more advanced warning if you're going to adopt a lifestyle change. No last-minute vegetarianism."

Peyton rolled her eyes and headed for the stairs, her brother bowing his head, avoiding eye contact and following her.

"Hey," she said. "Not so fast. How was school, Hayden?"

"Great," he said, in the same monotone he always did.

Always great. Never any details she didn't pry out of him.

"Homework?"

"Yeah."

"When are you going to do it?"

"Sometime."

They were desperate to get away from her and up to their rooms and she felt...like she should make them stay downstairs. Like she should make them talk to her.

But she couldn't make them want to spend time with her. Hayden wanted attention from David, who was too busy to give it.

And none from her, of course.

But she had some disgusting chicken to go make that Peyton would pick at morosely, so who said being a mom was a thankless job?

At least Peyton didn't leave any debris lying around for Avery to deal with. She should call Hayden back and have him pick up his things.

She knew that she *should* correct all of the attitude that had just blown through the room.

But sometimes it was just a lot less work to pick up a soccer bag than get into a fight with a fourteen-year-old.

She'd pick it up in a minute. She stared over at where he'd

thrown it and noticed that there was a chip on the wall behind the table, where he'd thrown the bag, and she frowned. The house wasn't that old. But old enough that they were starting to have some patching up to do.

She lost herself in sorting through the fabrics and looking at the copy of the design for the quilt Lark had sent home with her.

She started mentally mapping out her part, which fabrics she would use where to create the intricate design that required thin cut strips of fabric laid together to create a woven look.

It would look rich with the parlor curtains and some of the gold and cream fabrics that were also in her box.

She touched the curtains again and wondered about that woman, because it had to have been a woman who brought her curtains with her.

A woman who did what she and her sisters had just been talking about.

A woman who pulled up and left everything behind for a whole new view.

She heard her kids thumping overhead and suddenly realized that time had passed.

She jumped up and went back into the kitchen, just in time for the smoke alarm to inform her that her chicken had been left in for too long. She let out a sharp curse and jerked the oven open while waving her hand in the direction of the smoke detector.

"Dammit," she hissed as she grabbed a dish towel and an oven mitt. She cleared the smoke out of the air with the dish towel as she removed the chicken. It wasn't bad. It was just that the skin was a little bit charred, and some of the juices had come out and burned in the bottom of the pan.

She was still staring down at the chicken when she heard footsteps behind her. She turned, and saw David standing there, holding a bouquet of flowers.

"I burned dinner."

His expression shifted, and he took a step toward her, those blue eyes, so familiar, intent on hers, the flowers clutched tightly in his hand.

There was no point thinking about new views. She had this view. It was everything she needed.

8

*I said no. I want to go to California. Where it's sunny and warm.
I want to go to Hollywood, where they make movies. I talked to a
man who passed through town and he said they're always looking for young women to be in films.*

Ava Moore's diary, August 1923

Hannah

When they all convened at The Dowell House a few days
later, Avery turned a focused eye and lifted eyebrow to Hannah.

"I noticed, via the invoice on the counter, that you hired your
ex to do the household improvements?"

"You did *what?*" Lark asked.

Hannah looked at her sisters, discomfort shifting inside her.
She hadn't intended to talk to them about this. For a few reasons.
The first being that it shouldn't matter. The second being…she
hadn't talked about Josh with them.

Not ever, really.

She sighed. "I didn't *know* it was his handyman business when I hired him. But his bid was really reasonable, and there's no reason to not hire him."

"Sure there is," Lark said, eyes round and earnest. "He's your ex."

"My high school ex," she pointed out. "It's not like he's my ex-husband, or something. It was years ago. Many men have passed through my life since Josh Anderson, and I imagine he's had a few women himself. No use making a monument out of teenage fondling."

The only reason he was significant at all was that he was the first. That was unavoidable. Firsts tended to change you. They'd been new and tender at that great mystery between men and women.

She doubted he was new at it now.

Because he had been handsome in high school, then he had grown up to be something else altogether. And that had nothing to do with the conversation at all.

Avery was literally standing on a counter, dusting the top of the cabinets and throwing random things down onto the floor. "Seriously," she said from where she was standing. "I think there are old pieces of artwork up here that we gave Grandpa when we were kids. It's ridiculous."

There were so many unnecessary nooks and crannies in the house. It hid all kinds of things. Dirt. Memories.

She didn't like it. She preferred the smooth edges and open spaces of her own apartment.

You couldn't stash anything in there. It had to be neat and organized.

"Hey, you brought this up," Hannah shouted up toward Avery. "You can't muster any concern?"

"You said he wasn't your ex-husband, like that meant it didn't matter. Is it an actual dilemma?"

Avery dusted her hands on her jeans and hopped down from the counter. Then she winced.

"You know, you're thirty-eight. Not eighteen," Hannah pointed out, just being mean because she did not feel *seen*, and her sister was the one who'd brought it up in the first place and then wasn't even indulging her. "You can't go flinging yourself off of countertops."

"I do yoga," Avery said.

"And do you do *cabinet cleaning pose* in yoga?"

"I won't jump next time," she said. "And I *am* listening. And I'm sorry. About the awkwardness."

"You don't sound particularly sorry."

"Hey. I live in the town we grew up in. I've run the gauntlet of high school ex-boyfriends routinely for quite some time. So I guess maybe I don't understand the magnitude of it."

Hannah stared at her sister balefully. "I literally have not seen him since I broke up with him."

At this point it wasn't about if it was awkward—because she'd decided it wouldn't be—it was about forcing her sister to admit that it *could* be. Because Avery always did that thing. Where she acted like everything was just fine, completely manageable and lalala.

And maybe Hannah had just tried to do the same, but it was her situation so she was entitled to her pretense.

"Okay," Avery relented. "Probably awkward."

"You still don't sound convinced."

"It's been a long time."

"I get it," Lark said. "You don't feel awkward about things that you did nineteen years ago?"

Avery frowned. "I don't know. Not particularly."

The response was classic Avery.

She just wasn't the kind of person who second-guessed. Which could make her sort of obnoxious sometimes.

"Well, were you in love with any of your high school boy-friends?" Lark asked Avery.

"I don't know. I guess I must've felt like I was at one point," she said.

"I mean, I should be over it," Hannah said, trying to sound sage. "It's just that I'm not."

The words fell flat in the air, and her lungs felt flat right along with them. She didn't want to admit that to herself, let alone her sisters. But now she'd said it.

"Did he hurt you that badly?" Lark asked.

She sighed. She didn't know how she'd managed to get into this conversation but she was in it now. The only way was through. "No. I hurt *him* that badly. And that… That really was terrible. The worst thing. Awful."

It was. And she bet Avery had no idea how that felt. She could be sanguine about her nice high school relationships. Hannah's hadn't been nice.

"I don't think I've ever broken anyone's heart," Lark said.

"Well, I haven't since. I don't recommend it as an experience. Anyway. Things are fine," she said. "Now that we've established I have a right to have a feeling."

"You're just usually very pragmatic," Avery said.

"I'm being pragmatic," Hannah said. "I hired the man."

"Do you still think he's hot?" Lark asked.

It was Lark's turn to receive her most evil glare. "That doesn't have anything to do with anything."

"So you do," Lark said, her tone obnoxiously knowing and not wrong, sadly.

She gritted her teeth and refused to show her sister that she'd irritated her.

"There are worse things," Avery said, "than enjoying the look of the man you hired to work on your house."

"Sure," Hannah said, glaring at her sister. "Maybe I'll hire one of your exes too."

"What does the yard look like?" Avery asked, abruptly changing the subject, and Hannah had to wonder if her sister was being kind to her, or not wanting the conversation to rebound.

And without waiting for anyone to respond, Avery charged out of the kitchen and into the little add-on sitting room. Hannah followed after her, taking in the layout of the room. The purple velvet couch and the bright rug. Definitely furniture her grandmother had had brought in. She hadn't spent very much time sitting in the house since coming back.

"I wonder what Gram was planning on doing with this place," she said.

"I don't know. I never got the impression she wanted to live here again, did you?" Avery asked.

"Not really. I suspect there were memories she didn't necessarily want."

"That's what I always thought."

Avery pushed through the double French doors, and out onto the deck. There were some chairs, with no cushions on them, but the green lawn was looking nice if a bit overgrown. At the edge of the lawn was a trellis with grape vines that grew over the top of it and cascaded down the side. Another fort.

A smile touched Avery's face, and she made her way down the porch and onto the grass, Lark following after her.

Hannah stood for a moment on the porch and felt another strange pull backward. Like when she'd seen Josh the other day.

Her sisters running around the backyard like they were kids reminded her of being with their grandparents—either here or with their grandmother at The Miner's House. The only time they'd gotten along. Without friends or violins or *Mom likes you best* between them.

Avery disappeared beneath the vines, only her feet visible in the gap between the twisting greenery in the ground.

"Did you find any badgers in there?" Lark called.

"No badgers," she said. "I can confirm no small mammals of any kind."

"Thank God."

Hannah relented and walked down the porch steps, stepping lightly on the grass because parts of it were spongey and she didn't want her boots sinking into the mud. Then she stooped down and went beneath the vines, a strange, tightening sensation in her stomach. It was because they had been talking about Josh. And that brought old memories up, twisting around her heart like grape vines.

Lark entered the canopy behind her. "I used to love playing in here," she said.

"I lost my virginity in here," Avery said.

Hannah nearly snapped her neck turning to look at her sister, and saw that Lark had done the same.

"*You.* You lost your virginity in here?"

Avery shrugged. "Yes."

"What? *When?* When you got back from college?"

"No. When I was sixteen. I…okay, so I was thinking about the yard because you brought up my exes. I don't know that I loved him. But man, Danny Highmore was hot."

That shocked Hannah down to her core. She'd sort of assumed Avery had waited for her one true love. Like maybe she'd been a vestal virgin when she'd married David.

"No way," Lark said. "I didn't know you ever did anything sneaky."

"Because I'm very, *very* sneaky," Avery said, tossing her blond hair, and tragically for her, still looking every inch the suburban mom that she was in her skintight black hoodie and black leggings.

"This really bums me out," Hannah said, looking around.

"Why? It was a long time ago. It's not like you're going to catch anything standing here."

"Yeah. But I went to third base in here with Josh." She frowned. "It just feels wrong."

She was hoping the easy admission of the fact she and Josh had gotten up to no good here might do something to ease the mystique of it all.

"Why am I standing here?" Lark asked, sounding distressed.

"Are you emotionally scarred?" Avery asked.

"Yes," Lark said. "I used to have tea parties in here."

"Right. So you were pure as the driven snow when you were a teenager?" Hannah asked.

"I did exactly what was asked of me, thank you."

"Lark," Hannah said, shocked. "Were you a virgin in high school?"

"I was! I was under the impression we all listened when Mom gave awkward talks about knowing when to say no and respecting ourselves and speaking softly, but carrying a can of mace."

Hannah shot Lark a hard glare. "Did you really think I was *that* well behaved?"

They stood there, underneath the vines, the sunlight barely filtering through the green, casting them in a golden glow.

"I thought you were mostly in a serious relationship with your violin. I guess if I thought about it—and I didn't—I would have figured you and Josh did it."

Hannah snorted. *"Did it?* Are we in high school now?"

"Well, we've never really talked about this sort of thing!"

It was true, they hadn't.

Though, Hannah had to admit she hadn't exactly taken a keen interest in Lark's personal life as a teenager. Her own had been too consuming.

"But it really never occurred to me that you would do anything like that, Avery. I thought only Hannah snuck," Lark said.

"Hey!" Hannah said.

"Well," Lark said. "You were sneaky. But I thought it was just cigarettes more than boys."

"There was *one* boy," Hannah said.

Not sure why she was being defensive since there had been many since, and she wasn't insecure about it. Maybe because Josh hadn't felt like sneaking around to her. He'd felt dangerous and thrilling. Wonderful and terrible.

Even now, what she'd shared with him wasn't like anything else ever had been.

And it killed her to admit that to herself.

"I didn't want to get caught," Avery said. "Mom would have killed me. But I wanted him. I...wanted things." Avery frowned, then shook her head. "Might as well have been another life."

"I mean, I didn't consider myself rebellious," Hannah said. "Not at the time, anyway."

She had just felt *so much*. That had been her problem back then.

The need to leave, the need to stay. The clawing desperation to do whatever it took to get to her preferred school. She had been consumed with it. And in the end it had burned her to ash. But the bonus of being ash was that it was much harder to set her ablaze now.

That utter destruction had been beneficial in some ways.

Like going from lava to obsidian. She was hard now. And if she ever regretted the loss of that bright burning girl that she'd been... Well, she let herself have a moment, and then she moved on. She also let herself remember that that girl had *hurt*. All the time. It was better to be the person she was now. Sleek and shiny with no vulnerable surfaces.

There were no loose ends here, not for her. There was only her life back in Boston. This was...funny. Interesting in a way. A chance to be home without really being home. This was just a stopover for her.

"You really loved Josh, didn't you?" Lark asked, an open sweetness in her voice, a sentimentality that scraped Hannah raw.

"Yeah. I did. Which was a good thing because I learned some-thing valuable. Love sucks, and you don't need it."

"Seriously?" Avery asked. "That's a bit cynical, even for you."

"Okay, how about this. I've had love. And through that discovered it wasn't for me."

"Don't you miss...men?" Lark asked.

Hannah laughed. "Um. No. When I want one, I invite him home. Add that to the list of things I've learned. You can have sex without being in love."

"Sure," Lark said. "But...companionship with sex is nice."

"No," Hannah said, crossing her arms like it might block out any feelings her sisters were trying to project onto her. "I don't want companionship, I want an orgasm. And then I want whatever dude I brought home out the door."

"You don't wonder what you're missing?" Avery asked.

"I've been in love," Hannah said. "I haven't been the principal violinist for the Boston Symphony Orchestra, though. So, that's next on the list. And anyone in my life has to go beneath that as a priority. I don't know very many people willing to do that. Do you?"

"A job is just a job," Avery said. "Love is... It's important. You build a life with somebody and... And it matters. It means something. It becomes part of who you are."

Avery had a way of making her choices sound superior even when she was trying to be nice.

"You say that like I don't know," Hannah said. "I just don't want it. I know that's hard for you to understand, but I like the person that I am. I don't want to change for anybody."

"I just think that's sad."

"Because you can't see that somebody could be happy with a different life than you have. Just be happy with your situation and don't worry about mine."

"Okay, Goody Two-shoes," Avery said, turning to Lark. "Why weren't you sneaking off with boys?"

Lark looked like she'd swallowed a rock. "I don't know," she said, lifting her shoulder in a way that made Hannah almost certain she knew exactly why. "I couldn't have… It would have destroyed me. Like, can you imagine? I would have imploded. It was way better to only have romances in my head. I had to go…grow up."

It was easy to look at Lark and see a boundless optimist, but Hannah had to wonder if it was…just the opposite to what she did. If Lark used a sort of untouchable facade of joy to keep people from digging deep, the way Hannah used barbs and prickles to keep people at a distance.

Lark seemed to let things roll off now, to an almost maddening degree. Had gone from screaming over every insult to waving a hand and smiling.

And Hannah had missed the transition between those two versions of her sister.

"Are you happy with your life?" Hannah asked, directing the question at Lark. "I mean, since you're lecturing me about my happiness and all."

"No," Lark said. "I wouldn't have uprooted everything if I was happy."

"Why aren't you happy?" It seemed only fair that Lark should have to share, since Hannah had been forced into talking about Josh.

Maybe this was…building bonds, though Hannah hadn't imagined it could be so uncomfortable.

"I don't know. That's the crazy thing. I don't feel like I found my place. So, I'm in awe of the two of you and the fact that you're so certain of yours."

"I think you have to decide to know where your place is," Hannah said. "It would have been easy for me to decide to stay here. I loved Josh and all. But I knew logically that it wouldn't do anything for me, so I decided to break up with him. I had to choose, and I did. There's no drifting into the place I'm at, Lark."

Lark looked miffed. "Maybe I'm not drifting. I didn't drift back here. I drove."

"It's not about perfection," Avery said. "It's just about commitment."

Hannah nodded, the truth of her sister's words sinking in. Maybe she hadn't spoken marriage vows to her violin or anything half that insane, but it was about the commitment to the dream. To the future. That she knew she had chosen the right life for herself.

"I guess I've never felt that committed to anything."

But there was an odd note in her sister's voice. Lark, for all her sunny openness, was difficult to pin down. Like trying to put a sunbeam in a jar.

"Do you feel that committed to the Craft Café?" Avery asked.

"Yes," Lark said. "Yes," she breathed the word the second time. "This is what I want. And I'm here. I'm home and I... I need to lean into it." She leveled her gaze at Hannah. "I need some of your certainty."

Yes. Her certainty. Which often cut like a knife, slashing at anyone who might be in her way. It had certainly done its job disemboweling Josh.

She'd wasted more time questioning that than she cared to admit now.

Crying in her dorm at the University she had dreamed about all of her life. Curled up on the floor, her face wet from tears. Her soul feeling depleted at the cost it had poured out in order to be there.

She'd thought about cutting herself open then. But instead she had lain there and repeated the mantra that had gotten her there in the first place. She was special. She was meant to be there.

She was going to achieve her dreams.

She had paid the price. The cost of admission.

Regrets were for other people, and Hannah wasn't like other people.

She never had been. Her drive, her feelings, had always mystified her family. Her parents had been utterly bemused by her certainty that violin was all she wanted to do.

She'd had to walk herself to lessons, and when things had gotten too expensive she'd had to take odd jobs to pay for all the lessons she needed. She'd started taking the bus to lessons with Marc Deveraux because he'd been the best. And when it had become clear that the school she wanted to attend would be too expensive for her parents, she'd set her sights on doing whatever she had to in order to get a full ride scholarship.

"Do you know what you're looking for?" Avery asked.

Hannah startled, because for a moment she thought that Avery had been talking to her. And for some reason the idea of trying to answer that question made her uneasy.

"I know what I want to feel," Lark said.

"You can't only rely on feelings, Lark," Avery said, her tone sage.

If it rankled Lark, she didn't show it. Which Hannah thought was a feat, since it wasn't even directed at her and she found it maternal and annoying.

"How did you go from vine trysts to domestic life, Avery?" Hannah asked.

Since they were all standing there in a place that very much represented *before*, standing in a place of tea parties and first times as women and not girls.

"It's what you do," Avery said. "Right?"

"Not what *I* did," Hannah said.

"Well, no. But you…you have the violin and I don't have that. I didn't have art. I wasn't particularly great at…anything. I did the young and wild thing and now I'm doing real life."

"Do you really not think you're talented, Avery?" Lark asked, frowning.

Hannah appraised her older sister, who had always been… contained. It had never occurred to her she'd once done wild things. Had she wanted to do something other than get married and have kids?

"I'm very organized," she said. "And I use it to my advantage. Anyway, it's not like any path is a wild, raucous ride. Eventually even dreams are work, right?"

Hannah had to agree with that.

Lark nodded slowly. "Yes and sometimes you outgrow dreams."

Hannah looked at her sisters and felt the strangest sense of recognition wash over her. The girls they'd been here, the women they were now.

"That's when you change," Lark added. "I'm on a quest to happiness. Via quilts and flower crowns. And memories of Gram."

"It's as good a path as any," Hannah said.

This was all well and good. This nostalgia. Even if it was sharp and uncomfortable sometimes for her. But it didn't change anything.

Because Hannah Ashwood hadn't done much changing in recent years, and that was by design. She wasn't that bright burning girl who had destroyed herself here. And she wasn't that weak, sad creature that had wept on that bathroom floor.

She'd put all that away.

She had emerged from all of it stronger. With some very clear decisions made.

Lark might be on a quest to find herself. But Hannah already knew who she was. She might have been momentarily diverted by the nostalgia of Josh Anderson. But momentary was all it was.

It was all it could ever be.

9

I don't have words. I don't have tears. My whole body is pain, and I don't think it will ever end. He's gone. He will not return home. I will not have my love. And our baby will have no father.

Dot's diary, June 1944

Lark

The café had been bustling all morning, and Lark had been busy, wearing her flower crown, which was now a little bit wilted. Her encounter with Ben had her a little bit...jittery, but her conversation with her sisters yesterday had put something whole and hopeful in place in her heart.

A promise of the healing she'd come here looking for. Avery being a sexual rebel had been something of a shock, and Hannah's...softness over Josh had fascinated her.

It made her feel a kinship to her sister. Of course, she hadn't shared about her own heartbreak. She felt a little bit guilty about it, actually.

She'd just found it easier—for years—to let them have their own narrative about her. Lark the youngest, so carefree.

It kept her from having to talk about the things that hurt her. The things that she had cared about desperately.

As if her thoughts had conjured *him* out of the air, she looked up and out the window and saw him through the wavy, antique glass.

She didn't even have to see him clearly to know it was him. Her body recognized him. Her heart fully lurched in her chest.

And it took her a moment to realize he was with someone. He bent down and hugged a small, slender figure with blond hair, the same color as his own.

Keira?

No. Keira was a brunette, not that hair color couldn't change, but she wouldn't look good as a blonde. Not being rude, it was just true.

They parted and he walked past the shop, toward his garage and out of Lark's view, and by the time she realized she was staring after him, the door opened, and the person he'd hugged walked in.

She was a teenager. A girl who had been in a couple of times in the last few weeks but suddenly it was like everything crystalized and she could *see it.*

Oh.

She had his eyes. The same blue, and her hair the same sandy blond. Her nose was like Keira's, so was her smile.

Seeing Ben's and Keira's features blended together was a particular pain she hadn't been prepared for.

For the first time, she wished her mother were a little bit more of a gossip. But the woman was resolutely closemouthed about the people in the community. Or maybe… Maybe she just knew that the topic of Ben would not be overly welcome.

But oh, Lark wished she would've known this.

Right. Ben and Keira have been married for sixteen years, and you figured they wouldn't have kids?

You went out of your way to not know that. It's why you don't talk to anybody. It's why you're happy to let them all think you just breeze through life and don't think about a thing. So they won't talk to you. So they won't ask.

"Hi," Lark said. "I… Hi."

She suddenly had no idea what to say. This girl had just been a customer—granted she was thankful for every one—a couple of days ago. One she identified by the latte she ordered and the bracelet she was working on.

And now…now she knew that the girl was Ben's daughter.

Ben's daughter.

"Hi," she said, looking at Lark like she was a weirdo.

Well, Lark felt a little like a weirdo at the moment.

"Did you want your honey latte?"

"Yeah," she said, undoing her backpack and getting out the small kit of beads that she had bought from Lark over a week ago.

Lark had given her and some friends a brief tutorial on how to do beading, and they had all been excited by how easily she picked it up, and had jumped right in.

Of course, her friends weren't here today.

"Don't you have school?"

"I guess. I'm skipping."

"And your…your dad is okay with that?"

The girl shrugged, laying her beads out in front of her, and her work in progress. "I don't think he loves it. But… You know, he's one of those parents. He would rather I tell him than have me hiding things from him so he makes a big effort not to freak out when I tell him something. This morning I told him I wasn't in the mood to go to school."

She had *not* imagined Ben would be some new age dad.

"Admirable," Lark said, ignoring that this was an extremely uncomfortable conversation for her in many ways. "Although my mom would skin me alive."

"Well, if my mom had bothered to stick around, then she would get to have a say in whether or not I went to school. But she didn't. So, it's up to my dad. Who is terrified that I will sink into a life of sex and drugs. He likes rock 'n' roll, so he doesn't seem all that worried about that one."

The girl's sudden anger was shocking, but not half so much as the revelation that Keira had left. Keira had left Ben. And her daughter.

"Keira." Lark hadn't meant to say it out loud. "Your mom, Keira?"

She frowned. "Do you… How did you know that's my mom's name?"

"I'm sorry. I… I saw your dad when he dropped you off this morning and I… I know him. I knew him. And your mom. In high school."

"You don't seem like you're my parents' age," she said, looking extremely uncomfortable.

Lark didn't know if she was complimented by that or not. But right now she couldn't make much sense of anything.

"I don't want to pry, and I don't want to push you to talk about something that you don't want to, but your mom…"

"She left. Like three years ago. She just… Left us. Sometimes she'll text or something. But not really. It's like she went crazy. Like she turned into another person. Everything was fine, and then she… She just… She quit. Like it was a job. A job she didn't want anymore."

Keira and Ben.

So much of her world was shaped around them.

Around their inevitability.

And now they were just…*divorced*?

Keira had won. She'd gotten Ben. She'd had his heart, his

love, since they were teenagers. He'd *married* her. Had a child with her.

She'd gotten Lark's dream and she'd walked away from it.

"I had no idea," Lark said. "I… Is your dad… Is he okay?"

"No. Of course, he would never say that. He doesn't like to talk about feelings."

"No kidding," Lark said.

"You knew both of them. Both of my parents."

"Yeah. You know. We had a friend group."

Her head was pounding. Lark wasn't a terribly angry person. But it was like acid in her gut, in her soul, filling her with rage. Keira had quit them like a job. That's what the girl had said.

"That's weird," she said, "to think of them…having friends. Or being friends. They didn't like each other very much in the end there. He really doesn't like her now."

Those words twisted in that cavern carving itself out in Lark's chest. Cut a deep groove in her soul.

They didn't even like each other now.

She felt betrayed.

Deeply.

Utterly.

"Did you want a cookie or anything?" Lark asked. Because she didn't know what else to do or say.

"Oh. I…"

"On the house."

"Sure."

She took a cookie from the glass jar on the counter and set it on a plate, pushing it toward the girl. "My name is Lark, by the way."

"Taylor."

"I'm sorry you're having a bad day."

She nodded. "Some days are okay."

Lark looked at that young face. She was probably fifteen and she'd already experienced a cut that deep. That some days you could breathe, and some you couldn't. Some days you felt normal and other days…well other days you skipped school and talked to strangers about your pain while eating a cookie.

"Yeah," Lark said. "Some days will be. And eventually more days will be okay than not."

She looked down. "That sounds more realistic than what a lot of people say. That it will all be okay."

Lark shook her head. And this time she thought of her mom. Her mom who had been abandoned by her mother. "No. It won't *all* be okay."

Taylor smiled, just a slight lift of the corners of her mouth. "Thanks. I mean it."

Here she was, giving Keira's daughter the life advice her former friend wasn't here to give. Lark could hardly breathe past that.

Another customer came in and took Lark's attention for a moment, and then Taylor sat absorbed in her work, and Lark let her have it.

Around dinnertime, the girl hopped off the stool. "I'm going to go get my dad for food. He forgets to…you know, eat. He'll just work."

She had to take care of him, and that made Lark feel a host of things too.

"Yeah, I… Nice to meet you, Taylor."

"You too."

But even after Taylor left, and the shop emptied out, Lark didn't feel alone.

Because her every heartbeat seemed to say his name. Over and over. After all that time of doing her best not to think of him at all.

She had her business up and running. She had a flower crown, wilting thought it was. And ancient history was exactly that. Ancient history.

Seeing him the other night when she'd gone to the garage

had thrown her, and meeting his daughter had been a shock. Finding out about his divorce was a shock.

She wasn't here to walk along old roads, she was here to find new ones in old spaces. She didn't want to go back to the person she was, she wanted to find a better version of the person she was now.

But this was exactly why when she came back to visit her family, she didn't loiter around town. This was why she made her visits brief. And infrequent.

And of course, she had moved back home without fully taking that on board.

She turned to the sink full of dishes and began to scrub angrily at some of the mugs. And slowly, clarity washed over her. Maybe it was the physical labor. Maybe it was the flower crown. Maybe it was the confrontation—so quickly—with one of the thorniest bits of home.

It was a good thing. This was exactly the kind of thing she needed to face down. Because she couldn't let old memories and feelings matter that much.

Because disconnected from the source a real life memory could become a fantasy. Hazy, fuzzy, and mostly lies. A fantasy didn't have boundaries. It could build itself into the most unobtainable joy, or the darkest of nightmares.

Ben Thompson was neither.

Taylor.

Apparently, his daughter was Taylor.

And her mother was gone.

She swallowed hard past the lump in her throat.

She looked around the room. "You would think this was funny," she said to the air, hoping that her grandmother's spirit was lingering in the walls, just enough to be amused by all the drama.

Gram would have popped a piece of candy in her mouth, adjusted her glasses and smiled. "Life has a sick sense of humor. The trick is to make sure yours is even more twisted."

That's what she would've said.

It was just too bad she wasn't here to say it.

But even if she had been... Even if she had been, Lark wouldn't have told her it was what she needed to hear.

And suddenly it made her sad that it was so much easier to talk to a ghost that it was to talk to somebody living.

10

We circle the wagons at night for safety. The men keep watch. One in particular is always watching. I'm told his name is John.

Anabeth Snow's diary, 1864

Avery

"We can have keto friendly snacks at the trivia night."

Avery was trying to listen to Alyssa talk about the upcoming event. But since it was intermingled with humble bragging about the progress on her diet and her daughter being student of the month, Avery was finding it difficult. She should be enjoying the respite. She was having a rare afternoon coffee, after all.

She'd considered going to the Craft Café, but Alyssa had wanted a very specific gluten-free something at the coffee house.

And as happy as she was to have a coffee break, Avery was antsy to get back to the quilting project. There was something about it that soothed her right now.

Maybe it was how it reminded her of Gram. How it connected her to those days she'd been aching for so much lately.

Simpler times.

Just her and her sisters sitting at a tiny table in the back of The Miner's House, beading and bickering, but united under the watchful eye of Gram, who had a counter full of candy, and an endless stash of gum.

The quilt brought her back to that.

She had gotten quite a bit of the fabric cut, but she wanted to finish. Because then she needed to iron it so that it was precise, so that when they reconvened in a couple of days she would be ready to start sewing the square.

She could already predict that Lark wouldn't have any of it finished, and whatever fabric she ended up choosing—unsurprising to Avery that she hadn't committed to anything—would then be fantastic and she'd finish before everyone else, somehow producing something perfectly lovely and more creative than whatever she or Hannah had put together.

Hannah was a dark horse. And it would depend on if she had decided that she cared about the quilt or not. If Hannah wanted to do something, then it was always done. Precise and when she said it would be. But if she didn't, then… Well, she wouldn't.

Their mother had been uncertain, though it wasn't wholly unusual when it came to things with links to Gram. They'd done Sunday dinner once a month for years and Mom still got a little wound up when things weren't turning out. Like she had to perform for Gram, which had always made Avery feel sad but then…didn't everyone want their mom to be proud of them?

"How about we have options?" Avery asked, forcing her mind back to Alyssa's conversation and trying not to roll her eyes.

"I'm not sure we have the budget for options."

All Avery could think was that if she had to sit in a room with these people, and there was no sugar, she might chew her own arm off.

"Not everybody is on a keto diet."

"But everyone could benefit from it," Alyssa said.

Honestly, there was no arguing with her. "All right. You take care of that. I'll probably bring some cupcakes or something."

She was a martyr, but there were limits. She wasn't doing trivia night without cake.

"Will we be able to expect David at the party?"

"It depends. You know how it is." Alyssa's husband was also a doctor. Notorious for arriving at school events in his scrubs, which Avery found disgusting, given that oftentimes there was food present, and she didn't particularly want MRSA getting in her awards banquet dinner.

"I know," Alyssa said. "Sometimes I feel like a widow. Or a single mom. He's doing such important work, but still, it's hard when your husband can't be at everything because his job is so important."

She was bragging even while complaining. And what made Avery uncomfortable was it sounded incredibly similar to what she had said to her sisters not that long ago.

He has an important job.

It was strange how much that defined her.

It felt even larger now that she was spending time with Lark and Hannah. Lark and Hannah were themselves first, and what *they* did came first in the conversation.

Avery thought of how she talked about her life.

My husband is a doctor. I stay home with the kids.

Except her kids were hardly home and when they were they didn't speak to her.

That girl she'd been, who did crafts and had all kinds of dreams, had never thought she'd define herself by what someone else had accomplished.

And hearing it said back to her only made it that much more clear. A husband with a job like David had gave her a certain amount of cachet with the other moms at school. The other doctor's wives were often smug in a half circle with each other at school events. It had become an integral piece of her identity. It made her feel...validated.

But right now it just felt small. Petty.

That what he did for a living somehow made her more important.

And at the same time made her less important as well.

She hadn't seen it until she caught her exact reflection in the woman across from her, who happened to be irritating her, which really made the whole thing a lot more confronting.

"Right," Avery said, agreeing rather than betraying any of her thoughts, because she didn't know what to do with them.

She left coffee feeling weird and sad, and she wasn't sure what she was supposed to do about it. So she shoved it all to one side as soon as she walked through the door of her house. She went into the kitchen and pulled a package of hamburger out of the freezer. While she was bent over the open drawer, she saw a piece of glass shoved beneath the edge of one of the cabinets. She must've missed it when she cleaned up that broken bowl the other night.

There was always something.

And it felt like an endless treadmill. Not an accomplishment that she could stand on. Cleaning just started over the next day. It wasn't like finishing surgery.

She stuck the hamburger in a bowl of water, and then went into the living room, taking out the bin that had the fabric in it. She got the ironing board down and started to fold each precisely cut swatch. Then she ironed them so that they were perfectly flat, so that her stitches would be straight and even.

At least sewing a quilt had real progress. Real progress she could see. When she finished pressing it, she decided to sit down and begin work on the first square. She had already assembled the backing, and was ready to begin the design.

She threaded the needle slowly, and lost herself in the simple, rhythmic work. She had never loved sewing machines. She used them for ease, but what she really loved was sewing in the silence like this. It reminded her of sitting next to her grandmother and sisters on the porch at The Miner's House on warm summer evenings. They would snap green beans, and when they were finished, they would sew. Sometimes quilting like this. Sometimes needlepoint.

And all of it did something to quiet that gnawing sense of never quite accomplishing enough inside of Avery.

Every stitch made its mark. Every stitch added beauty.

She took a strip of the parlor curtains, all velvet burgundy and floral. A series of triangles and stripes would create a classic heritage quilt design. The rich color of the curtains contrasted with the ivory backing beautifully, and she shrank her world down to the needle entering the fabric. To each stitch. As neat and tiny as possible.

And she smiled, imagining Lark working on her square, and Hannah. She wished she were sitting with them now.

Tears filled her eyes, and she blinked them back. She didn't know why she was being so ridiculous.

She heard the sound of a car door, and she stilled.

Then she looked down at her phone, and saw the time. She had lost herself completely in quilting, and she hadn't done anything with the hamburger that she'd gotten out. She hurriedly put the quilting square away, and stashed the bin behind the couch where it wasn't visible, then went into the kitchen.

Her brain was turning on a loop. She didn't know how she could have lost track of the time. There was really only one thing that David asked her to do for when he was home from work. He was always hungry. She needed to have dinner finished. And it wasn't like she had a job.

And she had been distracted lately. She had burned dinner just last week, and now she had forgotten it altogether. Which was probably better than burning it, because at least when it was finished it wouldn't be terrible.

She heard the front door, and then his footsteps heading to the kitchen.

"I'm sorry," she said, before he could say anything, moving to the kitchen doorway. "I had coffee with Alyssa today, and then I came home and lost track of time. I just need maybe forty-five minutes and I'll have spaghetti."

He didn't say anything. He didn't have to. She recognized the look on his face. But for some reason, she didn't have time to brace herself.

Pain burst over her cheekbone, and her head hit the door frame, sending off a shower of stars in her head that glittered like broken glass.

And that glitter shifted and turned into images. A young woman in a wedding dress and a young man in a tux. Babies and a new house and stress from work. Being kissed. Being hurt. Shattered bowls. Chipped door frames and dented walls.

A perfect house that was crumbling slowly.

Flowers and fists and those blue eyes she'd loved for more than seventeen years.

11

Sam, the man I met at the diner in Bear Creek, helped me find a small apartment to share with three other girls. It's so different here. Vibrant and the buildings light up at night and the air is warm, even in late winter. Sam says he can get us jobs on a set. Even if it's just fetching coffee. The prospect of it is thrilling.

Ava Moore's diary, September 1923

Hannah

Hannah leaned over the wooden countertop at her sister's Craft Café and stared at the shot of espresso coming out of the manual machine. Dark brown with a caramel crema over the top. She could have made a pot of coffee back at The Dowell House but she wanted the real deal.

"You can't rush perfection, Hannah," Lark said, her tone sage.

"I'm dying."

"Maybe you should go to sleep earlier instead of staying up all night playing your violin?"

"I wasn't up all night."

"Late enough. It reminded me of sharing a room with you."

"Sorry." She wasn't really that sorry.

"No," Lark said, steaming a pitcher of milk, her concentration focused on the white froth. "I like listening to you."

Emotion turned in Hannah's chest like a key. She didn't particularly like it. But it forced her to look around her sister's café. At the scarred wooden floors that were still so familiar. The same as when Gram had run the candy store here. The counter, which was different, and the Edison bulbs that hung from the ceiling like pendants. Also different. Her sister's quirky brand of art mingled with some of the classic paintings that Gram had always had on the walls.

"Do you remember how Gram would set a table in the back and give us paints or crochet hooks or needlepoint samplers?" She didn't know what had brought that on. But with the memory came a wave of nostalgia.

"Yes," Lark said. "I do. It was about the only time I felt settled. Calm. Otherwise it was just always like there were a million ants marching underneath my skin, so many feelings I couldn't get them out. It was when I realized what making things did for me."

"I used to think it was a distraction. But, it was about the only time I ever sat with you and Avery." She frowned. There was so much self-isolation involved in the life that she lived. She'd been doing it for so long that it was a habit she wasn't even aware of.

It was a strange thought on the heels of her realization that maybe she wasn't as different from her sisters as she thought.

And she could remember, sitting in this space, while they all sat quietly and worked on different things, but next to each other.

The quilt would be like that.

And that made her chest feel slightly bruised, and made her wonder if it was one reason she'd been avoiding it.

Suddenly, she missed Addie. She had missed her, the entire time. A sadness that settled into everything she did. A sense of loss. But this was keen and sharp, different in that way.

Lark set the coffee up on the counter in a reusable travel mug. "Are you okay?"

Hannah frowned. "Yeah. I was just thinking about Gram." And that floor caught her eye again. The floor with the scars in the exact same places they'd been when she was a child. This place was so full of memories. And Lark making this Craft Café was keeping them alive. Keeping them here for the entire community.

It made Hannah feel connected in the strangest way. To this place that she had separated from so many years ago. Before she'd even left.

But you're back. And you're rehabbing the old house...

To turn it into something that would keep existing, yes, but she wouldn't have to be here every day.

"I'm glad that you opened this," Hannah said, feeling uncharacteristically soft and vulnerable. "I mean, I'm glad that more people will have the chance to come here. Use it."

"She was so special to me," Lark said, the smile on her face getting sad. "Sometimes I would just sit with her, and we wouldn't talk. But I felt like she understood me."

Another memory that Hannah had suppressed. "Me too. I felt like she was maybe the unacceptable part of me. The part that wanted to leave." She blinked, her eyes feeling dry. "She'd gone on all those adventures, and she told me about them. All the places she'd seen in her convertible. And I just let myself forget that in all those stories Mom was sitting at home without her mother. Because I liked the image of a woman with red hair and a red car cutting a swath of terror through the countryside."

Her eyes met Lark's. "I guess we both kind of did that," Lark said.

"I guess."

She'd always felt like she and her sister were a world apart. But standing there in this space she wasn't sure it was true.

"I have to go. I... You know, renovations and things."

"You should play," Lark said. "I mean, while you're here."

Hannah shifted uncomfortably. A long time ago she'd enjoyed messing around and playing folk music at bars with friends, but she didn't really do that anymore. It was all work now, and she could never quite justify wasted time spent...messing around.

"The Gold Pan has an open mic night on Fridays," Lark pointed out.

"Yeah. Not sure that I'm going to get in on open mic night at the Gold Pan." She wrinkled her nose. "But, thanks for letting me know."

"You should play here. I'd love to have some live music here."

She let out a short breath. "Sure. Maybe. Just let me know."

"I will. I want to have some fun evening things. I think it would be great. Music and crafting and wine."

Hannah had to admit it didn't sound terrible. But that was as far as she was willing to go.

"I'll see you later," Hannah said, taking her coffee and walking out of the Craft Café. She paused at the porch. Another spot filled with memories. Where they had snapped peas with Gram, another group activity. Gram had forced them to play together. To be nice to each other. In a way their mom and dad didn't.

Hannah's dad had always been indulgent of her specifically. For the first time she wondered...

She wondered if it was because she was like her mom.

He was good with Mom, too. Who didn't like fuss or muss, and who'd always preferred action over talk.

She smiled as she turned and began to walk down the street, heading back toward The Dowell House.

It was made of bright, cheerful yellow brick. Large green trees covered part of the facade, swaying gently in the breeze. The stark, white balcony that led out to a widow's walk, as well as the gleaming columns that stood sentry by the crisp door gave it the look of a Jane Austen fantasy. At least, it always had to Hannah. Whether it was an accurate fantasy or not was another matter. But it had always made her think that dukes and ladies might not be terribly far away.

But she had always dreamed of bigger things.

She walked up the sidewalk, and paused, planting both feet firmly on the marble heart that was laid into the pathway. She had always been curious about that. Because while her grandmother was eccentric, as far as she knew, she came from very practical people.

The Dowell family was well regarded, and had been for years. Their family history was written on many a plaque about town. The first Dowell in town had not only built the largest house the community of Beak Creek had ever seen, they'd bought a newspaper, built up the school system and been active in the politics of the town. Of course her grandmother's behavior had put a slight dent in the family history.

But then, Addie had more than made up for it in her later years. As far as the community was concerned.

Not as far as Hannah's mother was concerned.

And Hannah understood. She did. But then, her mother didn't make mistakes. So maybe she didn't understand that sometimes people do desperate things in low moments.

Hannah did.

She began to walk forward, moving slowly up the stairs, and pausing when she saw that familiar truck parked against the side of the house. Right up against the picket fence, a mockery of sorts. Of something, though Hannah didn't particularly want to think of what.

She paused for a moment and let out a slow breath, then pushed open the front door. "If I would've known you'd be here already I would have brought you a coffee."

She didn't hear anything in response except for the sound of a hammer against drywall. "Are you breaking my house?" she asked.

"Sometimes you have to break it to fix it," came the reply.

She rolled her eyes, then followed the sound of the hammer into the parlor. "That's cute. Did you get it in a fortune cookie?"

"No. I learned it. From life. Also, your drywall here is moldy. And it's beyond saving. So I have to put in a couple new panels and I have to break them out to get new ones in." He shrugged. "So it's not a saying so much as just the situation here in your house."

"Great. Good to know."

He was sharper now than he'd been.

She crossed her arms, resting her latte against her elbow and leaning against the doorway. She stared at his profile, at the solid motion of his shoulders, his arms, as he swung the hammer. He was... Well, he was good at this.

Practiced. His every movement was forceful, but economical. He didn't waste energy or movement. He found the most direct path and took it. And she could tell herself that she enjoyed that because what she appreciated was professionals. In any capacity. People who worked hard at what they did, and found a way to excel at it, whatever it was.

She was not looking at him because the way his muscles shifted beneath his skin fascinated her. No. Not at all.

"Did you have something to say?"

"No." She felt weird and caught. "I just..." She hated this. This weird *in between*. The way he made her *feel* in between. The woman she was, the woman she'd been. Because it shouldn't be possible. Because she had ample experience steering conversations the direction she wanted to. Because she had all the experience she could possibly want with good-looking men. And she didn't do tongue-tied. Didn't do dumb, ridiculous staring at a nice pair of arms. Because arms were just arms, and if she wanted them wrapped around her, she didn't have any problem asking for it. And if she didn't, she had no problem looking away.

She also wouldn't look away out of embarrassment. If she wanted to look, she would look. There was no call making this weird. And she mentally was. So, she was going to stop that right away.

"So how did you end up as a handyman?" She wasn't feral. She knew how to have conversations with people.

"Well, there came a point when I realized that I was good at a hell of a lot of things, and the collection of those things was quite handy."

"Right. Great."

"So you really went and became exactly what you wanted to be?"

"Almost," she said. "I'm first chair. This principal position is open. I'm hoping for that." She wasn't quite sure why she told him that. Maybe because he'd said she wasn't confident last time they'd talked, and that was patently ridiculous. So if he needed to see a little bit of confidence, she was happy to show it.

"Well, I'm my own boss," he said, setting the hammer down and turning to look at her. Something glinted in his eyes that made her feel...it made her feel, which she wasn't that big on.

"Good for you." He hadn't mentioned a personal life at all. And hadn't asked about hers. And she was trying to figure out if she would have asked someone else. Because what she wanted was to treat him the way that she would anyone. Any friend that she ran into. Of course, you had to be careful. Because people could have just gone through a breakup or divorce or something like that. So there were definitely pros and cons to asking about somebody's personal life, even if they weren't an ex-boyfriend.

Not that that mattered. It was just she wanted to be no more or less curious about him than she would have been about anyone.

Her phone started buzzing in her pocket and she grabbed

onto it, her heart slamming against her chest when she saw the familiar phone number. "I have to take this."

She pushed to answer, quickly walking out of the house, out the front door so that she could get some privacy. "Hello?"

"Hello, Hannah."

It was the Board of Directors for the Boston Symphony Orchestra. She knew Peter's number and his voice well enough that she didn't have to ask who it was.

"How's the weather in Boston?" She hated herself for that inane salvo into conversation, but she also didn't want to jump right into asking him about the principal position. Even though they both knew that was why he was calling.

"Getting to be too warm already. How is your family? I know that losing someone is tough. And often sorting through years of possessions isn't any easier."

The scarred floor of the Craft Café swam into her vision. Walking in when she'd been a child and had run to the candy counter. Shuffling in as a teenager, knowing Gram would make her knit. Coming in today, knowing Gram wouldn't be there.

And she shoved it to the side.

"Yeah." She nodded, focusing on one fluttering leaf on the tree in the front yard. The sunlight filtered through it, and it wiggled on its branch as the wind picked up. "Definitely tough. But we are making progress. And everything is on track, so... I'll be home in September just like we talked about."

"Good. I'm glad to hear it. In regards to that, I wanted to be the one to call and tell you that we decided to go with Ilina Voychek for the position of principal violinist."

"Ilina plays in LA." The words fell from her lips before she could process them. Before she could make sense of what he had just said.

"She did. But she indicated to us that she was ready to make a move and... She came out and played with the orchestra. We were very impressed. She has a lot of experience."

I have a lot of experience. It's all with you.

She didn't say that, though. Because she felt like the sky was caving in on top of her, pressing her down into the ground. It was impossible. It was just impossible.

She had done everything. Absolutely everything. Gone to the preferred school, put in the hours. She had… She had given up everything to end up in this position before she was forty. And now she felt like there was no guarantee she would ever get it. Ever.

To be passed over for someone who wasn't even part of the Boston Symphony…

It didn't matter that she'd seen it before. It didn't matter that these things happened. They didn't happen to her.

Because everything went her way. She did the work. And she was… She was special.

That sounded so stupid when she thought it, but it had to be true. Because how else could everything she'd done be worth it? She'd paid the price for her destiny. And the asking price was steep, but she'd done it.

It didn't make any sense. That she could lose this. This position that was absolutely hers for the taking.

"You're still a very valued member of the orchestra. And of course your position in first chair is secure."

"And I appreciate it."

"I wanted to take the time to call you myself. Before it was announced anywhere."

"Thank you." She took a deep breath, and stared at that leaf like it was the thing that had betrayed her. "I have to go. I have a… There's a handyman here fixing things. And he needs direction."

She hung up, and felt like there was a vortex beneath her feet. She couldn't breathe.

Her hands were shaking, and she opened the door, standing there for a moment, knowing that she couldn't face Josh. Josh of all people, who was here during this crushing low. She grabbed her purse from the hook and dug her cigarettes and lighter out of it, then shut the door, lighting one and collapsing onto the porch step, each breath of tainted air promising to bring some kind of emotional relief that it ultimately couldn't deliver. Not when she was so close to a breakdown.

She heard the door open behind her, and looked even more determinedly off to her left, drawing a deep, smoke-filled breath before letting it out slowly, willing the nicotine to do its thing, and if not the nicotine, then the routine beauty of the habit itself.

"You still do that?"

She didn't look at him. Instead, she took another defiant pull on the cigarette.

"I thought that was just something to do in high school to seem edgy."

"I don't do it to seem edgy," she said, archly. "I do it because I like it."

"Hey, do you. But you know they make patches for that."

"Do they make patches for annoying exes?"

"What's up?"

"Nothing. Just intrusions from home." She was not in the mood to have the discussion. And he didn't...he didn't deserve this. It was *way* too good.

This isn't why you broke up with him. It was more than that. And the reason is still solid.

Also, she hadn't lost anything. She hadn't. It was just the possibility of something.

But it was her goal. It had been for so long. And it felt...

It didn't matter what it felt like.

It wasn't fair. That much was true.

"Right. You have a... A husband? A boyfriend?" Her scalp

MAISEY YATES

prickled. She was genuinely shocked that he had asked the question. The one that she had been avoiding asking him. And annoyed. Because now was not the time.

"No," she said. "By choice, thank you."

"I wouldn't have thought anything else."

She wasn't going to ask him now. Because she didn't care. She didn't care about anything. She ignored the strange, messy sensation in her chest that told her she might be lying.

"I have to go practice." She stabbed her cigarette out on the porch step and stood. "Just finish up in here. I'm going to be upstairs."

"Will the pounding disturb you?" The way that he asked that... She could tell he didn't actually care.

"No," she said. It probably would. But she wouldn't give him the satisfaction of knowing he had the power to annoy her. Just like she wouldn't let him know that she was crumbling inside.

Because she just didn't let people see her crumble. Much less him. Never him.

She walked past him, into the house, up the stairs, and into the peacock blue bedroom that she had been sleeping in. She closed the door firmly behind her.

Her violin was resting in its case, on the mantel. She swallowed hard and picked it up, unzipping the case and taking out the bow, tightening it before taking out her rosin and making sure it was coated with just the right amount.

She lifted the instrument up with her left hand and braced it underneath her chin, holding it there with no hands while she finished fussing with the bow. And then she played.

Long slow notes at first, then fast and electric. She played until she couldn't breathe. Played with her eyes screwed shut, so she could ignore the tears falling down her face. And she wrapped it all up in music.

The music filled up the room, and she waited for it to fill her up too. But it didn't.

And when she finished, she let her arms fall to her sides, holding the instrument tightly in her hand. And she didn't... She didn't know what this meant.

If Ilina Voychek was just as special as she was, or more, then what did that mean? What did any of it mean?

This was like falling into an abyss. This not knowing.

Not having any idea what was in her future anymore.

How could she even find solace in music when this was all wrapped up in music?

There's no reason music is all you should be able to do.

She remembered her grandmother's voice. And she frowned. She placed her violin carefully back in its case, along with its bow, and began to pace the length of the room. She could still hear Josh moving around downstairs. Which meant she was going to be on bedroom exile for a little while longer yet. She had no desire to see him again. Not when her eyes were red and her face was still wet from her tears.

He was still downstairs. And the only escape from this room would be to go up.

She opened up the bedroom door and went up the curved staircase that led to the attic. She pushed the door open, and was yet again surprised by the sheer volume of things stacked into the tiny space.

"Okay," she said, looking around. "Do you have answers for me up here? Because you always acted like you did when you were alive. And you said I was too focused and too intense. But I was right, you know. And you wouldn't know anything about that. Because you decided to do something, you decided to get married and have kids, and you didn't even keep on doing that. So really, what would you know about the kind of commitment it takes to see something through?"

She had the thought of going back to the Craft Café. Going to see Lark. But she didn't think she could handle that right now.

She felt spiteful and mean even knowing she was just talking to her grandmother's ghost that way. But she was so angry. She was angry and she didn't know how to have that conversation with another person. Because she had spent so much of the last nineteen years handling every thing by herself. And things had been good. They'd been fine. She didn't need anything. She didn't need anyone. She had only needed her music.

She went over to the stack of fabric, where they had mined their quilting objects from. There was another bin, nearby, but it didn't have only fabric in it. It had trinkets.

She wondered if Lark had seen all of this yet. She thought, briefly, about taking the box to her sister but she couldn't face... anything. Not right now.

She knelt down and opened the top.

There was a stack of old photos inside. The top one had a picture of a man with a mustache, wearing suspenders and blue jeans, holding a clearly deceased creature by the leg. The label read: Jason Dowell with Bobcat, 1919.

"Great. Great for you, not so much for the bobcat." There were more pictures, of The Dowell House in other stages of construction. Also a picture of an old barn with hides tacked to the outside. Fittingly labeled: Skunk Hides, 1918.

The best photo was of a man standing on top of a tree branch, his hunting dog on the branch as well. He was pointing his gun off into the blank space. Labeled, William Wesley Dowell, 1922.

She was fairly certain that was her great-grandfather.

If nothing else, her ancestors were certainly... Well, something.

She pulled the next picture out, finding more animals, buildings and men holding weapons. But there was another photo, smaller than the others. And she paused.

It was a young woman, her dark hair cut short, pinned into waves that framed a heart shaped face. Her lips were dark, and though the photo was black and white, it was easy to imagine that they were a deep red. She was standing in almost a ballet pose, wearing low heels, and a dark colored dress that fell down past her knees, with a dropped waist, and a spangle of shining beads over the fabric.

Very familiar looking fabric.

"The Party Dress." She touched it, and then turned the picture over, looking for a label as comprehensive as the others. But there was only a date. 1923.

She stared at the girl, at the dreamy look on her face. If she was a Dowell, then she was definitely an odd one in the middle of all these outdoorsmen. In the middle of all this... Practicality.

In many ways, Hannah had always considered herself practical. It wasn't that she didn't take the steps to make her dreams happen. She did. But there had to be more. That magic. The kind of magic that had a girl who might've been part of this suspenders-wearing family choosing a dress that looked like this. Something frothy and beautiful and ornate, that wouldn't have been at home here in Bear Creek.

"Maybe you weren't at home here either."

She shrugged off the vague disquiet that asked her if she knew where in the world she was at home now.

12

His mother says our child will be a bastard. And I know she is right. That there is shame I will bring on our child if I insist on raising him. I cannot tell my mother at all. I fear her disappointment too much.

Dot's Diary, July 1944

Mary

Lark was still at The Miner's House when Mary arrived for quilting night.

"I'll be out in a minute, Mom," her daughter called from the kitchen area at the back.

The Closed sign was turned, but the lights above the bar still glowed with warmth. And Mary paced around the room, taking in the changes that Lark had put into place since the last time Mary had been in.

She'd been busy the last few days—volunteering for morning reading for preschoolers at the library, taking Peyton to her evening ballet class and picking her up and making sure Joe had all of his gear together for the three day trek he was taking into the woods to take pictures.

Joe had wanted her to go, but she had too much to do here to go sit around in nature. She didn't have an interest in photography and she'd never been one for camping. She liked the outdoors, but it was something her father had always seen as being pretty foolish when a body had running water and electricity at home.

She agreed.

Plus, she didn't like sitting around being idle.

Lark had a display with local art under a glass case, and shelves with handmade ceramic mugs and local honey.

There was jewelry hanging from pegs, that Mary was sure Lark herself made. Tapestries hung from the walls, painted with images of naked women draped in flowers and sitting in fields with wolves.

There was a sweetness to the art, but something confusing in it too. Like her youngest daughter. Lark was sweet and always had been. She'd run errands with her without complaint, had spent time gardening with her, twirling and laughing in the sunshine. She hadn't helped with chores but she'd followed along, chattering behind her while she cleaned.

And when she wasn't sweet…she was a tempest. But it was part of all that Lark was.

But when she'd left home, she'd stopped all that. Like whatever thread had connected them had been decidedly cut when she'd left Bear Creek.

That was when she'd changed, and Mary had never been able to tell if it had been maturity or college.

She looked around the room even more closely, looking for clues about her youngest child. Who she was, why she was here.

If Mary were another woman, another sort of mom, she might

have just asked her. But that kind of heart-to-heart stuck in her throat, and she never knew quite how to approach it.

When the girls had talked, it had been to Addie.

That stuck in Mary's chest and burned. Addie had passed her over, and she'd come back just in time to teach her daughters the language of femininity, something Mary felt utterly clueless to.

Addie had made it so she couldn't quite relate to her own daughters. If she'd never come back…

If she'd never come back they'd have had Mary's influence and maybe then it would have been easier.

But then maybe Avery wouldn't have become the wife and mother she was.

Maybe Lark wouldn't have found so much sweetness.

Maybe Hannah would have had less of a sense of adventure.

She didn't want her girls to be different.

So her resentment always felt hollow, small and mean. And there was no use dwelling on it now. So she turned her focus back to the room she was in.

The place was cluttered, but in a very careful way. Everything designed to be beautiful.

But that was exactly how everything Lark touched turned out.

Another reason Mary felt reluctant to do any work on the quilt.

Mary didn't feel confident in any of the work she had done on her square, not even with the help that Avery had given her earlier in the week. Lark had told her that everything was fine, and that if she followed the guidelines carefully everything would turn out. But she was reluctant to make stitches, because even though they could be torn out, she was concerned about the fabric of the wedding dress, which seemed so antique and dear.

Even though she didn't know whose wedding dress it was, she still felt the connection to that fabric, and its time in history. A wedding dress was such a personal, important thing. Her own had cost a hundred and fifty dollars, and had been made by a friend, who had put together the fabric of her dreams into something that suited her perfectly.

Expensive or not, wedding dresses were so sentimental, and cutting up a gown with that much significance was horrifying enough, but attempting to turn it into something beautiful was quite another.

She wasn't a frilly type of woman. But her wedding dress had been. Getting ready for her wedding without her mother had been a deep, terrible wound. So many hurts had come up during that time. But Joe had been…

Joe had been the right kind of rock for her, as he always was. Strong and steady, but with a softness to him that her own father hadn't possessed.

She'd said she'd marry him in blue jeans. He'd said he'd marry her that way too, but if she wanted a wedding dress she should have one.

She'd gone shopping for it with her groom. Breaking all manner of tradition. But immersing herself in something so… girlie had been a whole different thing to what she was used to, and watching Joe's face as she'd come out in each one had done something to repair the cracks in her heart.

Her wedding day had been the most special, incredible day of her life and she'd felt like the princess she'd never imagined she could be.

Wedding dresses, for her, were sacred.

Just like weddings.

Just like the way she loved Joe.

But when it came to the quilt, all she had managed to do was cutting and temporary tacking. Anything else had her feeling far too…it was like anger, but it trembled inside her.

The fabric squares she would be sewing the dress pieces onto were a lovely wine color that complemented the parlor curtains Avery was using on hers. It was also a nice contrast to the midnight blue that Hannah was working with.

For all her fussing and instruction, as far as Mary knew, Lark hadn't chosen anything yet. But once she did, she knew that whatever her youngest daughter produced would be perfect. When inspiration struck her, just like lightning, she could create. It always amazed Mary, because she didn't have that ability inside of her.

And sometimes... Sometimes, a very small part of her that she felt ashamed of found it unfair.

Because it was something that Lark had gotten from Mary's mother. When Mary felt as if she had gotten nothing from Addie herself.

And she couldn't see much of herself in Lark at all.

For all that she'd been her little sunshine fairy, Lark hadn't admired enough of anything in Mary to take on any of her hobbies.

No gardening or baking for Lark.

"How is your progress?" Lark appeared from the back, her honey blond hair piled on her head in a large, messy bun. She was wearing a long white dress, her shoulders bare, a silver band painted onto her upper arm.

"It's not a tattoo," she said, poking at it.

"I know that," Mary said.

"But you looked very concerned."

"Well, I do know what a tattoo looks like."

"That's good."

"You don't have any. Do you?" That was another thing she didn't know about her daughter.

"Don't ask questions you don't want the answers to," Lark said, winking.

"Have you heard from Hannah?"

Lark frowned. "No. Not today."

Hannah was distant in a way that seemed deliberate. Mary made sure she stopped by to check in on her middle daughter most days, but she always had the sense Hannah was busy. She didn't say that, but her manner was brusque and she would stand rather than sitting, like she had half her body in the next room.

"Is Avery coming? She said that she was feeling a little bit under the weather the last few days. I haven't seen her." It was unusual. She saw Avery most days, even if was just to share a half a large carton of eggs or some other farmers market find, plant starts or just a quick visit with her and the kids.

"She said she was. She texted me earlier."

"Well. I barely made any progress."

"I'm sure it looks great, Mom."

"Well, I'm not."

"Let's see."

Lark leaned over the bar, and Mary reluctantly put her squares on the counter. "I don't want to sew them on. I'm afraid I'm going to ruin the fabric."

"You won't. And anyway, there's plenty of it."

The door pushed in, and Hannah breezed into the room, holding a stack of squares in her hand. "I sat down today and finished a couple of them," she said. "For your inspection."

She set them on the counter, right next to Mary's.

Hannah's were precise and perfect, the blue fabric, and the beautiful, glittering beads looked wonderful on the cream colored fabric. Each neatly sewn diamond looked brilliant, next to some of the accents that she had done in triangular shapes right next to it.

"Wow," Lark said. "I didn't expect you to come with that much done."

"Well, I had some time today."

"You did all this today?" Mary asked.

"Yep. Hey, do you have some wine, or something?" Hannah asked Lark.

Mary did her best not to take a lot of notice of the smell of nicotine on her daughter. It reminded her of her mother, a piece of her that Mary would have rather Hannah hadn't picked up.

The artistic gene was preferable. But that smell of cigarettes with a slight sweet scent layered over the top of it was stronger than usual. Hannah was dressed in all black, a stark contrast to her sister's ethereal white dress. In spite of the heat outside, she was wearing formfitting leggings and a tight top.

Of her three daughters, Hannah was the slimmest, and Mary sometimes worried that she replaced meals with cigarettes and coffee.

Mary was too like Hannah to pry, and they were both like oysters that were sealed shut tight and couldn't find a way to connect. Joe could. But then, Joe could reach Mary too. He was the only one.

It made her feel better for Hannah, that she had Joe at least.

"Yes. What do you want?" Lark asked.

"I dunno. What's open?"

"I have a rosé."

"Basic. Sounds great."

There was an edge to Hannah tonight, that was always present, but it was definitely a little bit more out in force than usual.

If Lark noticed, she didn't acknowledge it, and instead produced a wineglass, and then poured some rosy liquid inside of it. "Some for me too?" Mary asked.

"Of course," Lark said, waving her hand and pouring a measure for Mary too. "Shall we retire to the circle?"

Lark went through a door behind the counter, while Hannah and Mary walked around, to the little sitting room. Lark had lit candles at varying heights, and instead of flower crowns, there were flower decorations, garlands hanging from the wall, and some blossoms hanging from the doorway that connected the sitting room they were in with the next.

"There's a local artist who does these dried flower decorations," Lark said. "I absolutely fell in love with them."

"Very cheerful," Hannah said, though her tone was slightly scathing.

"Very," Mary said, only she made sure to keep her voice sincere.

"I've actually had customers this week," Lark said, taking her seat in the chair and fussing with things. "I might have some profits to split sooner than anticipated!"

"Well, that's good," Mary said.

Hannah snorted. "You don't need to share your profits, Lark."

Lark ignored Hannah's scathing tone. "I had done a lot of research on all of this but...you never really know. You can't really expect to make a profit for a while in a town like this—everyone says. But I'm surprised by how excited people are to have something new to do here."

Hannah rolled her eyes. "In my opinion, there is nothing to do here. No offense. But if I'm going to go out, it's not going to be to craft." She stabbed at her quilt square with no irony.

"Except you did come out to craft."

"Because you're my sister and you're making me."

"I," Lark said, eyes wide, "cannot make any of you do anything you don't want to do."

"You used to scream until you turned blue and got your way."

"No I didn't."

"Yes, you did."

"You did," Mary confirmed.

Lark was a sunshine girl. Unless she'd been a thunderstorm. And when her mood had turned, heaven help everyone. She'd worn her every emotion out in the open for the world to see.

"Well, I guess when I was little," she said, grumpily.

"Pretty much until you were fourteen," Hannah said.

"I am not fourteen now, Hannah. And have had nary a tantrum in your presence in the last week. Anyway, you used to lock me out of our room and not talk to me."

"Also not true. Sometimes I locked myself outside."

"Unless you were too lazy to go outside and then you smoked cigarettes hanging halfway out the window."

A reflexive pang reverberated in Mary's chest. "You did not smoke in my house."

"No," Hannah said, measured. "I did not smoke in your house. I smoked with my ass in your house and my head hanging out the window."

Mary frowned. "Can you not swear?"

Lark grinned. "Yeah. Don't swear, Hannah."

"This is not me swearing," Hannah said. "Trust me."

It was strange to see them like this. So like they had been, and so different too. Because they were beyond her reach now. She couldn't actually get mad at Hannah for smoking. Well, she could, but she had no jurisdiction in her life. She couldn't really yell at her for swearing either.

Or at Lark for having a tattoo.

Just another way she both ached at the distance and felt pride that they were more adventurous than she would ever be.

"So have you chosen your fabric?"

"Not yet," Lark said. "Nothing is speaking to me."

"Do you *need* the fabric to speak to you?" Hannah asked.

"I would like it to." Lark sighed. "It was my idea to start the project and I want to be in love with what I choose. I'm fast at sewing so once I find it I'll catch up."

"I found a…" Hannah sighed, and fussed with the square on her lap. "I found a photo of a woman wearing the dress. I was wondering if it was someone from the Dowell family. The picture isn't labeled. And the ones of the family all are, so I'm not sure. And I didn't see this woman in any of the other pictures. But, it was all men and dead animals, so it's really hard to say."

Mary frowned. "I don't know." She didn't know in part because her mother hadn't shared stories about her family. Not personal stories. What she knew, she knew from plaques around town.

More that she'd missed. Not just the keys to connecting with

152

her girls, or mother-daughter wedding dress shopping. The layers of family. Of what made them…them.

"I should've brought it," Hannah said. "I took it to my room. But I didn't think…"

"I probably wouldn't recognize her anyway," Mary said. It made her feel sad. That she couldn't ask her mother now. That she probably wouldn't have if she had been here.

She looked down at her unfinished squares. And she wondered what her mother would say about that. She would probably wave her hands and tell her not to take everything so seriously.

That made anger burn in her chest. Because it was exactly what her mother would've said. And Mary would have wanted to ask her if she had any idea why Mary took things so seriously. Since clearly her husband had been fine to live with, her sons had been fine to live with, but once she had her daughter, she had no choice but to leave.

So how could a person not take things seriously, when they knew that something they'd done had been part of their mother walking away from them?

She'd done what she could with the girls. She'd been there.

She hadn't done everything perfectly. Her biggest regret was probably the lack of support they'd given Hannah. But music had seemed like such a farfetched goal and Mary had focused on drilling the concept of hard work into Hannah, had made it so Hannah had to be self-sufficient with it because Mary felt like if that was too much for Hannah she wouldn't be able to make a career from it anyway. Then she'd worked to pay for lessons, earned herself a scholarship, and when Lark had said she'd wanted to go to school for art…

Well they'd been different parents. Who saw things differently. Because of a trail Hannah had blazed.

Sometimes she wondered if Hannah was angry about that. But Hannah, being Hannah, would never share.

"What time is Avery arriving?" Mary asked.

She would take comfort in her oldest daughter's presence. Because yes, having children hadn't actually taken away her pain. But having Avery had gone a certain ways in making her begin to feel complete. And she had done... She had done right by her daughters. And maybe she wouldn't have chosen all of the same things that they had, but they were all right.

They were all right.

"She's probably baking a four layer cake for a school fundraiser and sewing costumes from scratch for a school play with nothing but a pack of mice and birds and her own martyrdom for help," Hannah said.

"Hannah Elizabeth," Mary said.

She didn't have to say anything else. Her daughter looked reflexively chastised, and she knew that Hannah hated to be chastised. But she also knew that first name middle name was an undeniable whip to crack, even over her spiky middle child.

"Sorry. But if she walks in with frosting on her face, you owe me an apology."

Except Avery would never look disheveled. Even if she had been baking right up until she had arrived. That was when the door opened again, and Avery came in. She had her blond hair in a bun, similar to Lark, except it was much neater, and any disarray was artful in its arrangement.

She was wearing her standard uniform of leggings and a flowing top, but there was something about her that didn't look right. And it wasn't until she got closer, and came into the sitting room, that Mary saw the large, purple bruise showing up as a ghost of itself beneath layers of foundation, just beneath her daughter's eye, running the length of her whole cheekbone.

Mary felt pain radiate in her head, down her neck and in her teeth. To her chest. As if she was feeling that bruise. As if the impact it had taken to leave a bruise like that echoed in her own body.

"What *happened*?" Mary asked.

Avery stopped in her tracks. "What?"

"Your *face*," Hannah said.

"Nothing," Avery said, frowning at Hannah like her sister was crazy.

"You have…a bruise," Hannah said.

Avery blinked, then squeezed her eyes shut for a second, like she was remembering. "Oh," she said, touching the affected spot. "My makeup must've faded. I… I did something really stupid last night. I tripped and I basically fell down the stairs carrying a laundry basket. And fortunately the basket saved my arms. I was cushioned by a whole bunch of clothes. But I knocked my face against the banister."

It didn't matter that her daughter was thirty-eight. That her youngest was thirty-four. Mary could still imagine a freak disaster around every corner, like she'd been able to do when they were children. The dark, careening panic in her chest was an homage to motherhood past.

"Avery," Mary said. "You have to be more careful. That's how… I'm so glad you're all right."

"Yeah," she said, slinging her oversize bag down off of her shoulder and setting it down next to her chair. Then she began to dig through it, producing her quilting squares, and a small bag filled with fabric scraps. "I got all the quilting done that I wanted to, though. And I still managed to make all the protein bars that I said I would make for Hayden's practice. It's crazy how much falling like that scares you. You know, when you're old."

"You're not old," Mary said. "You make it sound like I should worry about fracturing a hip if I bump up against the door frame."

"I'm just saying. I don't have time to have a broken arm or anything."

Lark looked concerned, but had gone back to a beading craft that she'd had sitting on a small end table behind the chairs. Hannah, meanwhile, was looking at Avery with intense focus.

"What?" Avery asked Hannah.

"You fell walking down the stairs?"

A shiver of unease began to grow in Mary's chest, widening with each passing moment until she found it difficult to breathe.

"Yes."

"And hit your face on the banister, which would have been on your left-hand side. But bruised your right side."

Avery's face took on an air of flat judgment. "Yes, CSI Boston, that's exactly what happened."

It took a moment for Mary to get exactly what Hannah was digging at, but once she understood, a strange sense of disquiet rolled over her. She pictured Avery's stairs, the banister on the left-hand side, the wall on the right, just like Hannah said.

"Did you do a somersault?" Hannah asked, her words flat and dogged, like a police officer conducting an interrogation.

"I'm not actually sure. I don't really remember it."

"You don't?"

Mary felt frozen, and she could see from the look on Lark's face her youngest daughter was just as stunned. But Hannah was pushing. Acting. Demanding. While Mary sat tongue-tied, afraid to connect the dots.

"What is the matter with you?" Avery asked. "Why does my injury demand a full-scale investigation?"

"Because I think it's weird," Hannah said. "I'm sorry. It's a weird story."

"I don't know what to tell you, people get weird injuries."

"And lie about them if they're trying to hide how it happened. Like if they were having sex in a shower or..."

"Yeah. I was having sex in the shower," Avery said, her tone dripping with enough scorn to make it impossible to tell if she was agreeing with Hannah or mocking her.

It was the anger in her tone, though, that seemed off. Hannah, for all she was edges, sarcasm and elusive emotion, was concerned, and her concern was making Avery mad.

"What happened?" Mary asked, her tone level.

It wasn't so much the story that was bothering her at this point, but the way Avery was reacting to being questioned.

"Nothing. Or I fell. I told you already. I'm not sure why you're all acting like this."

"I'm worried," Lark said, the words choked.

"I wasn't day drinking, for all your soccer mom jokes, Lark," Avery said, her tone acid. "You don't need to have an intervention."

"That's not what I was saying," Lark said. "I've never seen you drunk. I would never assume that's what happened."

"So what are you saying?" Avery met Lark's eyes directly. "Because it seems to me that you're skirting around something offensive and ridiculous, and I'd rather you just said it."

"Did he hit you?" Hannah asked, the words hard and sharp, her eyes glittering with sadness, anger and the intensity of a person ready to march into battle.

"How *dare* you?" Avery asked, her words carrying no less intensity, and a dose of venom. "Hannah, you don't live here. You barely *know* him. You barely know my kids or even me at this point. You breeze into town when you feel like it and act above everyone else while you sit outside smoking, just like you did when we were kids and you went and played violin instead of talking to anyone because you thought you were so much better than the rest of us."

Color had flooded Hannah's face, but she didn't break eye contact with Avery. Mary was shaking and she'd never felt like more of a coward. More ineffective.

She felt like she was drowning, right there in the middle of the shop.

Because there were things that needed saying and she'd had so many years of not talking about real, serious things with her daughter that now she needed to she couldn't find the words.

Avery took a shaking breath and continued. "You don't know

me at all and you think you can accuse my husband of something like that?"

Mary's breath suddenly exited her lungs in a gust and she stood. She couldn't just sit there. Not while her daughter was there, wounded.

She was shell-shocked, and she was hurt, but it was Avery who needed support.

She wasn't a mother to run when things were hard. Not like her own.

She was here. She would be here. No matter what.

It didn't matter if she knew what to do. It didn't matter if she was perfect, she just had to do something.

Mary got off of her chair and walked over to where her daughter sat. She sank to her knees and took hold of Avery's hands, and looked her daughter square in the face. Avery had never been able to lie. She'd been terrible at it. She knew that Avery didn't know that. That Avery was still convinced Mary had no idea she'd been fooling around with Danny Highmore—now Pastor Daniel Highmore, who Mary could not look in the eye—in the ivy at her grandfather's house. That she still thought she had gotten away with having a beer at a friend's house when she was fifteen.

"Avery," she said. "I want you to look me in the face and tell me that David didn't do this to you."

"Are you kidding me, Mom?" she asked. "David. David who I've been with for seventeen years. Your son-in-law and the father of your grandchildren."

She was daring her to push. Daring her to prove her wrong.

Mary had never pushed, not when Avery was sixteen and not in the years since but she would do it now.

"Did he?" Mary pressed.

"Don't ask me about my marriage," Avery bit out finally. "It's mine. And it's none of your business, not any of you, what happens in it."

"Dammit, Avery," Hannah shouted. "He hit you."

"Leave it alone!"

"Why did you come here if you didn't want us to know?" Hannah asked. "If you wanted us to leave it alone you should have stayed home sick."

Avery looked back and forth, like a hunted animal calculating her next move. And Mary wasn't sure if she was going to fight or run.

"I went to school today," she said. "Had coffee with my friends. No one asked me."

"Well your friends suck," Hannah said, fractured emotion showing through in her tone, even as her words sharpened them into a finely pointed anger.

"Why do you suddenly get to pass judgment on my whole life?"

"Since your life looks like *this*."

"It's my business. My life is perfect! I am married to a doctor and we have a boy and a girl and they get amazing grades and I plan the gala every year!" she shouted, her voice rough and frayed.

"Who. Cares. About. A *small town school gala*?" Hannah shouted back. "You act like you're head cheerleader of town, and *it's so damn weird*. Your life isn't perfect. You're a battered wife!"

Avery stood, her breath coming out in a rush. "No, I'm not. I'm Avery Grant. I'm Doctor David Grant's wife. I'm not... I'm not a battered wife."

"What do you call it then?"

"Nothing you would understand, Hannah. You don't love anyone but yourself. You barely know my kids, you barely know me. How dare you come in here and start labeling me? Telling me about my life? You think I'm hurting myself in some way? I think living in Boston, sleeping with half the men there and not having any sort of real relationship is self-destructive but you don't see me in your face."

"I didn't say I was perfect, Avery, I said what's happening to you is unacceptable." Hannah's expression got darker. "Is he hurting the kids?"

"I would die for my children," Avery shot back. "And I'd kill anyone who touched them. If he touched the kids I'd be gone. He's a good father. He is."

I'd die for my children.

Kill anyone who touched them.

Mary knew that truth. She felt it now.

"Avery," Mary started.

Avery whipped around to her mother. "Don't start, Mom. I don't need your opinion on this. I'm not like you were. You didn't do things you didn't get or make friends with any of the parents or…or do anything to help me make friends and be involved in school. I don't just…garden and make halfway homemade meals while my husband works a nine to five. David is a doctor and I have to go to events and I look a certain way and act a certain way. The kids go to an amazing school and we both have to do work to support their position there. I work for what I have, for the life I have. You just put me in thrift store clothes, not because we couldn't afford them, but because you didn't care about what was important to me and you never even tried."

Her words were bitter and acid and they hit Mary with unexpected force.

"Honey," she tried again.

"No," Avery said. "No. You wanted…a family that was together and just…not like yours and you did that. Fine. But *I did better.* I'm doing better." She moved closer to Hannah. "You can't look at one issue in a seventeen year marriage and think you know…think you know the whole relationship. *I love him.* I gave things up for him. You don't know anything about that. You had Josh and what did you do? You dumped him. So you could go off and live your life by yourself, but that's not what loving someone is, Hannah. You give to the people you love and you don't run when things are hard. You wouldn't know anything about that. Neither of you would." She rounded on Lark then. "You're barely ever here. All you do is run. Good for both of you that you have nice jobs, but who's here supporting Mom and Dad? Who's here being a good daughter? A good wife. A good mother. All things to all people instead of a…trash heap of an island unto myself. Don't tell me how to live my life when you're both such disasters."

She turned, holding her bag tight against her body, then walking out the door. Mary went after her, stumbling out onto the porch.

"Avery, don't go home," she said.

"I go home to him every night, Mom," she said. "I'm not… I am not leaving my husband."

"Avery, your dad…"

"Do not get Dad involved," she said, her voice trembling. "Don't. Just stop. I know you need to be involved in my life to feel like yours matters, but this is my life. It's mine. I want… I don't want to leave." The last word broke, and she turned on her heel and stomped down the sidewalk. And Mary watched, as she passed beneath pools of golden light, getting farther and farther away.

And she'd never felt so helpless.

She couldn't fix it. Couldn't pick her up and kiss her bruise and make it better. And she'd never wished more that she knew what to say. But she hadn't ever known exactly what to say in all of history and now when she needed to most…

She didn't have it.

Hannah and Lark were by her side, Hannah putting her arm tightly around her shoulder. "She's being an idiot," Hannah bit out.

"She's scared," Lark said softly. "And you didn't help."

"I'm not going to be the person who enabled her," Hannah

shot back. "She's in denial, and someone has to just say it so that she sees it."

But what Mary really couldn't believe was that she hadn't seen it.

That her daughter had been quietly falling apart, and Mary hadn't known.

And even if she had seen it…

She wouldn't have known how to talk to her about it.

All the lights in the house were off. Mary sat on the couch, Joe's comforting warmth next to her. Like it had been for forty years. And in the middle of all of her sorrow she was grateful. She was grateful for this man. She had thought that she and Avery had a lot in common. But Joe was a good man. Joe had been the best father, always. And an incredible husband. Mary had been so wounded by the abandonment of her mother. Marriage had frightened her. Love had frightened her.

And Joe had made her feel safe. Always.

"If the police don't do right by her they're going to be looking for his body."

Joe's voice was rough. Emotion like this wasn't easy for him. He wanted to do things, fix things. He wanted to fight with them, and there was really nothing to be done. Nothing that wouldn't put Avery in a bad position, because she hadn't committed to moving out. Nothing that wouldn't end up with Joe in jail, or potentially harm his relationship with their grandchildren.

"How did this happen?" Mary asked.

"I thought she was too young to get married," Joe said. "I always thought she was too young."

"She wasn't any younger than I was," Mary said. "I thought it was perfect. I thought David was perfect. I thought… I thought what I did was enough. I was there and I…"

"You are a good mother," he said. "It's not you that made the choice to hurt her. It was him."

Joe had always known how to get right to her heart.

"I know that," Mary said. "How could I not see it?"

It sat uncomfortably with her. Reminded her too much of the lack of relationship with her own mother. And how could that be? How? When being there for her girls had been everything to her. She had known that she couldn't always reach Hannah. And she had felt Lark go from being open and honest with her emotions to starting to hide. But Avery... Mary had been so certain she was happy. Was safe and settled. It was terrible to discover that she was wrong. That the son-in-law they had let into their lives, into their homes, the son-in-law that Joe had shared countless beers with, that Mary had grown to love like a son, had been hurting their daughter.

"They're their own people," Joe said. "The three of them."

"I just wish that they were little again. And I could fix everything." Fix everything in the way that her mother never had. Not for her.

Except it was clear now that whatever those kisses on their bruises had done, it hadn't fixed *everything*.

And she had no idea what would begin to mend the cracks running through Avery's life now.

There was no Band-Aid for this.

And it was the one thing that Mary had a difficult time sitting with. Knowing that there was something she couldn't make whole. And she couldn't help but wonder if it was because there was something missing in her. Something her mother should have taught her but didn't.

Or maybe it was missing in her either way. No matter what.

It was like that sampler all over again. Like waking up and finding out her mother had left and wondering if her mother was wrong...or if she was.

13

I have many regrets. But right now my deepest regret is that this family has not learned to share our secrets.

A letter, unsigned and unsent

Lark

That Ben got the parts for her car and wanted her to come in the day after Avery's whole situation seemed unfair. It was the tail end of the day, and she had managed to hold it together to work at the Craft Café, but she was pretty much just done. She was raw as it was, still processing everything that had happened. She didn't know if there was a time frame for that. Her sister was being abused by her husband. By Lark's brother-in-law, who had been part of their lives for so long it just felt...

Lark wasn't a stranger to secrets. Her family didn't know everything about her. And it was by design. But she had no idea that Avery was keeping secrets.

Avery.

So sanguine and calm, and always holding the answers. Avery who had seemed perfectly together to Lark for all this time. Who was always measured and matter-of-fact, and who had fought tooth and nail against last night's revelations. She didn't want to leave him. She didn't want to leave the man who was harming her.

But Keira had left Ben.

And here Lark was tangling those things up in her head as she pulled her car up to Ben's garage.

It was stupid.

She shouldn't even be worried about him. Not now. Not with everything as it was.

But she was. Her skin felt like it was on fire.

The garage door opened, and then he walked out, wiping his hands on a rag. Those tattoos caught her eye again, and she wondered. If he had gotten them before the divorce or after. What they meant.

He hadn't told her. He hadn't even told her that he was divorced.

But then, her own sister hadn't told her that she was having problems with her husband. And then hadn't let them help.

You just stood there. You barely said anything.

She felt guilty. Insanely guilty about that. Hannah had launched into Avery, giving no quarter and no mercy, and Lark had sort of just...

She detached. It was what she had years of practice doing. Pulling away. Retreating.

She looked up at Ben. And then she realized that she needed to do something. Get out of the car. Not just sit there.

"Hey," he said.

"Hi."

She felt shaky. She looked at his hand now, and saw that he wasn't wearing a wedding ring. She had noticed that before, casually, but had dismissed it because he was a mechanic, and it made sense that he might not have a ring on. But now she knew it wasn't because of his job. It was because he was divorced.

From his soul mate.

Great.

She was not in the kind of emotional space to handle this. It made her feel like young Lark. That girl who didn't know how to control her emotions. Who had been impulsive and reckless. And not the bohemian queen she had trained herself to be. The woman who let things roll off her back. Who pretended that nothing wounded her too deeply.

But she was wounded. She was wounded from last night, and she still had no idea what to do with the whole Keira thing.

Not to mention finding out he had a daughter in the first place.

"It won't take me very long."

"I hope that your daughter isn't sitting at home by herself."

He paused. "She's fine."

"I met her the other day."

"Well, I figured you might. Since she's been going to the café."

"Yeah, you just didn't mention that when we talked the other night. You didn't mention that you're divorced either."

His hands stilled, a muscle in his jaw ticking. "It didn't come up."

"I asked you to say hi to Keira. You said you would."

"And I will. If she gets in touch. She probably won't." His voice was hard. Bitter. It bore no resemblance to the Ben that she used to know. She could remember that night he and Keira had broken up clearly. Not just because of what had happened after, but because of how sad he'd been. Not bitter. Just broken.

But he was bitter now.

"It just seems like something you might have mentioned."

"I haven't talked to you in sixteen years. I'm not sure why I would mention the state of my marriage to you. You came to me to have me fix your car."

"We were friends, Ben."

"Yeah," he said. "We were. But we haven't been. Not for a long time."

"Did we… Stop being friends?"

"Don't give me that. Don't play games. You never spoke to me again after that. Never. You left town. You didn't come to the wedding…"

"You expected me to come to your wedding?"

"Why not? We had sex, Lark, and you didn't call."

"Wow. I didn't call."

"I did," he said.

"You got back together with her. So. I don't know what you expected me to say. Ever."

"I tried to talk to you first. You avoided me."

"I needed some time to think. You didn't give me any time. That's… It's ancient history. It doesn't matter. That's not what I'm here for. I'm here to have you fix my car. I am not here to talk to you about the one time we had sex. I'm sure that we've both had sex many times since then, and there's absolutely no reason to have a postmortem about one encounter."

"Except you're still mad."

"Yeah. I'm mad. Do you know why I'm mad?" And she could feel her grip on her temper loosening. She could feel herself moving toward a place she hadn't been in a very long time. Actually, since the last time she was with him. The last time she had been that stupid. The last time she had thrown caution to the wind. And she had learned. She had. All the years since then she had been so… Different. But he took her right back. "You were meant to be. You and her. I loved you both. So much. But I… Then I wanted you. And when she broke up with you I couldn't… I couldn't not have you. There's a reason that I waited. There's a reason that I gave you my virginity as quickly as I did."

"I'm sorry, what?"

"That's not important. Let's not get hung up on that. But I just… I felt so awful after. I felt so guilty. And I saw Keira and she was so… She was so broken up about you, and I couldn't tell her what I'd done. And it was just that… She wanted to be with you. She did. She was scared of being married, scared of committing so young."

"Are you telling me that you told her to get back together with me?"

"No. I'm not that… I'm not that nice. But I did listen to her while she talked herself into it. And I knew that she was going to tell you she wanted to be together. I couldn't get in the middle of that. I had tried for a very long time not to be in the middle of the two of you. You just seemed inevitable. And I just never wanted to be in the way of inevitable. But I guess…"

"Yeah," he said. "She left me. So, if you're going to get angry at me, you can't possibly say anything that I haven't said to myself." He sighed heavily. "I thought we were fine. Maybe I was a bad husband, I don't know. But Taylor is a damn good kid, and she deserves better."

Lark let out a slow breath, forcing herself to expand her scope. Here she was, yelling at Ben about the frustrations she felt about his marriage. Maybe she needed a little perspective. And the mention of his daughter did it. "Do you really think you're a bad husband?"

He laughed, and it sounded bitter. "No. I was a good husband, actually. I don't know what happened to her. It's like… Like she became a completely different person than the one that I knew for more than twenty years. So there. That's what happened. I don't have any deep insight for you, and I don't have anything to say about whether or not we were meant to be, then quit being meant to be, or anything at all, really."

"Have you considered therapy?" She tried to ask that in a measured tone, tried to find her way back to that emotionally even space she worked hard to exist in. The look he gave her would have been funny if the situation weren't so decidedly unamusing.

"No. I considered continuing to work to support my kid. And just... Dealing with it in the best way I can." He let out a slow breath and leaned back, gripping the edge of the workbench, the muscles in his arms flexing. And she couldn't help but notice. "Sometimes I think I didn't have a thought in my head until I was maybe... Twenty-five years old. And everything before that was just acting and reacting. I was with Keira so I thought that I should be. And I was sure that I was in love, because we slept with each other and had been together since we were fifteen. I thought that I should marry her because of all of that. It seemed like the right thing to do. And then there was you, and the way you were with me when I was heartbroken. And that confused me. Then you were gone, and she wanted me back. And I just reacted." He shook his head. "People show you who they are, and you ought to pay attention. She left me once, and I think she probably should've gone with her gut and stayed gone. But I think like me she was scared. Scared not to take the next step because it was our plan. Because it was what everybody thought we were going to do. And I just... I just thought it was right. I thought it was right because we had done it. We got married. We had Taylor."

The speech left her bruised, but it was honest. She could tell that it was honest. And fair, because he was right. About the way expectations from other people made choices for you before you were old enough to figure out what you wanted, and what the whole world was. Who you were in it.

"Were you happy?"

He looked up, the lines around his eyes suddenly seeming deeper. "I had everything I thought I should have. I owned my own business, bought a house, a really nice house. I enjoy my job, Lark, even if it's not a fancy job. I like fixing things. I like working with my hands. And the whole time I didn't notice my relationship was broken. But when you live with somebody for that long you can forget to talk to each other. And we just didn't. I mean, we talked. About the day, about how Taylor was doing at school, and Taylor's friends, and when we would let her get her driver's license, and if she could get her nose pierced. But we didn't really talk. And there was a point where I thought we had everything, and she didn't. I wish like hell that she would've just talked to me, but I can't really blame it all on her."

Lark held her breath. "But were you happy?"

He looked up at her, those familiar eyes burning into hers. "I don't remember what happy feels like."

There was something about that statement, simple and flat that landed hard inside of her. She leaned against her car, with him still leaning against the workbench, a couple feet of empty concrete between them. And a whole lot of years. But he had been her best friend once, and she had been his. And mostly, she just… She felt the same way sometimes. She wanted to tell him about Avery. There were a lot of things that she wanted to tell him. But as they looked at each other, the air between them seemed to shift, and her breath caught.

And this had nothing to do with emotions. With bad feelings or what had happened with Avery. With the fight they just had, or with what had happened all those years ago.

It was just still this.

It was just still there.

"When will you have the car done?"

"Tomorrow sometime. Do you need a ride back home?"

She shook her head. "The walk will be good."

He took a step toward her, and she took a step back. "Okay," he said.

"Bye."

She walked out the door quickly, shoving her hands in her

pockets and moving down the street, away from him. Away from… All of that.

There was too much going on in her life to indulge in any kind of attraction to him. It was too much of a minefield.

Ben Thompson had only ever been a path to heartbreak. And she was here to heal.

And now, Avery needed her. It wasn't the time to be focused on herself.

Too bad her heart was still beating twice as fast as it needed to be. Making a mockery of all of her common sense.

He always has.

At least she hadn't kissed him.

But oh, how she'd wanted to.

14

I lived in the same city all my life. Even moving from my parents' home to my husband's was not so different. Here, everything is different. But I am learning to find the familiar in each new place we stop. The grass, the flowers, and John. The sun and his friendship make me feel like less of a stranger in this world.

Anabeth Snow's diary, 1864

Avery

Avery was up and out early with the kids, on the promise of breakfast at the diner near the school.

"This is weird." Hayden didn't look up from his coffee. He drank coffee, because he felt like it was grown-up, but Avery knew that he would still rather have a hot chocolate. But she never argued with him when he ordered it.

She ached for both of her kids. And that was her focus right now. Not thinking about what she was doing. Not thinking about herself. Or about what had happened last night with her family. But about them.

Yes, things weren't ideal right now between herself and David.

Her stomach went sour.

She replayed the reel of *not right* that had been happening for years now.

Being pushed against the wall.

Shoved backward.

Her head cracking against the side table by the door, sending it hard into the drywall and leaving a gouge in the wall.

Last night it had felt like the world had unraveled. They knew. They knew.

She had no idea how she'd made it through the night and she'd thanked God that David was out late, because if she'd had to talk to him she didn't know what she'd do.

She'd sat in the bottom of the shower, letting the hot water pound on her skin, letting steam fill her nose and lungs.

And she'd convinced herself that nothing had to change.

That they could gloss this over.

She'd carefully taken the whole evening and begun to cut pieces from it like she was dividing up a scrap of fabric for a quilt.

She could rearrange it then. Leave parts out.

It's what she'd been doing for years, she could keep on doing it. When a few years of happily married turned to a strange, passive-aggressive meanness that started eroding Avery's confidence. When that had shifted to naked insults and two years ago finally...

Violence.

It had been a slow shift to get there, but it could change. It could. Anyway it wasn't always bad.

Her parents wouldn't blame her if she stayed, not if they understood.

David was their son-in-law and had been for so long they'd... if Avery was happy they would have to let it go.

If Avery was happy.

"Aren't you eating, Mom?" Peyton asked.

Avery had only gotten coffee. She couldn't stomach anything solid. She shook her head. "No. It's too early for me."

Peyton started in on the pancakes in front of her, Hayden picked at the bacon on his plate.

If she left David, the kids wouldn't have their life anymore. If anyone knew that he'd lost his temper with her a few times...

He could lose his job.

And then where would the money come from?

How could they afford the house?

The kids' school?

She was doing this for the kids.

"You have a bruise on your face, Mom," Hayden said. Shockingly angry teenage eyes connected with hers. "I know he's mean to you."

"I..."

"He's not that good at hiding it. He thinks he is, because he thinks he's smarter than everybody else."

Peyton didn't say anything. She just sat there, staring straight ahead.

"Hayden," Avery said slowly, "it's complicated."

"It's not complicated. He's a dick," Hayden said, his voice shifting from boy to man in that sentence. "He always has been. He doesn't care about anybody but himself."

"That's not true," Peyton said, a tear sliding down her cheek. "Don't say that about Dad."

"Yeah well he likes you, Peyton, because you get straight A's and you don't talk back to him, and you'll probably go to medical school. But he doesn't care what I do, and he doesn't care about Mom either."

"He has a hard job!" Peyton exploded. "He has a lot of stress. If you weren't such an asshole to him all the time, Hayden, he'd like you better."

Avery felt like she'd been stabbed in the chest. Hearing her daughter issue the same sorts of excuses for David's behavior that Avery herself had repeated over and over again. For every slight. Every hurt.

How had she not noticed that they were part of this? Peyton's excusing him. Hayden's anger. She'd told herself that because they'd never seen any of his violent outbursts they were protected.

But they weren't.

"He's hit me before," Hayden said.

Avery's stomach lurched. "He what?"

There weren't words. Just a deep groaning in her heart, her soul. She nearly doubled over with it.

He'd hit Hayden.

You weren't protecting them.

You were protecting you.

Your perfection.

Your life.

"Not like he hit you. But he slapped me once. When I got mad at him for not coming to my soccer game."

"Why didn't you tell me?" she whispered.

"For the same reason you didn't tell me."

That stabbed her. Right through her heart.

He'd been protecting her.

He'd been protecting her. Her son. Her little boy. And he was a boy. Not a man, like David, who should be held responsible for his actions and should not have the people he'd hurt bending over backward to keep him safe.

Peyton was weeping silently, there in a diner booth. Hayden was looking angry and defiant and she was...

Defeated.

Soul deep.

She'd failed her kids.

Her family.

Her husband, the man she'd married was gone. And it was like mourning a death. The man he'd been. The man she thought he was.

Maybe he'd never been the man she'd thought.

She didn't know.

And then there was her.

The woman she'd thought she was.

She hadn't seen herself as a battered wife. She'd seen herself as a warrior. Fighting to hold her home and family together.

She was proactive. A fixer. A doer.

Who'd convinced herself that taking a punch somehow went along with planning the carpool for soccer practice.

She hadn't been doing or fixing anything. She'd been desperately bailing water out of a ship with a hole blown through it, fighting a losing battle and refusing to see it.

"I'm your mom, Hayden, it's my job to protect you."

"I had to protect you. Because nobody else was. And I didn't know yet that he'd actually... Done more than just yell at you like he does. And when I realized... I want to kill him," Hayden said.

The sorrow that broke apart in Avery was debilitating. Because she hadn't known. She hadn't realized how much of the toxicity had already gotten onto Hayden. She hadn't understood that it was already seeping into other parts of her life. She had been convinced that it was only her. That she was standing there, taking it and protecting her children.

But they weren't protected.

"I don't know what to say," she said, because she really didn't. Because this all felt awful.

"Are you going to go to the police?" Peyton asked. "Are all my... All my friends going to know?"

"Who cares about your stupid friends?" Hayden asked.

"*I do,*" Peyton said.

Avery's heart squeezed tight. Because she cared too. She cared

about her own friends, the way that this would affect their normal. And she shouldn't.

It hurt to remember that moment in The Miner's House when
she'd realized they knew. And not…not just suspected, knew.
When she'd realized she was standing there burning alive and
claiming she didn't smell smoke.

If it wasn't perfect, it was nothing.

She was nothing.

"Let's skip school today," she said, her voice rough. "I'm
going to take you both to Grandma and Grandpa's and then…
we'll figure it out."

They finished breakfast and then went to the grocery store
where she filled her cart with food she didn't feel like eating.
Cereal she never usually let the kids have. Chips. A lot of chips.
And then they loaded it all up and drove to her parents' house.

She couldn't say how she got up the walk, or when her dad
came out. He carried all the bags, she knew that. Her mom
hugged her and sat her on the couch and her dad stood in the
living room with his hands curled into fists then finally crossed
the space and hugged her.

Her head was a fuzzy blur.

"I should pack some things," she said.

But her dad wouldn't hear of her going back to the house,
even though David was at work, so he went and collected everything she asked him to.

"What do you need, honey?" her mom asked, squeezing her
hand when she stood there a few hours later, looking at her belongings, shoved into bags and boxes.

"A sedative?" She tried to smile. "I'm sorry, Mom. For what
I said last night I…"

Her mom squeezing her, touching her…it made her want to
break apart. She never showed affection with physical touch so
Avery must really look like a mess.

"No need."

Except she felt like there was. Like they needed to talk which…she didn't even know how to do that with Mary. But she was tired, and grateful for the out.

"The kids can sleep here," her mom said. "And we can get the air mattress out if you want. Hayden can have it and you can have the bed in your old room."

She nodded. "Thanks. I…"

"You should go stay at The Dowell House," her mom said. "You know we'll take care of the kids. And Lark and Hannah can help with…whatever you need."

"The kids might need me."

"*You* need to sleep. And worry about yourself for a little bit."

"I might go over there for a while."

"Go," her mom said. "We've got this."

Avery found herself back on the road, and then somehow inside The Dowell House, not wholly conscious of how she got there.

She just needed to sit. She was relieved that Lark and Hannah weren't here. Glad for a chance to sit by herself for a while. To let the reality of the last few hours wash over her. Without omitting anything. Without rearranging or cutting or making a new story.

And as she sat, she looked out the window, at the new view.

And she thought of her quilt square. Something strange echoed inside of her then, something deep and resonant that she couldn't put words to. Like a melody without lyrics.

It was familiar, and warm. It made her think of something, the edge of a memory that she couldn't quite grasp onto.

She felt broken. She felt battered, but she remembered thinking about that woman, who had brought her curtains with her, who had left home and had brought her possessions with her. Who had made an entirely new life in a strange, foreign land.

And she was suddenly desperate to know more.

She got up from the chair, and walked up the stairs, heading up to the attic. There was an eclectic pile of boxes, but there was one that caught her eye in particular. It didn't have fabric in it, but an assortment of things. And she just wondered. Because there had to be information somewhere, more information about the fabric. About the people who'd owned it. Because why would there be any information at all, if the rest of it wasn't...

And maybe it was just her desire to be distracted for now. Maybe it was just a desperate attempt at making herself feel better. But she wanted to believe that there was something up there. Something in here that might give her more answers than she already had.

The boxes mostly contained junk. Weird junk, too. She went through one that had mostly candlesticks, but also Pez dispensers. And then another one that had old candy jars. But then finally she stumbled on one that had some silver in it that looked old. What era were the curtains from? It was 1864. During the Oregon Trail. The rush of it, if she remembered correctly, and anyone who had been through elementary school in Oregon knew their Oregon Trail history.

So maybe this was her bin. Or, just a collection of things from that time.

There, in the bottom of the box, was a small leather book. A Bible, maybe. Though, family Bibles were usually massive. Small Bibles like this she more associated with preachers who had to travel around the countryside.

But when she opened it up, she saw that it wasn't a Bible. Rather the words inside were handwritten. The first entry was from 1863. And was signed *Anabeth Snow.*

"Anabeth," she said, touching the book.

Maybe it was hers. Maybe not. But she would read it, and she would find out.

Lord knew she didn't have much else to do.

Because when word got out of her new situation, everything was going to fall apart.

Everything was going to fall apart.

There was nothing she could do about that. It was the baseline truth of the place she found herself in.

She wouldn't be a doctor's wife anymore.

That made her feel like she was drifting off in space, wholly untethered from the woman she'd fashioned herself into for the last seventeen years.

Disconnected.

Afraid.

Then she saw herself, a little girl snapping peas on her grandmother's porch. Dreaming of the life she could have.

Maybe it's time to make a new place.

Maybe it's time to make a new view.

Just then the front door opened and Lark came in holding a white canvas bag. Hannah followed in after her and the three of them just looked at each other in silence for a moment.

"We were grocery shopping," Lark said, holding the bag up.

Hannah looked away.

Avery realized she should explain why she was here, but the words stuck in her throat.

"I got green beans," Lark said. "Why don't we go sit on the back porch and snap some."

Pressure built behind Avery's eyes and she could only manage to nod. And that was how she ended up sitting down on the worn wood in the back of The Dowell House doing something old and familiar while she faced a future that was terrifying in its uncertainty.

And she was thankful for a moment that didn't need words.

Eventually she'd explain.

But for now, they just sat and enjoyed the moment.

15

Sam says we can come to set, and that we'll have parts in the back-ground of an actual film! He bought us new dresses and they glitter like the lights outside the Vista Theater. Mine is all midnight blue with silver sequins, like the stars at night. This is every bit as magical as I dreamed.

Ava Moore's diary, 1923

Hannah

Hannah was vile, and had nowhere to channel it. She had been a little bit of a bitch to her sister last a couple nights ago, but she was... She was just so angry. About everything, really.

She was glad that Avery had moved out, glad that she was here, and that the kids had joined her after a couple of nights at Mom and Dad's.

Hannah and Lark had spent the last two nights mostly not talking about things and pouring wine, letting Avery sit there pale and shell-shocked. They hadn't really talked about anything. About next steps or what all of this meant.

About the fact Hannah wanted to kill David with a spoon.

She bit off her rage as she put her violin away and picked up her quilting square. Then she carried it downstairs into the kitchen, just as Lark walked through the front door. Her sister was carrying bags of what looked like fake flowers, and several balls of yarn.

"What exactly are you doing?"

"Thinking on some things," Lark said.

"Are you going to start your square?"

"I need time. I haven't found the right fabric."

"You really are ridiculous," Hannah said.

Hey, she had been the worst that she could possibly have been with Avery last night, she might as well take Lark's head off too.

"Excuse me?"

"You just expect that everything is going to fall into place for you, don't you?"

"No I don't," Lark said. "This is a quilt, not... I don't know. Something with a deadline."

"You don't even know what it could be."

"Fine. Illustrations for a book. I'm not doing that anymore. I'm not doing it right now. I'm leaving myself open to creativity. So quit trying to put me in a box."

"You wrangled all of us into it and now you're not doing it. That's just very typical of you."

"And are you mad that you're doing it? Or are you enjoying it? Because it seems to me that you've made more progress than anyone else."

"Oh... Bite me," Hannah said. She stopped into the kitchen and sat down at the table.

"Did you just say bite me? What is it, 1996?"

"You don't remember 1996."

"I absolutely do. I have a deep and abiding love of crop tops to prove it."

That was the problem with Lark. She was irritating, but it was often impossible to be mean to her because she was... She was pleasant even when she was a frustration.

Lark sat opposite her and pulled out one of the balls of yarn, and a pair of knitting needles.

"It's summer, so you figured you would... Knit something?"

"Well, I'm going to do an introduction to knitting course at the café. And I needed to make some samples."

She really couldn't be mad about that, because it was work. So she had to put her bad attitude away. She didn't want to do it at all. She wanted to let it fly.

"Have you talked to Avery today?" Lark asked.

"She's here, and the kids are here. But I haven't really seen much of them. They've been straightening up their bedrooms and getting things organized. I got the feeling that they're not very social."

"Have we heard anything from David?"

"Are you expecting him to come pound the door down?"

"I don't know what to expect," Lark said. "I didn't think he would ever hurt Avery, but he did, so I guess we can't exactly rule out him coming here and trying to get to her, can we?"

"Guess not. She needs to go to the police."

"You can understand why she hasn't."

Maybe she could. But she was being stubborn about it. Not on purpose, really. It was just that... Life wasn't easy. Not for anyone. And sometimes you had to make hard choices.

"Gossiping about me?"

Hannah turned and looked behind them, and saw Avery standing on the staircase.

"Not intentionally," Lark said.

"How are the kids?" Hannah asked.

"I don't know," Avery said. "Weird. I think Hayden is protective and angry with his father. And Peyton is sort of angry with me, but shocked also. And I can't really blame either of them for their reactions."

Avery sat down on the couch next to Hannah, a decent amount of space between them. She propped her feet up on the coffee table in front of them, and sank into the white cushions. She closed her eyes, her blond, wavy hair fanning out behind her. "I just keep thinking... This is not what I wanted for them. This isn't what Mom and Dad did for us. They worked so hard on their marriage. And they gave us... Mom did so much to make sure that we grew up in the kind of household she didn't get. One with both of her parents together."

"Your house wasn't the same," Hannah said, frustrated that Avery was taking so much blame.

"I know that," Avery said, sitting up suddenly, her hands clenched into fists. "I do know that. I really do. And it... It kills me. It kills me that I'm going in circles like this. But it's just not that simple, Hannah. And I know that you think it should be. Because you're strong in this one really particular way, and you go for the things that you want, but you do it by yourself. And there are less gray areas when it's just you."

"I'm not by myself. I have friends."

"No. Everything you do, you do it... Come on, you were never that close to anyone when we were growing up. I mean, not to us. Not to Mom and Dad."

Hannah itched, the microscope now on her, making her want to crawl out of her skin.

"Why are we talking about me?"

"Because you think you just... Know what you would do. If you were me. But you don't. You're a different person than me."

"I'm well aware."

"I don't think you are. And you know what, it's not even that we're different people. It's just that you don't know what it's like to have your life wound around somebody else's like this."

Lark was silent.

"What do you think?" Avery asked Lark.

"I don't know either," Lark said. "I don't have anyone."

"Well, what would you do?"

"I don't know," Lark said, looking flustered. "I don't. I would... I don't know. Maybe pretend it wasn't happening for a while." Lark's blue eyes filled with tears. "I'm just really sorry, Avery."

Hannah thought maybe there was something broken inside of her, because she didn't want to cry. She wanted to break things. Preferably her brother-in-law. And she didn't know why it was so difficult for her to offer sympathy. Why it was so difficult to be like Lark and sit there and tear up and look sorry, and just say that she didn't know what she would do.

The idea that you might not know what to do is way too scary.

"Why did you keep it a secret?" Lark asked. "I know you were scared, I know... I just wish you'd told us."

"You don't know," Avery said, choked. "It's not just not knowing what to do, or loving him still. I'm so... I'm so embarrassed. I didn't ask to be this woman. I didn't ask to be her."

"Of course you didn't," Hannah said.

"You know, everybody says... They all say that they would leave him if he hit them. If he cheated. And I used to think the same thing. That if my husband ever did anything like that to me there's no way I would stay," Avery's voice was low, shaky but strong at the same time. "But that was before. Before I'd been with him for so long I couldn't remember what life was like without him. Before I was... Comfortable, and dependent in so many ways on the way that we structured our lives. Hannah, the violin is your dream. David was mine. You tell me that you could walk away from a dream that easily even if it hurt?"

Her words were sharp, and they stabbed into Hannah's chest. They tangled around inside her with all kinds of words she'd called herself. All kinds of fears about dreams and what she might or might not be.

And what it looked like when everything unraveled...

That was what Avery looked like.

Hannah's worst fear.

Avery leaned forward, clasping her hands in her lap and letting out a slow breath. "He's so smart," she said. "And handsome. And he's funny sometimes. And when he smiles at me I feel like someone turned a light on inside me. And those are the reasons I fell in love with him. Those feelings, those reasons, they didn't go away the first time he hit me. And since he did I've spent the last two years telling myself that he was still the man I loved. Not the man he was when he got angry, when he berated and belittled me... That it wasn't him. Not my husband. It was someone else who... Made him do those things. He became someone else when he did it. And when he didn't, he was completely that man I fell in love with in the beginning. But it is him. It's as much a part of him as his blue eyes and his humor and that smile. Now I think I'm finally not so in love anymore. Or at the very least I realize I can't keep on loving him like I have."

A tear fell down her cheek. "I really did it. I left. And now I have to... I have to make more choices."

"We should go to the police," Hannah said, her chest feeling sore. "I just think it's probably the safest thing for you to do."

"I don't know. I don't know what that's going to mean for me." She crossed her arms, closing her eyes, another tear sliding down her cheek. "Seriously. I think he's going to lose his medical license."

"Yeah, and maybe you're not going to have a lot of money," Hannah said. "But you'll be safe."

"The kids go to private school."

"And they can go to public school."

Avery doubled over, and Hannah had never seen anything quite so scary as her most confident sister...undone.

"This is what I was afraid of," she said, straightening, her fists pushed hard against her eyes. "You guys know and now I have to...oh I have to go to the police. He hit my son."

"What?" Lark asked.

"Hayden told me that David slapped him." She wiped her arm under her eyes, sniffing loudly. "I can't let it go. I can't hide it. I have to do this. I just... I want to go back and hit Pause. I just want to go back to a week ago. Two years ago. I want to go back to before, and I can't." She breathed out, slow and strong. "It's today. And I wish it weren't. I want to be in the future or in the past, but I don't want to be here."

"We are here for you," Lark said, leaning forward and putting her hand on Avery.

"Yes," Hannah said. "Lark can be... Soft and sympathetic, and I can get angry for you, when you can't. Also, admin."

Avery opened her eyes, and surprisingly, laughed. "Well, those are your individual strengths."

"Let's go to the police station," Lark said, squeezing Avery's hand. "We're here for you. Mom and Dad can come over here so Peyton and Hayden don't have to shuffle back over there."

"They don't need to be watched," Avery said, but Hannah knew that her sister wouldn't want the kids to be alone right now.

"Great," Hannah said. "I'll call Mom and Dad. Get your coat."

Hannah suddenly had the vivid memory of Avery babysitting her and Lark on their parents' date nights. How she'd been cool and calm and mediated all fights. How she'd cooked for them and scolded Hannah for going out in the dark and cold to play violin without properly bundling up.

Hannah had found it annoying then. But she could see now it came from a place of love. Of caring.

And Avery needed Hannah to take care of her now.

"Okay."

"Are you ready?" Hannah asked.

Avery's eyes met hers. "No."

"That's okay."

"We have to do it anyway."

"Yeah," Hannah said. "Sometimes that's how it is."

16

His wife and little girl died of fever. He told me after he took me for
a ride to a field where he said we'd find bluebonnets. He gave one
to me and told me his story. Right now bluebonnets feel like home.

Anabeth Snow's diary, 1864

Avery

The last time she was in the police station in Bear Creek,
she had been there to help her daughter sell Girl Scout cookies.

She had been walking on her own two feet, letting Peyton move ahead of her. Peyton had been skipping, her pony-
tail bouncing as she had approached the uniformed officers and
asked for their support in helping her earn an owl keychain, for
which she had to sell one hundred and fifty boxes.

She had walked out with a full order form and Avery had
listened to her chatter the whole way home, her excited voice
filling the car.

It had felt perfect.

Not now. It was dark now, and Hannah and Lark were on either side of her, their arms linked through hers, bracing her. It was only their strength that held her up, that propelled her forward. Without them, she didn't know if she would be able to stay standing.

For two years she'd taken it. More than taken it, she'd hid it for him. And for more years than that she'd pretended their relationship wasn't corroding.

One day she'd been cleaning the silver glasses they'd used at their wedding and had noticed a black blotch at the center and for some reason, she'd quit polishing it. She'd watched it grow. For years she'd watched the tarnish on that silver spread, grow, and there had been something satisfying in it.

It was them, she realized now.

That silver had been her private homage to their degradation.

So she was here now, making public what had been a shameful secret.

On some level she had known. She had known that it was getting to this point. She had hoped—no, she had prayed. She had prayed that it would be an anomaly. That it would stay that way. That it would happen once. Twice. But it was escalating.

He had cared, at least for a while, about making sure that none of his fits of rage were visible anywhere on her body. That nobody would know that he had vented his frustration, her body a journal of his professional disappointments, his personal inconveniences. Sore muscles and bruises on her arms, impressions of his fingers dug deep into the upper part of her arm. She had learned to carry that over the last couple of years. Had learned to push it down and just not think about it.

She had compartmentalized. Turned him into good David and bad David and made sure they were never the same man in her mind. But now, everything had collided. And as she'd been looking at herself in the mirror and laying on as much concealer as she possibly could, she had to actually look herself in the eyes while she contended with a mark left behind by her husband. And that was so much harder. So much harder than putting on a sweatshirt and covering it up.

And it was a testament to her denial, and perhaps to the kinds of friendship she had or didn't that she had been convinced all she needed was some makeup and a backup story and nobody would ask questions. And no one had. Not at school. Not in the drop-off or pickup line. Not at coffee, where she had continued to have discussions with a whole group of women about trivia night.

What Hannah had said about her being head cheerleader of town had been echoing in her head. Was that was she was? Just…this sad woman clinging to being popular like she'd been in high school?

And all the good it had done her. She couldn't talk to any of the people who were part of that piece of her life.

It was her mother, her sisters who had seen. Who had pressed. She should have known she couldn't hide it from them.

The next steps of the process went by in a blur. Hannah did most of the talking as she made arrangements for Avery to speak to a police officer. She was taken into a room, and given paperwork. She was questioned, and she was given a form that said Victim Statement on it.

Victim.

It was so difficult to see that word and know that she needed to write below it. Know that she was a victim, and this was a form for her.

"Do you need any help?"

The female police officer with a sympathetic expression and a name tag that read L. Dempsey was staring at her.

"No," she said, shaking her head and staring at the blank page, doing her best to try to fill out the specifics of everything that had happened. She focused on the other night. Not on the escalation, or on any of the other days.

"We need to take pictures," the woman said softly. "Of where he left marks."

She closed her eyes. "Everywhere?"

"Yes."

Officer Dempsey was gone for a moment, and when she returned she had a mirror, and some facial wipes. Which was when Avery realized, she needed the bruise to show. It certainly didn't need to be partly covered up. There was a small mirror next to the chair she'd been sitting in, and she looked into it, as she slowly dragged the cloth over her face. As she removed the layers of makeup, the bruise bloomed darker, like a perverse rose.

She looked at the officer, nearly defiant. But the other woman's expression was a study in neutrality. There was no pity there, no sympathy. But no judgment, either. And Avery found she was thankful for that. She photographed her face quickly.

"Anywhere else?"

Avery nodded slowly. And with glacial movements, took hold of the hem of her sweater, pulling it up over her head. She had a tank top on underneath that, but she pulled it up over her head as well. The room they were in was completely closed off from the outside. She was almost certain there were bruises down her back, from where she had been thrown up against the wall the other night.

Tears pooled in her eyes as she pushed her leggings down her hips, exposing the bruises on her hips, her thighs. She held her arms out, extended slightly from her sides. She closed her eyes as the police officer circled her, taking pictures. She listened to her own breath, echoing in her ears, and her heartbeat, moving quickly, terror making her limbs weak.

Her heart beat, and the camera clicked.

Victim.

It was documented, all those bruises.

Avery had gotten really good at living for the moment she wasn't in. At just moving herself outside of her body. Which was what she did now. She felt like she was standing with her sisters, staring at this thin, bedraggled woman in her underwear. Having pictures taken of her body. Exposing herself, but not just her skin. The way she'd been living for quite some time. The things she'd been hiding, desperately.

Here it was all out in the open.

She was caught somewhere between power and devastation.

"We have enough to make an arrest," the officer said. "We're able to hold him for about twenty hours. And in that time, we will submit all of this to the district attorney. That will decide if the case proceeds."

Avery nodded, as if that made sense to her. None of it really did. That she was standing here didn't make a whole lot of sense. That her life had brought her to a police station.

That her marriage vows had become… Nothing. They weren't anything.

It wasn't a marriage. Not anymore.

She went to bed every night with the man that hit her. She let him kiss her.

After those hands hit her, she let him put them on her body.

And it wasn't good David and bad David, it was all just David.

"I'll let you get dressed."

Avery dressed, her fingers cold as she pulled her shirt back on, tugged her pants back over her hips. Then she just stood there in that room, the fluorescent lights buzzing as she tried to orient herself.

She breathed in deep. Felt her feet connected firmly with the floor. Felt the air fill her lungs.

She was still here.

She hadn't fallen apart.

She swallowed hard, then turned and walked out of the room. Lark and Hannah were standing outside, both standing, holding

193

the straps of their purses, their right legs bent, left legs straight. And it was so absurd, the two of them standing just the same with concerned looks on their faces.

She wanted to laugh, because it would horrify them to know they looked so alike.

But she didn't have it in her.

"What do you want to do?" Lark asked. "Do you want to go buy cake?"

"No," she said. "I think I just want to go home. To The Dowell House."

"Then let's go home."

As they walked out of the police station, and out onto the darkened street, she felt like she'd left her pride on the floor in there. That when she'd picked her clothing back up and put it on her body, she hadn't been able to reclaim that. And she wondered how long it would be before she felt... Good. Certain that she'd done the right thing. Proud. Like a survivor. Like something other than a woman staring at a life that was shattered beyond recognition.

You weren't the one who shattered it.

She clung to that. Like a diamond in the middle of lumps of coal. She hadn't done this. She wasn't perfect. But she had never abused his trust. And he had done it to her now, countless times. Over and over again. He demanded better of her constantly while giving nothing more of himself. He had pushed it here. He had done this.

She tried to feel angry, and didn't have the energy for it.

But someday she would.

Someday, she would think about that, and she would feel... She would feel angry. Angry like Hannah. At him, and maybe at herself. And she would cry. She would cry just like Lark was. But for now, she found she couldn't do either. So she let her sisters take her by the arms again, and let them feel all the things she couldn't quite yet.

17

The best part about being in the studios is we get invited to the parties after. Champagne and brilliant food. Everyone is so beautiful. Sam says he's going to help me audition for a role that's more than just background and I can't wait.

Ava Moore's diary, 1923

Hannah

Hannah felt completely drained by the time they brought Avery back home. They poured glasses of wine, but then Avery had suddenly been overcome by exhaustion, and she and Lark had helped her up to bed. She wanted to be unconscious when the police went and handcuffed her husband.

Hannah couldn't blame her for being tired. It echoed inside of her. It was just such a helpless feeling, and Hannah didn't like helpless. Selfishly, she had it up to the very top of her being with helplessness. Because even though she knew it wasn't the dissolution of the marriage, or abuse or anything like that, she was still so… She was so angry about the principal chair position, and there was nothing she could do about it. Nothing at all. She also had to put it on hold while they dealt with Avery, which was fine.

Except it was eating at her.

Her own secret that would never be as important as the one Avery was dealing with.

One that still had the power to cut and wound.

She had others. But they were like scars. Hardened and raised and like armor, not wounds.

And it was just… She wasn't used to this. She wanted to fix it. She wanted to make things change with the force of her… Her feelings. Her deep conviction that it shouldn't be like this. She wanted to knock David sideways, and she wanted to tell Avery to quit being sad about him. That was it. She just didn't want her to be sad. Because he wasn't worth it.

But she had a mortgage and kids and all kinds of things that made it complicated. And even if Hannah didn't fully understand it, she could sort of get how… How it was complicated for Avery to lose that marriage even though it clearly wasn't a great one.

But Hannah just wanted it to be fixed for her. And she couldn't do it. Any more than she could fix the situation with her career. Well, at least that was… No. There was no *at least*. She had been working for years for that. And it was just… It was just a no. And there was no way of knowing when another seat would open up. Yes, she could start applying to other symphonies. But there weren't very many that paid as well. Maybe she could go take Ilina's spot in LA. But it still wasn't a principal spot. And it wasn't what she had set her mind on.

She took her violin off of the mantel.

She went downstairs, and saw Lark lying on the couch, holding her knitting above her head, making slow stitches.

"I'm going out," Hannah said.

"Don't do anything I wouldn't do," Lark said.

"Which would be?"

Lark shrugged. "I don't know. I'll get back to you."

"It will be too late by then."

Hannah stepped outside and looked down the street. She could drive. But then, she wouldn't be able to drink. She started walking toward the Gold Pan. She had avoided that place. She had avoided... Honestly, anything that made her feel like she was back in town. Really back.

But her future was... She didn't even know what it was now. Her plan was upended. And she was here. She wasn't in Boston. She couldn't fight her way into the position she wanted, apparently. Any more than she could dedicate herself to the symphony for years and earn it. So maybe for now she would just... Live in the present. It was a strange thought, one that honestly wouldn't have occurred to her just a couple of days ago. Because the future was what everything was about for her. Planning. Making sure that she got where she wanted to go. That she hit the target she'd been aiming at for all these years.

But she missed it. Somehow. She'd done something wrong, but she didn't know when or where. She'd had a sense of destiny. Like it was...meant to be.

And that made her feel stupid. Because if she had ever talked to anybody about how she'd gotten where she was, she wouldn't have said destiny. She would have said that it was hard work. That it was all the lessons that she'd taken, that it was getting that scholarship and going to that college. Making the connections that she had. She would have said that she was the master of her fate, the captain of her ship. And that anyone who wanted to get where she was had to be too. But underneath all of that she had a sense that she was destined for it. And never had that been more clear than in those moments of futile outrage after she found out that she hadn't gotten the principal position.

So here she was storming down the street in her hometown,

headed to the bar holding her violin, which seemed to represent everything that was broken in her life at the moment.

You still have your first chair position.

But it wasn't enough. It wasn't.

And she had been so close to having her goal. And close to feeling like...enough.

Like she had done it. The reward for all the work she had put in.

She shook her head, looked both ways, and crossed quickly at the crosswalk, and then again, making her way down the street, across four blocks to the Gold Pan.

She stopped in front of it, looking through the windows, at least, as well as she could. There were stickers on them. Mostly for energy drinks, ATV companies and truck logos. There was a guy with a guitar sitting on the stage, singing. Avery pushed the door open, and walked in, just as he finished his song. He set his guitar down, and walked off the stage. She did her best to close the distance between them. "Are you jamming?"

"It's just open mic," he said.

"Well. Perfect."

There were a couple names on the sheet at the end of the bar ahead of her. And she ordered a shot, taking it in one gulp as she took her sweater off, and hung it on the back of the chair. And as she did, she looked up, and locked eyes with Josh.

Because of course Josh was here.

She couldn't really lie to herself and say that he was the last person she wanted to see. Because she... She wasn't really unhappy to see him. He was handsome, and familiar, and right at the moment that was a lot more desirable than she would like to admit.

Familiar. This place was familiar. Not because she had spent a lot of time here. She had vacated town before she was of legal drinking age. Not that they hadn't tried to sneak in. But the real problem with small towns wasn't so much the difficulty of landing fake IDs, as it was the probability of running into somebody who knew full well that you weren't old enough to be in the bar. A teacher from the school, or one of your parents' friends. Yeah, that was likely. She had walked by the Gold Pan often enough, and looked inside.

But she had never planned on becoming a regular. Not at all. She'd been too busy planning to escape. So it was weird to be here now. At the same time as Josh.

He said something to the guys that he was with, then stood and started walking in her direction. She vaguely recognized at least one of the people he was sitting with. Caleb or something. She had... Maybe science with him or something. But she was too distracted by Josh to think too hard about Caleb. Really the only thing Caleb's presence accomplished was proving that Josh had aged very well. Because while he had grown into a broader, more masculine body, Caleb had gotten wider at the gut, and his hairline had migrated backward. Not that some people couldn't work that look. It was just that Josh was one of those guys who would work for anyone.

"Hey," he said.

"Hi."

"You look tired."

"That is literally the worst thing you could say to a woman. Okay, not the worst thing, but it's a pretty terrible thing to say."

"Okay, let me try again. Is everything okay?"

She sighed heavily. She didn't actually want to talk about anything meaningful. "Yes. It's just been a day." She didn't want to get into everything with Avery. Eventually, it was going to be common knowledge. Eventually, it was going to sweep through town.

But it wasn't right now.

And here she was with her own crap, and no one knew about any of it. There was something freeing in that. Here and now she could give all the space she wanted to her own disappointment.

Maybe it was the chance to take a wound and make it a scar. She was good at that.

She could do it on her own, no confessional required.

"Great. I heard it was open mic night." That was a lie. But really, there was no way to explain why she was here with her violin otherwise. Not without letting him into her head. Which she wasn't going to do. He didn't belong in her head, in her life.

This moment, sure. And right now, this moment was all there was.

"Are you going to play?"

"Yeah. I am." She tapped the clipboard. "In a couple of songs."

"Do we get a country song?"

"No. Irish folk, though. Which, people seem to think pairs nicely with beer anyway."

"I didn't know you played folk music."

"I can play anything," she said.

His gaze held hers for a minute, and his lips curved into a smile. But she didn't let memories invade, because the past didn't matter. The future didn't matter. The thought filled her with a sense of power. Adrenaline. She knew people lived like this, it was just she wasn't one of them.

"Do you want a shot?"

"Sure," he said.

"I'm buying."

"Well, since you asked me, I figured you were," he said. "I'm equal opportunity. I'm happy to let you buy the alcohol."

"Great."

She ordered two more shots, then handed one to him, and held hers aloft. "Cheers."

"What are we toasting?"

"Tonight. Because it can be absolutely anything we want."

She knocked it back, and as the alcohol burned down the back of her throat, his eyes burned into hers. And she realized that the open-ended toast sounded a whole lot like an offer. The idea… The idea only added fuel to the adrenaline fire sparking through her veins.

It would be a very bad idea. Doing anything with an ex. But then, that would require acknowledging the past. And worrying about the future. And that just wasn't what was happening tonight.

"Is this what you always do on a Friday night?" she asked.

"Not every Friday, no."

"Tonight."

"Yeah," he said.

"What do you usually do?"

"Go to dinner at my mom's. Hang out with my niece and nephew."

"So, you're single."

A slow smile spread over his face. "I did wonder when you were going to ask that."

"Why would you think that I would?"

"Because," he said, his grin way too tempting for her to deal with, "you wanted to know."

"You don't know that I wanted to know."

"No. I do."

"You *really* don't."

"But you asked."

She made a scoffing sound. "But I waited a very long time. Which means I really was not curious."

"I think you are."

She looked around the bar, full of people laughing and having a good time. It was…nicer than she'd imagined it would be. The whole place was. "Fine. I was a little bit curious. You're single. Have you… Have you been married?"

He shook his head. "Nope."

"Why not?"

"The same reason you haven't been I imagine."

"You're in a committed relationship with a musical instrument?"

"Haven't found the right person."

There was something about that statement that cut into her, and she didn't know why it should.

"That is not why I'm single. I've never looked. I don't think there's a right person for me."

That was far too true, and it echoed weirdly inside of her.

"I think that's pretty sad, Hannah."

"Why? Not everybody wants to be in a relationship. I figured out a long time ago that there was no way for me to put everything that I needed to put into violin and into a relationship."

"Did you decide that around the time we broke up?"

She shrugged off those memories. No past. She was just talking to him like two people who might meet in a bar. And given the amount of sparks that were going up between them, him being single was absolutely a relevant point of conversation. Because she wasn't going to let anything happen with a man who was married, engaged, or otherwise committed.

"Here's an idea," she said. "Why don't we pretend we just met each other. I'm just a girl in a bar. And you… You're just a guy in a bar. Nothing happened when we were teenagers. And everything that's happened since… Well, what would you want to know if you just met me?"

"What's your favorite thing about playing the violin?"

It was a strange question, and it cut right to the very heart of who she was. He might not realize it, but it wasn't a casual question that a stranger could just ask her. It felt deep and intimate, like he was searching beneath her skin.

"It's when I feel like me," she said, and she left it at that, because there was more. There was a way to explain that. A way that it felt. But… She didn't want to tell him. She didn't want to say it out loud. Not right now, not to him. Really, not ever.

"And all the other times?"

"I don't know," she said. "It's hard to explain."

It wasn't. Not really. She just didn't want to explain it to him.

"I'm not in a hurry."

"I am," she said. "I'm on in about a minute."

"Then give me the one minute version."

She shouldn't find that dogged persistence of his charming.

"I could never figure out how to explain myself to my family. What I wanted. What I felt. And when I first picked up the violin, I found a way to do that. It's everything I want, it gives me a way to express what I feel. It gives me the way to earn a living. It's everything that I am. So that's... That's what that means."

He didn't say anything, he just stared at her, those blue eyes different than she remembered them. Because when he'd been a boy, they'd been beautiful, and they'd made her stomach flutter, but she hadn't felt like he'd seen something in her that she'd never shown anyone before. And he'd been the first person to see her naked.

"It's my turn," she said.

"Good. I can't wait to hear."

She swallowed, and walked up to the stage, positioning herself in front of the microphone as best she could, and angling. And then she started to play. Slow at first, building, until it was fierce and fast, the rhythm of her heart. The song itself was joyful, a celebration song, and nothing inside of her felt joyful or celebratory. But it was like the music created it within her. Carved out a space for something new, something different, and allowed her to experience something that she didn't have in her. It was magic, and it was wonderful.

She stomped her foot in rhythm as she played, spinning and turning and not caring about the microphone anymore, because she knew that the sound was carrying without it. And people in the room got up and danced with her. Her hair fell out of its bun, vivid red in her face and sticking to her forehead as sweat beaded there, heat from her movements, and adrenaline from the performance building through her, and when her song was done, the whole bar erupted, and asked for more. So she played. And she kept on playing.

And somewhere in the middle of that, she realized that she hadn't played in her own town before.

Her own town.

When had she started thinking of Bear Creek as anything other than an old home that she had outgrown?

It wasn't her town. Boston was her town. But Bear Creek was something, and she couldn't deny it. And she had never done recitals or talent shows or anything like that, because it had never felt like something she could share here. She had played at home, she had played for her teachers.

When she was finished, she was breathless, and she was smiling.

And Josh was waiting for her just off the stage.

"You are amazing," he said, his voice low.

"Yeah," she said, grinning wide. "I am."

He shook his head. "You're something else, Hannah."

"That's the point." She nodded in affirmation of herself. "I mean, that was always the point. To be something else."

"It's pretty impressive," he said. "But you know, I liked you just fine back then too."

"I didn't. So."

"Fair enough."

"I'm going to kiss you," she said. Then she got up on her toes and did just that.

He wrapped his arms around her, and she gave herself up to it. Absolutely. Completely. And she wasn't really sure if this was something Lark would do or not, but Hannah didn't feel like that was a binding agreement that she'd made with her sister. And this was a moment that she wanted to live in.

This was a moment she wanted to extend.

"I hope you have room for one redheaded violinist at your place."

"I'm sure I can find a spot for you," he said, his voice rough.

"Then let's go home."

This wasn't the memory lane she had intended to walk down tonight. In fact, nostalgia hadn't been the reason she'd gone out at all. But somehow, right now, the chance to be with the first man she'd ever been with seemed... Right. Like it might be the exact thing she needed. She didn't know why.

Or maybe this was just a classic case of arousal making you act a little bit stupid.

Either way. She was okay with it.

"All right, Hannah," he said. "Let's go home."

18

I have agreed to be sent away for the remainder of the pregnancy. I told Mama I got a job. It was a lie. I know why his mother wants me to go. I have time to make up my mind. I could just never come home.

Dot's diary, August 1944

Lark

Lark was in the process of turning the Closed sign when Ben started up the sidewalk. She stopped what she was doing and just kind of froze. She had picked her car up from the garage, but they had only exchanged a few words, and they'd had the counter between them. It had been a cordial conversation, and there had been none of the tension that had been present in the previous interaction. At least, that's what she told herself.

In reality, she hadn't been able to breathe. But she had done her best to ignore that.

And to make sure that he didn't realize it.

But now, the air was sucked right out of her.

He pushed the door open to the Craft Café, and she was still standing there with her hand on the Closed sign.

"Am I too late?"

For some reason, it felt like that question had deeper implications, and she did her best not to do that. Not to make more out of this than need be. Because she really didn't need to make anything out of it at all.

"Taylor isn't here," she said.

"I know," he said. "She just left the garage. She walked home."

"Oh. I figured… I just figured maybe that was why you were here."

"No. I came to see you."

"Why?"

He paused, for just a second. And she felt like that meant he either had no idea why he'd come to see her, or he did, and he didn't want to say it.

"Well, last time we talked, we didn't actually talk. And I kind of found that I preferred fighting with you to just exchanging pleasantries."

"Is a fight required?"

"No."

"That's good."

He stepped inside, the door closing firmly behind him, and she felt like the place had gotten two times smaller. He looked at her, his gaze assessing. And her heart rate increased twofold. Great. She was not doing a good job of remembering what she had decided about him.

She felt churned up still, about the whole thing with Keira. She had been going through a list of what ifs in her head, and trying not to. But it was there, in the back of her mind. Because *what if.*

You know you can't do that. It just makes you insane. You can't go back. You can't change what is.

No. She couldn't, but he was standing in front of her right now, and that felt like something. Even if it shouldn't.

"Are you okay?"

"Why do you ask?"

"You just look… You don't look okay."

"How would you know? We haven't spent significant time together in over sixteen years."

"But we spent a lot of time together before that. And I remember." He got closer to her, and she took a step back, but she hit the bar, and it stopped her progress. And he kept on coming. He smelled good. Or maybe he didn't. But she interpreted it as good. Because it was him. And yeah, maybe a lot of years had passed, but she still recognized that. She still recognized him.

She ached then. Because she had loved him in so many ways. Because knowing him, caring for him, had made her and broken her several times over.

But he was still Ben. And when she looked at him she felt…all those things. Heartbreak and caring and trust. And right now, it was that trust she needed.

"Avery's husband has been hitting her."

He straightened up. "What?"

"It's been going on for a while, and she didn't want anyone to know. We just got her moved out. It's been… Awful."

"Hell. Does she need anything? Does anyone need to go handle that bastard husband of hers?"

"While I'm sure my dad would lead the angry mob, the police are involved. She went to the police." Her heart squeezed tight. Avery's humiliation had been clear, the fact that it wasn't a pure victory for her hitting Lark in a way that reality never had before. She was risking her life, but in ways that she had never considered. Her livelihood. The way people saw her in the community.

"I'm just sorry," he said.

"Me too."

He moved to her, and her heart jumped. Her breathing became labored.

"Ben…"

"I thought about us. I did. Maybe I *was* a bad husband, Lark, because I wondered if I did the right thing. I wondered if I should have married her. I thought about what it would have been like if I would've chosen you. If I would have gone after you. I thought about you… I thought about that night. And you know when I would think back on what it was like to be young, and to not be burdened by how heavy life is, I thought about you. I thought about your smile. Thought about the way you… The way you saw things. You were so enthusiastic about everything. About the world. You wanted things. You dreamed about things. You didn't just look around you and see the way things are and accept them. You think about how you could make it more beautiful. I remember… I remember when we were like… Fourteen. And you thought it would be the best idea to take sidewalk chalk into town and color the squares in front of all of the businesses, and Mrs. Wilson got mad at you and said it was basically graffiti. And I remember you were so mad after, and you were lying underneath that ivy canopy at your grandfather's house and talking about how you were being persecuted for your art. And I just… I remember so many things like that."

He reached out and tucked a strand of her hair behind her ear, and she shivered.

It was the first time Ben Thompson had touched her in sixteen years. And she felt even more now than she had been.

"What else do you remember?" she whispered.

Because she wanted to hear it. He had memories of the girl she'd been before. The girl who had never been hurt. And she wanted to hear him say them out loud.

"That for a year when you were eleven you wore a gymnastics outfit everywhere."

"*No.*"

"You did. And you never took gymnastics."

"That's not fair."

"It was silver, if I remember right."

"No. I want more flattering memories about how I was fighting the establishment with nothing but my creativity and chalk."

"Okay, how about the time you protested the dress code at school by having a visible bra strap day."

"Dress codes are a tool of the patriarchy, Benjamin."

"That's what you said then."

"I stand by it."

"You were unexpected. You always were. I went for the expected. I regretted it."

"*Keira* was fun."

"I know," he said, his voice rough. "I'm not rewriting this, I promise. It would be easy to do that. But I'm not. I just wanted you to know that I wondered if it should've been you."

"You can't rearrange life. You can't... You don't get a do-over."

"I know. You can't do anything over. I'm well aware. But we're both standing here right now."

"Ben..."

And then he touched her face. His hand, callused and rough, brushed over her cheek, and her heart beat an unsteady rhythm. His blue eyes were intense on hers as he leaned down, kissing her. Deep and hard. And it was like fire. Like magic. Like a deep bliss. She had told herself stories about his mouth. About his kisses. She had one night of them. One night of them and years of fantasy about them before, and a whole lot of weaving together dreams out of memory and wishful thinking in the years since.

It wasn't as good as she remembered.

It was better.

His lips were firm and warm, and most of all, he was still Ben. Years hadn't changed it. Time and pain hadn't changed it.

She was a before and after, but this wasn't.

It was everything it had always been. And then some. Because the first time he'd kissed her she'd been a virgin who hadn't understood exactly what she wanted.

But she was a woman now, with a lot of experience in her rearview mirror, and she knew.

Oh, now she knew.

But there was more than physical desire here, and the memories of that first time made her pull away. Made her think twice as she fought to catch her breath.

"Ben... I..."

"It's okay," he said. "We don't need to jump into anything."

She wanted to. She wanted to drag him back to her Gram's bed, and she didn't even care how weird that was. But it was the memory of the consequences that stopped her. Of the fallout.

And Keira loomed large. Because fundamentally, she had been the person to mop up his heartbreak before. And it just hadn't worked. She needed to be sure. She needed to be damn sure that she wasn't just a sexual surrogate, not again.

"How many women have you been with?"

"What kind of a question is that?"

"A valid one, I think. How many women have you been with?"

"Two. You know them both."

"So, nobody since her?"

"No," he said. "But that doesn't matter."

"What if it does? What if this is just the same as last time?"

"It isn't," he said. "Because I'm not eighteen. I'm not eighteen, and I know what I want. And I'm brave enough to fight for it. I don't need to be with anyone else to know that I want you right now."

"Can we... Wait?"

"I might not want to wait, but I will. For you. I've waited sixteen years. Now you're here. I'll wait some more."

"You didn't, though. Wait. You married someone else."

"I did. And I have a daughter that I can never regret. Ever. But there were other things I did regret, and you're just going to have to believe me. You're just going to have to believe that I know what I want now."

"Time."

"Like I said. You've got it."

"Okay."

He touched her chin, her cheek, and then he turned and walked back out of the Craft Café. Leaving her standing there, shaking, aroused and bruised. Her heart hurt. Because she wanted to jump in with both feet. And it just seemed... Impossible and ridiculous and unfair.

That in order to do that, she needed to get back to who she'd been.

But she wasn't that girl anymore.

And it was because of him.

19

I said I was a widow. People in this town believe me. There are too many widows. Too many wives who will never hold their husbands again. Too many children who will never know their fathers. My child may not even know his mother.

Dot's diary, October 1944

Mary

It was quilting night.

Mary and Joe had handled picking up Hayden and Peyton from school in the days since Avery had moved out of her house. Had eaten dinner with the grandkids every night before taking them back home. Avery had joined them three times, and each time had been quiet.

Neither she or Joe wanted to bring the subject of David up in front of the kids. But he loomed there like a ghost.

She'd only gotten a small window of time to talk to her

daughter without the kids around and they'd only had a brief exchange about Avery's decision to press charges.

It was obvious Avery didn't want much more than a brief exchange, and Mary wasn't sure if Avery would come tonight, all things considered.

But right on time, she saw Avery walking toward The Miner's House at the same time she was, a large, full bag slung over her shoulder.

Mary said nothing, she just walked quickly toward her oldest daughter and pulled her in for a hug. Avery was stiff for a moment, and then went pliant. She didn't return the hug, but she received it. And for now, Mary would take that.

"Let's sit out here for a moment," Mary said, nodding toward the wooden rocking chairs that were just outside the front door. She watched as Avery hesitated.

Mary sat, and Avery finally followed suit.

The bruise on her cheek was fading, even with the makeup over the top of it, Mary could tell. But the circles under her eyes were darker than usual, and grooves around her mouth looked deeper.

Avery looked straight ahead, and Mary looked at her daughter's profile. Mary wanted to fix this. Wanted to find the right thing to do. She wanted to carry it for her, and she knew that she couldn't. Knew that it was impossible.

She was fractured inside, but Avery looked determined to hold herself together. And that made Mary feel even more broken.

"I'm sure that Lark wants to get started quilting," Avery said, clutching her bag close to her chest and moving to stand.

"I wish you had told me," Mary said. "I understand why you didn't know if you could go to the police. And I understand that... I just... I thought if it was really important you'd tell me. I know I've never been good at chitchat and talking about boys or...manicures. I know I'm not like you are with Peyton. I know. But I was sure that if you ever needed me you'd tell me."

The corners of Avery's mouth turned downward. "I don't tell you things, Mom."

And how could she? Mary didn't know how to talk. She didn't know how to share. She'd kept her own feelings bottled up inside her all growing up. The only person she'd ever figured out how to open up to was Joe and even that was hard.

Even with Joe she didn't like being too vulnerable. It was why it was so hard to just go off and try new things with him.

"But why not?" Mary asked, knowing she wouldn't like the answer.

"Mom, you always taught us to pick up and carry on. Sitting around and moping doesn't fix anything. You have to do things and be active. I've done that. I've tried so hard to do that and I didn't know how to tell you nothing I did was…fixing anything. That my life was out of my control. How could I tell you that when you always told us we were the ones with the power to make things better or worse?"

Mary had never wanted to hurt her kids by telling them that. She'd wanted them to feel in control. Because for all of Mary's childhood she hadn't felt she'd had any. She hadn't chosen to be abandoned by her mother and sadness hadn't helped.

Her dad had taught her to pick up and carry on and she had.

It had been the best thing for her.

She'd wanted to give her daughters that same sense of strength, of control in a life they couldn't control. But she hadn't known how to balance that.

With sensitivity Avery clearly needed.

That she hadn't believed she could get from Mary.

And maybe she'd been right.

"Avery, I don't know how to do this, you're right. But it's not because I didn't want to hear it, or because I thought you shouldn't have struggles. It's because it was the only way I learned to deal with mine."

Avery nodded, tears welling in her eyes. "I guess I'm the

same. I guess… I just wanted to be able to act okay and to have it be okay. But it's not. I'm a mess. I wasn't there for the kids. I didn't mean to be distant from them, but it was easier to get… wrapped up in schedules and doing things because it helped me not focus on what was happening with David. I was too tired to see what was right in front of me. I just… I just wanted everything to stay the way that it was supposed to. Because I can't… I can't see a way forward here. I don't know what I'm going to do. I don't know who I am. I don't know if I'm going to be okay. I don't know if I can go on without all this and if I can't stay strong and move on, I don't know how to face you when I'm broken apart like this."

Mary felt like she was barely holding herself together. Like she had cracked into a thousand pieces and only her indrawn breath was keeping her from disintegrating right there. Because there weren't words. She could tell Avery that it wasn't what she wanted, that it wasn't what she had intended for her to feel, but it didn't matter. Avery felt it. She felt it now. Mary could see it. In the anger and hopelessness radiating from her.

"All I want is for you to be safe. All I want is for you to be happy someday and you don't have to be strong now for me to think you're…you're doing a good job, Avery."

"That doesn't mean anything when I don't know who I am," Avery said. "I'm like superwife and supermom. And the person who volunteers for every committee. And now I don't have any of that."

"Avery, none of that is what makes you special. It's not what makes you, *you*. Did you think I wouldn't love you anymore?"

"It isn't that I think that," Avery said. "I just didn't want to disappoint you."

"I'm sad, Avery. I'm heartbroken *for* you. I'm not disappointed *in* you."

"I'm sorry. About what I said. I… I shouldn't have said all that to you. I was angry and I was embarrassed."

"Avery, I obviously made mistakes I didn't mean to make." She shook her head. "I wanted to be there for you. But that you didn't feel you could come to me...it makes me feel like I just being here hasn't been enough."

"I could have told you what I needed," Avery said. "The fact is, I didn't know what I needed. I still don't know."

She sucked in a breath and forced her lips into a smile. "We should go quilt, Lark will start making flower gowns for us to wear if we wait too long."

Mary reached out and stopped Avery's movements. Then pulled her in for a hug. "I'm sorry," she said. "I'm sorry I let... feeling like I didn't know how to do this keep us more distant than we should be. I'm sorry I hurt you."

"It's okay, Mom," Avery said, her voice muffled against Mary's shoulder.

"I want to make it okay," she said.

They looked at each other, and she felt a heaviness there because she knew neither of them could name promises.

So they just walked into the Craft Café together, where Hannah and Lark were whispering in the corner.

"You better not be whispering about me," Avery said.

"We're not," Hannah said. "You know, *we* have lives."

Avery looked chagrined.

"Be nice to your sister," Mary said.

"No," Avery said. "Don't be nice to me. Don't treat me like I'm broken. I *am* broken. I'm... I think I might actually be broken. But if you go treating me like I am I don't think I'm ever going to be able to... I will never be able to get past it. And I would like to not be broken forever. I would like for that to not be the end of who I am. I want to believe that there's something after broken. I need to believe it. So don't be nice to me. Just be... Just be yourselves with me."

Avery laughed suddenly, hollow. "Be yourselves. I don't know what that even means. I don't know how to be myself. I don't know who that is."

Hannah softened. "You do. Of course you do. You're the person who's giving me crap right back when I dish it out to you even though things are hard. You're tough, Avery."

"I don't feel tough. I don't know what I'm going to do. Very seriously. What if he loses his medical license? I know I'm not qualified to do anything that makes that kind of money. And I haven't had a job in… It has been a long time."

"What kind of job would you want?" Lark asked.

She looked blank. "I don't know."

"You could work at the furniture store, or a bookstore. That place down the road that sells candles," Lark said.

"I said I don't know," Avery said, sounding frustrated. "This isn't like an era of great new beginnings for me. I just feel lost."

None of them said anything for a while. They got out their quilt squares, and Mary stared down at hers, at the white lace, brushing her fingertips over it. Perfection. That was her problem with this, wasn't it? And she had always felt like it was only to do with her. The fact that she wanted to do the right thing for her girls. It'd been directed at her, never them.

She sometimes felt paralyzed by her fear she might look like she didn't know what she was doing. She had never wanted her daughters to feel that way. It was why she couldn't make a real stitch on this thing. She was just so afraid that she would make a mistake. And she…she had. Not on something as mundane as a quilt square. But with her daughter.

Her *daughter*.

Who hadn't believed that she could tell her that she was being abused because somehow that would make her less than perfect, and if she were less than perfect then Mary might not feel the same about her.

"Do you know that I love you?" Mary said, looking from

Hannah to Lark, to Avery. "Do you know that I didn't need you to be strong all the time? To brush everything off and move on?"

"I don't mind," Hannah said, her tone flippant. But in it, Mary could sense the weight of pain. "There's no point dwelling on crap anyway."

Avery and Lark said nothing. "I don't need you to be strong all the time," Mary repeated. "I want you to be happy. I want you to be...yourselves. And I know that..."

"You had definite ideas about what happy was," Lark said. "That wasn't a bad thing. But... We know what's important to you. And what you wished we would do."

"I..."

"You definitely didn't want us to end up like Gram," Hannah said. "She was too emotional and thought only of herself. You wanted us to be stronger than that."

"I only meant," Mary said, "I didn't want you to leave your children after you already had them."

Hannah looked slightly stricken. "Well, sure. It's just also, you had definite ideas about behavior and things like that. Anything that you thought seemed too much like Gram."

"To protect you," Mary said. "My mom's life was not smooth. And I know that she came back here and made a relationship with you, but this was the best part of her life. All those years that she spent away from us... She wasn't happy. She would come into town sometimes, and she was frazzled and upset over some man, or she was drinking too much. Her emotions were all over the place."

"That doesn't even sound like her," Lark said.

"No. Because you don't really know. I do. I know what it was like to have a mother who didn't care at all. Who only cared about herself, and who came to visit only when she needed things. So no, I didn't want you to be like her. And I know that you think you know what that means because you think you knew her. But you didn't. I remember her... Just leaving me home alone all day. Going out to drink at the Gold Pan while my dad was at work. Forgetting to feed me. My brothers used to have to fix my hair for school because my mom would still be asleep. No, I didn't want you to be like her. But that didn't mean I needed you to feel nothing. To be strong all the time and keep everything bad and hard inside you."

They were all staring at her like she had grown another head. "I'm sorry," Mary said. "I'm sorry if you thought that. I was scared, but more for me than for you. Scared to lose you, scared... I was so scared maybe I had that in me. I don't know why she left. To this day I don't, and I can never ask. I was afraid it might creep up on me someday and I was vigilant to make sure it didn't. On either of us. I wanted to be perfect, and wanting that so much, being so afraid of mistakes... I made it worse."

It didn't matter, did it? How much she had wanted to be a good mother. Because in the end, she had messed up. In the end, Avery felt lost, and she hadn't been able to go to her when she needed her most.

"We didn't know, Mom," Lark said, softly. "I didn't know that side of Gram."

"I know. She changed when she came back and stayed. She stayed for the three of you."

Not for Mary. Never for Mary.

But that didn't matter. Not now.

"Avery," Mary said. "We talk now. What do you need?"

"I need a plan," Avery said. "The only plan that I've had for the last two years is to just... Hold everything together. And now it's blown apart. Completely. So now I need to fix it. I need to do something."

"Have you told your friends yet?"

"No. But his arrest is going to show up in the news. You know it is. It'll be in that column under arrests."

"Yeah," Lark said. "So what will you do?"

"What can I do? I'm going to have to tell everybody." Avery

looked down at her square. "I just kept thinking maybe I would find a way around this. Some magic solution. I started reading a diary that I found in Gram's attic. The woman who brought these curtains. And I thought that maybe I would find something there. But I haven't yet. I just kept thinking about how brave she was. Coming to Oregon from Boston. Changing everything. She was a widow." A tear tracked down Avery's face. "At least if I was a widow there wouldn't be a choice. At least I wouldn't feel like it was my fault." She shook her head. "I need... I need to get to the place where I want to have something new. Where I'm excited about it. But I don't know how to get from here to there."

Mary curved her hands around her quilt square, balling it up in her hands. "Avery, I know that I've made mistakes. And I'm so sorry about that. I think some of it is that I didn't share with you... I didn't share with any of you some of what happened in my life. I didn't know how." She swallowed hard.

She knew how to express anger about her mother and she'd done that. She knew she'd made plenty of tight comments over the years too. But she hadn't shared. Not really. And it gave her that same feeling as trying to figure out how to quilt.

A naked, sort of exposed sense that all her flaws and deficiencies were revealed by what she couldn't do.

"Your grandfather was a good man," she said. "I loved him very much. But he was so hurt by your gram leaving. And he couldn't bear my hurt on top of it. I had to be strong. And I thought being strong helped me. It did help. But I never meant for you to keep your heads down and tough it out through hardships without seeking help."

She cleared her throat. "I'm not great at this. At sharing. But I know a little bit about before and after. Even though Gram clearly didn't want to be my mother, I was so sad when she left. And I didn't think I could ever enjoy anything again. But I found a new way to live. And it doesn't mean that I didn't miss her. I did. If I hadn't missed her I don't think I would have been half so angry. But no matter what happens, you find a way to live your new life. Even when you have to start again because someone else failed you. Even when it's not fair."

"So what if I just… Burn it all down," Avery said, leaning back in her chair. "Quit every committee. Quit volunteering for anything."

"Yes," Hannah said. "Do it. You're nobody's suburban sock bunny. You are a new woman. You are whatever you choose to be. And maybe it isn't perfect. But none of us are perfect." Hannah took a deep breath. "I didn't get the principal position. And I wasn't going to say anything because it's nothing compared to what you're going through. But… I'm really upset about it. But… I'm just… I'm going to figure out something else. I'm going to find a new thing."

"I'm sorry, Hannah," Mary said. "I know how much that meant to you."

"Yeah," Hannah said. "It did. It does. But… I'll figure it out. We'll figure it out. Maybe it's not perfect but it's… But we're still here. And we can make it what we need to make it."

"A new view," Avery said. She didn't look exactly triumphant or happy, but she didn't look quite so crushed as she had before. "We can make a new view."

"We can," Hannah said. "And we will."

"And I'm going to support you," Mary said. "Whatever you need. It's okay if we don't know what we're doing. We'll just figure it out."

And Mary knew she needed to hear that as much as they did.

20

*He let me ride with him today, though I said I shouldn't. He said
we are not in Boston society and won't cause gossip in a wagon
train. I don't know what I'm doing. Right now sitting on his horse,
with his strength behind me, feels like home.*

Anabeth Snow's diary, 1864

Avery

The discussion she'd had with her mother last night had been
surprisingly therapeutic. She had vented her guts, even though
she couldn't dump her need to deny anything was wrong completely on her mother. Because she should be worrying about
practical things, like housing and money, and emotional things
like her children's well-being. And instead she was freaking out
about having to tell her friends everything that was happening
before it hit the paper.

So she was committed to this coffee date. Where she was

going to tell everybody, and she was going to take a step back from… Everything.

It was perfection or destruction, as far as she could see. There wasn't another option. If the secret was out, then why not destroy it all completely? Why not just lay it all out there?

Another time, she might address this issue. This internal feeling that there was nothing between perfection and failure. But right now, it was propelling her forward, and she needed that.

Karen, Alyssa and Sandra all walked in the same time, pushing their sunglasses up on their heads in tandem. Avery felt like she was watching a scene happen outside of her body.

She curled her fingers around her coffee cup and tried to take some comfort. But it was limited. She felt like she was sitting there naked, or might as well have been. Because she was about to peel everything back and reveal all of who she was. She was trying. She was trying. But it was a lot of time of keeping all of these things protected. Hidden.

At least, she *had* tried. She had tried so hard to protect her secrets. She had tried so hard to protect her children. She had tried so hard to protect herself.

And here she was. Telling the key members of the PTA exactly what had been going on in her life. That she was getting divorced.

Because of course that was where this was headed. She had left him, and it would be divorce.

It would be court. It might even be a lot of court, if charges were brought up against him by the district attorney.

She started humming to herself, softly, as she watched her friends wait to get their coffee. Then, her nervous energy became too much to bear and she reached into her bag and took out her quilting square. She looked at the place where she had left off, the crimson strip of fabric halfway tacked to its white background. She stabbed the needle through the fabric, making one neat, even stitch. Perhaps she couldn't control this interaction, but she could control her stitches.

That was something.

Her stitches, at least, were in order.

Her friends each retrieved their coffee, crossed the room, and sat down at the empty chairs at her table. As she looked across at them, she suddenly realized she had forgotten to put on makeup this morning.

And that was the weirdest thing.

She put it on every day. Like armor, like a shield, and she would have thought that she would want even more of it on a day like today. But it hadn't even crossed her mind.

She had gotten ready in a fog, pulling on her usual uniform of oversized sweater and black leggings and she had put her hair up, but then she had…walked away from the mirror. And she hadn't done the rest. She had taken the kids to school, but she'd been lost in her thoughts. Rehearsing an interaction that she had no guidebook for. No script.

"Are you okay?" Alyssa asked.

"I…" She really didn't know how to answer that. She was sitting there. She was upright. She had been dry eyed for days, and generally functional. She had endured the humiliation of having her mostly naked body photographed in a police station. She had revealed to her family that her husband of so many years had been hurting her. She had found out that she had failed at protecting her children, that her son had been hit by the same man who had used his fists on her and that her protection had only enabled that, and not shielded them from anything.

She had no idea what her future looked like. She wasn't even really sure what her present looked like, considering that she hadn't even completed her typical morning routine—and she hadn't even noticed.

So she decided not to answer the question. Because to say no would make it seem like she'd crumbled—and she hadn't. Of all the miracles that had come out of this, it was that she was here. Sitting right there, completely un-crumbled. It almost didn't even seem possible.

But she couldn't say yes either, because that implied a certainty that she didn't know if she would ever have again.

"I need to talk to all of you." She looked down at her hands, down at her wedding ring. She didn't know why she was putting that on every day. Maybe because somehow she hadn't quite accepted until she had been sitting here in the coffee shop the divorce was the next step.

Divorce.

She didn't like that word. Not at all. On her wedding day, she had been so certain that it would never be a word used in her life. In her marriage.

She had spoken vows that she had meant as she had looked into those beautiful blue eyes. But the man behind those eyes had changed. And he was not a man she could be with anymore. And *divorce* still felt like the wrong word, because she had not made vows to that man. She hadn't made vows to the man who hit her.

To the man who would strike their son.

No. This was a death.

And that had been in their vows.

Till death do us part.

Their love had died.

The man she believed him to be, was dead.

And she needed to take that ring off.

"I've been… I've been keeping something from everyone. I… I had David arrested. And… It's going to come out. It might go to trial."

She felt like the dorky girl who'd shown up at school in a seasonal denim vest her mom had gotten from Goodwill, not understanding how important fitting in was to Avery. Not understanding that would make her stand out.

Bet you wish it was a denim vest with a snowman on it now...

"David was arrested?" Sandra asked. Her unlined face didn't move, only her tone expressing shock.

"Yes. I... I really don't know how to say this. I really don't. But I've been pretending for so long and I can't anymore. I can't. When he gets angry he's started being physically violent with me. And a few days ago he hit my face. That's where my bruise came from. And my mother and sisters confronted me about it. I thought... I thought it would get better. I thought that it would stop. Or at least that it wouldn't escalate. But it did. And I don't know what to do. I don't know what to do except... I can't be with him anymore. I can't be with him."

There was utter silence around the table. And all at once Avery wished for Hannah's rage. Or even Lark's tears. Both things that had made her uncomfortable at the time, but they were genuine. This silence wasn't about shock, it was as if they were trying to come to a consensus with their eyes. As if they were afraid of giving an answer that didn't line up with each other's.

"Have you...have you been to counseling?"

It was Karen who asked that question.

"No," Avery said.

"I'm not saying it's easy but he's a...he's a good man, isn't he? It's...maybe he's going through something and he needs to see a doctor or a counselor."

"I'm sorry, Avery," Sandra said, but she looked wooden as Karen. Like there was a shield up. Like they wanted to draw back from her and not lean in. Like she might be contagious. "I really don't know what to say."

"Counseling?" Avery asked. "Like you think counseling will fix it?"

"I'm not saying that," Karen said. "I just think maybe there are things you should try, that's all. I mean, the kids and...and... you know?"

"Is that what you think?" she asked Alyssa. "That we should go to counseling or something?"

"Marriage is hard," Alyssa said slowly. "I mean, being with someone forever is never going to be easy. You have to make the decision that works best for you. I've forgiven Micah a lot. But you know, he is a doctor like David. And it's a stressful job. Truth be told, I haven't always been there for him like I should've been."

"Does he hit you?" she asked.

"No. He's… He's gotten close to one of the administrative assistants. I mean, it's over. But… I didn't talk about it because I feel like people are very judgmental when you don't leave. But, sometimes the only thing you can do is stand by him. And that's a choice that only you can make."

Avery felt like maybe she should get angry. Like Hannah had. Because Alyssa was right about that kind of subtle blame that women put onto themselves for all of the flaws in their marriage. But she had never hit David. And she never would.

Here Alyssa was blaming herself for her husband's affair, and Avery didn't know anything about their marriage, but she knew enough to know that it was entirely possible to talk to your spouse without first sleeping with another person.

You could be angry without hitting. You could be unhappy without betrayal.

She waited for rage to build inside her. For her anger to sweep in like a tide. But it didn't. Because when she looked around the table she just saw herself. Smooth, made-up perfection.

Three beautiful women. Who had poured themselves into their husbands. Into their marriages. Their children. Who had made the successes of the man they were linked to their own. She knew what that was like. How futile it made everything feel, how she felt untethered. Like there was nothing holding her to the earth, because what he was *she* was. And if he was no longer a well-respected doctor, but just a disgraced wife beater, then what was she?

And she supposed that went for Alyssa too. He was an adulterer, then what did that make her? If he was a bad husband, then how could she be a perfect wife? And how could her life be enviable?

That ugly, unspoken component to all of this bloomed in her chest just then, and she couldn't ignore it or deny it.

She wanted to be envied. She wanted people to look at her and think Avery Grant had it all.

That she was a good wife, and a good mother. That she was selfless and sacrificing and did all these things for all these other people, that she was beautiful and fit and looked so good for her age. And why? She had put so much focus on the facade of the house that she had ignored all the drywall crumbling inside.

And the problem with that was, when the facade was compromise, then there was nothing left. Nothing. The outside of the house wasn't where you lived. No matter how beautiful it looked, no matter the curb appeal, if it was falling apart inside then who could call it a home?

And that was her.

So perfect on the outside. With this enviable marriage, and so desperately broken inside.

And her friends couldn't deal with the fracture in her marriage, because they might have to look deeper at their own. She was breaking rank.

She was the thing they feared the most. The revelation of emptiness, the degradation of that artifice.

They weren't her real friends. Not because they hadn't told her what she wanted to hear. Not that at all. But how could they be? They didn't know each other. Everything between them was based on the lies they told the world, and the lies they told themselves.

She didn't want to fit in anymore.

Not with them.

Not in their world.

"I am really *fucking* miserable," Avery said. Four heads turned at the table next to her. And her friends' eyes widened. "I hate all of this. It's awful. You know what, I hate trivia night. I hate it. I hate that I spent the last two years sleeping beside a man who hits me. *He hits me.* I hate the plastic robot that I've become. I used to be interesting. And I used to want things. For myself. Now... All I want is for people to look at me and wish they had what they *think* I have, which isn't even what I have. It's *bullshit*."

Alyssa startled. "People are looking at us."

"Fine. You know what, I don't care. Because I'm not perfect. And I can't be perfect. I can't hold it together anymore. I'm falling apart and that's got to be okay, because holding it together was going to kill me. And maybe... Maybe I'll just try to be happy instead." She stuffed her square back into her bag. "You have anything else to say?"

"I think you maybe are having a psychotic episode," Sandra said slowly. "I have a Xanax in my bag if you want it."

"I don't want a Xanax," Avery said. "What I would like is a life that doesn't require a low level of self-medication to get through the day. And I don't know how far away I am from that. I really don't. But I'm going to get there someday. Because this isn't what I want. Not anymore. It's not what I want to be. I'm quitting all the committees."

"You can't do that," Karen said. "We have a lot to do."

"I have to go earn a living. And I'm not going to be able to do that. Everything is so messed up. I may have to take the kids out of school. They might have to go to public school. I don't know. I don't know. But I... I am a mess." A bubble of hysteria welled up in her chest. "I'm a mess. I'm not perfect. I'm not even close."

"Where you going?" Alyssa asked as Avery stood and began to head toward the door.

"I think I have to go get a job."

She walked out the door, and into the sunshine, and she looked around at the very familiar view of Bear Creek's Main Street.

And suddenly, it felt new. And since everything around her was the same, she knew that the change had to be coming from inside of her.

21

It didn't feel right, what happened at the audition. Sam says it's normal for a director to need to see more of an actress. He says so many girls would be thrilled at the opportunity and he was mad at me for my lack of gratitude. Maybe he's right. Maybe I just need to be tougher. This isn't a small town. Things are different here.

Ava Moore's diary, 1924

Hannah

She'd been out in the back having a sneaky cigarette and in general trying to avoid *him* after the horror that was three nights ago. And while she'd been standing out in the back, with the breeze rustling through the trees she'd found there wasn't anything, nicotine or the vanilla perfume she put on her wrists, that smelled like Gram.

They'd gone back to his place.

They'd kissed. And oh…it had been amazing.

But it had hurt. The moment his lips had touched hers she'd been seventeen and thirty-six at the same time and she'd never felt anything like it.

She'd turned the casual hookup into an art form over the years. But where he'd touched her with his hands had burned like fire and her chest had felt like it was splitting in two.

And she'd run.

Literally had run away from him when his hand was halfway up her shirt because she'd been overcome by feelings. And she'd sneaked back into her bedroom, running from sex with Josh Anderson like she'd once sneaked out to have it with him.

And that was ridiculous.

Now she was trying to strike the balance between hiding from him like the coward she was and acting like that night hadn't rocked her to her core.

She supposed facing him was the only option.

She looked around the backyard and then turned, slinking back into the sitting room, and then walking into the kitchen, where Josh was working.

He stopped what he was doing and looked at her, his blue gaze absolutely scalding.

"Hi," she said, the word a stammer, which ruined everything.

One syllable had completely destroyed her intent at being cool. The cigarette was pointless now.

"Are we going to talk about what happened the other night?"

"Oh, wow. Read a room, Josh. I was clearly avoiding that."

"Did I hurt you?" His expression was flat, focused and she had to look away from him.

"No! No. You kissed me, you didn't… It's just that…" She cleared her throat. "It's…" Then something caught in her throat and she started coughing.

"It's the damn cigarettes."

"It's you, *dammit*," she shot back. "This town."

"I didn't do anything to you. You said you wanted to go to my place, you did. You wanted to stop, we did."

She looked at him, his face covered with dark stubble, his jaw so perfectly formed and beautiful. And she had to be honest with herself, that maybe it had been easy to keep herself from getting involved with other men because no one had ever seemed quite so exceptional to her. Maybe the problem was her sexuality had imprinted on Josh Anderson a long time ago, and no matter how much she might wish it were otherwise, no matter how much she could find a guy who was close enough, and handsome or amusing, he just wasn't him. And the other night had been...

It had been intense in a way she hadn't been prepared for.

Isn't that always the problem with him?

And do you really think that you deserve it?

Think about everything he doesn't know about you...

"I thought... I thought we could just have some fun, okay? But you and I weren't fun when we were seventeen," Hannah said. "When we were all earnest and crazy and could only see things in terms of breaking up or staying together forever."

The space between his eyebrows crinkled. "What are the other options?"

She blew out an exasperated breath. "Well, I guess there aren't any."

"So you were just thinking we'd hook up and...that's it. We'd hook up. Get off and go on our way?"

"Yes," she said, the word was lodged in her throat like a cement block. "You're a single, attractive man in his thirties. A booty call shouldn't be a foreign concept to you."

"I don't do that. I don't hook up casually, and you know...it pisses me off that I was willing to do it for you, Hannah."

That made her feel angry and small, and she didn't like it. "I don't believe you."

"If I meet someone, and I'm interested, I have a relationship. I'm not averse to commitment. I just haven't met the right person to keep me in it." He shrugged. "But I don't go into it thinking it will be temporary."

"You don't? Well, you're a lot less jaded than I am."

And she felt bitter about that. Really, quite bitter. Because her heart felt hard like obsidian and so much of it was related to what had happened between the two of them. To the way they had broken up. And he... He still believed in love? In the potential for forever?

Wow. You really are a horrendous bitch. You like the idea that you ruined him.

But maybe you just ruined yourself.

She wasn't ruined. She was first chair for the Boston Symphony Orchestra, and maybe not principal chair.

If it isn't everything, it's nothing.

"You don't believe in forever?" he asked.

"I told you," she said. "I'm committed to my music. I wouldn't ask anyone to try to compete with that."

"I don't know, Hannah. I... I'm in awe of that. I'm in awe of you, a little bit. Because I never had dreams that were much bigger than this place. I'm happy here. I have a piece of land that I'm happy to work. I have my family. I've always believed that I would find somebody, fall in love, have some kids. That feels like something to me. I know it never did to you."

"It isn't that it's nothing. I just don't think that you can have both. I don't think that you could be exceptional and ordinary at the same time."

He nodded slowly. "Right. Because you always thought that was ordinary. I just never thought we were. I really thought we were something else."

Special.

The word whispered through her like a curse this time.

He shook his head. "I wish... I wish there was something to make it go away. Because let me tell you something, Hannah Ashwood, I am damn sick of wanting you." He rounded that bar, and nothing was between her and his anger, his height, his broad male body that was harder, and even more beautiful than it had been at seventeen.

He took a step toward her, so that they were only a breath apart. "I'm sick to death of it. But I'm weak. I'm weak as hell. Because I wanted you all this time you were gone, and you're here now. I still want you so much."

It was the rawness in his voice that caught her. It made it impossible for her to be cynical and she hated that. She wanted to make a joke. She wanted to push him away.

She couldn't.

She could have cried. With how much she wanted him. Not just because she was attracted to him, though there was that. But because he was...him. Solid and real and right there. A link to a past she hadn't wanted. But now it just made her...

Everything was such a mess. Gram was gone and Avery's life had crumbled.

Hannah hadn't gotten the position she'd spent her whole life sacrificing for.

Josh Anderson was the one thing in her life she'd let distract her.

She wanted that distraction now. But it scared her.

That was the problem. Sex with other men was something easy.

A touch from him never could be.

This didn't feel simple at all. Or fun. Or like embracing nostalgia. And she felt like he was asking her for something that there was no way in hell she could give.

But she couldn't resist taking a step closer.

She could feel his breath against her lips. She put her hand on his chest and could feel his heart raging there, a furious beat that matched her own.

"Hannah..."

She stretched up on her toes and kissed him.

The storm that brewed between them burst into thunder and lightning and every sharp, painful thing she told herself she would never want ever again. But she let the past burn away, and she let the future go right along with it.

He was here right now. He was kissing her right now. And he might be angry, and he might have every right to be. Right now she would just take it as passion. All the passion that she could feel coming from him. The hope that he still had inside of him that she didn't have anymore.

She just wanted to take it. Just for a little bit.

And it would never be anything else. It never could be.

Because Avery wasn't the only keeper of secrets. But some were better left untold. Because it was too late to do anything to make it better.

Because he wanted her now, and if he knew the truth, he would never want to touch her again.

He pressed her back against the kitchen wall, hard muscle pinning her there. She opened her eyes and the expression she saw on his face took her breath away.

She could see him, sixteen years ago. When she'd told him all the reasons they couldn't be together.

You're not good enough for me.

She closed her eyes again and kissed him harder. Deeper. Trying to blot out the memories. Erase the past with the present.

I'm special.

Her own words, so sharp and horrible, cut through years and desire like a knife.

Just because you're happy with your sad little life, doesn't mean that I will be.

She pushed her fingers through his hair, arched her body against his. His hand moved down her back to cup her rear end.

You're holding me back.

She pushed away from the wall, and he held her, kept them both from falling.

"Upstairs," she whispered against his mouth.

He grabbed her hands, pinned them down at her sides. "Are you sure? Because I already told you who I am. How I do things. And how I don't."

"Please," she said, her chest tight, her throat throttled with so many emotions it was all she could do to force the word out.

He picked her up. Like she weighed nothing. Like all her problems and baggage weighed nothing. She took a breath but it turned into a sob. But he didn't ask what was wrong and she was so grateful for that.

They went to her room and he shut the door hard behind them, peeling his T-shirt up over his head. His body was familiar and totally new all at once. The years had brought a blessed maturity to his chest and stomach that sent a kick of arousal through her.

He was perfect.

She felt clumsy as she tried to take her own clothes off, but his movements were decisive as he stripped her bare, his lips firm against hers. His hands were rough in a way they hadn't been sixteen years earlier. Changed by labor and time.

She moved her own hands down his chest and wondered if he could feel her calluses. If he'd always been able to. The rough edges of her fingers from years of building up defenses against her strings.

It was who they were. The roughness on their hands.

He kissed her neck, her shoulder. She shivered. He'd always made her shake, but this was more. Better. He was better.

And he knew her body. They were different now and years had passed but he knew where to touch her and how. He was more confident now. There was no hesitation.

This was why she'd run.

Because this was something perfect that she'd never experienced before. This rush of new exciting sensation with an intimacy that lingered, even though before that night three days ago it had been years since he'd touched her, kissed her.

He kissed a path down to her breast, down farther still, pushing her back on the bed and spreading her out for him like a feast.

And then she couldn't think. Not anymore.

Not with his lips and tongue creating wicked music that echoed inside her like magic.

She had the strangest urge to cry.

Music. What a funny way to think of pleasure, but it was like that.

Music he made for her, rather than music she had to create for the world. It was effortless and wonderful and it made her feel like she was flying.

She was gasping for breath when he moved up her body and captured her mouth again. When he surged inside her. She squeezed her eyes shut and held on to his shoulders. Whispered against his neck. Begging for more. Afraid she couldn't possibly handle more.

This was more than a wave of pleasure. Than the crash of an orgasm. It was that and more. Deep.

Everything she had been right to fear.

And want.

And need.

And when he held her afterward, a word, deep and quiet echoed inside of her.

Special.

22

The baby came last night. She's so small she terrifies me. I look at her and my heart feels bruised. I thought I might have a son. A son could bear more shame surrounding his birth. But not a little girl. The world is unspeakably cruel to women. Men die in war. We die in our hometowns, crushed to death by expectations we could not meet.

Dot's diary, December 1944

Lark

Lark had made some new flower crowns, but angrily. She was finding it hard to concentrate on… Anything, since she had full on *made out with Ben* the night before. She was sitting on the purple chaise in the living area by the kitchen, when she heard the front door open. She heard the thunderous footsteps of her niece and nephew, followed by the less thunderous footsteps of her sister. And then, the clear sound of boots, which was her other sister.

"Hi," Lark shouted, not quite able to keep the irritation from her tone.

"Hi, Aunt Lark," the kids chorused.

"Hi. Did you go viral today? Or whatever it is the kids are aiming to do these days."

"No," Peyton said, looking vaguely appalled.

Hayden grinned. "You know, if we could film a clip of you dancing, it might do it."

"I'm gonna pass on that. Thankfully, when I was your age, all humiliation stayed between the pages of our diaries."

"Where's the fun in that?" Peyton asked.

"I worry for your generation," she called as her niece disappeared into the kitchen.

Hayden waved, and then went up the stairs. Hannah and Avery appeared in the door a moment later. Avery was wearing an open, pink hoodie, a T-shirt and leggings. Hannah in black on black on black, her red hair a beacon.

"How was your day?"

"Fabulous. I met with a lawyer." Avery did not look like she thought it was anything like fabulous. "Division of assets is not sexy."

"Good," Hannah said. "Make the separation from that illegal."

"It just sucks. The whole thing sucks."

"Yeah, that's why we need a wine and attic party after dinner," Lark said.

"Which kind of wine is that?" Hannah asked.

"Any kind. Whine. Wine. Red. White."

About an hour later, they ate a very nice chicken dinner with the kids, who then went up to do their homework, and that meant that the sisters could go upstairs.

Lark had brought her bag with her, filled with some of her various craft things, and the swatch book that she was still perusing, looking for her fabric piece.

And just then, with all that was going on, Lark didn't have the ability to hold in what had happened with Ben. Not now.

"Okay, let's talk about everything that's terrible. I'll go first. I made out with Ben Thompson."

She kept thinking about that moment. And about the realization she'd had that she lost the bravery that had once enabled her to do things like that.

She wanted him, and couldn't have him, because of him, and it was a circle that she kept on going in.

"You *did what?*"

"You heard me."

"Isn't he married?" Hannah asked.

Avery lifted a finger. "No. Divorced. She left him."

"No kidding," Hannah said. "That's actually pretty shocking."

"Right?" Lark asked. "They were like this golden couple. Meant to be." She poured herself a generous glass of wine. "So meant to be, mind you, that I never... I mean I didn't... I didn't tell him I was in love with him."

"You were in love with him?" Avery asked.

Hannah snorted. "That was obvious."

"How was it obvious?" Lark asked.

"I read your diary. That did make it obvious. Because you wrote that you were."

"Hannah! You are terrible."

"You left it open. It's not my fault."

"I thought you were only interested in the violin."

"Mostly. But I did enjoy tormenting you."

Lark digested that for a moment. "But you never said anything about that. I mean, you never teased me."

"Because you were fifteen, and he was dating Keira, and actually that just seemed too mean. So I never read your diary again, and I never looked at it, and I didn't make fun of you. Because at that point I knew what it felt like to have my heart broken."

"Josh..."

"I know I broke up with him. But it hurt and it's complicated. But, the sex with him now is amazing."

"I *knew* you were having sex with him."

"We're not that subtle. Do you honestly think he's patching holes in the wall at ten o'clock at night in my room? More like making more."

"And what are you going to do about it? I mean… Are you actually going to…"

"I have a life in Boston. I have a career. It's no more practical for me to give it up now than it was then. So no. And he knows that." But her sister suddenly looked sad.

"Enough sex talk," Avery said, pulling a face. "It's not fair."

"I didn't have sex with Ben," Lark said. "I kissed him."

"Yeah, well, you're going to sleep with him," Hannah said prosaically.

Lark's whole body tensed up as excitement and fear poured through her in equal measure. "You don't know that."

"I pretty much do," Hannah said.

"Stop it, you don't know."

"I do. Because you're not twelve, you are thirty-four. And you made out with him. You don't just make out to make out when you're thirty-four."

"Maybe *I* do. You don't know my life. Maybe I like a little sensuality. Maybe I don't need for it to be all about… You know."

"Not even I believe that," Avery said.

Hannah took another sip of wine. Lark did the same. Avery had gone through three quarters of her glass without Lark even realizing.

"Why wouldn't you sleep with him?" Hannah asked.

"Because last time I ended up devastated."

"Last time?"

"Yeah." The wine was working through her system, making her both reckless and decisive. "You want to hear virginity stories. Since I had to hear about your vine tryst, let me tell you mine. Ben broke up with Keira for five seconds. I went to his house to watch a movie, and we had sex. Then, he got back together with her."

"Oh my gosh," Avery said. "That's why you didn't come back for the wedding."

"Yes," Lark said. "It was… Horrible. Humiliating."

"Why didn't you tell anyone?" Hannah asked.

"Why would I?"

"Because you… Never kept secrets." Avery shook her head. "I didn't think you were capable of it. You were always sounding off about every little feeling you had."

"I wasn't. I kept plenty of things to myself, thank you very much. Including the fact that I was terminally in love with him."

"It was literally the only thing in your diary I didn't already know," Hannah said. "You didn't keep that many secrets."

"You just… You don't know everything about me."

"Well, clearly not everything," Avery said. "But plenty. I mean, let's take the quilt for example. You haven't even chosen the swatch yet. You roped us into doing this, and you're working on everything but the quilt. It's classically you."

"What does that mean? You keep saying things like that. You make all these proclamations about my life, and I don't even know what any of it means."

"You don't know what it means? I think you do," Avery said. "It's just how you are, Lark. You're enthusiastic, but you don't really commit to things. You… I don't know. You coast. You drift. And the drift carries you to fortunate places. Look, it even brought you back to making out with the guy that you used to be in love with."

"You don't know me," Lark said, suddenly filled with the kind of righteous indignation that she had not felt since she was eighteen years old. Since before.

"I have known you for thirty-four years."

"No. You know exactly what I show you. Which is not everything. Because do you know what happens, Avery? Life kicks the shit out of you. And then you just quit being who you were before."

"I am well aware of the fact that life kicks the shit out of you, Lark, thank you."

"What, are you the same? Are you the same as from before?"

"No. But are you honestly comparing some guy you slept with forever ago with my abusive marriage?"

"No. You don't know what I'm... You don't know what I'm comparing. Because you don't know me. Not really. Both of you. You write me off all the time. You talk about how I'm all these things, but you don't actually know. And yes, I let you think so. But I have a successful career as an illustrator, and I'm running the Craft Café just fine, and you both still think that I'm...some kind of feckless wonder."

Venting like this felt surprisingly therapeutic and she was ready to embrace it. Ready to let it all out.

"Well, what do you think about me?" Avery asked.

Lark narrowed her eyes. "I think that you're boring. You were pretty and popular in high school and it made you feel good, but instead of growing up you just...decided to try and keep being that. Which is *boring*. And I think that you decided to get married and play it safe because you didn't actually want to go for your dreams. Because you wanted to be a writer. But you didn't think that you could actually do it."

"Yeah, real safe. My life turned out real safe," Avery said, taking another sip of wine.

"Great! *Do me*," Hannah said, looking ready for a fight.

Lark rounded on her sister. "You try to pretend you don't care about things because you're consumed with angst. You have convinced yourself that you can't love anything but your violin. But it doesn't love you back. And you're so consumed with your all-or-nothing attitude that you don't even realize you're already successful. Because it's not the exact thing you want you don't think you have anything. Also, you're a slut."

"You should be more of a slut," Hannah said. "Then maybe you wouldn't be tied up in knots over some guy you kissed. And there's nothing wrong with having goals. And there's nothing wrong with being a stay-at-home mom, either."

"I didn't say there was," Lark said. "I said Avery *specifically* sold herself short. On purpose. Because she was too afraid to go after what she wanted."

"So, Hannah is wrong for going after what she wanted," Avery said. "And I'm wrong for not going after what I wanted. I just think you're spoiled. Mom coddled you, because you were wild. And she was afraid that she would lose you. Because she was afraid that you would be like Gram. So she tried to give you everything that you wanted so that you would be happy and you would stay, and then you didn't. And she'd never say it, but it broke her heart. I stayed, I stayed for both of you. And neither of you have given me any credit for that."

"Get down off the cross," Hannah said. "We need the wood."

"Oh you're both awful," Avery said, standing up with the wine bottle and heading out toward the exit to the attic.

"Stop," Lark said. "I didn't want to be in a fight." She stomped her foot. "I don't want to be in a fight. I'm sorry. But I'm upset. And I'm a coward. And I don't know how not to be. And you all think that I'm this one thing, and I'm not. I'm miserable. I have been for a long time, and it's so ridiculous to feel this bad and to have everyone in my life think that... Like you just all think it's going to be okay for me, and I don't know that. I don't know. I don't know if it's going to be okay for you, Avery. Or you, Hannah. I don't know if we're going to be okay. And we've been... Split apart for all these years, off doing our own things, and not... Not having this fight. We needed to have this fight."

Hannah's shoulders sagged. "Lark," she said. "You're not stupid, and we don't think so. It's just… You're the baby. And I don't mean that in a mean way. I mean… Of course Mom and Dad were easier on you. And of course we have kept a running tally of all the ways in which they were easier on you. That's how that goes."

"I don't feel like I had it easier than the two of you. I felt incredible pressure to be good and to never disappoint them. And I was always living in hell not able to control my emotions and knowing it made Mom sad, always wanting to follow rules and finding it hard. I did not have it easy."

"Of course you don't think you did," Avery said. "The baby never does."

"I'm sorry," Lark said. "I'm just… I'm sorry that I was off on my own, and that I wasn't here to see you and the kids as much as I should have been. That I wasn't in a place where you could tell me about David."

Avery sighed. "It wasn't your fault. I didn't even want to know about it. Nobody could have been close enough to me to know about it."

"I'm sorry, Hannah, because we could have known each other a lot better. And we could have supported each other. But we were both too busy trying to show that what we did was the most special."

"It hasn't been all bad. We haven't been as close as we could have been," Avery said. "But we're here now. And without you… I never could have left him. I wouldn't have gone to the police. You were both there when I needed you. Even when you were being a bitch, Hannah."

"Some say it's part of my charm."

"It is. Because if you hadn't been a mean bitch, if you had been nice to me instead, I think I just would have fallen apart. And I don't think I ever could have faced it. It was the anger that got me through."

"You know, this was Gram's doing," Hannah said. "She was always trying to make us talk." She laughed. "Look at us now."

"I wish she and Mom could've made up."

"Me too," Avery said.

They sat in silence for a moment, looking around their little circle at each other, each holding their wine and looking sad.

"That was like old times," Lark said. "Me freaking out and being a brat."

Except nothing bad had happened. They were just still here with her, and she felt better.

"We're all brats," Avery said. "Or, we all can be."

"No, it was good. I need... I want him. And I need to be brave enough to take a chance."

"You should be more of a slut like me," Hannah said.

"I mean, the problem is it's him. Right? It's not sex. It's that it's Ben."

Hannah made a disgusted sound. "Sadly, I relate to that."

"Well, you came back here for a reason," Avery said. "Maybe he's part of it."

"Maybe. Or maybe I'll get my heart broken again."

"Maybe," Avery said. "But in a few years, I hope that I need you to talk me into trying something again. And I hope that you'll tell me it's worth the risk."

Lark nodded. "That's fair."

"Now," Hannah said. "Are you ever going to choose fabric for your quilt square?"

"I don't know." She pulled the swatch book out of her bag, and turned to one of the back pages. There were a few swatches in there, but there was a yellow one, butter soft and pale, unlabeled. "I keep looking at this one. But it's yellow, and I'm not sure."

"Lark," Hannah said. "Whatever you choose, you'll make it into something beautiful. That's what you do."

"You really think that?"

"Yeah," Hannah said. "It's one of the very annoying things about you."

"Well, thank you."

"But also, know that I think you're amazing," Hannah said. "And that I think the Craft Café is brilliant. And that might be the wine talking, so don't ask me tomorrow when I'm sober."

"Oh I will. I'm going to make sure that I get all compliments from either of you in writing for posterity, forever."

"I'll give it to you gladly," Hannah said. "If you take a chance with your guy."

"Why does it matter to you?"

"Because," Hannah said. "I'm out here dealing with some old drama. Avery is starting over. It seems fair."

"Remember how Gram used to give us a candy bar, and have us divide it into three pieces. But whoever did the cutting had to pick last?"

"It had to be equal," Avery said.

Lark looked around at her sisters. It was really too bad that life didn't work like candy bars. Everything could never be equal. But they could be there together. And that was what mattered.

And with them, she could be brave enough to let her emotions go. To make it a little bit messy.

Maybe now, she would be brave enough to try with Ben.

There was no maybe. She would be.

Because life was too short to be this indecisive.

"I will. And I'll use the yellow fabric. When I find it." She kicked over a box, as if it might magically reveal the fabric, but it didn't, just pictures. And an old, red leather book.

"What's that?" Hannah asked, she swooped down and picked it up. "Ava Moore." She flipped it open. "1923. I wonder... I wonder if this goes with my dress."

"It might," Avery said. "The 1860s diary went with my curtains."

"Well, I'm going to keep it. Now, I say we raise a toast to

Gram. For bringing us back here, for bringing us the quilt, and for bringing us together."

"To crafting and togetherness," Hannah agreed.

"And to red lipstick and spearmint gum."

"Cheers."

23

The love in my heart for my husband isn't gone. But there is room now, beside the love, beside the grief. For bluebonnets and horse rides, and for the vast mountains that have replaced the endless prairies. And though I know it is wicked to even write it, John's arms feel like home.

Anabeth Snow's diary, 1864

Avery

She had gotten a job.

When Avery walked back into The Dowell House that evening with bags full of takeout hanging off of her arms she felt triumphant. She felt free. Her kids went upstairs, without saying more than three words to her. "You're coming down for dinner," she yelled at them. "Ten minutes. I'm not doing silent treatment." The house was warm, the work that Josh was doing to fix the place up making it look inviting and absolutely perfect for a vacation rental. Though the idea made her a little bit sad now. Since it was beginning to feel like a haven in ways she hadn't expected.

Of course, she hadn't known what she would need.

Hannah passed the kids on her way down the stairs, and Avery was about to say something to her when her phone buzzed in her purse. She dug for it, maneuvering the bags on her arms as she did.

"Let me take that," Hannah said, unburdening one side of Avery as she grabbed her phone and lifted it to her ear.

"Hello?"

"Mrs. Grant. This is Officer Dempsey from Bear Creek Police Department. I'm calling to let you know that the DA has decided to press charges against your husband. There will be a court date to follow." Everything went into white noise in Avery's head. The officer was still talking, making suggestions about restraining orders, and what she should do if she didn't feel safe. But Avery was finding it difficult to concentrate.

A court case.

"Okay," she said. "Thank you."

"You'll probably be brought in to testify, and so will your children."

"Okay," Avery said, the word a whisper. She gave the officer her current address, and other information, before getting off the phone.

"Was that the police?" Hannah asked.

"Yes," Avery said, walking past her sister, through the living room and into the kitchen. She set the takeout bags on the counter, and Hannah followed suit.

"This has been a very weird day."

"What are they doing?"

"Prosecuting. And I think I'm supposed to be really happy about that? But I don't feel anything. I actually don't know which of the two options is worse. Because I hate all of it."

"I'm sorry," Hannah said, standing with her arms awkwardly at her sides. Hannah was not going to hug her. And that was actually fine with Avery. When Hannah graduated to hugging people, then Avery knew something was really wrong.

"I got a job. I was feeling really excited about that until a minute ago. Now I just feel gross."

"Where did you get a job?"

"Oh at The Roaming Pika." The quirky store sold furniture, clothing, candles and gifts. It was eclectic and bohemian, and really not traditionally Avery at all. But it was on Main Street in town, was extremely cute and was within walking distance of The Dowell House. They were also able to work with her kids' school schedule. So it was perfect as far as Avery was concerned. Didn't pay enough to help her afford a whole lot, but when they did the whole divorce thing...

Well, if he was in jail or didn't have a job, she supposed she wouldn't have child support.

There were no good options.

There's the house.

Their house.

She could sell it. She could sell it to pay for the kids' education. As long as they moved in with her parents.

"I'm thinking too far ahead," she said. "I need to stop it."

"Hey. Understandable."

"But there's nothing I can do about the future. I can't fix it or foresee it or any of that. All I can do is just... I got a job. And I told my friends. And they were awful."

"Why doesn't that surprise me?"

"What didn't surprise you?" Lark came breezing into the kitchen. "What's for dinner?"

"Tikka masala," Avery said. "And rice and naan. David hates Indian food. And he doesn't like me to get takeout too much. And screw that guy."

"Hear hear," Lark said.

Her kids finally came downstairs, and since Aunt Hannah and Aunt Lark were something of a novelty, she actually got a little bit of human interaction out of them. They liked Indian food. And they were happy with the choice.

Avery added it to her list of small wins.

She was going to take every win, no matter how small. Because there were some big unknowns looming. Her kids reacted strangely when she told them about the job, but she supposed they probably didn't know quite what to think. She hadn't done anything but be there for them since they were born. That they were going to have to share some of her time was likely not their favorite thing. But then, their whole world was full of change right now. And she was going to have to tell them that their dad was going to court. That they were going to have to tell a judge what they had seen and what they hadn't.

But she was sitting here, at this unfamiliar kitchen table, eating food that she'd chosen, and her kids were there. Her sisters were there.

So maybe she couldn't see into the future. But she could see this. And she felt... Safer than she had in a long time. Happy might be a stretch. But she did feel like maybe... Just maybe things would be okay. And as assurance went, she would take it.

Later that night she went upstairs and took out Anabeth's diary. Because she found courage in those little passages written by that woman so long ago. Courage in her strength to start over.

And for some reason, that connection with the past brought her a greater connection with the present than just about anything else.

24

*The girls and I had a falling out because I got the part and Elsie
didn't. Sam says I can stay with him. It'll be easier anyway. I'm
sick of their complaining. They act like children. You can't be a
child here.*

Ava Moore's diary, 1924

Hannah

Hannah had been out buying groceries, which felt like a novelty experience. But now that Avery and her kids were living
here, she did feel like maybe it would be best if there was actual
food in the house. And it kind of felt nice to do a favor for her
sister. She didn't go grocery shopping. Sometimes, she got groceries delivered to her house, but mostly she just brought takeout home. She was busy.

Cooking and buying food didn't really have a place in that.
But she felt cheerful as she walked through the door of The

Dowell House, and then a little bit confused when she saw that it was empty. It was evening, and she had expected everyone to be there. The Craft Café would be closed and Avery should have gotten the kids from school. She was used to walking into empty houses. She lived alone. And she liked it. And being in close proximity with the amount of people she had been with for the past few weeks really should make her feel claustrophobic. But instead, the lack of them felt strange.

She had felt separate from her family for a long time, but these past weeks, and their wine soaked shouting match had made her feel…

Part of them.

She liked it.

She walked through the living room, and stared through the kitchen to the back door that led out to the yard. And she saw lights. Curious, she moved forward. Rope lights. Strung from the rafters of the house, to a pole at the center of the yard. And underneath that was a table. Set for dinner.

Dinner for two, though. Definitely not for all the people that lived in this house.

Her heart thundering, she went outside, and she saw Josh. Dressed in dark jeans and a black T-shirt, which she had a feeling was dressed up for him.

She spent a lot of time around men in suits. Very nice suits. Well tailored suits.

Nothing beat Josh Anderson in dark jeans and a T-shirt, when it was especially for her.

"I made dinner," he said.

"Did you also tie my family up and stash them in the basement?"

"No. They took a generous gift card and went out to dinner."

She looked around. "Really?"

"Yes," he said.

She was stunned for a moment. Absolutely stunned. Because

they had been sleeping together, certainly. And the way things were between them, it wasn't like she could pretend it was casual. No, the need between them was far too sharp for that.

She also couldn't stop being with him, so she was willing to deal with the emotional ups and downs she felt every time they shared a bed.

But this was like *dating*.

No, this was like something she hadn't experienced in… Ever.

Because she just didn't. Men didn't do things like this for her.

You never stay with them long enough to give them the chance.

"Thank you," she said, cautiously. "But I'm not sure I understand."

"I wanted to do something nice for you," he said. "There's no catch."

"There's always a catch, Josh, or have you not heard the one about the free lunch?"

"This is a free dinner. And since I'm the person that made it I think I'm the one that gets to decide whether or not it's free, don't you?"

She tilted her head and looked at him from the corner of her eye. "I don't even have to put out?"

"No," he said. "Anyway. You put out for nothing, Hannah, so, I don't know why you would think I made you lasagna to get you have sex with me."

"I think mostly because I'm not sure what you want."

He looked at her, and something in her melted. Outright melted. And she felt… Like she was in more danger than she had ever been in before.

"I just want your time. That's it. Do you think you can give me that? For a little bit?"

She nodded, mute. He pulled the chair out, and she sat down at the table, where there was lasagna and salad.

"Did you really cook this?"

"Yes. Basic survival skill."

"One I don't even have."

"What do you do?"

"There are many apps that allow you to push buttons and have food magically appear at your front door."

"Not here."

"Yeah. One of the many reasons that I find this place to be a hellscape." But she looked up, at the string of lights, and the rosy gold sky, at the green trees and the tips of the mountains that she could see beyond the yard. At the man across from her. And she had a very hard time applying the word *hellscape* to any of that.

"I think it's pretty beautiful." His eyes were on her, and her heart squeezed. "I did think about leaving," he said. "You know, for a while there. But then Dad died, and that left ranchland to run. And I love that, Hannah, I found out I really loved the ranch. It doesn't pay the bills on its own, and that's one reason I started this business. It's better, to not have to worry about your land sustaining you. Better to have something else to help out, because one thing I can guarantee you is that pipes will start leaking, but I can't guarantee you that we're going to get a good crop of hay. I can't control the weather. And then Jamie got married and started having kids, and I get to be an uncle. That makes me happy. My family makes me pretty happy."

It made her ache to see him like this. This man, who had a capacity to care about the land of his family in this deep way. Who made his roots here seem steady and solid and right, instead of limited and small like she'd seen them all those years ago.

It was her life that felt small suddenly. An apartment and a violin. Yes, she had friends. And yes, she cared about them. She had fun. But it didn't resonate, not right now. And for some reason this did. For some reason he did.

She had always thought that if she ever came back and had a confrontation with him she would be fancy and superior and he would feel like a damn fool. Wish that he had followed her, or something.

Even though you made that impossible.

"I've dated other women, Hannah. But I don't think any-thing's ever come close to us."

She tried to choke down the lasagna, but it suddenly tasted like sawdust. Because he still thought she was someone she wasn't. And that was the problem with that little fantasy she just had. That he might someday wish he could have her back, or wish that he'd gone with her.

She'd done her best to kill that. To end it. She really had. She'd been mean, but she hadn't told the truth.

And that secret was so deep, so buried inside of her that even thinking it made her head hurt.

She thought of Lark and Ben and how much she wanted Lark to be able to find her happiness with him. How she'd pushed her the other night to have her own reunion fling and...

And she just wanted to run away from hers now.

Because this wasn't a fling.

And it wasn't casual.

She'd known it wasn't. She'd known it when she couldn't sleep with him that first night and she was still here.

It had still come down to this.

"Dance with me," he said, taking his napkin from his lap and putting it on the table.

"No," she said. "That's silly."

He took his phone out of his pocket and opened up the music app, put on a song about a woman looking perfect tonight, and held his hand out.

And she sat there frozen, staring at that hand, her mind flash-ing hard between the past and the present.

And when she looked up at his face, it wasn't his face that she saw.

You want to get into that school, don't you, Hannah? If this is about that boyfriend of yours, I thought you were different. I thought you were driven. That's why I feel the way I do about you. Because you're like me.

You're special.

Her skin crawled, and she stood up, moving away from him.

"No, Josh, this is a mistake. I'm going back to Boston. I'm not starting something with you."

"Hannah, I can't explain what I feel for you. After all this time. I'm actually pretty pissed off about it. That I wasn't angry when I saw you, I just wanted another chance to see what we could be."

"Nothing," she said. "Nothing. Because you love it here. And I... I hate it." But those words felt like a lie. "I thought that I would've made you hate me effectively enough nineteen years ago."

"It's too bad you didn't," he said. "God knows why."

"Well if you knew the real reason I broke up with you, you probably would."

"And what's that?" he asked, his face stone.

"I slept with someone else, Josh. I slept with someone else, and when I broke up with you I couldn't bear to tell you that. But it's true. You shouldn't want me. Because that's who I am. You loved me, and I betrayed that. You can't trust me. At the end of the day, if you know one thing, you should know that. You can't trust me."

25

She has arranged for the baby to go to her cousin. She will send for her later and claim she is the child of her niece, widowed by the war and unable to care for her. She says this is right, for she has a piece of him, and our daughter will endure no shame. I don't know what it means for me.

Dot's diary, February 1945

Lark

Lark stumbled into Ben's garage, still feeling high off of the shouting session she'd had with her sisters. It had clarified things. She'd worked the whole day and done what needed doing at the Craft Café, but she'd been buzzing with energy, anxious to see Ben again.

She'd learned something in that attic. That sometimes outbursts made you closer to someone, not more distant.

Ben looked up when she came in and her heart stopped. But her words wouldn't be.

"I have a whole lot of speeches for you. Saved up. Rehearsed. Some of them are angry, and some of them are tearful, and some of them are about how I have a lot of regrets. And some of them are about how I don't have any. I've gone back and forth a lot over the years. But now that I'm here, I don't actually want to give any of them. I just…"

She crossed the distance between them, and it felt like walking across years. Then she wrapped her arms around his neck, and she kissed him. And he kissed her. He dragged her into the garage, shutting the door behind them, and turning the lock. It was fierce, and hard. A storm that had been brewing for sixteen years.

"Ben," she whispered.

There was nothing to say now. Nothing at all.

"I want you," he said, his words filled with gravel. She pushed her hands beneath his shirt, grateful that he had already drawn the blinds on the windows. His skin was hot, his muscles more densely packed than they'd been when they were younger. And those tattoos. She peeled his shirt up over his head, her heart stuttering as she looked at his body.

"I want you," she said. And then they were kissing, and he peeled her shirt up over her head, casting it onto the washed-out gray and white floor.

He walked her back, behind the counter, and through a door that led to a tiny room with a very small bed inside.

"A holdover from the end of my marriage. Things were not going well."

"Oh."

"Convenient."

It was all a little bit much. It tangled the past and the present, and she didn't know what the hell it said about the future. But that all melted away as easily and quickly as their clothes did. His touch was like magic, perfect in every way. The first time they'd been together, she'd been young. She had no experience at all. And more than that, she hadn't known what it would be like to live in a world where she knew what it was to be with him, and not have him. She knew now.

She'd lived in it for years.

And she wanted to take the risk. Knowing what she did, she wanted to take that risk. And somehow that made everything more intense. More powerful. His lips, his tongue, his hands. All of it traced dark magic over her skin, made her feel like she was burning.

Made her feel alive.

As if that wild thing that had roamed around inside her chest all of her life, when she was a young girl, that thing that made her spontaneous and willful and irrepressible, was now crackling over every inch of her body. Only he could ever do that. Take that feeling and make it focused. Take it and make it matter.

Take it and make her...

Feel more like her than she ever had before.

Not before. Not after. Both things.

Together.

And when he surged inside of her, she gasped. Because it was good. And it was perfect. He was Ben.

And she was Lark.

And maybe in the end, they were the ones that were inevitable.

Maybe they had been meant to be all along.

It didn't matter that the bed was small, it didn't matter that it was a glorified cot. It was perfect for them. Because the moment was right. Perfect in every way. As tangled and messy and difficult as it was. It was still perfect.

And when it was over, he held her, tracing shapes over her hip, and she looked at the ink on his forearms.

"What do they mean?"

"I got them after the divorce."

A smile curved her lips. "I wondered about that. I didn't think that Keira would be into tattoos."

"Not especially."

"I like them."

There was a pause. "Somehow, I figured you would."

"Really? Like... In the last couple weeks?"

"No. When I got them." He shifted, and that was when she saw it. The bird resting in the mountains on his upper biceps.

"Ben..."

"It's a lark."

"I know," she whispered. "I don't... Why?"

"Because you're part of me, Lark. You always have been. And I wondered, for a long time, if it was just me... Romanticizing something that I couldn't have. You know, married men like to do that, I think. Pretend that there's some great, unobtainable love out there that's keeping you from fully being present in your marriage, or whatever. I don't know. I just always thought about you. Even after I wasn't with her anymore."

"What about the other ones?"

He turned his arm over, and there was a rose, embedded in a thorny vine. "Taylor's middle name is Rose. The thorns are pretty self-explanatory. The mountains are Oregon. The bear is Bear Creek."

"Nothing for Keira?"

He shook his head. "No."

"Are you that mad at her?"

He shook his head. "No. Not for myself. But the part of her that I carry, is Taylor. That's the piece I don't regret. The piece I know means something. And beyond that..."

She touched the bird on his shoulder. Where she wasn't sharing space with Keira. At all.

"Is this really something that we get to try?"

"Yes. I think we need to. I really do."

"Me too."

"You know I was in love with you, right?"

"Yeah," he said, the words sounding heavy. "I think I was in love with you too. I just didn't know what love meant yet."

"What about now?"

"I know what it means now."

So did she. And for the first time in a while, she felt a very real bubble of hope blooming inside of her chest. Maybe she had come back not to put the past away, but to find a way to redeem it.

26

Today, we crossed into Oregon. Today, I feel new. I started off to Oregon to find a new life, but I did not expect to find so much more. Of all the things, it is hope that surprises me most. For it was always there, or I would never have started on this journey. If not for hope, I would never have made it this far.

Anabeth Snow's diary, 1864

Avery

All the kids were sitting outside eating ice cream and in general creating a scene. They'd gone into Medford to meet the kids' school friends and to give Hannah privacy for her date with Josh. Avery had always liked him, and she hoped—she really hoped—that her sister made it work with him this time.

The teenage boys were being crazy, and the teenage girls were pretending to be above it while staring and giggling.

Avery watched the scene from her car, smiling slightly. She

remembered this. When watching a boy that you liked felt dangerous and fun in a totally different way than that thing between men and women had turned into for her.

When the world was full of possibilities, and you played games with your friends to try and predict the future. Folded notes that offered glimpses into what could be. But nowhere and never had she predicted that she would find love, find the man of her dreams, only to have him turn into some kind of monster. Only to have it become something deadly and dangerous and quite the opposite of a dream.

She didn't know what you did after that.

And she missed being sixteen right then.

When you were so convinced that becoming an adult was a destination, and you wouldn't just be continuing on the journey. Having no idea what you were doing or what you wanted, or where to go.

It was *like* being sixteen in some ways, actually, except knowing all the things she didn't know. She felt like she had just gotten her first job. And she felt confused and like the popular girls hated her. So yeah, maybe it wasn't being sixteen she missed. Maybe it was just feeling like there was a future ahead where she would know everything. When she was convinced now that didn't exist.

Her phone buzzed and when she looked at the screen and saw the name on it, everything in her went cold.

David.

She looked up, and that was when she saw him standing there in the parking lot.

She felt an icy sliver of fear, because she kept remembering what Hannah had said about how things escalated. About how she might actually be in danger.

And she wanted to scream. Because this was the father of her children and she was afraid of him. And right then, she hated him as much as she had ever loved him.

She got out of her car, because they were in public, and she was going to make sure that if he did anything, or thought about doing anything, there were going to be a hell of a lot of witnesses.

She crossed her arms and stood as tall as she could. "What are you doing here?"

"I tracked your phone," he said. "We need to talk."

She hadn't even thought of that. Her phone. They were on the same account because everything was meshed together. So deep and in too many ways to count.

"We don't need to talk," she said. "All of the talking between the two of us is going to be done between law enforcement and lawyers."

"Lawyers, Avery? Really? You had me *arrested*. I was at work."

"You hit me," she said. "In my kitchen."

He didn't flinch. He didn't pause. It was like she hadn't said anything.

"You didn't even talk to me about it."

"Is there anything to say? Is there anything to say at all? How can I talk to you. How can I talk to you when it's going to just end up with me being injured. I can't do anything to stop you, and you know that."

"I'm not that guy, Avery, don't make me sound like I'm some psychopath."

She was thankful the car door was between them. "I'm sorry, what guy aren't you?"

"I am not some wife beater, and the cops treated me like one. And it was in the damn paper, everyone knows."

"I'm sorry, are your own actions embarrassing for you?"

She searched his face for something. Some shame. It wasn't there. There was just the cool, low burn of his anger.

"You know that this isn't a one-way street. Marriage never is. We've been married for a long time, and it never came to that until recently. Didn't you ever ask yourself why that is? I'm stressed, and you like spending my money, but you've never done a damn thing to try and help me out when my job got more stressful, and started paying better, too, which you benefitted from. What are you off doing? Having coffee with your friends, working on this quilt thing with your mom and your sisters. We're your family. We are more important. I'm more important. And if I come home from a long day of work and I don't have my damn dinner..."

"You hit your wife." She felt like she was having an out of body experience. "When you come home from work and you don't have your dinner you hit your wife. And you hit your son. And you know what, David? I might have been weak enough to be talked into going back to you a couple of times if he hadn't told me that. But so much of what I was doing was to protect them. Because I'm scared. Because if you go to jail what am I going to do? You're right. I do spend your money."

She let out a ragged breath. "I've let you take care of me. But because I did that, I started to belong to you, and the more that you thought I belonged to you the more you thought you could do whatever you want with me, and the more I thought maybe you were right. Some women... Some women can trust their husbands to take care of them and they really damn well do it. They don't lay a finger on them. They're safe, and their homes are sanctuaries and their kids are treasured, and I wanted that so much I *decided* that we had it. We had it except that I didn't feel safe. Except that you hurt me. And I decided it was a separate thing. So separate that I walked into a quilting session with my mom and my sisters with a bruise on my face and had somehow convinced myself that I could talk my way around it. That I could justify it away. But you hit me. In the face."

This was her moment. No matter how scared she was, no matter than it hurt. This was her chance to say what needed to be said. "The drywall in our house is crumbling from the places where you shoved me against the wall. None of it's normal. And none of it's right. And you *are* that man. You are. It doesn't matter that you're a doctor. It doesn't matter that you're successful. You hurt me."

"Let's talk about it, then," he said, his tone suddenly conciliatory. "I never felt good about it, Avery."

"There's nothing to say. We passed talking the first time you used your fists instead of your words. The opportunity to fix it was done. I wish it were different. I really do. I wish you were different. But you're not. And that's what I've had to accept. That's what I'm working on accepting. And if I were you, I would leave now. Because whatever happens after this there's going to be a divorce. And if the police have to come arrest you again, none of that is going to go your way."

"Are you threatening me?"

She bit back a wave of rage. Because escalating it wasn't going to help. But she wanted to. She wanted to hit him, but she wasn't going to. But oh how she felt free. And gloriously justified.

She was just bitter and angry now. That she had been made to feel afraid of him. And none of it was her choice. It was all him. He had dumped this on her, on her life. And she had never thought that accepting she was a victim could be any kind of position of strength. But it felt like one now. Because it made everything clear.

All the confusion, all the conflicting emotion that she had felt for the last couple of years was melting away.

Being his *victim* meant that she wasn't his *wife*.

It meant accepting that whatever he might call love, it wasn't love. It meant accepting that he couldn't be her husband. And it meant releasing herself from her obligation to him. From any guilt she felt over not fixing it, over not being better.

There were gray areas in marriage. But not when one person was a predator, and the other person was prey. He was the one who had demolished that other lane. He was the one who had turned it into a one-way street. And she wasn't going to feel guilty about it.

She just felt… Uncoupled. Brilliantly. Gloriously.

"Go away. I am considering getting a restraining order, and I really would hate to have to, but if I do, then this is going to be a crime."

"Avery, you bitch."

"Yeah. Maybe. I should have been a bigger one earlier. The man I love isn't real. He was a fantasy that I spun out of my own dreams. And I'm halfway to hating you for what you did to me. To your children. But I'm not going to let myself hate you. Because I'm not going to let you make me into a toxic person. I'm not going to let you make me into anything. I'm going to make *myself* into something. And it's going to have nothing to do with you. Now go away. And don't make this unpleasant because there are a lot of people here. And all these kids over there, their parents know you. So don't make it worse."

And it was the one bit of power she had, that much was clear, because he took a step away from her, and she could tell he didn't want to. That was another thing that hurt, right then.

He could control it. When he was more worried about the consequences, he could control it. Which meant that he had never really cared all that much about her, and never seen her as a threat. Just an outlet for his temper tantrums. If he could stop himself now, he could have stopped himself any of those other times.

"Goodbye," she said, forcefully.

And he left.

He left, and the kids never noticed that he was there. He left, and she stood there, watching them. Smile and laugh and be kids. This was new, and it was scary. But there was normal in it. And it would be better. She wasn't mourning her marriage. Because the marriage that she believed in for so long didn't exist. She was sad about something she never really had. She had constructed dreams and fantasies and had been convinced that her desire to make them real had done it.

But it had never been real. Not really.

It had never been perfect.

And neither had she. That melody that had pushed at the edges of her mind a few weeks ago came back to her, like sunshine pushing through storm clouds.

And it suddenly became clear. It was a song her mother sang to herself often, usually while washing dishes.

Avery had never once, in all of her adult life been tempted to sing it, least of all while doing dishes.

I sing because I'm happy.

I sing because I'm free.

For His eye is on the sparrow, and I know he watches me.

But it was there now, suddenly like an anthem in her soul.

I sing because I'm free.

27

*I had a new audition and I didn't get it. I haven't had anything
new since that first role and Sam is getting harder and harder to
live with. Whiskey makes him mean, and there's always whiskey. When I look out the window, the lights still glitter, but they
feel dim now.*

Ava Moore's diary, 1924

Hannah

"What do you mean you cheated?"

"There's not a whole lot to tell," she said. "That's what happened. I had sex with someone else. And I had been doing it
for a while before I broke up with you."

She was shaking. She felt sick. Dirty and disgusting and everything she always felt when she dragged this up. She had spent
a lot of years justifying it. Telling herself that it had to happen.
It was the price she paid.

And there was no use being upset about it. No use regretting it. There wasn't.

And it was his fault, because he had pushed it here. Because he was asking for things that she couldn't give. Again.

"You just never really knew me, that's my point. So while this has been... It's been really good. I'm not going to lie to you about that. But you never really knew me. You thought you did."

"I don't know what to say, Hannah. I don't really know how to react to that. But it was nineteen years ago. I can't think that what you did when you were seventeen has much to do with what's happening between us now."

Except she could see on his face that it did.

That it had reshaped the image he had of the girl he had once loved.

God knew it had reshaped her image of herself.

And she had spent years trying to twist it and tease it to make it into something else. To make herself feel different about it. And then she had just quit thinking about it altogether. And she had turned it into fuel. Because there was nothing she could do about it. There was no other choice she could go back and make. So it just had to be. She had to accept it. And she had to use it. And she would use it now.

It was the only way to survive this. She needed him to hate her.

"What happened? Who was it?"

"Doesn't matter," she said, wishing she hadn't eaten. She was going to go ahead and say this, she should've known that she needed an empty stomach. Because she wanted to be sick.

"I mean, you're the one that brought it up, so I'm not sure how it's supposed to matter. You're trying to make it so I don't... What, want to get to know you better now? Because I'm not proposing. I'm telling you that I have feelings for you."

"Based on someone you thought I was. But I was keeping

secrets from you. That's the point. It doesn't really matter what happened."

"Bullshit it doesn't. It matters. It matters because you're still hanging on to it, at the very least. If you thought it meant nothing, why would you tell me?"

"Because I know it means something to you. Sex doesn't mean all that much to me. I hate to break it to you."

"You're a liar. You're just a liar."

"I'm not a liar. I don't care about this kind of thing. I told you, relationships... I don't believe in them. Not for me. Not for people like me."

"What is people like you? Because before when you said things like that, I thought that you meant people who were really driven. People who had goals, and all of that. But that isn't what you mean, is it?"

It tore at her, ripped at her stomach. Her skin was crawling, and she wished it would go ahead and just crawl off.

"I wasn't going to get the scholarship," she said. "I had to get an extra letter of recommendation. I had to have intervention. I wasn't good enough. Marc said that... He said that it wasn't that I wasn't good enough. It's just... Other people had connections. And I didn't have any. And about how I was going to have to do a little bit more to prove how much I wanted it. I didn't want to. Because of you. And he... He said that that was just me being like every other stupid teenage girl. Giving all this stuff up for a boy who didn't even support her." She shook her head. "I couldn't get that out of my head. Because I knew you didn't want me to leave. I knew you didn't. I... I knew you didn't want me to leave. But Marc did. He wanted to help me. And he kept telling me that I was meant for it. And that he... he said I was different. Special, and that my music made him feel things that...that were wrong but he felt them, and I owed him. For making him feel that. For what he was doing for me. And eventually I just... I couldn't see why I wouldn't? Because he was offering me something and somehow the way that he talked about it, it didn't feel like it was cold or calculating to hold the letter back if I didn't sleep with him."

"I'm sorry," Josh said, his voice shaking. "Is this your violin teacher Marc?"

"Yes," she said, the word a whisper, and she hated her solar plexus for not backing her up on this. For being filled with shame when she was trying to be defiant.

"He was in his forties," Josh said. "He was older than we are now."

"It's not... That's not the point."

"He coerced you into having sex with him. You were seventeen. Dammit, Hannah, he raped you."

"He didn't," Hannah said, that word echoing in her head like a gunshot. She hated that word. "I said yes. I said yes every time I went for a lesson in the end because he was doing what he said he would for me. Going to get me the scholarship. And I... It felt good. When I said yes it was because he was touching me. And it didn't feel bad, and he kept offering that letter. I said yes. I'm not a victim. If anything I'm a prostitute. I paid for my schooling, just not the way I planned on it. But he wrote me that letter, and I got that scholarship. And because of that I got my job in the orchestra. I was supposed to have everything. Everything. Not just first chair. Principal chair. I was supposed to get all of it. Because I proved it, didn't I? How much I wanted it. I wanted this more than anything."

"Hannah," he said. "I wish you would've told me."

"Are you joking? If anyone would've found out, that would've ruined everything. That would've compromised my scholarship and... It was already done. It was done. And I needed you to not mourn a girl who didn't exist. A relationship that didn't exist. Because that's who I am, Josh. I took something that was really special to you, and that was a first for us, and I made it currency. And I... I was still with you while it was happening.

And I felt so awful. I really did. And I wanted you to be absolutely free of me. I did not want you to miss me. And that's why I was so mean. That was why I ended it like I did. I didn't want this. I didn't want you to imagine some sweet romance where there wasn't one."

"I'm not mad at you," he said. "I am furious at him. If that asshole is still alive I'm going to drive out to wherever he is and tear his head off."

"Stop it," she said. "Stop trying to put the blame for what I chose to do on someone else. I'm not saying that he wasn't inappropriate, or out of order in some way. But he didn't hold me down and do anything to me."

"He held your dream over your head like a bully and asked you to jump for it, Hannah. He might as well have held you down. He might as well have."

She covered her mouth with her hand, trying to keep the sound of distress that was building in her chest from escaping. This wasn't working. It wasn't going the way that she wanted it to. None of this was okay. It was supposed to push him away and it wasn't.

It was supposed to make her feel... She didn't know. She was searching for some way to be hard-edged and confident about it. Like she was a woman who'd made a choice with the asset she possessed at the time. Because it was worth it. Because the end goal was worth it. But instead she felt small and sick and dirty. Instead, she felt seventeen and scared.

And she wanted him to hold her and tell her that he loved her anyway, and she hated that. She hated all of this.

She'd stopped being scared a long time ago. Stopped being sad.

At first she'd felt devastated by how easy it had been for her passion to be twisted and used against her that way but then... she'd found the right story. One that didn't make her feel small or afraid.

One that made her feel powerful. Special. And she'd clung
to it.

"I can't see it your way," she said. "But I have to... I have to
succeed. Or it was for nothing."

"Your life is about more than trying to justify the actions of
one bastard. If you want to succeed because you want to, that's
fine, Hannah. That has always been part of you. But the thing
is, it's only part of you. You were never special to me because
you were going to be successful. You were just special to me
because you were you."

"That's not enough for me. It's never been enough."

"Hannah... We need to sit down and talk about this. Have
you ever told anyone about this?"

"No," she said. "I put it away, and I left it here. Along with everything else. Along with you and everything, and the only reason I'm even thinking of it now is because I was stupid enough to
get sucked back into this. Because I was weak. Because I didn't
get the principal chair position, and everything started to feel
like it was falling apart. And none of it matters, because Avery
is a victim. Avery's husband hit her. And we have to deal with
all that. This isn't the time for me to go picking at old wounds.
It's just... It's just the principal chair thing really sucked. And
it's you. And otherwise I never think about it. I'm fine."

"Is this supposed to push me away?"

"Is it not?"

"No. It's not. I should've been there for you, Hannah. I wish
I would've known." He shook his head. "I don't know. I was
seventeen and an idiot. Maybe I would have been mean to you.
I hope to God I wouldn't have been. I really do. But I can't say
for sure that I would've been what you needed. But I want to
be. I want to be now."

"What I need is space. And if my story doesn't make you want
to leave, then maybe me saying this is done will."

"Please don't do this."

"I said no."

"Okay," he said, holding up his hands and taking a step back. "I'm not going to try to talk you into anything. But if you need me, you come to me. If you decide you want me, you know where to find me. I know it's easier for you to try to burn it to the ground, to pretend that you don't have an option. So that you can focus on that one thing out in front of you. But I'm always an option, Hannah. Even if it's just as a friend. If you need something, I'm there."

She turned and walked away from him, into the house, shaking.

And she tried, she tried so hard to see that one goal, that one end point, that one thing that had been driving her all this time.

That prophecy of her being special come to fruition.

And she could still see it.

But the problem was, she could also see this house.

And she could see Josh.

She could see him standing there, waiting for her to come back.

Waiting for her to come home.

28

I've gotten myself in trouble. That's what Sam says, that I did it to myself. Women are supposed to know how to prevent these things, but I didn't know. He says it will ruin everything. He says it ruined me.

Ava Moore's diary, 1924

Hannah

Hannah was just about to hide when her niece and nephew burst through the front door and ran up the stairs, blocking her access to her bedroom before her sister walked into the room and saw her face, blotchy and red from crying like a child.

"What happened?" Avery asked.

"Nothing," Hannah said, wanting nothing more than to drown in her own misery.

Was this what all these years of restraint had earned her? Josh had pulled a foundational Jenga brick out of her tower and now she was crumbled. Reduced in her living room.

At least he wasn't here anymore.

"I'll make some tea," Avery said.

"I don't want to talk about it."

"We spent way too much time not talking in this family," Avery said. "I'm getting quilt squares and tea, and we are going to sew and you can tell me why that bastard made you cry."

"It wasn't him," Hannah said, scratchy.

"I had a run-in with David tonight," Avery said conversationally as she walked into the kitchen. Hannah craned her neck from her position on the couch.

"Did he do anything to you?"

"He was…" Avery appeared in the doorway. "I don't love him. I'm glad I got to see him. Because that was… That was clarifying. It's like now that I see everything I can't go back to how I saw them before. And it's good. I'm glad of that. Because part of me felt so conflicted, and now I just don't. I'm scared. Don't get me wrong. And I'm far from happy. Or joyous, I guess. But I know that I can't go back there. I cannot go back to that life I was living. I just see it too clearly now."

"That's good," Hannah said, knowing she sounded miserable.

"Tell me what's going on?"

"It's stupid," Hannah said. "Because you're going through something that's real. And I'm mad that I didn't get the position that I want in the orchestra."

"And that's why you're crying on the night you had a surprise date with your ex-boyfriend?"

"It's part of it."

"Tell me. As long as you still want tea."

And Hannah knew that she had an out. She could pretend that this conversation hadn't begun. But as she sat there holding the book, she felt that for some reason she shouldn't. That for some reason, she should sit with her sister, and talk. Talk for the first time.

"Something happened," Hannah said. She looked up and met Avery's eyes. "To me."

Phrasing it that way felt strange. And when she told the story about Marc, her sister's face stayed smooth. As if she knew that what Hannah needed was an impassive listener, who would offer neither judgment nor sympathy. Or anger.

Because telling the story, listening to it, paying attention to how it made her feel... That was what she needed.

To hear her own story come from her mouth, to experience it not as a seventeen-year-old girl who felt wise in the ways of the world and filled with ambition, but a thirty-six-year-old woman, who knew quite how young seventeen was, and was well aware of all the life experience the girl she'd been hadn't had.

And when she was finished, she just sat for a moment.

"Did Josh get angry at you?" Avery asked softly.

Hannah shook her head. "No. He said it wasn't my fault."

"And what do you think?"

"I don't know. I feel closer to knowing something now. But... I don't know."

"I had a confrontation with David tonight, like I said. And there was something... Something kind of magical that happened. I realize that I am a victim. And you're the one who told me I was, Hannah, with all the conviction of someone standing outside the situation. But it hurts to hear that. Because to me a victim is someone who's weak. But that's not how it works. I'm not a victim because I'm weak, I'm a victim because a person that I trusted very much took advantage of that trust. Abused it. Broke it. And recognizing that I'm a victim lifts an immense burden off of me. And it doesn't mean sitting here and feeling that forever, but it does mean finding a way to take it and use it. To use that label, to use that feeling."

"I didn't say no," Hannah said.

"And I stayed with David. But sometimes you're so deep in a situation you can't see it for what it is." Avery looked at her.

"It takes someone outside of it to see it for you. You did that for me. Can I do it for you?"

"But you didn't… I mean, this was years ago."

"Does it hurt still? Is it why you didn't feel like you could take what Josh was offering you tonight?"

"I always felt like I took what he gave me and destroyed it in a really kind of awful way. I think we probably would have broken up anyway, I think we had to. I had to get out there in the world and see what else there was." Her mind went blank then, her emotions blank. And it was good. It was like seeing everything impartially. Clearly.

"I think I stayed in Boston, with the symphony, longer and with more single-mindedness because I felt like I paid for it. And I had to… I couldn't turn back."

"You earned it," Avery said. "You wouldn't have done what you did for all these years if you hadn't earned it. You can't let what he did reduce your success to you… Paying for with your body. It isn't fair. If it was so right why does it hurt all this time later? If you wanted it, why are you so ashamed?"

It was so different, sitting across from Avery and having this conversation. Because Avery was strong, she wasn't weak. And Hannah realized… She had been yelling at herself, when she had yelled at her sister, defending the person who had hurt her. Screaming at that girl from long ago who had pretended everything was fine. Who had been too afraid to say no, because the consequences might have meant her not getting her dream.

That was why she was so angry.

She was angry at herself.

Because she had spent so many years convincing herself that every choice she'd made had been hers. That she was strong enough to move through anything, even if it was unpleasant. That it didn't touch her. But the ends were always worth the means.

That she had been a seventeen-year-old girl who had acted

with clarity of mind, and made a trade. That she could handle being a whore because she'd gotten what she wanted.

"If I'm just a girl whose music teacher held a letter of recommendation over her head based on whether or not she would sleep with him… Maybe I'm not good," she whispered. "Maybe I'm not special. I had to believe that I was, Avery. I really did. Because I was distant from all of you, because I worked, because I broke up with the only person that I have ever been in love with to pursue this. And I had to believe that it would work out, but now it's all falling apart. I didn't get the position that I felt like was guaranteed. And the reason I believed in it was because I bought into my own self-delusion, all those things that he said to me, about how I was special and I had to do these things to prove that I was worthy of that specialness. And you know, he couldn't help himself when it came to me because I was just… So unique. But that's not it, is it? He has probably stripped a hundred teenage girls naked and said exactly the same thing to each of them. It was a casting couch. And in the end, I happened to get a scholarship out of it. So maybe I'm the lucky one in one hundred who got what was promised along with it. But it was never about my music. It was about my body and the fact that he was a predator. I just never wanted to believe that."

"Both of those things can be true, you know. He can be awful, and you can still be special."

"But I don't have what I wanted. And you know what? I don't even know if I'm happy? I don't know if I've been happy for a long time. I'm obsessed. I'm obsessed with trying to take this broken piece of my life and make it mean something. And I just don't know how anymore. I don't know if I belong there anymore. But I sure as hell don't belong here. Because before I left here, before Marc, I believed a lot of things. I believed in love, and I believed in fate. I didn't know how to reconcile the fact that I loved Josh with what I felt was my fate to be this violinist, because he felt like fate too. And I went away and I did it, and I have done it for all these years. And there was just one next thing. And now it's out of my reach again and I have to keep working toward it, and I just don't know if I want to. And I don't know who that makes me."

Avery reached out and took her sister's hand. "I never wanted to be sitting here," Avery said. "Facing divorce. Facing the fact that my marriage is broken. That my husband is broken. But I'm not. And neither are you. We might be a little bit banged up, but we get to choose. That's the thing. We get to choose where we go from here. And you're not stuck on a path. You're not." Hannah looked down at the diary still in her hands.

"I guess I should get some tea," Avery said. "Since I promised it to you."

"Why don't we read?" She held up the diary. "I love that fabric for the quilt. I want to know more about the person who wore the dress."

"Okay. I'll go get Anabeth's journal. We can read together."

And Hannah suddenly felt like she had been stitched together with her sister, in a way she never had been before. Felt like they maybe weren't so different. And like she wasn't so alone.

Special had meant being singular. And it had meant isolating herself, too. And she was done with that. Tired of it. She opened up the diary and started to read.

He asked me to marry him...

29

I am home. I keep telling myself that. When you are not home, even in your own heart, where can you go? I gave her away to save myself. But there is nothing of me left to save.

Dot's diary, March 1945

Lark

Today Lark felt hungry. For Gram's face. Her smile. Her smell. For cigarettes and perfume and her laugh.

After being with Ben she felt...she felt good but also so... shaken. Like her world had been tilted on its axis and she wasn't sure which way was up.

The door opened, and she hoped that it was Ben.

She wanted more of him. His touch. His kiss.

But it wasn't Ben. It was Taylor, looking wide-eyed and upset.

"Taylor," Lark said. "What's the matter?"

Lark and Ben were proceeding with caution. They'd slept

together a couple of times, both times at the garage, since that first time, but as far as she knew Taylor had no idea anything had happened between them, so she hadn't been expecting a visit filled with teenage drama.

"She's here," Taylor said.

"Who?"

"My mother. She's back in town."

Fear twisted Lark's heart. "Oh," she said.

"I don't want her here. I… I can tell my dad likes you. A lot." Well, so much for subtlety, but she and Ben had been around Taylor a few times together and it wasn't like they were actors. And maybe Ben had said some things about her. And she tried not to let that warm her. Besides, it wasn't the point. "I like that you're both happy and I was happy."

Lark tried to keep her expression neutral. "Has your dad seen her?"

"No," Taylor said. "He's at work. She came by the house. I yelled at her. And then I…ran away and came here."

Lark wanted to yell at Keira too. For everything. For hurting Ben, for being part of something that had hurt her, for hurting Taylor. For coming back.

But Keira was Taylor's mother, and no matter how much Lark didn't want her around because it complicated everything, she also couldn't… She couldn't deny the fact that she was Taylor's mother. That she had loved a woman who had also abandoned her daughter, and who hadn't been able to make it right with her before it was too late.

This was *Keira's* daughter. And no matter what Lark thought about anything, no matter how she had been hurt, from the past until now, no matter what she hoped for with Ben, Keira had been her friend. And Lark was the keeper of her own complicated decisions.

"Did she say what she wanted?"

"To see me. She wants to see me."

"Are you going to be angry at her forever?"

"I don't know. Maybe."

Lark sighed. "I… I don't think that I'm the right person to talk to you about this, but I'm here. I cared about your mom a lot when we were teenagers. We were all friends, and I hate that she hurt your dad. But I don't know why she left. She's a person, like me. Which means that…she has reasons for her mistake, or she thinks she does."

"But she left me. She left him."

She paused. "Do you know who else left her family?"

"No."

"Addie. My grandmother. She left my mom when she was just a little girl. Left her husband with three kids."

"She did?"

"Yes. And my mom never got over it. Addie came back, and when she did, my mom made sure that we had a relationship with her, but she never really did. I don't blame her. I don't think she was wrong for that. Not really."

Her breath caught. "There are some wounds that only time can heal. But some wounds are so deep there isn't *enough* time. Not for time alone to do the job. And Addie died before they could ever… Before they could ever talk. Right now, my family is untangling a lot of unsaid things. And what I can tell you is this. The same woman who worked in this candy store is the same woman who left her husband and children behind. The same woman who was a wonderful grandmother for me, who supported me and loved me and influenced me in the decisions that I made in my life was the same woman who hurt my mother deeply and desperately. Who hurt the grandfather that I loved so very much, made him bitter about love to his dying day. She had both things in her."

Lark looked down at her hands. "There are certainly things about me that your mom doesn't know about. Wounds that I have, burdens that I carry. I'm certain that she has her own.

And I don't know… It was wrong of her to leave you. It doesn't change that. It was wrong of my grandma to abandon her husband and children. But it doesn't mean they're all bad. You've seen that. And I guess it's up to you to decide if you want to try and find the good things. It's not fair. It means you have to be more mature than she is. And you're only fifteen. It's not fair. And you don't have to do it now."

"I don't know if I can."

"At the very least you should go back and yell at her more. Say what needs to be said. Say what hurts. Because I think in the end the unspoken things can create hurts that never needed to be there in the first place. I thought my mother would disapprove of something that I did, and I never told anyone because I was ashamed. Because I thought I knew how it would go. She never talked to her mother, because she didn't think there was any fixing it. And maybe there wasn't. That's the thing. Maybe we were both right. Maybe telling wouldn't have been better. But you know, there's something definite in it. And in the end, it's really awful to be left with a lot of what ifs. And I think it leaves more space. For bitterness, for wondering. For everything. A whole lot of things that hurt a whole lot worse."

Lark forced a smile. "And the only reason that I'm giving you any advice at all is that it's about the only use you can get out of pain. You can try to use it to help someone else. You can try to use it to build yourself something new. Otherwise it's just pain."

But if Ben wanted to be back with Keira, she didn't know how she would survive that a second time.

Well, maybe you go say something? Maybe you quit assuming that you know how it's going to go, and stop being passive.

"You should go talk to your dad. Give him a heads-up. I mean, *I* can, but…"

"I will. For all I know she's there. Trying to talk to him."

"Well. Let me know."

"Okay."

When you get a chance, I want to talk to you. Face-to-face. You can come here or I'll go there.

She hit Send. And then she put her phone away.

She wasn't going to drift off. Not this time. She was ready to fight if she had to. She was ready to be a little emotional, a little reckless.

Because he was worth it.

They were worth it.

30

We married as soon as we arrived in Oregon City. There is more travel ahead, to get to a newly incorporated town called Bear Creek, where John's land is. I have written to the school to let them know they will need to find a new teacher. Bear Creek has need of one, and I will teach there.

Anabeth Dowell's diary, 1864

Avery

It was her third day at her new job, and she was finally feeling less… Well, like less of an idiot. At first the whole register situation, which was just an attachment and a stand on a tablet, had made her feel about hundred and fifty years old, and completely incompetent. But it was beginning to make sense to her. She was starting to learn a little bit about the stock, and actually remember some prices and information. It was a quirky place full of handmade, artisan goods, and she really liked all of it, plus all the people.

And she had taken off her wedding ring. She had also found a lawyer, one of the women at her kids' school, to represent her when the divorce proceedings started. And she was overall feeling pretty positive.

There was one other person—a woman named Suzette, who had a nose ring and purple in her hair—but she was running back and forth doing inventory while Avery managed the store. Suzette was Avery's age, which had shocked her at first.

She liked Suzette. She'd had a couple of shifts with her, and she was funny and talked about the deathly dating situation locally with gothic tones.

Suzette didn't know anything about Avery's life. And Avery found that freeing. They talked about general things, not specific things.

Politics—Suzette's tended to be on the fringe, any fringe, she didn't seem to care which—essential oils, gel nails and the great lettuce heist of '09, when one of the restaurants in town had set up a camera to discover who was stealing their lettuce shipment, and discovered it was the smaller restaurant next door.

Mostly, she was just happy to have someone to talk to like that. Someone who felt like a friend. Someone who didn't feel sorry for her, or treat her like she was a tragic disappointment, or a potentially contagious pariah.

They were in the middle of discussing the parking space scam one of the older men on the city council was constantly running—talking new business owners into buying parking spaces from him that he didn't own—when one of the most striking men Avery had ever seen walked into the store.

He was tall and broad with golden brown skin and black hair, eyes that were so dark they almost looked nearly black, but were in fact a very deep brown.

"I'm Nathaniel Oak," he said. "I have an account here. I just came to collect my check."

"Oh," she said, blinking. "Oh. You're one of the...the artists."

"I suppose so," he returned. "I make the antler handle knives."

"Those are very popular," she said. "Which... I guess you know. But, I'm learning. I'm new. I'm... Avery."

He smiled, slow and laconic. "Nice to meet you."

"You too."

It was weird, talking to an attractive man without a ring on her finger. Without any obligations at all. And that... Well, that was interesting. No, she really didn't want to be in a relationship, and the sight of a handsome man wasn't going to make her forget that. But she was suddenly giddy with freedom and she couldn't quite do anything to tell her body to settle down. She dug through the files, and pulled out an envelope with his name on it. And when she handed it to him, his rough fingers brushed hers.

She felt an arc of heat, and she really didn't know if it was just because he was attractive—which he was—or if it had something to do with suddenly realizing what it really meant to not be tethered to David anymore.

That there was another life, and other men, and an endless possibility for happiness in all the forms that it could take, because she had chosen to walk through that door and out of perfect, into a field of endless wildflowers. And she could pick any one of them. She could be single, and go out with friends, and go back to school, figure out what she wanted to do for a job. She could date someone. She could date a lot of someones. She could marry someone else. But she didn't have to. She could be as blissfully happy as she wanted to be. She could be whatever she wanted to be. And that... That was what was going to make her a better mother. A better sister, a better daughter. The very best Avery that she could be.

And somehow, it had all hit her in the brush of those fingertips against hers.

"I hope I'll see you in here again," he said.

"You will," she said. "You definitely will."

He turned and walked out, and she felt Suzette watching her. She turned and saw the woman leaning against the doorway.

"You said there were no men," Avery commented.

"No. I said the dating situation was tragic. I don't date men."

"Right," Avery said. "Well."

"Even so, I think he's kind of a rare find."

"Well I'm not in a space where I want to find someone."

Suzette shrugged. "Well, who knows?"

Who knows.

And suddenly, unknown didn't seem like such a bad thing. Unknown seemed like a gift. "I guess we will."

31

I wonder how long you can keep sorrow inside you, how long you can pretend things are well, when each breath makes it feel like you're crumbling. Things should be better now. But I am not healed.

Dot's diary, 1958

Mary

They'd gone out to dinner to celebrate Avery's first day at work. Hannah had claimed a headache early and had gone back to The Dowell House, while Joe was headed back to work on signs and Avery and the kids went to do homework.

That left Mary and Lark standing there in front of the Craft Café. "Do you want to walk down to The Miner's House?"

"Sure," Mary said, delighted to get to spend a few minutes alone with her daughter. There had been a time when her youngest had been her constant companion. Avery had gotten a couple years to herself, Hannah never had, and then Lark had again when her sisters were both in school. She wondered if that was what had carved the very different relationship between them. Or if it was just how she was.

Lark, her open, sunny girl who had taken her light elsewhere.

And now she just didn't know. They walked into the small building, engulfed by warmth.

"You probably shouldn't keep the heater so high when you're not here," she said, as they walked in.

"It's just the heat from the day," Lark responded, giving her mother a look. "I never turn the air-conditioning on. I just opened the windows. It was so pretty."

"Sorry," Mary said. "It's a habit. We all do treat you like the baby, don't we?"

Lark lifted a shoulder. "I act like it sometimes. But, I also live on my own, away from all of you most of the time, and have for years."

The time for holding her tongue, hesitating...it was over. She wanted to talk to her daughter.

"I've missed so much of it, Lark."

Lark looked away. "I was going to pull out some of Gram's boxes in here. I still haven't found what I want to use. There was a square... It's in the swatch book. But it doesn't have a label. It's this really pretty yellow, and it's so soft. And I thought... I thought I might want to use that. But I couldn't find it in the attic."

"Well, she may have gotten rid of it during one of her purges."

Lark shook her head. "I just don't think so. There was something about the quilt that mattered to her. And I think anything that she earmarked for it... It's been here. Avery even found that diary."

"I don't know," Mary said. "You definitely understand her better than I do." She stared at her daughter. "Sometimes I think you understand her better than you understand me."

Lark jerked and looked at her mother. "I don't, Mom."

"You had an easy time sitting and talking to my mother. After you quit talking to me."

There was a ripple in the air between them, and Lark's brow creased.

"There were things that Gram understood about me," Lark said. "She was… An artist. And, I know that it's hard for you that I have that and you don't. That it's something I shared with her. But I never needed you to do the same things I did. You always cared about what I made, and that was what mattered."

Mary could feel the weight of things they hadn't said to each other before, settling in this room, and she didn't know where it came from. If it was all that regret from the things she hadn't said to Addie. All of the air they couldn't clear, resting here, choking her. There wasn't room in her throat for it, and more unspoken words.

Her mom wasn't here.

Lark was.

"Why did you leave? I don't mean for college. You've just been gone for a long time, and you know, I don't just mean your body." She looked at her daughter. "It's something about you."

"You've never asked me before."

"No, I didn't. I was afraid, with all of you, that I would ask the wrong questions. I was jealous, Lark, of how my mother understood you all. I felt like I would never be able to connect with you the way she did. I felt like I didn't learn how. That if she'd taught me I could have been a better mother. I… I shouldn't have let that stop me. I caused you pain, didn't I?"

"Mom…" Lark said, pain reflected in her eyes. "There are some things that don't get better when you talk about them." She cleared her throat. "Now, I want to dig through those boxes that I found back here."

She walked away and Mary felt that with it, Lark was taking the chance for them to talk. And it wasn't on accident.

Lark made her way through the back of the darkened building, into the tiny bedroom that used to belong to Addie Dowell.

Mary had avoided this, and anything like it. She had avoided being around her mother's things. At least, in this personal sense. She had been to the house, but that house was filled with memories. She had both of her parents there for a time, and then after that, it was where she had grown up with her father. The memories there were layered. The things her mother had stored in the attic were part of other people. Things from the past, and not directly tied to Addie herself. But this room... It was all Addie.

A shoebox full of lipstick, and she knew that every single one was on the red spectrum. She didn't even have to look.

Bottles of perfume and hairspray, some wigs. All red. It smelled faintly of cigarettes, even though she knew her mother hadn't smoked in here. It was just... All of her things. There was a tin that had once contained cookies sitting on top of the vanity, and Mary took the lid off of it.

Inside were pieces of broken costume jewelry.

Earrings with no backs, gaudy bracelets that were missing some of their rhinestones. "She probably saved these for projects," Mary said, sticking her hand into the tin and holding the gems up. "Either that or she just liked them, I guess. She was a magpie."

She wondered if her mother had worn those to parties.

All the things she'd done during those years that she was away.

Off being a woman instead of a wife.

Instead of a mother.

"I bet she just liked them," Lark said. "She was... She wasn't practical. Not at all."

"I never understood it," Mary said. "People from her generation, they were supposed to be some kind of sacrificing and self-serving. She never really was. It was like she was lost half the time when she was home, halfway to somewhere else even when she was with us." Mary shook her head. "I'm sorry. I shouldn't say these things about her to you. You loved her so much."

"I love you," Lark said. "That she hurt you hurts me. I think she really did feel bad about it. Later. But, she didn't know how to tell you about it. How to apologize to you."

"Did she ever tell you? About the things she did when she was gone?" Mary had never asked. And she'd never be able to now.

Lark shook her head. "Not really. She talked about her red convertible. And sometimes she would talk about having been to this state and that state. And I thought... I thought it was really interesting. And now I've kind of done the same thing, I guess. Roaming state to state. Did she tell you?"

Mary shook her head. "I didn't want to know."

Part of her regretted it now.

There was a large box at the foot of the bed, that was taped shut. And Mary moved over to that spot, pausing when she looked at the quilt on Addie's bed. "Do you know if she made this?" she asked, feeling suddenly sad that she didn't know the answer to the question.

"No," Lark said. "I don't. There's just a whole lot I never asked her. Because I was waiting for her to tell me. I guess I'm not that good at talking about what matters either."

Lark was looking more and more large eyed, and slightly upset. But she still didn't speak. She grabbed the edge of the packing tape on the box and tore it open, and when they opened it, they found folded material inside. A lace tablecloth, which Lark took out and set aside, and then under that, a yellow blanket. Lark frowned. "This is it," she said, taking it out and spreading it on the bed. There was part of a bumblebee embroidered on one side, and in the center, part of a tree. Though it wasn't finished. Mary watched Lark stare at the item, watched as she got yet more pale.

"What?"

"Nothing," she said, dragging her fingertips over the soft

material. Mary looked back down into the box, where she saw two books, and an envelope containing what looked to be more envelopes.

"Maybe there's explanations in these."

There was a nondescript blue book with a clasp that appeared to be broken. She opened it up, and saw the first page.

Dot's diary.

Mary frowned. "Dot. Dot's diary."

Then Mary picked up the envelope, and leafed through the envelopes inside. It was unsealed, just keeping the rest of them together, she imagined. And then she flipped the envelope over.

"Lark," she said. Her daughter looked at her, and she held the envelope out to her. "These are for you."

32

Sam drove me to a friend who said he'd make it go away. They gave me something that made me sleep and I woke up bleeding and in horrible pain. Today I still feel awful and I'm lying here, looking at that midnight blue dress trying to remember that night when it looked beautiful. When I felt beautiful. When this all seemed like a miraculous dream. Now home is a dream. But I do not believe it can ever be real for me again.

Ava Moore's diary, 1924

Lark

Lark stared at the letters in her mother's hand, and she looked down at that little yellow blanket with the unfinished embroidery, and dread climbed up into her heart and took hold there. Made it feel like she was frozen.

"I don't want them," she said.

"You don't want your letters?"

"No," Lark said. "No. I don't want this. Let's put it back in the box."

"Why?"

"I don't know," Lark said. She stared at the blanket, and she didn't know how she knew. It was only that she did. And the amount of raw grief inside her made her feel like her lungs had been torn out, left her empty and gasping.

Because it was easy, far too easy to imagine the tiny little pink body that should have been wrapped up in this blanket. She knew. She didn't know how she knew, only that she did.

"I just want to put it away."

Her mother took out the first letter, and Lark reached out and grabbed them, holding them to her chest, her heart beating fast.

Secrets.

The secrets were starting to unravel. All around them.

Quilt pieces, lying everywhere. Quilt pieces that could never actually be put together into one cohesive picture.

Avery had secrets.

Lark had secrets.

None of them knew who each other was. And they never had.

And they were trying to build something together that she didn't think they actually could.

She thought back to the scrapbook, and how this had called to her.

And she didn't want to believe in any of her metaphysical nonsense just then, because if she did, then she was going to have to acknowledge that there was a spiritual connection to this fabric. That it was what she was supposed to use. That it was something she was supposed to uncover. That the letters were something she was supposed to open, and she so desperately didn't want that.

Instead, she pulled the first one out, the paper on the envelope odd and stiff. She opened it, and it sounded loud in the stillness of the room.

Lark,

You have never gone so far that you can't come back home again.

There was nothing else. Nothing more. She simply stared at it. At the blanket. And she felt like she knew. She took out the next one, her hand shaking, and she could feel her mother's eyes on her.

Lark,

I keep starting letters, and I cannot find the words to finish them. But I know we'll talk about this one day. In the meantime, I'm sewing.

Lark sat down hard on the bed, nearly crumbling.

She put her hand over her mouth and pressed hard as tears overflowed her eyes.

"What is it?" her mother asked.

"It's mine," Lark said, words and violent grief all tangled together in her throat and fighting to be the first one out. "The blanket was for me."

"Lark?"

The question, a single word, contained a thousand more.

"It's sixteen years old." She touched it. And for some strange reason a smile curved her lips. "*She* would be sixteen years old."

The silence that stretched between them echoed in the stillness of the room. It mirrored the silence in another room, all those years ago. Not a word. Not a sound.

Not even a baby crying.

Still.

Horribly still.

Horribly quiet.

She looked up at her mother, and a rolling through her chest, leaving tiny cuts all inside her. It was worse than grief, this unbearable regret. She had grieved her loss. Over the course of years, in many towns, in many places. Left tokens and tributes and pieces of herself behind. For the child that she had only held once.

Cold and still.

The child who had never cried.

The child who had gone from pink, for only a few moments, to a deathly, ashen blue and been still. So still.

Her baby.

She had cried enough tears to flood a river for that baby. She had sent lanterns to the sky and flower petals into the water, and ashes into the sea.

She had never known the true regret of not telling her mother. Her mother, who had children of her own. Who would have been able to imagine the loss. Her mother, who had never known that Lark had carried a baby inside of her.

And Addie had *known.*

Gram had known. All this time. And never spoken a word of it to her.

Had never reached out and done a thing to see if she could ease Lark's grief.

She was there for you. She just didn't ask you about this.

But they could have. They could have.

It's your fault, isn't it? You kept the secret.

She was so sick of secrets. She was so done. What had it given her? Nothing. Absolutely nothing. It certainly hadn't brought Mara back. The child she'd named after she was already gone.

Mara.

Bitter.

She remembered that from Sunday School, the meaning of that name. That in the Book of Ruth, Naomi had changed her name after losing her husband and sons.

Bitter.

The loss had been bitter.

And she thought… She thought that she could make sense of this, on her own. She'd been certain that she'd been missing something on her healing journey.

And she'd been right.

She'd been right.

It was only a shame that this made her feel cut open fresh again. That it made an old wound feel new. The staring down at this blanket, this possibility, this piece of another future, made it all feel so keen.

And Taylor… Ben's daughter.

His *living* daughter. Barely even a year younger than the one he didn't know about. The one who had never lived.

Seeing her didn't help either.

You came back. You came back to this place where it would be hardest to keep it to yourself. What were you really hoping for?

Maybe the same thing Avery was hoping for when she had walked into the Craft Café with a bruise on her face.

A lifeline she hadn't even known she needed.

"What happened?" Mary asked, sitting on the bed beside her and grabbing her hands. "Lark, what happened?"

This was the moment. Her chance. To finally say it out loud.

This was what Addie had left her. Not just The Miner's House, but these letters. This blanket.

This knowledge that she'd known, but that she'd never had the chance to share. So it felt right to do it here.

These were the words she'd been keeping inside ever since she'd taken that test and seen those two pink lines bleed into being.

"I got pregnant. The summer before college. And I kept thinking… I would tell you. Because you can't keep that kind of thing a secret. Except, I couldn't decide what to do. I couldn't decide, and I waited until it was too late to…to have an abortion. I figured I didn't really want one anyway. I went all through classes, and I just didn't talk about it. And some people asked, and I would shrug and say that I was a surrogate or something. I just lied. A lot. I told someone I was married and he was in the army." She scrunched her face. "I just… I didn't want to tell anyone. And I started to feel her move. They told me it was a girl."

Her breath caught. "I realized it was my chance. To be great at something. I could be her mother. But I didn't want to tell anyone. I wanted it to be mine, and I kept thinking the time would come when I'd feel ready. And then she came. Early. I was sure it would still be all right. But I had… I had a placental abruption. And she died. She was… She was born dead, really. She never cried. She never cried, and it just felt like another way I'd failed. Another way I wasn't… Avery who's just so perfect and wonderful, and Hannah who was so brilliantly talented. You were so worried my big feelings would get me in trouble. And then I got pregnant. I made such a big mistake, and I proved I was just as…silly and irresponsible as everyone believed, but I thought maybe I could be a good mom. I thought it was my chance. And I failed her."

"Lark," her mom whispered, tears in her eyes. "You didn't fail her, you didn't fail anyone."

"I was so embarrassed. Because you warned me. You told me being impetuous and spontaneous and emotional like I was could hurt me. And I knew that you would be disappointed that I got pregnant when I was eighteen. And I couldn't marry him. I couldn't marry him because he got engaged to someone else." She shook her head. "I didn't know how to tell you. I didn't know how to tell anyone. What was I supposed to do? He got back together with her, and I found out I was pregnant. And I just wanted to stay away forever. I wanted to stay away forever because I thought I could never hurt as bad as I did knowing that he was going to be with someone else. But I was having his baby. Until I didn't." She put her hand on the blanket. "She knew. She figured it out. And I don't even know how. It must've been one of the times I came home. I did come home twice when I was pregnant. It didn't really show, and I just didn't say anything. Gram knew. She never... She knew I lost the baby and she never said anything. Maybe she thought I got rid of it. Gave it up for adoption or... And... But we never talked about it. And we never will."

Mary grabbed her and pulled her in for a hug. "But I know," she said. Her mother was smaller than her and had been for a long time, but her fragile frame held Lark with all the strength that she needed. "I know, Lark." She could hear tears in her mother's voice. "And you can tell me whatever you need to. I am so sorry I didn't ask you. I'm so sorry we couldn't talk."

"I know. If things had been different...with him..."

"Ben?"

"Yes," Lark said.

"You could be with him now."

She nodded. "It scares me, though. He conveniently doesn't have a wife, and has a daughter so close to the age that my baby would be. Our baby. And it all feels a little bit neat. Like the kind of thing that might actually be poison." A tear fell from her cheek onto her mother's hand. "I wanted her, you know. I loved her. So much."

"Nothing is going to replace your baby. His daughter wouldn't be the same. Just like you're not the same as Avery or Hannah. One of you does not replace the other. And never could. It just sort of expands, that's all."

"But we're not in that space. Not at all."

"How did you survive?" her mom asked. "Without any help?"

"I just... Kept on breathing. And in the end, that's all it takes to survive. But somewhere in there I lost something of what I wanted to be. I lost my connection to all of you." She looked at her mom, emotion bubbling in her chest. "Mom," she said. "I really did think that you would look at me and think that I was... That I was broken like her."

Guilt lashed at her, because she could see that her words nearly destroyed her mother where she sat.

"This is never what I wanted," her mom said. "It's not what I thought we had."

And she couldn't say who was at fault. Because it was like they had all allowed each other to be guests in each other's homes, showing only the very best of themselves and hiding their secrets in a closet. Choosing to believe that each other couldn't handle them rather than actually putting it to the test.

Even Gram had done that. Gram had known, but hadn't reached out.

It was like they all felt so tentative in their position in the family. Gram knowing she was barely forgiven by her daughter, their mother wanting so desperately to be perfect in a way her own mother hadn't been. And her daughters in turn wanting to make sure they didn't disappoint that effort. And as for each other... As for the sisters...

They had let that same tendency keep them apart from each other as well.

Separate rooms, full of secrets.

Separate quilt squares.

Separate stories.

"Did anyone ever cry with you?" her mother asked, putting her hand on Lark's face.

Her mother, who had never been able to show emotion, had tears on her cheeks. And Lark wanted to share this.

Needed to.

Lark shook her head, and Mary lowered hers, tears slipping down her cheek. This hurt. But it was a gift. This shared grief. The shared tears. And even though it was painful it was like a balm. Like a disinfectant poured onto a deep wound.

Because this pain, this grief, deserved the tears of others, because it was that deep. And she had carried it by herself all this time. Carried it inside of her, a piece of her story that she never spoke out loud.

And when they were done crying, Lark's eyes were swollen, but her heart felt new.

"I'll drive you back to The Dowell House," her mom said, pushing her hair back from her face.

"Thanks," she said.

"I feel like I have so much work to do, Lark. Getting to know you. Getting you to trust that I want to."

"It isn't just you," Lark said. "You've just started sharing all the ways that Gram hurt you. You wanted to preserve our relationship with her, so you didn't tell us how much it hurt. We knew it did, but it wasn't… We knew it did. But I'm beginning to understand. And it's complicated. Because I love Gram, but she hurt you."

"I couldn't ask you to sort through that when you were children."

"We have to start trusting each other to handle these things that hurt. Because otherwise… Otherwise we just have to face them alone."

Mary nodded, and they walked out of Gram's bedroom and turned the light off behind them. Lark was holding the blanket, pressed firmly to her chest, but she didn't notice until they were out the front door. But she kept on holding it, this blanket in her arms. That her grandmother had made for the great-grandchild she never held. That her mother now knew about. And even though she was holding the blanket now, she felt like she was carrying less than she had for the last sixteen years.

33

Sam threw me out. I have nowhere to go. I have nothing. Elsie says I can't come back to the apartment. I'll have to go back to Bear Creek. I don't know if I can bear the shame of it. But I remember the girl I was there. She had hope. I want that hope again. I want to be loved again.

Ava Moore's diary, 1924

Avery

It was sunny, it was summer, and Avery didn't have to go into the store today. Consequently, she had dragged Hayden and Peyton to the Craft Café with her. *Dragged* was maybe a strong choice of words, but of course Hayden had to pretend like he was a little bit too cool to go to a Craft Café with his mother. Peyton... All of this had been difficult for her. It had been a little bit rocky with her friends, and she was still torn over feeling betrayed by what her dad had done, and loving him. And

Avery didn't have an easy answer for that. Because it wasn't as if she had stopped loving David the day that he had hurt her.

She was thankful the school had been supportive. They'd offered the kids scholarships for next year if she couldn't afford to pay, and it went a long way in soothing some of her worries.

But it didn't ease their pain.

She still loved the idea of him. She could still see the man that she had walked down the aisle toward, and that man, she loved.

But she did not love the man that he became, and that was the only man left.

But he was Peyton's dad, and it was never going to be simple.

But just because it was complicated, didn't mean they couldn't be happy.

And Avery didn't feel tired like she had before.

"Have a seat," she said, gesturing toward a table and chairs in the corner. It was larger, of course, than the one that Gram had kept set up for herself, Hannah and Lark. But it was in the same place. And it made her smile.

Lark came out from behind the counter and walked over to the table, grinning.

"Hi, Aunt Lark," Peyton said.

"Hi," Hayden mumbled.

"Anything to drink?"

"He'll have a hot chocolate," Avery said, and laughed at his scowl. "It's what you want. Stop drinking things you don't like just to be cool."

"What tea do you have?" Peyton asked, straightening and trying to look grown up.

"Chai," Lark said. "Others too, but I bet you'd like the chai."

"Okay. I'll have that."

"Do you know what craft you're going to do?"

"I want to do those bags that people do here," Avery said. "Where you carve out your own stamp."

311

"Linocut," Lark said. "I'll get you the supplies for that. You two?"

"I don't know," Hayden said.

"I'll do the same as Mom," Peyton said.

"Linocut all around, how about? And I can help if you need it."

Lark turned to get the supplies, and Avery stopped her. "Just a second," she said. "I think we need…flower crowns."

"What?" Hayden looked horrified.

"You don't have to wear it. But I'm feeling celebratory."

"What are we celebrating?" Peyton asked.

"Whatever we want. And that in the future we can be whatever we want. All of us."

Lark returned with crafts, drinks and flower crowns, and the three of them set to work. She and Peyton wore the crowns, Hayden's sat in front of him on the table.

It was amazing how being a happier woman, one who let herself want things, and feel things, was making her into a better mother. Because this didn't feel hard, or like too much. It felt like joy. And it had been a long time since she had felt anything like joy.

Lark came and sat at the table for a while, assisted where assistance was needed.

"Do you want another drink?" Lark asked, after a while.

"Sure, I'll go help you carry them."

"You're good at this," Lark said, when they were out of earshot of the kids.

"It turns out that I'm good at a lot of things," Avery said. "It's amazing how much more you can appreciate that when you don't always feel like you're failing at something." She studied Lark's profile, and saw that there was a stillness, a sadness to her sister.

"Are you okay?"

"Yeah," she said, forcing a smile. "I… Keira is in town."

"Ben's ex Keira?"

"Yes."

"And that scares you."

She nodded. "There are things...there are things I have to tell him about and this is going to make it even harder."

"You're not scared of hard, Lark Ashwood."

"I'm not?"

Avery shook her head. "No. We all underestimated you for a long time, but look at you. Look at this place. You set your mind to something, and you seem to make it work. I think you'll make this work too."

Lark ducked her head. "Well. You too. You were always an overachiever."

"I don't know about that. But I liked a lot of different things. A lot of things that I forgot I liked. I used to really enjoy writing."

"Well," Lark said. "I would say that you have a lot to write about."

Avery looked around the Craft Café, this building that housed so much of what she was. What she'd been, and now, who she was going to be. At her sister, who she was beginning to realize was strong and brilliant. Like they all were. Like all the women that had come before them. Who were with them now.

"I do. I really do."

Lark

Lark had spent the whole next day feeling like she was floating. It wasn't as though she felt entirely unburdened, but she felt like something. She couldn't quite pin it down. She was about to close the shop, when Ben walked through the door.

"Hi," she said.

Something shifted in her, when she looked at him. And she knew that she was going to have to tell him.

"I just came to find out if you wanted to have some dinner," he said.

"Dinner?"

"Yeah. I brought…" He moved his hands out from behind his back. "A picnic basket. I know you have food, but I didn't think it was a very good offer if I had you make it for us."

"That's… Actually I did want to talk to you."

He cut her off though, kissing her. And she just wished that she could kiss him and not talk because between Keira being back and having to face dealing with her secret…

She didn't want to. She was too bruised. Too battered.

Because her *one* had up and married someone else. But he was the person that her heart cried out for, no matter how much distance, no matter how many years. And she had been certain it was that grief that she carried, the fact that she'd had his baby. That it had done something to her, but she didn't think that was it. Not now. Not while he was kissing her.

When they parted, he was breathing heavily, and so was she. She pressed her fingertips to his chest and felt his heart beating beneath them.

"Keira is back," she said, resting her hand against his chest.

"Yes," he said, his voice rough. "It doesn't matter. I mean, not like that. She came to talk to me and I sent her away."

"You can't do that. You have to talk to her."

"I don't," he said.

"You do. Because she's Taylor's mom. And because frankly, we have to deal with this or we can't…we won't be able to work, Ben. We can't pretend. We can't pretend that it was us all this time. Not when it wasn't." Emotion throttled her voice. "I can't pretend Taylor is mine. I mean, I can be in her life but I can't pretend… Ben, I have something to tell you," she said. "I just don't know *how*. And it's the real reason I have avoided you for all this time." She breathed out deep, taking his hands in hers, letting a tear fall down her face. "Ben, we didn't use a condom when we had sex that night."

She could see confusion flash over his face as he tried to place her comment with a point in time, and realized what she meant.

"I got pregnant, Ben. But by the time I found out you were already back together with Keira. I didn't want you to leave her because I was pregnant. Or not leave her when I begged you too. And I just felt like I couldn't win."

"Lark, what the hell?"

"Let me finish." She held her hand up. "Please. Please let me finish. There's not a kid out there. I didn't keep a kid from you. I thought that I would have time to tell you. And figure out ways to do it. And it was one of those things that seemed inevitable. And definitely part of me was tempted to keep it from you. Just forever. Give the baby up for adoption or something. But... I stayed at school, and I hid from everybody. And I went into labor." Her face crumpled. "She died, Ben. The baby."

He stumbled back, his face stone. "She?"

"A girl. She would have been a year older than Taylor. At that point I just... What was the point? I was never going to tell you. I was never going to tell anyone. But here we are, and here you are. And I didn't mean to get in this deep with you and not tell you."

He looked at her. Like he'd never seen her before. And she realized that this was so much more complicated than she would like it to be. It was huge for her, this confessional. But he was having to stand there and rewrite his own personal history. Because what he knew about his own story had just changed.

Because what she had just told him would have changed everything at the time. Or maybe nothing. But the potential for change remained, and it couldn't be denied.

If he had known...

How would things have been different?

And she could see him trying to do that math.

"You can't," she said softly.

"I can't what?"

"You can't rework it in your head and figure out where we would be if it had been different. I know, because I've tried. A hundred times. To figure out what it would be like if I had gone back and made different choices. If she would have lived. If I would have told you. If not having her would've been my choice, rather than something that just... Happened to me. I have tried over and over again to figure out how I would feel. Where I would be. And there are just too many things I don't know. Too many things I'll never know. If I had told you that I loved you, even before I found out I was pregnant..."

And there was something a lot like regret in his eyes, because they both knew that they couldn't go back and unpick the stitches.

How could they?

Because their own personal quilt square might be unfinished, but he had one of his own. And it included Taylor.

There was a whole human being that existed because of the choices he'd made. And she knew that he loved his daughter. And that he didn't regret her.

That there was no possible way for him to regret the last sixteen years of his life, and he shouldn't.

And she didn't regret hers.

Because it wasn't as if she hadn't done a great many wonderful things with all these years.

She had lived so many places and met so many people. She had grown, as an artist, and as a woman.

She had in many ways found the center of who she was, and that was what had propelled her here. She was strong. Artistic. She loved her grandmother, her mom and dad. Her sisters. This place she'd left behind because it hurt too much to be there.

"It hasn't been perfect," he said. "But..."

"You had a life. And so did I. We can't wish we were in a different one." She cleared her throat. "I realized that I was illustrating all these books for other parents to read to their children, but part of me would imagine it was for her. That the drawing was hers. That the story was hers. And that I was sending it out into the world. But I would never read it to her."

She gulped air into her lungs, and it burned. "I won't say that the grief is as sharp now as it always was. But I felt like as long as I was doing that, as long as I was going into that space, I was never going to find a way to heal. I feel like in so many ways it doesn't make sense to mourn a person you didn't know. But it's the loss of all that could have been. That's what keeps me up. It's all that *what if.*"

He took a step toward her. "Above anything else, you were my friend. I would never have wanted you to go through that by yourself."

"It was my choice. I chose to go through it by myself."

"But you didn't give me a choice, Lark," he said, his voice hard, anger burning through.

"I know. I thought... I thought I handled it. But what I really didn't think about was that I wasn't just going to go through it by myself in that moment. But for all the years after."

"I don't know what I'm supposed to say," he said. "I had another daughter, and she died."

His words were broken, and he had bent slightly, as if the weight of the news had broken something inside him.

"I know that you didn't ask to be part of my journey to healing."

"I hate to break it to you, but this isn't just your journey. That baby was part of me too. And you... I cared about you."

"You didn't come after me." She lashed out then, because how dare he? He went back to another woman and he thought she should have done something else? "Should I have come to your wedding with my baby bump, Ben? What should I have done?"

He stared at her, his expression stone. "I don't know, Lark. I don't know. But you've had sixteen years to decide how you feel about this, can I have more than five minutes?"

It was reasonable. What he was asking for. But she felt desperate. For understanding she didn't know if she deserved. To be held and comforted by a man who needed some comfort of his own.

"Ben, please don't be mad at me."

"I am furious at you," he said, his eyes blazing. "Furious at life. At…at not even being able to regret this properly because I can never regret the choices that led to Taylor, not ever. But this… We had a baby."

"Yes," she said, helpless anger fueling her now. At everything. That she had to do this. That Keira was back. "We did. I carried her, Ben. *I lost her.* I have lived with that every day and I… You just went on and had your life. You got to have a life. And I know Keira hurt you and left you, but I…lost you. And I lost Mara. And I have never been the same. I have carried this…" She took a sharp, jagged breath. "And I love you, Ben. I do. But I don't know. This is too hard. It's too hard."

"Lark…"

"I just… I love you and I'm mad at you. And I'm mad at her. And I'm mad at me. For indulging in this fantasy."

"It's not a fantasy," he said, his voice filled with grit. "I'm here." He grabbed her hand and put it on his chest. "I'm right here. And no, it's not simple. But we don't have to run."

She shook her head. "I have so much… I just don't think we can make this work."

"I do."

She shook her head. "I'm sorry."

Lark waited for the truth to make her feel free. But instead she just felt broken.

And she was so very tired of broken.

34

I will beg him if I have to. I will get on my knees, like he got onto his. It became clear to me on the train home. I turned down some-thing real for a fantasy. The stars in the sky for beads sewn onto a gown. I want the stars again.

Ava Moore's diary, 1924

Mary

It was quilting night, and Mary was holding not only her quilt square, but Dot's diary.

She'd read some of it to Joe last night, who'd listened while he'd worked on his projects in the shop. She was trying to share more. And it started with this.

Mary had been casually reading the diary for a while, an entry every time she sat down to work on the wedding dress. She was... It was heartbreaking to read the story of the young woman who had lost the love of her life. This wedding dress...

Mary was beginning to understand that it had never been worn. That it had been a symbol of love, and the promise of a union that had never occurred.

And it made her feel a sense of purpose with the quilting that she hadn't before.

To turn the stress into something. Because Dot had loved the man she'd lost in World War II very much.

And she had suffered. Having to give up her baby as she had.

And the stress… Turning it into something more felt like Mary was honoring that sacrifice. That loss.

There was something beautiful about the diary. Even though it was tragic.

Because it made her think. About all the things that people before her had survived.

And her family would survive all these things too.

They'd uncovered a lot of secret sadness in these past weeks, but revealing it hadn't created it. It was just forcing them all to deal with the hidden things, brought to light now.

It was hard, but good in so many ways. And it was changing Mary.

Making her face some things she'd shoved down deep years ago.

When she walked into the Craft Café, Avery was there already. And Hannah followed right behind her.

Hannah was also holding a diary. That red one they'd found among her mother's things.

"Have you been reading?"

"Yeah," she said. "A little bit. It sounds like she was kind of a movie star. Ava Moore. I wonder if that's why Gram got her dress? She was definitely in some silent films back in the twenties."

"That sounds like a nicer story than the one I'm reading."

"Really?"

"The wedding dress was never worn," Mary said. "The young man that she was supposed to marry... He died."

Hannah frowned. "That's awful."

They all sat in the circle, and Lark put a tray of cheese out on the tables, along with some wine.

"Anabeth lost her husband," Avery said. "The woman who had the curtains. And she had to go make a whole new life. Reading about her journey I realized that I've had this...sense of dread now for a really long time. It was so much a part of me that I didn't even realize I had it. And now I feel like I can make something completely... Completely new if I want." A smile touched her lips. "It's the most incredible thing. Because I started this quilt, and I felt so connected to this fabric. And it's this woman's journey. From grief to something new. I feel like her, arriving at that new place."

Silently, Mary picked up Dot's diary, a marker where she had left off. The discussion about all the different fabrics, the different women, made her feel compelled to look at it now.

"I think I ruined things with Josh," Hannah said. "But I wasn't going to stay anyway." She looked up.

"Are you all right?" Mary asked.

Hannah shook her head. "I don't know. Maybe my square's telling me I'm destined for greatness and to run away from home. Because as far as I can see that's basically the point of it."

But she sounded sad.

Lark looked around, and then she stood, and Mary's heart squeezed because she could see, in the tremble in her daughter's hands, the pale color of her face, just what she was about to say. "I have something to tell you all."

Her story, the one that Mary already knew came spilling out, along with the fact that she'd told Ben today, and then sent him away. "Gram knew," she said. "The whole time. And she understood. But we didn't talk. We didn't talk ever. I could have told her. She could've told me. We could have helped each other heal.

We were so busy trying to protect each other. But I think we're all a whole lot stronger than we've given each other credit for."

Hannah was stoic, Avery was wiping tears away from her cheeks.

"I just think we need to… I think we need to stop trying to be the version of ourselves we think each other wants us to be. Or even just the version you think you have to be." She directed that last part at Hannah.

"You don't have to be anything except for you," Mary said. "And it's up to you what that is." She looked around. "That goes for all of you. I'm so sorry that we didn't talk. Not before all of this. Maybe things would've been easier."

"Gram wasn't good at it either," Lark said softly. "I don't think it's a magic gift you have, talking about things that are hard. You just have to choose it."

Mary nodded. "Like doing any hard thing. You have to be willing to stumble around in the darkness, and make wrong turns." She took a breath. "I was so hurt by your grandmother. By the things she didn't teach me, and I tried to pretend I didn't need any of it. I tried to pretend I was fine. To take on my father's lessons so I wouldn't miss hers. It's why sewing was so hard. It's not just that I don't know how, but that I was angry she didn't teach me. That she taught you. Like a secret language she kept from me."

"Oh, Mom…" Avery said.

"But I can't blame her, not forever. It's up to me to make the relationship I want with the three of you."

She looked down at the book that she was holding in her hands, and then she turned the page. And that entry stopped her cold.

I've received a proposal from another man. He's kind. He's offering me something more than what I have. I like him. Perhaps that will be enough. But I can't allow him to call me Dot. Dot is who I was to George. And it will always be his name. Our secrets will al-ways be ours. Our love will always be ours. I asked him to call me Addie, for my middle name. Maybe I can simply be someone new.

Dot's diary, July 1946

"It's Mom's," she said, looking up around the room. "This is my mother's."

"What?"

She felt light-headed, the full realization of what she was read-ing echoing inside of her.

Dorothy Adaline Dowell.

"We always called her Addie, and never... And I never knew... I never knew."

"What?"

"She was in love before my dad. And he died. She had a... She had a baby." She found Lark's eyes and met them. "She had to give her up. She was forced to give that baby up. She was raised here in town."

"Oh my gosh," Avery said. "Mom, do you have a half sister?"

There were so many unanswered questions, and Mary didn't know how to go about getting the answers. Because her mother was gone. Because they had never talked. Because this was what happened when you didn't talk. Secrets touched everyone. What if they had known? What if they had always known that her mother was forced to give up a child?

What if never telling was why she had never healed. If it was why she had run away.

And she had known about Lark. About Lark's baby. What kind of comfort could she had offered her granddaughter. She could see that very same question reflected in Lark's eyes.

It was grief, fresh and bright and new. And it burned like a flame.

"Poor Gram," Lark said. "Poor Gram going through that not being able to tell anyone."

Of course Lark would have nothing but sympathy.

"But if she had told," Mary said. "Maybe it would've changed things."

"But she can't now," Hannah said. "Gram can't make it different now."

"We can," Lark said. "We can find out who it is. We can find out who the man was. Who the baby was."

And Mary's first feeling was resistance. A desire to keep things from changing, because they'd already changed so much.

But there were so many wrongs, so many things that had happened that couldn't be changed.

She couldn't go back and raise her girls so that they would feel like they could talk to her. She could only talk to them now.

She couldn't go back and know her mother better. She could only try to understand her now. Just like she couldn't bring Lark's baby back, or go back in time and sit with her in that hospital and hold her through her grief. No, she couldn't do any of that.

She could make the life she wanted now though. Learn what she wanted. Forget being so afraid to fail.

She turned to the next page in the diary, then the next, and shifted it, and when she did, a photograph fell out.

Lark crossed the room and picked it up. "George Johnstone," she said, looking at the picture. "That was his name. I bet this was him." She held it up, the photograph of a handsome young man in a military uniform.

"Maybe we can find the family. Maybe they're here. Maybe they can give us a name."

"What if she doesn't know?"

She looked around the room at her daughters, and it was Avery who spoke.

"Well, it's been my experience that the secret itself is really the problem. So much as what happened to make you keep it. And in the long run, secrets don't really do anyone any favors.

So maybe she won't want to know. And maybe it will cause problems. But what if... What if she could really use some family? What if she has questions too? None of you could help me until you knew the truth."

"All right," Lark said. "Let's find her. At the very least... At the very least she can know that Gram loved her."

And it wasn't so neat for Mary, because this had given her an entire new way to see her mother. A dimension of who she was, as a woman. As a person who was broken and flawed. But it didn't answer the question of whether or not she had loved Mary. Or if she had just loved that beautiful young soldier, and the daughter she had with him.

But eventually, that had to stop mattering. She had to stop being angry. She had to choose how she wanted to live.

She took a deep breath. "We'll see what we can find out."

Avery

It was late, and Avery was reeling from the revelations of the night.

Lark's baby.

Her grandmother, the loss of the love of her life and her child.

The weight of tonight was heavy. So heavy.

She couldn't sleep. So she pulled out Anabeth's diary, and sat at the foot of her bed, looking around the room. At the beautiful, textured wallpaper and the intricate wainscoting. And she sat there, holding the book in her hand, feeling the history pressing in all around her.

The generations that had lived here before her.

The lives that were here now.

They all carried so much pain around with them.

Her grandmother, with her bright red hair, and easy smile, had clearly spent years consumed with grief.

And so had her sister. Her sister, who had run in much the same way Gram had.

And she hadn't blamed Hannah for not making an announcement about what had happened between her and her violin teacher. There would be a time and a place to talk about it, but she knew that Hannah needed to sort through it in herself first.

Her kids would carry pain too. From their childhood. From their father. And no doubt from her, because they each carried a piece of baggage from their own wonderful, loving mother.

It was a frustrating and dark revelation, coming on the heels of all of the good that had happened earlier today.

But maybe that was just it. Everything didn't need to be perfect for hope to exist. There could still be light even when there was a little darkness.

And they were all just doing the best they could.

She opened up the diary, and started to read. She made it to their marriage, and her breath caught when she saw Anabeth's new name. And when she finished the last entry, tears were streaming down her face.

The house is finished and it is beautiful. I told him we didn't need anything so grand, but he insisted on making me feel at home. I told him my home is anywhere he is. I have learned the heart can heal in such miraculous ways. I have a new home now, Oregon. I have a new husband, and he has my heart. This house is a new view, but with John's blessing I kept the parlor curtains. The view is new, and pieces of the life I had are part of how I see that view. For we are both what our past lives made us, and we are living this new one together. What a wonderful thing, to realize there can be new life after sorrow. To know you can build a new home, always.

Anabeth Dowell's diary,
in The Dowell House in Bear Creek, Oregon, 1866

"Because of course. Of course you are, Anabeth," she said, touching the pages.

Anabeth Dowell.

Who had left home, started over, endured loss, and been brave enough to find love.

Who had made a new view.

A new view.

I hung the parlor curtains in our window. And the view is beautiful.

They had hung here. In this house. And they had belonged to her great-great-grandmother. And so did her spirit. It belonged to all of them. To her, to Lark and Hannah, their mother.

To Gram.

It was why they still stood; it was why they forged on. It was why they still hoped.

Because this strong, brave woman, who had endured the loss of the man she loved and left everything she'd ever known, shared her blood with them.

Her story was part of them.

Her story. The curtains.

The quilt.

The wedding dress was Gram's.

It was their story. The story of their family. Coming together.

She thought of the man who'd come into the store, and the thrill of sharing a moment with him. It wasn't about him. It was about the possibility.

It wasn't just one new view, it was many. Not about finding perfect, or neat or certain. But embracing this wide-open path, as broad and big as the prairie.

The grass is like the sea...

And she could follow it in any direction she chose.

She stood from the bed and went and looked out the window, at the night sky, scattered with stars.

She couldn't see the future. And she couldn't take away the bad. But she could move forward. And make all the good that she could.

And she would. She would.

35

There's an honesty to being sixteen. You think about your feelings. You let yourself and everyone around you know exactly what they are. But then you start wanting to look a certain way. Have a certain life. You can lose yourself somewhere in the middle of it. I lost myself. I let myself believe that joy was a house, a position in the community, the envy of others, rather than a glow in my heart. I would rather have myself and my joy.

Avery Grant's diary, to be given to her children, June 2021

Mary

It hadn't taken long to track her down. Linda Meriwether-Johnstone. Mary's half sister. They talked on the phone in the afternoon, and then later that day, had met in the coffee house. There was a lot of grief and hurt to untangle, but as far as the sisters went, there was nothing but a desire to build a bridge across a chasm made deep by generations of grief and separation.

They had talked about how Linda's parents had always told her that George was her uncle. She knew his story, but had never realized he was her real father.

They had *talked*.

She had invited her to the quilting circle.

And now Mary was back home in her house, the place where she had raised her children. Where she had made her own life, one as separate from the grief of her childhood as possible. But of course, she had always carried it with her. Going through her mother's diary was a study in reopening wounds. And then allowing them to heal in a way they never had before.

The last entry in the diary had been an extremely bitter pill. Because it had been about her mother's life right before she decided to leave.

It was not about a sampler, about Mary's inability to make beautiful things the way that Addie had done. Not about her being a frustrating child.

Not about her inability to needlepoint, or learn quickly enough.

It was not about Mary at all.

And of the many great things she had imagined that had driven her mother away, that it could possibly have been demons entirely contained within her, had never occurred to Mary.

She had read about women with postpartum depression, and that was what it sounded like. Well, depression. Maybe. This endless certainty that everyone was better off without her. That she was failing.

And the truth was, had her mother said any of that to her face, Mary wouldn't have believed her. She would've thought she was deflecting, being dishonest. Trying to make herself sound like a victim.

But she couldn't look at her mother's full story and not... Believe.

★ ★ ★

I feel like a ghost. I walk through the rooms in the house and don't touch anything or anyone. I can't feel anyone touching me.

He's a good man, but I can't love him.

Not the way I loved George.

I look at my children and see how I failed her, and I know I'm failing them too.

How terrible for them, to have a mother like this. It would be better if I weren't here. He could find a better wife.

They could have a better mother.

How well Mary knew the fear of falling short.

Because her mother's wordless abandonment had transferred those feelings to her. And maybe sharing, maybe being honest would have changed things.

What if she'd said those things out loud, instead of just to her diary? What then?

What if she were brave?

Mary had thought that being steady and measured, that hiding her emotions, was being brave. But it wasn't. It wasn't hiding them in a journal and running away either. She wasn't so different from her mother than she'd thought, though.

She had never bared her heart. She'd let her anger simmer over sometimes, but she hadn't told her girls why certain things hurt, and in return they hadn't been able to speak to her about their own pain.

In many ways, she had abandoned them.

It was such a difficult thing to realize that much of what she had lived for was in vain.

But not the love of her girls, never that.

She hadn't been perfect.

She had made mistakes. She had stayed though. She had been there the best she knew how.

And her life wasn't over.

She didn't need to leave her husband to try and satisfy the ache in her. No, of course she didn't. She had this life, this wonderful life. And she was just more free to live it now.

It was like an incredible burden had been rolled away from her shoulders, and she could... She could breathe.

She stood up, and set her mom's diary down on the couch. She stroked the blue cover.

"I love you, Mom. And I forgive you."

Blinking back tears she walked out of the house, down the little path that led to Joe's shop.

Her husband of forty years was bent over his workbench, measuring something. A signpost, perhaps. It didn't really matter. She crossed the distance between them and wrapped her arms around his broad back, resting her head between his shoulder blades. "I love you," she said. "Our time together has been a gift."

He straightened, turning around to look at her. "Are you leaving me?"

"No. Just making sure you know how... How happy I've been. And how thankful I am that you gave me the family that I always dreamed of. Joe, we've had a wonderful life. Not perfect. Better than perfect. Real. I'm sorry if there were times when my fear held me back."

"Did things go well with your half sister?"

She nodded. "Yes. But... More importantly I just... I got some answers. To these questions that have hounded me all this time. It's late but... But at least I did. I look at you, photography and camping and making furniture. You're not slowing down. And I... I want to do all of these things with you. I want to do new things. I... I'm not scared of them now."

"Even if you can't do them perfectly right away?"

"Especially then."

He leaned down and kissed her. "I'm glad to hear that. What do you think of doing that big Colorado hike. Staying in cabins on the trail."

"Yes," she said. "You can bring your camera. Maybe I'll... Maybe I'll bring some quilting. Or a good book."

"Bring whatever you want. So long as you bring you."

Hannah

Hannah looked at her violin, and she didn't want to play. She was the only one who hadn't participated in the family confessional. But she just didn't... She didn't see the point.

She was still sorting through everything that she and Avery had talked about. Sorting through her own complicated feelings about what had happened to her. About how it changed the way she saw herself.

She had punished herself. And punished herself and punished herself for years.

Like she was on a mission to make sure that she could never really come back home.

As if she was afraid that if she did she would never want to go back to Boston. Like she was protecting herself from going back to Josh, and she had to ask herself why.

For the first time she wondered... If her future was actually here. And not in Boston. And the girl that she'd been for so many years rebelled against that. She lay down on the bed, and looked at Ava's diary. She pulled it closer to herself, and looked at it. Then she opened back to where she'd been, and started to read.

And of course, it wasn't a happy story.

Were any of them? Her grandmother had lost everything, and then this poor woman... With all these hopes and dreams. It felt way too close to Hannah's own life.

And when she talked of home, and how it was a dream she could never have, Hannah lowered her head, and she cried.

She had never wanted to be the girl who crawled back home. And she didn't have to. But what did you do when a dream

332

didn't satisfy that hollow ache inside of you? What did you do when you were chasing something you didn't think existed?

There had been a time when she had believed so firmly that satisfaction would come from her career. That she would reach a place with it where she finally felt special enough. Where she finally felt like she had shown everyone, like she had proved that she has everything she had set out to be.

But she wasn't finding it.

And she was starting to think there was just something missing from inside of herself.

And in these quiet moments here, and when she walked the streets of Bear Creek, when Josh held her in his arms, she had felt a resonance that she hadn't been feeling in Boston. Not anymore.

After she dried her tears, she read on.

About the time she got to the end, she was breathless, desperate to see if Ava would make it back home.

He didn't ask me to beg. He brought me to my feet and wiped my tears away. I told him everything. Everything. He said: You have never gone so far that you can't come back home again. And he will be my home. We married quickly after that. I have not returned to simple living defeated. Rather I have seen enough of life to know there is beauty in the quiet. And that special is not what the world thinks of you, but rather what you carry in your heart.

Ava Dowell's diary, 1925

Ava Dowell.

Goose bumps stood up on her arms.

"Ava Dowell."

She pulled out her computer, and started searching, and there it was. *Ava Moore Dowell.*

"Great-grandma." This was her grandmother's mother. The mother that her grandma hadn't wanted to confess her shortcomings to. This woman who had made mistakes, who had needed forgiveness, and who had found it with her husband. They would have given it to Gram. They would have. Because they knew. They knew what it was to love through all those things.

How would things have changed if Ava had given this diary to her daughter. If Gram had known that her mother had gone away to Hollywood, had found herself pregnant and alone. Had been so badly treated by people she'd trusted, had come back home and found forgiveness with the man who had loved her first.

How would everything have been different.

If they had known not that they had come from a long line of well-respected people in the town of Bear Creek. But that they had come from a long line of women who were flawed and loved anyway.

What if they had known their whole history.

You can *always* come home.

Hannah dried her tears, and sent a text to her sisters.

36

I thought I would try writing some of my own story. To keep, and maybe someday to share. I never thought I could learn something new in this small town that I hated so much. But I have. I am not what happened to me. I am not only music and mistakes. And coming back home isn't giving up.

Hannah Ashwood's diary, June 21, 2021

Lark

When she walked into the garage that night, it wasn't the sight of Ben that sent her heart slamming against her breastbone. It was the familiar figure, with the petite frame and glossy dark hair. And Ben looked up, his expression weary.

And when Keira turned around, Lark could see she didn't look any better. She'd been crying, that much was obvious. And Lark felt like she was standing very much somewhere she shouldn't be.

Except… Ben was her… Well she'd told him they were nothing. That it was too hard. But Ben was hers. Ben was hers, and she loved Taylor. And she had a right to be here.

"I was just… Hoping to talk to you," she said, directing that at Ben.

"We'll talk," he said. He didn't ask her to leave.

"Lark," Keira said. "I… I didn't realize that you were back."

"Yeah," Lark said. "I… Heard that you were back. When I talked to your daughter."

"Oh, she talked to you? She didn't talk to me." Keira was instantly defensive and Lark had no idea what to do with that.

"I asked her to, but she didn't feel comfortable with it. I've been here. You have been gone for the last three years."

"You've been here?" Keira asked. She looked over at Ben. "How long has she been here?"

"I'm not your husband, Keira. So it's not really your business."

"Oh, it's not my business. Right. Is this where we all pretend that I don't know that you two had sex?"

Lark looked up at Ben, whose face was set in stone.

"When Ben and I were broken up. Before our wedding? I know you did. I know you'd been after him for a long time. You were probably happy when we broke up, while you were pretending you were still my friend."

"Keira," Lark said. "I'm sorry. But I don't think what happened sixteen years ago matters." It did. To Lark. It always would. But it had nothing to do with… This tangled disaster that was happening now. With the fact that the man she was in love with's ex-wife was back, when her wanting him back had been the thing that had dragged them apart the first time.

"Are you sleeping with him?" Keira asked.

"Yes," Ben said. "She is. And it's not any of your business anymore. Because like I said, I'm not your husband."

"We have a child, Ben."

Those words hit Lark like a bullet.

Because they'd had a child too.

Lark stood there, and she waited for the feeling that she was losing her grip on him. But it didn't come. This was the show-down they hadn't had back then. She hadn't asked him to choose, that was the thing. And she had a feeling she wouldn't have to ask him to now.

"I went crazy," Keira said. "I just… I lost my mind for a while, and I don't want to be away from you anymore."

Ben shook his head. "I want you back here for Taylor. Not for me. *We* weren't happy, Keira. You know that. You were the one that told me that. How can you stand there now and tell me you want to be back in that?"

"Because I… I tried being out there, I don't know who I am. I don't like it. I miss this town. I miss you. And…"

"You can't fix some things," he said. "I hope for Taylor's sake, you can fix that. But I'm not in love with you."

"Because of her?" Keira asked.

"Because of us," he said. "My feelings for Lark are separate."

Keira turned and rushed out of the garage. And Lark felt torn. Keira had been her friend. And she was angry at her, weirdly, mostly because of Taylor. But she still… She couldn't hate her.

"I'll be back," she said to Ben.

She left the garage, following after Keira. "Wait," she said, two paces behind her on the sidewalk. "Let's talk."

"What's there to talk about? You were always, always wait-ing on the sidelines to take him. You slept him when we broke up just after high school. And you immediately started sleeping with him now."

"You've been gone for three years. And I didn't come back for him. But even if I did… You're right. I love him. And I have loved him for a long time. It's not to spite you. It just is. And I love your daughter too. And you hurt her, you hurt her really badly. So… If you want to have something here, it's not going to be with him. If you want to repair something it has to be with Taylor, and you have to mean it, or you have to leave now."

"She's not your daughter, Lark, you don't get to tell me what to do."

Lark breathed through that pain. "But it's our life," she said. "Mine and Ben and Taylor's. We are... We're trying to make something. And we can include you. Because of Taylor. Because... You were my friend too. But you don't get to stand there and be angry, not when you're the one that walked away."

"You would never have left him, would you?"

Lark shook her head. "No." A tear slid down her cheek. "Except I did. I wasn't going to fight you for him. And in hindsight, I kind of think I should have. So this is me, standing my ground now. I don't want to be enemies. But you have to be realistic. You can't just come back and expect to slip right in to the life you had. If you want to come back here, you have to make a new one."

It was what she'd done. It was what she was doing. And maybe she and Ben would be able to work this out. She didn't know. Because it was tangled and messy and complicated. But he was the one that made her whole. That brought together all the pieces of who she was.

"This just... It's too hard," Keira said.

Lark could relate to that feeling. She'd said it herself only recently. "All the good things are."

"I just feel like I... I've made so many mistakes, Lark. Coming back means that I actually have to deal with them."

And Lark had no idea if they would untangle this. If they could all find a way to be happy. But she'd learned one thing.

"We all make mistakes," Lark said. "But you've never gone so far that you can't come back home again."

Hannah

"Did you really call us all together to have a picnic at a graveyard?" Avery asked.

"I did," Hannah said.

She hugged the picnic basket to her chest as they walked along the trails of the hilltop cemetery. They had all been to Gram's grave after the funeral, but she didn't know if any of them had been up here since.

It was a great spot. With a view of the entire town below.

It looked like a miniature, little brick buildings with green trees on every block.

She sat down, right next to Addie's grave. Dorothy Adeline Dowell.

"Hello," Lark said, putting her hand on the gravestone. "I wish I would've known you better."

Avery looked at the other gravestones. "Anabeth Dowell," she said, pointing to one. "Buried next to John Dowell."

"And Ava Dowell." Hannah sighed. "Right next to William Dowell. That's why I wanted us all to come up here. I finished Ava's diary. The story of the dress." She took her quilt squares from her bag, glittering with pieces of Ava's dress. "She had a dream of being famous. Of getting away from here…but it all went wrong. And she had to come home. If I'd read that story at a different time I would have thought she'd lost. That she'd failed. She didn't, though. She didn't fail, she…she let herself be happy and she didn't let pride stop her. Didn't let a choice she'd made when she was young become the whole rest of her life."

Hannah looked around the cemetery, bright and filled with history. It wasn't creepy or sad. It was…alive, somehow, this place. With the memories of all of these souls. The lives that had come before them. Part of the fabric that made the town they lived in. For they'd built the foundations, the houses, the businesses. The streets that they all still walked on.

This wasn't a sad place at all, it was…brimming with hope. With truth.

"I could only let myself want *one* thing," Hannah said. "I loved too many things too much. And my music teacher…he took advantage of how much I loved the violin. He…made me think

I needed to give him my body to have my dreams. And I was so afraid that if I ever loved another thing I could be hurt like that again. But the violin was already a scar so I just...pursued it. Doggedly. Determinedly. Single-minded. But I've run out of steam on that now, and I can't be one thing. I have to be more."

She looked down at the quilt square in her hand.

The party dress nestled against plain cotton.

I want stars again...

Hannah was both. The girl who'd grown up in this town and the girl who'd run away. The woman who'd made a career for herself in the symphony, and who had fallen for a man in a small town where she'd never be able to have the kind of career she used to dream of.

"This is who we are," Hannah said. "All of us. These are the women that make up our history. And they were brave, and they were flawed. And we're *them*. They're part of our story. And we didn't know."

Avery frowned. Lark went to her knees next to Gram's headstone, brushing her fingers over the lettering.

"I wish I could have talked to her. About how it feels to lose your child."

"You can talk to us," Avery said. "That's what we have to do. Talk to each other. And I need to make sure I keep talking to my kids. So that they know me. The real me. Not some sanitized version that I'm trying to show them to make them feel better. Because it doesn't help, does it? You just end up thinking you're the only one with problems. You want to hide things and try to make them easier, but it doesn't make it easier. Mom didn't know Gram's history, and she just thought it meant Gram didn't love her. But that wasn't true. It was herself that Gram didn't love."

"They were all so desperately human," Hannah said. "And didn't want to be. I relate to that."

"Me too," Avery said.

"I don't want to go back to Boston," Hannah confessed. "And

340

this is the first time I've been able to say that and not feel like it's giving up, or failing. And not feel like it means the last nineteen years have been nothing. Because they haven't been. I needed them. I'm not failing by being done. Because that's it, I just… I want more than one thing from my life. I played, and it was wonderful. I loved it. And it gave me distance from here. From what happened."

She looked into the sun, squinted and pretended the moisture in her eyes was all from that. "I always felt like I bought my scholarship with my body. And if you're going to be a whore you better be a really great one. I'm good at extremes. And I think it made me get obsessed in a way… I love it. I love it, and I'm not sorry that I went to Boston." She ran her thumb over the beading on the dress. "I can't be one thing anymore. And that will mean…compromise I guess? I don't even know what that feels like. But I'm a woman, not just a musician. I've been a victim," she looked at Avery, "but that doesn't mean I'm not strong. I have to figure out what staying here means for my life. What I'll do. I mean, I'll still play. But, it's going to definitely be on a much smaller scale."

"Do you really want to leave Boston?" Lark asked.

She nodded slowly. "Yes. Because being back here made me realize how much I miss all of you. Maybe in a way I never did before. If you're just staying gone because you're trying to prove your own point, and prove that you're right…well, that's not really strong either. That's just rebellion. I don't think I'm ever going to be special until I decide what that means. And what I have here, that's special. What I have with all of you."

"Josh?" Avery asked.

"Yeah," Hannah said. "I think I want to stay for him too. Seventeen-year-old me is tearing her hair out."

"But you're not seventeen anymore."

She laughed. "And thank God. I can accept a whole lot more complication than seventeen-year-old me could. I can see a lot more about how the world is put together. With cotton and chiffon and glass beads, all beautiful together. Party dress fabric sewn into a heritage quilt."

She sat down on the ground next to Lark, and put the picnic basket in front of them. And then Avery sat down next to her. Lark put her head on Hannah's shoulder, and she put her arm around her younger sister.

"It's amazing," Hannah said. "How much talking changes things."

"It helps when someone is there to listen," Avery said.

"I'll always be here to listen," Lark said.

"Let's just all be here. For each other. Talking and listening and everything."

And then Lark and Avery both reached into their bags, and took out their quilting. Lark had a large yellow square, which she turned away from them, but began working away on.

The sun filtered through the trees and bathed the headstones in golden light, and them right along with it. There they all were, under the same sun.

Special.

This was special. They were special. And Hannah didn't feel like she was coming home again. Instead, home felt like something different than it ever had before. Home didn't feel like a prison, it felt like a gift.

And maybe that was the real lesson.

That you could change, but then you can keep on changing, and it might bring you back to where you started.

That you could make mistakes, and run away, and be hurt and broken, and find a way to feel anyway, to be reborn, while carrying those memories along with you.

And when you became that new creation, you had to be okay with where it might take you.

37

*Being afraid of showing my emotions, of failing, of being a bad wife
and mother and woman, has been my greatest enemy. It did more
damage in my life than simply asking for help, showing I didn't
know what to do, ever could have. I finished my first ever crafting
project. My first quilt squares. I was so afraid they wouldn't be perfect. And they aren't. But they are filled with love, and they brought
me closer to my daughters, closer to my mother. Brought me a sister
I didn't know I had. Lark was right about creating. It isn't about
struggling to make something that looks perfect, but about the joy
to be had in the journey. The same, I think, might be true of life.*

Mary Ashwood's diary, June 24, 2021

Lark

It was a shock to have Ben turn up at The Dowell House.
Her sisters, and niece and nephew were all inside, playing Go
Fish, in a ruthless fashion that had nearly drawn blood. Lark

had been feeling enervated since her confrontation with Keira. But there was… There were a lot bigger problems between her and Ben than Keira.

Like the fact she'd turned him away last time they'd been alone together.

"Hi," she said.

"Hi."

"Ben… I want this to work. I… I really need it to and if you're going to tell me it's impossible, I will understand. Because everything is complicated and I get it. But please make it quick if that's what you're here to do because I can't take it."

"No," he said. "That's not what I'm here to say. It's not too hard, Lark. Too hard is not being with you. And everything else… Everything else we're going to find a way to work through. But I needed to make sure that I did the thing I didn't do last time. I needed to make sure that I came for you. Because you… You matter to me. You more than matter to me. I love you. I love you, and everything else is just details."

She laughed, and launched herself into his arms, toward him. Not away. Right into messy. Right into the past, the present and the future.

She didn't run, not anymore.

She would stay, right here. With him.

"They are really messy details," she whispered against his neck.

"Yeah. They are. But I didn't get your name tattooed on my shoulder just because I thought a bird might look nice. It's because you're part of me. You're part of my life. My journey."

"We should've talked then."

"Yeah. But we didn't. But we are now."

"I'm not sure if we could've weathered that. Losing her."

"We did the growing we needed to do. And maybe we could have done it together. We didn't. But things are… They've come together now. We are together now. I choose this. I choose us.

Jumping in with both feet. Both eyes open. Not just because it's easy, not just because it's expected. Just because of love."

"You know," she said. "I remember how you got that scar." She touched the slashing line on his face. "And I remember you jumping off the rocks at the creek. And you hiding under Avery's bed after I told her a ghost story, so that you could help me scare her. And I remember that time that you came to my house, and you said that you loved me. And then you kissed me."

"Really?"

"It's my favorite one. My very favorite memory."

"Then I better make it happen." He moved closer. "I love you." And then he did kiss her. And it was like all the pieces of her life, every fragment, every girl she'd ever been, came together at that one moment. All the sorrow, all the laughter, all the journey that made her who she was, was wrapped up just then, in a neat little bow. And she realized then that it actually didn't matter. If they were meant to be or not.

Because they chose each other.

And that, in the end, was what mattered.

"Why don't you come inside."

"Really?"

"Yeah. We're playing a pretty violent card game, though."

"Is it Uno?"

"No. We save that for after the children go to bed. It gets too colorful. Avery curses like a sailor when she loses at cards."

"Well, I'm here for a little Uno after dark."

"Perfect. Does Taylor want to come over?"

"She's actually with… With Keira."

It surprised Lark, but it made her feel… Good.

"I'm glad," she said.

"But I'll let her know that we are playing cards. I think she'll be happy."

"I hope so."

"Well, I know I am."

"For now. But you haven't faced my sisters yet."

"I'm ready."

She had a feeling, that after all this time, they were more than ready.

38

Starting over is terrifying. But for me the worst thing was knowing how my life might end up if I didn't have the courage to change. The unknown became far less terrifying than what I knew for certain. To let go of a life that no longer fits is not a failure. Pride is a poor substitute for joy.

Avery Grant's diary, June 22, 2021

Hannah

The night of her thwarted hookup with Josh, she'd come to his ranch, but she hadn't really looked at it. And as she stood on the front steps of the modest, but exceedingly clean house, she felt guilty. She was coming to the conclusion that she had been pretty tunnel-visioned and pretty selfish back then. She had claimed to love him, even in her own heart, but everything had been about her. About what she wanted. She had belittled what he cared about because it hadn't mattered to her.

This ranch wasn't *nothing.* This life that he had wasn't nothing. He was a good man. He had always been a good man.

He pushed the door open, wiping his hands on a dish towel, his gaze assessing. He leaned up against the door frame. "What brings you here?"

"To talk."

"I was just doing dishes." He slung the towel over his shoulder and held the door open. "Come on in."

"You do dishes?" she asked.

"You seem easily surprised that I know how to do basic things that most humans do to sustain themselves."

"Well. I don't. I'm a terrible housekeeper and a little bit of a disaster. But I have someone clean my apartment and I have takeout places bring me food. And I am in general kind of miserable. And that's what I've been facing. That I'm miserable. That I'm hurt. But I'm not untouched by what happened to me back then. That I… Josh, I couldn't face that. Because I thought I had to make it mean something. I had to believe I was special, so I made it something else in my head. Instead of just accepting that it…that it was wrong. And that a man used his power against me in a way that he would have done against any student in my position, and probably has."

"Hannah, I don't blame you for not wanting to think of it that way. Maybe it wasn't my place to say what I did."

"Somebody had to. Because yeah, it is making me question a lot of things, but I needed to." She shook her head. "I needed to go to Boston. I am so grateful for all the years I had playing in the Boston Symphony Orchestra. Not just because it made me a whole lot of money, and when I sell the apartment that I bought with some of that money, I am going to have enough money to live here while I figure the rest of everything out. But also because it was my dream. It was my dream, and the whole time I was living it I didn't really appreciate it. I was waiting for the next thing. I'm tired of waiting for the next thing. The first time I was happy in a long time was when I just put everything aside and played violin in the bar. And hooked up with you. And it was because I was happy with the moment I was in. I haven't let myself feel that for a long time."

"Go back a minute," he said, his expression like stone. "You said you were moving here?"

"I did. And… I'm not going to use the house as a vacation rental. Because obviously my sister needs it now. I haven't talked to her about that yet. But I need to. So I'm going to need some form of income."

"You're moving here."

"Yes, idiot. Because of my family." She rolled her eyes. "And because of you. Because you know what's really special? When you're not the center of your own world. When you have people in your life that you love even more than you love yourself. When you can reconcile all that you are, all that you were. When you don't have to pretend anymore. *That's* special. I don't want to be special out there all on my own. I want to have a special life. And that's here. And I'm definitely falling in love with you."

"That's a damn relief," he said, holding her up against his body. "Because I love you too."

"All these years later, with a lot of learning, a lot of hurt, and a lot of work left to do, do you think that you can take me back?"

"With pleasure. With ease."

"Then I am very glad that I'm back home."

She let him kiss her, and she had to think that her great-grandmother had been right.

You could never go so far that you couldn't come back home.

Avery

Neither of her sisters were back at The Dowell House, and Avery and her kids had a card game set up on the table, ready for a family game night. A family that was a different shape than it had been a month ago, but one that she was learning to embrace. That was when she saw the package. Sitting on the table, with a letter.

She opened it, and saw her sister Hannah's neat script.

I realized at some point over the last week that this house was never being renovated for guests. It was for you. Because you need it, and this is part of our family history. Our family history was there, when we needed it, even though we didn't know that was where we were headed. So Mom, Lark and I all agree, that this place is for you and Hayden and Peyton. And of course we got you some curtains, for your new view.

Tears pooled in Avery's eyes as she tore the wrapping open and found red velvet curtains, almost exactly like the ones she had been sewing with. Just like Anabeth's.

A smile curved her lips, and she saw her future.

Not what she was doing, or who she was with. If it was perfect.

Perfect.

When it was time for Avery to go and get Hayden from his friend's house, she wasn't even nervous. And she didn't mind when things were a little bit awkward with a couple of the other moms who were there at the same time. They probably didn't envy her. Not anymore.

But she was happy.

So, she didn't care.

Because she liked her life. And that meant she didn't need anyone to envy it at all.

That word had been her prison for far too long.

I sing because I'm free…

There were no more prisons, not now. The only limit would be her hope.

And right now, it was overflowing.

39

There is a reason we love the story of the phoenix who is reborn from the ashes. Because in life, there will always be moments where we catch fire, and have to rebuild from what remains. The trick isn't to avoid the flames, flames are inevitable. The trick is choosing to rise again.

Lark Ashwood's diary, June 25, 2021

Lark

It was quilting night, and they had already been at it for hours. Because the squares were finished, and all they needed was to be joined together. Which was Lark's responsibility, since she was the one who knew how to use a sewing machine.

It was all fine and good to do the squares by hand, but when it came to the big task, she needed equipment.

She began assembly while her sisters and mother talked, while they laughed and shared passages from the diaries that they had each been studying. Taylor had joined them tonight, which made Lark's heart feel bruised, but in the best way.

This was bigger than them. That all the women who had come before them, and lived and loved and made mistakes and been redeemed, were right there with them. Wordlessly, she placed her square at the center, the square she hadn't shown anyone yet. With embroidery that had taken the better part of twelve hours yesterday.

But holding the blanket had felt good. Right and real. It had connected her with Gram in a deep, beautiful way.

There was no judgment in these stitches. It was love, pure and simple.

And ultimately, that was what she was holding close to her heart. That even though she and her grandma had never been able to speak of it, her grandma had been prepared to offer her what she herself had never been given.

Acceptance.

She felt the strongest sense of certainty as she worked, as she moved the fabric through the machine.

Because she was just ready. Ready to make the life she wanted, not just wish for it. Not just drift into it.

She was ready to build her home. With her own two hands. And his own two hands, too.

The conversation in the room hushed and the only sound was the hum of the sewing machine, just as Lark finished stitching together the last piece.

She looked up to see what had everyone so silent, and saw a woman with shoulder-length gray hair standing in the door-way, looking around the room.

"Linda," Mary said. "You came."

The older woman nodded, tears in her eyes. "I did. These must be your daughters."

"Yes," her mother said. "Lark and Hannah and Avery."

Lark took the quilt out from beneath the sewing machine and held it close to her chest.

"This is Linda," her mom said. "My half sister. Gram's daughter."

It felt right that she was here. And Lark felt hungry to know everything about her. Because they didn't keep secrets anymore, they shared stories.

"You're right on time," Lark said. "We just finished the quilt."

She draped it over the wooden rack she had set up earlier, the colors bright and rich. Interlocking triangles of blue and silver, cream colored lace and rich brocade.

The party dress, the wedding dress, the parlor curtains.

Those fragmented pieces joined together, telling a story, of who they were. And there, at the center, was the baby blanket. Lark had finished the tree that her grandmother had begun, and beside it she had embroidered the words: *You have never gone so far that you can't come back home again.*

Lark had always believed that it was art, creation, that healed. And this had healed them.

Their history. Their secrets. All right there, bright and brilliant and shared.

Lark's mother put her arm around her, a tear rolling down her cheek. "It's beautiful," she said.

"It is," Lark said. It was beautiful. Not just because of what it was, but because of all it represented. And Linda came to stand beside them, and Lark looked at her sisters, her mother, at her mother's newfound sister. "She gave us this. She didn't tell us all her secrets. She didn't ever find a way to ask you to forgive her, Mom. She didn't find her way back to Linda. We never spoke about the baby. But she left us this quilt. And gave us a chance to make it together."

To stitch together the rifts between them, like squares joined by the finest stitches.

She had been waiting. For this moment. When she'd looked

at her grandmother's pieces she'd seen that it wasn't finished, and she had been waiting for that word to echo in her soul.

Finished.

But that wasn't it. It wasn't about *finished*, or *unfinished*. For their work, their lives weren't done.

They would always grow and change.

But here and now pieces of their history were brought together. Each stitch like a path, showing where their ancestors had walked, and where they could walk forward.

And their stories would show the ones that came after them how to keep walking forward too. She could see it all in front of her now, all that history, all that time.

Time didn't pass on by, never to be seen again.

It moved through the earth, through all that they were, like stitches in a quilt. Each thread, each fabric creating a bigger picture, a bigger truth. Each piece an integral part of the story of what had created them.

The sorrow, the joy. The loss, and the chance for new beginnings.

And the certainty that home would always be there.

She stood there, with her family, with her future stretched out in front of her, bright and brilliant however it would unfold.

And the word that echoed inside her was better than *finished* could ever be. Sitting with her sisters, her mother, and making this quilt, reading about her ancestors, learning to love all over again...

It was as though joining each bit of fabric had restored a part of her she'd thought was gone forever.

Lark Ashwood was no longer a woman in pieces.

She was whole.

epilogue

Three months earlier…

Adeline Dowell knew she was dying. She was ninety-four. She could no longer ride her bike wherever she wanted. Her grandchildren were scattered and she couldn't run her candy shop. She loved her great-grandchildren very much, loved watching them needlepoint, even Hayden who pretended he didn't like it.

But she was rapidly losing independence, and it was even a chore to dye her own hair. That just made it seem like there wasn't much point going on. These days, she was pragmatic like that.

The years for fancy were long gone.

She had regrets. A mountain of them. She did her best not to dwell on them.

She hadn't finished that quilt, not ever. Now most of the fabric, along with her plans for it, were in the attic at The Dowell House and she couldn't manage all those stairs, not anymore.

She wished she had gotten her mother's diary down from the attic before it had gotten too hard for her to get up there. But she hadn't. It didn't matter.

She could see the beautiful, red cover in her mind even now. The stamped gold letters there. And she could recall the words of her father, as recorded by her mother, by heart.

You can never go so far that you can't come back home.

Those words had brought her back to Bear Creek years ago.

They were calling her now.

She felt it. Heard her mother's voice more strongly now when she recalled the words from her diary.

Then she picked up her own diary, blue and filled with failures. With heartbreaks. With business she had no time to finish now.

But she thought of Mary, of Mary's beautiful girls. The loving marriage her daughter had made with Joe. She couldn't take credit. Not for that. Not for the strength and talent of her granddaughters. For Lark's creativity and spark and perseverance in the face of loss Addie couldn't bring herself to ask about.

For Hannah's brilliant musical gifts, and Avery's certainty.

For Linda's happiness. The life she'd watched her have from afar. She might never have been able to be her mother in practice, but she'd been her mother in her heart.

She didn't need credit. They were her joy.

There were so many things she'd left unsaid. But as she finished putting curlers in her bright red hair, and lay down in her bed, she didn't feel regret.

She felt only love.

And a sense that someday all of the secrets, all of the mysteries, would be laid bare. That the things hidden in darkness would be brought to the light. And she had the strongest feeling of being forgiven.

Maybe not now, but there was a certainty deep within her that someday Mary would, and she could feel it even now.

But you're running out of time...

No. She wasn't running out of time. She'd had time. Time that had been good, time that had been painful.

And in the end she knew that all those heartbreaks couldn't be erased, couldn't be changed or easily mended. But they were not stains on her life, not now. They were part of who she was. Each broken piece coming together to create Dorothy Adeline Dowell.

She had thought as a girl she had to stop being Dot. For Dot had loved and lost, and felt destroyed by it. She'd become Addie, and that hadn't fit either.

But she was both. Everything. All the sorrow, all the triumph, all the joy.

It filled her now. Gave her a sense of wholeness. The good along with the bad.

Her daughters, her granddaughters, they were her legacy and they would carry on. Any scattered pieces she had left behind, fragments she had never managed to mend, they would.

She knew it as sure as she'd ever known anything.

As she let her eyes drift closed, a smile touched her lips. Clear as day, she saw George as he'd been the last time she'd seen him. In his military uniform. Smiling. So handsome. Perfect in every way.

And the deepest sense of peace she'd ever known washed over her, like the warmth of a quilt, all blue and silver and lace and rich red velvet.

Finished.

★ ★ ★ ★ ★

acknowledgments

I owe my thanks to so many people, as always. To Rusty Keller and Megan Crane, for always being up for a stay in a historic house. And listening to me read strange histories to you while we sit in them. And again to Megan, for reading this book when I finished it so I could have her greatly valued take. To Jackie Ashenden and Nicole Helm, who read this in chunks and took the time to help me get a handle on my characters. To my editor Flo Nicoll for her deep insight, which helps me take a book to where I really want it to go. To my agent Helen Breitwieser, who provides constant support.

The history of WWII is foundational in both sides of my family, as it is in many. Before this book came out, my grandfather, a veteran of the war, passed away at ninety-three. He was a walking, talking piece of history, and the world is poorer for his absence.

I owe a special thank-you to my family for this book, because the starting point for this idea came from our story. Though this story is entirely fictional, the initial seeds of it came from this history, and I want to pay it tribute. To my grandmother, who lost her first love July 15, 1944, in the Battle of Normandy, and was left a young widow with a baby. And to her first husband, my uncle's father, George. Who I know was much loved and has been missed all these years.

from the author

There's really no way around the obvious comparison that, for me, the pieces of this book came together like a quilt.

Lark and Ben, as characters, had been with me for a long time, and I knew I wanted to write their story, but didn't have a setting for it.

There is a historic house in my town that I drive past almost every day that I've been fascinated by since childhood.

And my grandmother's life story has been one I wanted to explore for a long time. And as time passes, and we get even more distance from that period in history, using it the way I wanted to felt even more important.

But these were all just pieces, and pieces don't make a story.

When I found out that home I've long been obsessed with is now a vacation rental, I jumped at the chance to grab a couple of writer friends and stay there for a few days. And it was in the house that my pieces began to come together.

There were books on the family history (including many, many pictures of the men with their hunting spoils, and men in trees holding rifles) and a lot of rich detail about the history of the house and when it was built.

The B.F. Dowell House became the not-so-disguised model for The Dowell House in this book. The Miner's House is a nod to another historic house in town that has been many different businesses, including an Ice Cream Shop and a Candy Shop, and most recently, The Miner's Bazaar, a Craft Café where I've spent a lot of time knitting and eating cheese. And while it too is altered for this book, the historic town of Jacksonville, Oregon, was the primary inspiration for Bear Creek.

These brick buildings are pieces of the past that still stand. Both changing, and unchanging all at once. The businesses and the people inside them are different, and yet they stand much the same as they ever have, proof that what's gone on before has a lasting echo through time.

And as I reflected on history, the history in these buildings, the history of a family, it became the binding thread of this story.

Mary, Lark, Avery and Hannah have all become the women they are in part because of the histories of the women who came before them. From Addie, going back into further generations. A history unseen, not standing on the main street of a historic town, but that is a part of the way these women are put together, part of the very fabric that makes them. But in the end the history they take forward is their choice. To dwell in pain and secrets, or move forward in strength, writing a new story, an open book, for the generations that come after them.

It's why I loved the idea of Addie feeling that sense of wholeness in the end, even though her daughters and grandchildren had yet to go on that journey. That in her final moments her past, her present, were all there, a complete story. And that in the end, it wasn't regret, or pain, or disappointment that she carried with her, but it was the love she'd given and received in her life that shone brightest of all.